CW00369913

Coven of

Kate Bousfield

Opening Chapter

First published in Great Britain in 2006 by:
Opening Chapter, 104A Ryder Street, Cardiff, CF11 9BU

www.openingchapter.com

A catalogue record for this book is available
from the British Library

ISBN 1-904958-04-4

Cover design by Ddraig

To Mum and Dad
I know you would have loved this.

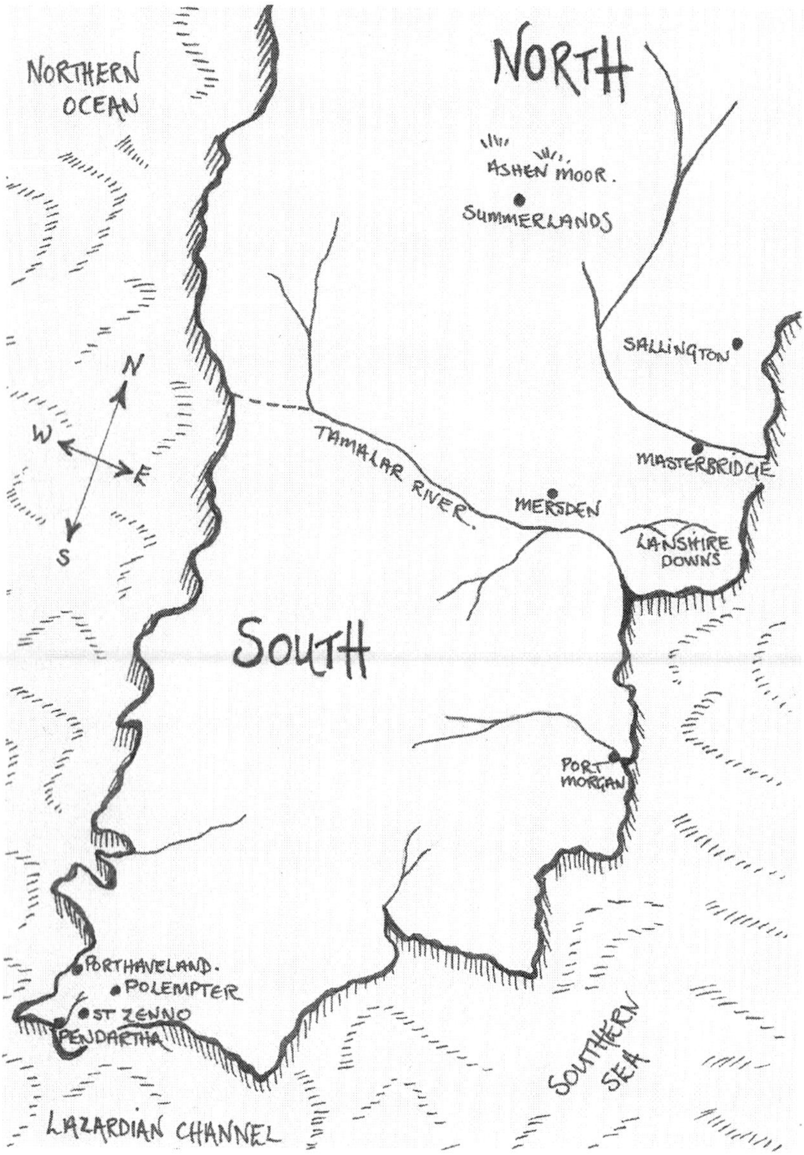
NORTHERN OCEAN
NORTH
ASHEN MOOR.
SUMMERLANDS
SALLINGTON
N
W
E
S
TAMALAR RIVER.
MASTERBRIDGE
MERSDEN
LANSHIRE DOWNS
SOUTH
PORT MORGAN
PORTHAVELAND.
POLEMPTER
ST ZENNO
PENDARTHA
SOUTHERN SEA
LIZARDIAN CHANNEL

An if ye harm none, do what ye will.'

Prologue.

'Mother! Mother Alice, come quick!'

The boy came charging up the lane and vaulted over the wall into the garden, his feet landing heavily on the flagstone path. He stood for a moment, hands on thighs, catching his breath.

'Joseph Figgins, I've told you before, use the gate' Alice said, stepping forward and giving him a swift clip across the ear.

'Sorry Mother but you must come. It's Mona, the bloody baby is coming.'

Another sharp slap followed the last.

'And I will not tolerate language Joseph Figgins no matter whose baby is just about to come into the world. Now fetch me bag. It's on the kitchen table. I'm all ready.'

Alice made her way through the village, as fast as her short legs and bent back would allow. Mona was about to give birth to her seventh child, she could do it on her own, and could probably cook a meal for the family in between the contractions, if she had a mind to. Alice did not even know why she was hurrying, the woman had no trouble popping the last six of her offspring out into the world, but if Mother Alice was called, then she would answer.

The small cottage at the other end of the village was damp, smelly, and cramped with too many busybodies aimlessly milling about. Alice shooed them all out of the door, clearing a space in which to look at her patient.

'It's a hard one' Mona breathed from the wet mattress on the floor 'been contracting since dawn. It don't want to come.'

Alice made reassuring noises and laid an expert hand and eye on the heaving stomach.

'She'll come out when she's ready and not before, now stop mithering. I'll boil the kettle for some tea, if you have any, that is.'

Mona heaved and groaned for another six hours until the last of the afternoon sun left the village. Alice lit the small mean lamps and put them around the room that served as a bedroom for the whole of Mona's large family. If truth be told, she had no time for Mona West, or her bullish husband. The pair of them should have stopped adding to the population years ago. The children they produced were small and skinny with attitudes they had no right to possess. They would never amount to anything much. Mother Alice, like many women of her position, had never acquired a husband or children of her own. She dealt with childbirth the same way she dealt with a stubborn boil. First time mothers were grateful for the aid you gave. By the second or third they thought they knew it all but still wanted you to nip in there and deliver it yourself. Mona squirmed on the dirty floor as another contraction ripped through her body.

'This bastard is going to kill me Mother, tear me to shreds from the inside out, it surely will.'

'Best use your strength to get the baby out then,' Alice said crisply 'that was a hefty contraction, it won't be long now.'

Mona screamed as another pain wracked her body. Alice wiped away the beads of sweat that had formed on her brow.

'Am I going to die? The Squire said we're all cursed. Am I next then Mother?'

Alice snorted. 'That is gibberish you're talking there Mona, let us get on with it shall we, I wouldn't mind a bit of sleep tonight if you don't mind, my back is killing me.'

An hour later, the troublesome baby made its difficult entrance into the world. Alice saw to the cord and wrapped the small, skinny baby in the cleanest blanket she could find. Alice then put the new baby in the wooden box that would serve as the baby's cot while she checked over the mother. She then took the girl over to the light to clean her up and give her the once over. In the dim room all had appeared well, but now, here by the light, she could see there was definitely a problem. She turned the baby this way and that.

'Another girl, he won't be best pleased' Mona sighed, sipping at the herbal tea that the midwife had prepared.

Alice took another cloth and wiped the baby's face again.

'What is it Mother? What's wrong with her? Let me see?'

Alice laid the baby at her side and held the lamp over the sorry sight.

*

Two days later Alice Bainbridge walked across the desolate moors. Her basket was heavy and getting heavier by the minute. She doubted very much that the contents would survive the journey; the nights were freezing and unforgiving out here. Alice cursed every mile across bracken, bog and river; this was not the time to be up here unless you were trying to catch a quick and easy death.

'Damn them, damn them and their petty beliefs' she cursed as her sturdy leather boots caught in yet another sucking mire.

This was just another occasion that Mother Alice had doubted her vocation. When this village had called, she should have turned a deaf ear, ignored them, and taken up with her original plan to join the coven in Baxton. This place was too far up in the mountains and too far away from civilisation. The villagers saw warnings and signs in anything and everything. Over the years, she had overridden many of their daft superstitions, replacing their stupid omens with good solid reasoning, but it was a losing battle.

'You are one that I cannot pass off I'm afraid, and there is only one thing to be done with you' she said to her silent passenger.

As Alice neared her destination, she took the baby out of the basket. The mark on the small pale cheek ran from ear to mouth in a vivid red line. To all intents and purposes, it did look like a knife wound, but it would fade with time, of that she was sure. It was a shame, apart from being very thin, the little girl showed promise of good looks, which would have been a novelty in her family. It had taken an awful lot of effort just to survive this far.

'She has been cut by evil, mark my words' Sedgely Pierce had said; and he was not the only one who had something to say about Mona's latest offspring.

She could not fight them, not about this, and rather than leave the baby to be drowned by her father, Alice had spirited the baby out of the village in the middle of the night. No one would miss her, the poor little mite, and it would bring her family nothing but relief to be unburdened from this stigma. It was a shame, Alice thought sadly, a dreadful shame, maybe one day someone, somewhere, would recognise the mark for what she thought it was.

*

The yellow-ridged fingernail reached out to swirl the inky water. With a sprinkle of chosen herbs, the scene burst into life once again. The shrouded face watched as the picture cleared, expanded, shuddered, and settled down to admit the truth...yes, she was coming.

Five ears in a row
Thoth, Amenhotep, Horemheb, Ani and Nakhte
Guide the knowing and make it so
-Pagan spell of news

Chapter One

Dorcas woke that morning with unusual anticipation, beating the cockerel's first call by a good five minutes. The others would not stir for a while; their gentle snores would remain undisturbed until the bird reminded them once again that it was time to rise. Even then, some would need a good sharp poke to get them going.

The first rays of the winter sun were just touching the eaves of the cottage as Dorcas crept out of her narrow bed and straightened down the sheets. Tucking in the corner, she took care to avoid the beams on the window side of the bed as she forced the eiderdown under the feather mattress and patted until she was satisfied. The warming wood above her head creaked and groaned, hiding her footsteps across the bare wooden floor, allowing her to open the attic door and make her way quietly down the spiral stairs. She stopped for a second at the bottom to check for movement from above before entering the kitchen. She so wanted just a little time to herself, a time to breathe and to prepare herself for the day's events.

'Good morning Dorcas.'
'Merrymeet to you Zarah. A good night then?'
'Prolific thank you.' the cat replied languidly, closing the bright green eye that he had deigned to open so early in the day.

Dorcas hopped over the cold flagstones and filled the heavy black kettle from the pump on the sink, lifting one foot and then the other while the water made its unhurried way from well to spigot. The warmth from the range never seemed to touch the cold floor no matter what time of year it was. Even Zarah, who had been outside on a night that had brought the first of the winter's frost, now sought refuge off the ground. He was balanced precariously on top of a pile of folded laundry next to the hearth, long limbs spread down either side like black lava. He did not stir as she waited patiently for the kettle to make its slow way to boiling point. Nothing happened very quickly in the kitchen. She pulled her Book of Shadows from the neat row on the dresser and opened it at the large wooden table. Her feet found their familiar place on the bar of the chair, habitually curling outwards to hug the legs. This would be the last day that she did this and it did not feel odd at all. Another flip of anticipation ran through her stomach as she scanned through the last observations she had made the day before.

The kettle 'blooped' its signal that it was preparing for the final push towards getting hot enough for tea. Dorcas retrieved her cup and saucer from their special place on top of the dresser. Her breakfast tisane was, as usual, pushed to the back of the cupboard and she had to get down onto the cold flagstones to dig it out of its hiding place. There was never any respect in this place and that would be one thing she certainly would not miss. With the tea brewing in her own small pot, she made a mental note of the possessions in this room that she would have to collect. She liked this kitchen and apart from the presence of the others, she would like to have one just like it of her own one day, large enough to move but compact enough to store everything to hand.

'And one where I don't have to hide anything.'

This kitchen had to be fairly big, there were twelve others to accommodate at meal times and that was something else she would not miss. The noise of all of them trying to do their work was enough to send Dorcas mad sometimes. On many occasions, she had retreated to the garden just to get some peace and quiet, sitting amongst the sage and mint to work quietly on her own. She relished these early mornings by herself, there were just too many other people around to get a grip on your own mind and that was something that Dorcas valued highly.

The list in her head grew as her eye fell on yet another box that belonged to her; did anyone else own anything at all in here? Gwenna's tubs of salves were already packed and stored in a wooden crate by the back door. She was good at ointments and the like, far better that Dorcas had ever been. Gwenna showed a real talent in the unguent department. Eliza's dopey frog was ensconced in its new travelling case, a jar with a handle on the top as opposed to a jar without one. The frog was not dopey. Eliza had let it eat wizenwood leaves and the poor thing had been drugged for over a week. Dorcas looked around. Apart from her own things, there was not much that belonged to anyone else. The specialised herbs on the windowsill would go with Ginnifer along with Zarah who didn't look as if he wanted to go anywhere at all at present. Many witches found that their cats returned to Summerlands, wandering the countryside until they found their way home again. Ginnifer had only had Zarah with her for a few months, so perhaps he would settle when they moved to wherever they were going.

'*And where am I going I wonder?*'

Dorcas pushed the thought away and concentrated on the cat. Zarah had been a present from Ginny's family and they could not have chosen a more suitable cat than this one. Black as night from the tip of his nose to the end of his regal tail, polite, mannered, and wise, as a cat should be. Dorcas admitted to feeling more than a little jealous at the arrival of such an exquisite creature and longed to own an exact replica when she finally gained her placement in the outside world. Ginnifer would be destined for great things with a 'Zarah'; the cat alone would open many doors for the girl. Dorcas had got on well with Ginny from the time that they were placed together as seniors and it surprised Dorcas as much as it surprised the rest of the students.

As soon as she had made her first appearance in this world Ginnifer Belle had been spoiled to the point of going rotten. Her family had indulged her every whim and supported her every fancy until the school eventually refused to let her father build a cabin in the forest so that they could visit more often. Ginny had the best of everything and the leftovers went to the rest of the girls in the cottage. Dorcas's new boots were courtesy of Squire Belle. If Ginny wanted a new thurible, then she got one by return of post, covered in precious stones or ornate carvings, along with a year's supply of Granidian incense. The pampering and cosseting should have been a bone in the throat of someone like Dorcas but the two girls remained good, if not close, friends. Dorcas knew that deep down Ginny did not really care a hare's foot about any of it, the hedgewitching or otherwise. She knew exactly what she was going to do when she finished here and that was more than any of the other girls knew at that moment in time.

There was a heavy thump from upstairs that let Dorcas know Maghda had just arisen. Dorcas finished her tea, washed up her cup, and put it back on the dresser. If she left it out then someone would use it and that would not do at all.

Maghda's heavy feet came down the stairs just before Dorcas

could escape to the bathroom.

'I knew you would be up first; beat that bloody cockerel for the last time then?' Maghda said, making for the kettle.

Dorcas felt that this statement did not need answering; it was obvious that she was up first, and had been up before all of them for the last thirteen years. A number of rude retorts swept through her mind but she fixed Maghda with a bright smile and handed her the communal tisane. She had nothing against the girl, Maghda was just Maghda, but the less she had to do with her the better. She just happened to be one of those people who got on your nerves when they had not really said or done anything wrong. She could be funny, in a sarcastic sort of way, and was excellent at puddings, but she got up Dorcas's nose much more than she ought to. Maghda Cotton was a moaner, an expert grumbler. She could moan from dawn until dusk about any subject you could think of and it looked as if she was about to launch into the first of the day. Dorcas beat a hasty retreat to the bathroom just outside the kitchen.

Their cottage, as so many others built around this small courtyard, had once been tithe cottages for the farm workers. When the new Summerlands College had taken over the estate, the old cottages were made fit for the students, but that unfortunately did not quite run to putting the bathroom on the inside. Once out in the bathroom Dorcas sent a silent prayer of thanks to the Goddess for giving her the foresight to have organised her clothes and wash things the night before. Stacked neatly on the bathroom chair was her outfit for the last day, newly polished best boots, and a piece of cinnamon soap wrapped in her washcloth. She had kept it hidden under her mattress in a small keepsake box that had been a gift from mother Lylas and was glad she had saved it for an occasion such as this. As with all things, Dorcas washed with speed and efficiency and knew that she would be dressed and ready before Maghda had poured the first of her morning cups. Dorcas scraped her hair into a tight bun at the back of her head and checked in the ancient mirror that no strands had escaped her competent fingers. The mirror had lost most of its silver so she tended to do everything by feel. There were a number of things that she could have done about this problem but that was just a waste of energy and besides the mirror reflected quite enough of her as it was. Dorcas had never been keen on her own reflection and didn't much like the face that looked back at her. She was aware of what the other girls called her and had listened intently when Amberlynne had suggested ways of making her look more attractive. Dorcas could not see the sense in this either but had put up with the copious amounts of eyeliner that the girl had slathered on.

'There, ten years younger' Amberlynne had exclaimed after working on her for nearly an hour.

'It would take more than a bit of make-up' said Joan

'Joan! There's no need for that' Ginny said, leaping to Dorcas's defence.

'Joan's right,' Dorcas said 'I now look thirty-five instead of forty-five which is a commendable improvement. I just don't think that I can waste the time doing this every day for no apparent reason.'

'No reason?' Amberlynne said dismayed. She spent at least an hour and a half preparing herself for the world *every* morning.

'Dorcas would have to get up before the cockerel even went to bed' Joan smirked.

'Well, I think you look lovely,' Amberlynne said, admiring her handiwork 'your hair looks so different when it's down.'

Dorcas could not imagine wearing her hair down every day. As a little girl she had even dragged it into a severe bun when she had hardly any hair to drag. As she got older, it seemed the only way that she could wear it; the hair had even started to look like it was growing upwards towards her crown. A woman in town had cut Amberlynne's beautiful titian tresses as it curled out at the sides when left to its own devices. Dorcas was not interested in fashions of any sort. Untidy hair and clothes got in the way of what one was supposed to be doing, and what one was, or was going to be.

'Thank you Amber, but I think I'll just stick to the old me.'

Dorcas gathered up her hair, coiled it neatly in one hand, and jammed in half a dozen hairgrips, before her make-up artist had even put her brush down.

'Well, you'll never get a man looking like that.'

'I'm sorry Amber, I didn't mean to offend you, it's just, well…'

'Dorcas doesn't want a man anyway' Joan chipped in.

Amber could not stand it any more and stomped off into the tiny workroom that adjoined the kitchen.

'I'm right though, aren't I? You don't want a man at all. You shouldn't listen to Amber, she is going to accept the first poor sod who proposes. After the first few babies, she'll forget all about the witching and settle down into being just a simple mother. She was only ever going to be a very basic hedgewitch anyway. '

Dorcas had thought this through for a long time. Joan was right, she did not want a man, but that was not the whole story. She so desperately wanted to be a witch, not any old witch, but a good one. She had wanted it for so long now that she could not remember a time when that feeling was not with her. They were all going to be hedgewitches of one sort or another, serving their communities in all winds and weathers so what was the point in having a good haircut? It was just going to be ruined underneath her hat of trade anyway.

Dorcas dumped her wet towel and dirty laundry into the basket and returned to the kitchen. There was much more noise from upstairs now and Bridget and Maegwyn had joined Maghda and were warming their backsides against the range.

'Meg and I have just been discussing you' Bridget said, rubbing her bottom where it had become too hot.

'Oh?'

'Not just you' Maegwyn said hastily.

'No, not just you, but we think you'll get Masterbridge. I overheard Mother Susan, there is an opening there for someone like you.'

'Me? I shouldn't think so' Dorcas said dismissively, although that would be the answer to all her prayers and more. She considered it bad luck to dwell on that particular possibility.

'Suit you down to the ground I should think.' Maghda said as she passed another cup of tea to Bridget 'If you're up to it, that is.'

'Of course she's up to it, they're hardly going to send the likes of Dorcas to some backwater place are they?'

'Who knows what they will do Bridget,' Dorcas said 'I'll get what I get and go where I'm told. They'll probably send me to Sallington!'

They all laughed at this. Maghda was born to deal with animals, and Sallington, a market town on the east bank of the Sallet canal, was the obvious choice for her. Dorcas often thought that Maghda had been clever in her choice of specialization. She could spend all day moaning at the animals, and they could not, or would not, answer back.

'Well, we'll see today won't we?' Dorcas said crisply 'Is everyone up now?'

The afternoon found Dorcas walking alone on the moor. She hitched up her clean dress, put on her old boots to stop the polished ones from getting muddy, and set off at a brisk pace. The morning rituals had been completed and all was ready and prepared for later. There was still over three hours to go before the ceremony started and she had escaped from the crowded cottage that was filled with too much energy. The chattering excited voices made her nerves worse and there were just too many people trying to squeeze past to get to the kettle. On an ordinary morning, the students were up at different times depending on their timetable and some would be just returning from a night expedition. They only ever all met together once a week and that was in the Hearth building for Pathworking or Esbat. This was the first and last time that this would happen and Dorcas breathed a sigh of relief at the thought. She could not imagine living with all those girls at the same time permanently.

Dorcas had chosen her 'thinking' walk; it would calm her nerves and let her put things into perspective. Up the valley to Grindle Point, across the southern tip of Ashen Moor and back down along the canal that would eventually meander its way through Brexham, the nearest town of any description to the college. The town had never crept any closer to Summerlands. Over the years it had spread out slightly to the west and to the south, but never venturing north. It would not dare.

Dorcas tossed things around in her head as she walked over the wet moors. She loved it up here, even in the depths of winter. The moor exuded peace and filled her senses with the smells of nature although damp bracken was now overpowering nearly everything else. This place allowed her to be herself, something that rarely happened when she was amongst others. A hawk passed high overhead screaming its annoyance at the lack of prey. Dorcas watched its progress until it swooped down and out of sight.

Thirteen years and it was nearly all over. Tonight she would find out where they were going to place her and it would all fall into place.

Dorcas sat on her favourite stile and surveyed the view in front of her. The deep valley spread out below her. In between the thickly wooded forest, parts of the college could be seen. Most of the Hearth building could be made out, its pentacle shape was too big to hide, but the rest of it snuggled into its surroundings, blending with tree, grass, sky, and moor. She could just about pick out the position of her own home cottage and the roofs of the other three that surrounded their yard but you only knew they were there if you knew where to look.

'That's exactly what I shall be doing,' she said aloud to the sheep, 'blending in, working with the coven. A sheep in sheep's clothing....at last.'

Dorcas was not given to impromptu bouts of giggling but her laughter rang out as she made her way back down the steep path to the valley floor. Today was Samhain after all, the end of one thing and the start of something new, the beginning of a life that she had been dreaming about for a long time. Today the Goddess would cast off her robes and take on the robes of the Crone. It was indeed a perfect time for new things to happen, and new doors to open.

Chapter two

'Samhain. Samhain.'
Dorcas rolled the word around in her head. The other twelve times
Samhain had come around it had signified only another year of life
at Summerlands. Today it felt different, tasted different, and
Dorcas felt herself caught up in the excitement of the Sabbat that
had infected the other girls all day. As she came into the courtyard,
Eliza and Joan came out of the kitchen door. They were dressed
and ready to go.
'Am I late?' Dorcas asked in horror, looking to the evening sky.
She was usually pretty good at estimating the time.
'No Dorcas, you're never late but some have gone on already to
take in the atmosphere and prepare themselves.'
'Ginny is waiting for you, we put your cloak and athame on the
table' Eliza added.
Dorcas hurried into the kitchen kicking off her muddy boots and
grabbing for the clean, shiny ones.
'Slow down Dorcas, we've got plenty of time. Cup of tea?'
Ginny had already placed a mug and a cup and saucer on the table
and was poised with the kettle in mid air.
'No, no, I want to get going.' Dorcas said, wrapping her cloak
around her and pulling on the flat starched cap. 'Are you ready?
You don't look it.'
Ginny rattled dishes in the sink and fussed with the tea towel.
'Umm, I can't go yet, Zarah has decided to go ratting, he felt it
appropriate. I must wait until he gets back. I'm sure he won't want
to miss it.'
'I'm sure he won't, but he does pick his times.'
'He has his reasons,' Ginny sniffed 'go on without me. He'll be
back in a minute. Go on.'
'Are you all right?' Dorcas asked.
'Of course, as excited as you are, now off with you.'
Ginny straightened Dorcas's cloak, gave her a quick hug and
pushed her out of the door. 'All the others are already there.
Maghda made some of that apple cake, go and join them before
they eat it all. I'll be there as soon as I can.'
Dorcas did not argue. She had no wish to sit in the kitchen
drinking tea waiting for his highness to appear, when she could be
mentally preparing herself for the Great Ritual. That would be best
done in the calm of the anterooms that surrounded the Great Hall.

She could not understand why Ginnifer would let her cat roam so close to such an important event, it was so disorganised. A cat could not be ruled, everyone knew that, but Dorcas felt sure that a few well-placed words would have done the trick. Ginny was like that though, she swayed with the lightest of breezes, bowing to the wants and needs of those around her.

Black figures appeared from the woods as she made her way across the stone courtyard towards the Hearth building. The colours of Samhain were apparent on all, with glimpses of red and purple beneath cloaks and caps. Dorcas herself had pinned her colours to the back of her cloak in the form of long ribbons that trailed down her back.

The Hearth was a true pentacle; the huge structure touching the low circular walls that surrounded it. Small gateways let the staff and students pass into the inner yards and through to the large entrance that was situated at the inward angle of the two southern points. Today the wide double doors had been pinned back, allowing a fresh flow of air right through the building. Dorcas could hear the quiet chatter of excited voices as she entered the Sacred Hearth and turned left to take the inner circle that ran around the middle of the pentacle. Thirteen students made a coven and five covens made up a year. Each had their own homeroom situated in one of the points.

Dorcas made her way down the long panelled corridor, pausing for a moment at the door to trace the familiar sigil carved into the wood.

'Dorcas, there you are, where's Ginny?' Joan asked impatiently. 'We're going to start the cleansing ritual in a while and all of us need to be here.'

'Zarah went hunting I believe, she'll be here in a minute.'

Joan stepped aside to let Dorcas pass, glancing up and down the corridor to see if Ginny was on her way. The hallway was hushed, most of the students were now preparing in their homerooms, but there was no sign of the last member of their coven. The girls were all gathered in the middle of the room and had already prepared and consecrated the circle. A bowl of incense simmered on a low table in the middle; the cleansing bowl next to it ready to receive the petals and herbs that would be added as the ritual started. Eliza and Breyone moved as one to make a space for her and she slid into her place. The circle sank into quiet contemplation to wait for their missing member.

The light had now dimmed outside and there was still no sign of Ginny.

'Where has she got to?' Amber asked.

'I don't know but we're going to have to do the ritual without her.' Joan said.

There were a few muffled gasps; they were not a full coven.

'I agree with Joan, the bell will start the Great Ritual in a minute and none of us will be prepared. Let's hope Ginny has done her own cleansing'

Maghda picked up the bowl and handed it to Eliza whilst she added jasmine petals, lavender flowers, and oil of frankincense and sandalwood. It was then covered with a purple velvet cloth as the coven said the cleansing mantra.

Blessed be these clean eyes,

To see the way,

Blessed be these clean hands,

To heal,

Blessed be this clean head,

To know what the hands and eyes do need.

The bowl was passed around until everyone had dipped their hands and wrists into the pungent water. As Manae was drying her hands, the bell sounded for the start of the last Great Ritual. The girls collected their athame from the table at the side of the room and waited to be summoned at the door.

'What if she doesn't come?' Nancy whispered, giving voice to twelve worried faces.

'Then Dorcas will have to make herself look like two people,' Joan said dismissively before adding 'if she doesn't mind that is.'

Dorcas raised an eyebrow but the rest of the coven looked unconvinced. Thirteen was the number of power and thirteen there should be. The door opened and Elsie, their coven Mother, ushered them across the corridor and into the Great Hall where they joined the rest of the covens to form a pentagram of sixty-four students and the mothers. Elsie did not appear to notice that one of their number was missing as she hurried them to their places.

The Mothers arranged themselves around the perimeter as the High Priestess Ellen stepped into the middle to address the students. Dressed from head to toe in garish purple velvet, she swished and jingled as she walked. Dorcas often thought that she wore way too many amulets. Her everyday jewellery was bad enough, but she looked like a child let loose in a treasure box when dressed for ritual. The woman was dripping in silver; arms, neck and ears heavily draped in every pagan symbol, amulet, and talisman that had ever been used in the craft. To cap it all she had even tied an Udjat on a piece of velvet ribbon and wrapped it around her forehead. Dorcas wondered why the Priestess felt the need to wear such a large talisman, especially over her third eye. Just what exactly was she trying to protect herself against?

As a follower of the highest of the high craft, Ellen revelled in the ceremony of the thing. She swept around her coven of students greeting them all in turn and offering wine from the sacred chalice. Mother Hedda dipped in and out filling the chalice as needed, and it was needed quite often. There were a few glances towards the door a number of times but Dorcas kept her gaze fixed on the Priestess. She could feel Maegwyn twitching silently beside her. There was nothing they could do; it was starting, and Ginny was going to miss the most important celebration of a witch's life all because of a cat.

'We are here. You have made it. Welcome Samhain, welcome the final Rite. The Goddess becomes crone and wise one, the year changes and so do we. Thirteen years ago you came, and now it is time to leave us and make way for a new generation. Before we can move forward it is time to look back.'

There was an audible shuffle as the students rearranged their feet and placed their hands in comfortable positions in front of them. The priestess twirled around in the middle and acknowledged the four elements of Fire, Water, Air, and Ether, coming to a standstill in front of the last point. There followed a long incantation towards the fifth point that was Spirit, thanking the God and Goddess for another year and wishing them well for the new one.

Dorcas hated all the pomp of these rituals and this one was going on a bit. Samhain was a lovely time of year but for many people it meant the start of hardship, hunger, and illness through the long dark winter months. Dorcas lost her focus and let her eye wander to the elaborate carvings that covered the walls of the Great Hall. One picture or pattern ran into another leading her on to the next panel. Dorcas knew each and every one of these pictures and symbols. Whoever had carved them had done so with a love and affection for the wood that he, or she, had worked with; that, and a deep understanding and knowledge of all aspects of witching. The eight festivals of the year were depicted along with the Goddess in all her incarnations. Interspersed with these panels were sayings drawn from the Book of Souls, blessings, and incantations framed intricately by the wood itself. They were a joy to the eye and had saved Dorcas many a time from the long boring rituals and ceremonies that dotted the Wheel of the Year.

With a flick of her hand, the Priestess signalled that the fire should be brought to the middle of the pentagram. The candles dimmed as the huge firebowl was carried through a gap by four Mothers and ceremoniously placed in the centre. Dorcas was barely aware of the communal indrawn breath of the sixty-four students and thirteen Mothers preparing to Pathwork. The candlelight faded into the background, the firebowl cast huge, wavering shadows across the walls and ceiling. Dorcas watched the shadows dance and old Mother Lylas came to mind; she was special to Dorcas; she was not surprised that she had come to her now.

'In order to scry, one needs focus' Lylas said, her voice overlapping with that of the Priestess.

Dorcas dragged her eyes away from the walls, drawn to the growing flames in the middle of the pentagram. She was back in the first term at Summerlands and was listening to a witch who had left the school some years ago. As she stared into the whitening flames, Mother Lylas's face became clearer. The communal Pathworking was strong, she had never looked back this far into herself, into her past. The rest of the room faded away and she found herself standing in the middle of a field, face to face with her favourite teacher and sometime guardian.

'Ah, there you are Dorcas, ready for this then?'

'If you mean what comes after I leave here then yes, I think so.'

'Think so, or know so?' Lylas asked.

'I'm not sure.'

'Better get used to it then.'

'Used to what?' Dorcas was growing confused as images started to overlap one another.

'The thing that you're not sure of.'

'You're talking in riddles Mother, I don't understand.'

'You'll know, the path is drawn, there are no mistakes. You are what you are. You cannot deny it. You will know who are and you'll do what you are supposed to do.'

Dorcas felt the ground lurch to one side and she reached out to Mother Lylas to steady herself but she was gone. In her place was the puzzled face of the High Priestess.

'We have been back for a few minutes now Dorcas, where were you?'

Dorcas brushed her skirts down, embarrassed that she had been singled out for taking too long and holding up the proceedings.

'Looking within' she said quietly.

'I see…'

The Priestess moved back to the middle of the circle.

'We will proceed then.'

After the proper incantations and a reading from the Book of Souls, the High Priestess visited all the students around the pentagram and blessed the proffered athame. The students then took their sacred knives in their right hands and repeated the Rites of Passage. It finished with a slicing of air as each student carved a slit in the ether and stepped through to her new life. The High Priestess stepped forward.

'I will not bore you with a long speech about the lives you are going to lead or the witches you are going to become. Suffice to say that you will find out on your own and in your own time.'

Willamina was the eldest witch at Summerlands and it was her honour to present the students with their new lives. Silence swept around the room as the old Mother stepped into the circle. Mother Sarah followed behind, holding the pile of cards on which was neatly written the name of each witch and the place where they would go. There was an audible crackle of anticipation in the air.

Dorcas planted her feet and locked her hands behind her back. The air of expectancy grew thicker as the bringer of destiny made her way slowly around the Great Hall.

'Frances Covington, you're going to Branfield Peak.'

The High Priestess moved on.

'Gerda Carpenter, Pickington.'

Pats on the back from her coven and as the Mother passed around there were nods of affirmation and confirmation as the students received their places.

Mother Willamina got to the start of her own coven. Masterbridge had not come up. There was hope, even though

Dorcas tried to push her strongest wishes out of her mind again.

'Gwenna Johnson, Halesmore Farm.'

Dorcas was pleased. Gwenna was going to a herbology farm where she could make salves, potions, and medicines from morning until night. Maghda, of course, was going to Sallington and Eliza to Peterling Infirmary to work at the newly founded hospital. She would need reining in on the amount of medication she administered but she would be useful to their research in botanicals. Everyone appeared to be going where they wanted to go and to where they were best suited. Even Amberlynne, to her surprise and delight was going to Connismere, a retreat of wellbeing in the Gretnor Mountains.

'Nancy Potter, Summersby.'

'Maegwyn Rogers, Castle Corton.'

Dorcas clapped and patted her on the shoulder, pleased again that another girl had won an exact placement for her skills.

Dorcas was next in line. She held her breath as the Mother drew close and sent a thousand silent pleas to the God and Goddess.

'Dorcas Fleming…you're…umm…that is…'

Dorcas snapped her eyes open as the old Mother hesitated and looked to the Priestess. Ellen nodded confirmation from the side of the room.

'You're going to Pendartha.'

There was a gasp of indrawn breath from the whole room and Dorcas's world began to unravel.

'Where?' she managed 'I...don't...?'

'We shall speak afterwards,' Ellen said behind her, putting a firm hand on her shoulder. 'Breathe now.'

Dorcas let her breath out but was barely aware of anything after that. Mother passed on to Breyone, Anne, Manae, and Joan and then on to the Elderflower coven. Her mind could not get a grip on anything and was casting around to make some sense of what she had just heard.

There seemed to be less enthusiasm in the clapping after Dorcas's placement had been announced and when the circle broke she sagged at the knees. Joan and Eliza helped her out to a chair in the corridor and her coven joined her, gathering around and fussing.

'Give her some air,' Joan said. 'This isn't going to help. Go and eat for goodness sake. She needs some space and there is nothing anyone can do.'

'But even the Mothers looked shocked.'

'Eliza, you're not helping!'

'Sorry Joan, I'll move everyone back into the Hall, shall I?'

Maghda and Joan drew up chairs beside her and offered some silent support but Dorcas was lost within the maelstrom that was spinning around her head.

'It couldn't be true, surely not where she should be going, there had been some mistake. Loston, Merrylake, or even Masterbridge. But not there, not there, and anyway where in Hecate's name was 'there'?'

She tried to imagine some sort of secret retreat that she had never heard of. Witches were always sent where they were meant to go. She had to keep faith, must keep her faith, there was nothing else to be done. After a while, she lifted her eyes from their fixed position on her knees.

'Did I hear that properly?'

'Afraid so,' Maghda said, patting her on the hand, 'nobody can believe it.'

'Well, I suppose I'll just have to get on with it then. Pendartha here I come?'

'That's the spirit, you're made of strong stuff Dorcas' Joan said.

'Perhaps it was Ginny's absence. Maybe it put a hex on the whole thing.'

'Not so Maghda,' Mother Elsie said from the doorway, 'Ginnifer Belle has left the college. She has run off with some local lad. She used the college to escape from that family of hers; she had no intention of returning home, ever.'

The news fell on ears that were already shocked.

'Did someone get Masterbridge then?' Dorcas asked.

Her fellow students looked at each other in dismay.

'Joan did' Elsie answered.

A few minutes later Dorcas was sitting in the private, overly decorated office of the High Priestess.

'You're in shock Dorcas dear, drink this.'

Dorcas sipped from the silver cup; the apple brandy made a warm river down her cold and shaking gullet. Her head felt as if it was too big and was going to burst. Ginny had run off with some lover from Brexham and she, Dorcas, was going to somewhere that no one had ever heard of.

'I...'

'Dorcas, listen while I explain a few things. Put Masterbridge out of your head, the runes have been cast, the Goddess has chosen, it is out of my hands. There is no 'why' for you, only 'how'. How can I achieve this, how can I make this work?'

'But I have never heard of Pendartha. How can I get my head around it if I don't know where it is I'm going? I assume Pendartha is something new or something remote'

The Priestess fiddled with a long tassel on her sleeve.

'This is going to be difficult' Ellen said shifting in her chair.

'I don't understand.'

'I'm not sure I do Dorcas. Pendartha is in the south.'

'South!' Dorcas cried jumping to her feet. 'South?'

'Yes, on the tip of the southern lands.'

Dorcas felt the blood drain from her face and her knees threatened to buckle beneath her.

'I can't. The heathen south? I can't go there!'

She flopped back in the chair her hands covering her face. This was worse than anything she could have imagined. What could she possibly have done to deserve such a punishment? Why her, why not one of the others? That Rosaria Tipton was a good all-rounder, she *came* from a community that was isolated. Why didn't they send her? Dorcas was a good student, she had worked all the hours that the Goddess had sent, had studied and studied and worked her fingers to the very bone. Why?

'No! I won't go, there's been some mistake' Dorcas moaned.

Ellen came around the desk and put her arm around Dorcas's shoulders.

'There has been no mistake. Pendartha has called, we must answer, and I am afraid that the answer is you.'

This was all too much. Dorcas gave in and sobbed for nearly an hour. The Priestess waited patiently for her initial grief to subside and wiped her eyes when she had finished. Dorcas tried to get herself under control and sat on her hands to stop them from shaking. The thoughts in her head ricocheted around like a pigskin ball in a courtyard. It was a long time before any words would come to her mouth.

'I'm to be a missionary witch then. On my own in the heathen lands. A coven of one. How will I survive? Can I really do this?'

The High Priestess nodded slowly. No words would help the poor girl now, nothing could be said that would comfort and reassure her. If the Goddess had chosen this path for Dorcas then that was what must happen. Ellen had reached this point in her career by being a wise, talented, and intuitive witch, but today, even she, was questioning the very core of her steadfast Pagan faith.

Raphael watch over me
Gabriel take me safely o'er the water
Auriel guide me safely o'er the land
And Michael take me safely there
- Pagan travel spell

Chapter three

Maghda poured another cup of tea.

'It's so quiet now, I can't believe that they are all gone' she said, handing the cup and saucer to Dorcas.

It had taken a week for the rest of the coven to depart. Eliza had left for Peterling only that morning and Maghda would be gone within the hour.

'It will be even quieter soon.' Dorcas said.

She could not believe that this was what she had been fighting for in the whole time she had been at Summerlands, peace and quiet. Now that she had it she thought she would give up everything to turn back the clock.

'You'll be alright though, now I mean, here on your own?'

'Oh yes, there's so much to prepare before I can leave. The Mothers are helping, gives them something to do before the new students start their classes.'

Both women spent a quiet few minutes taking their minds back over the last thirteen years. They could both remember clearly, how it felt to arrive at the college at ten years old. The new girls would spend their first six years in dorms to the north of the Hearth. Only when they reached sixteen would they move down to the cottages and become self-sufficient. It was part of their learning, a progression towards what they would eventually become.

'Thirteen years to find out that I'm good with pigs and puddings!' Maghda laughed.

Dorcas smiled. Maghda, above all, had been a steadfast support to her since Samhain. They had shared many midnight talks on any and every subject they could think of. The woman had kept Dorcas feeling positive where so many others could only see the dark side of what was happening to one of their own. The others did not know what to say or do and appeared to avoid her at all costs, wrapping themselves up in packing and preparing for their new lives. Maghda had just carried on as normal and that was exactly what she needed. In fact, Maghda had shown remarkable insight into how Dorcas was feeling, keeping those who felt the need to whisper behind her back out of earshot. Joan had thankfully departed for Masterbridge the day after the ritual; her presence would have been a constant reminder of things that could never be. Dorcas was trying to swallow her bitter pill but it seemed to be stuck in her throat, unable to go down no matter how many cups of tea Maghda put in front of her.

There was the sound of footsteps on the pebbles outside and Mother Elsie came into the kitchen.

'The cart is on its way down Maghda, are you ready?'

Maghda nodded and said that she would be out in a minute. Mother Elsie waited in the courtyard, leaving them to say their goodbyes alone.

'Dorcas, I know that you haven't always liked me very much.'

'Maghda, I....'

'No, listen, you have probably helped me in ways that you cannot imagine. I have put a keepsake next to your bed. When things get rough maybe you'll remember one of my puddings or something.'

Dorcas was surprised to find that she had tears in her eyes. She had never felt particularly close to any of her coven and it had taken thirteen years to find out that one of them was a lot deeper than she imagined.

'Take care of yourself Maghda, there are going to be some lucky pigs out there.'

Maghda laughed and hugged her tightly.

'You really shouldn't worry you know, with talents like yours you will manage wherever you go, even if it is to the end of the world.'

Dorcas watched as Maghda loaded up her bags on the back of the cart and climbed up beside the driver. She had a long journey ahead of her. She gave Dorcas and Elsie a cheery wave as the cart lurched out of the courtyard and down to the main drive. The Mother returned to the main building to check on her new girls and after Dorcas made a quick incantation for a safe journey, she went back inside for another cup of tea.

Later that day she found the small keepsake that Maghda had left for her. In the shape of a small pig, the silver amulet was no more than half an inch long. Dorcas recognised it as one of the many that Maghda had collected over the years and was touched that she had given it to her. Why now was she able to look back and say that she would miss all this when she had spent the last few years longing to be away from all of them? That was the way of things, perhaps you weren't supposed to know what you would miss until it was gone. Dorcas stifled the rising loneliness by throwing herself into making lists for her own journey.

The next day she accompanied Mother Hedda to Brexham to pick up the last of the supplies that she would need to take with her. By the end of the week, the cart would come to pick her up and take her to Mersden where she would join a trade convoy that made a twice-yearly journey to the south. After that, she would be completely on her own.

The empty workroom was now piled high with Dorcas's belongings. She could not see how she was ever going to get all this stuff onto a cart without some judicious pruning. The trip to Brexham had added considerably to the load and there were now crates of seeds, root vegetables, grains and a stack of other consumables that should see her through the first few weeks in her new home.

'Are you sure that I will need three hundred candles?' she had asked the High Priestess.

'The trouble is that we just don't know what is available down there Dorcas. The Mayor, who requested a witch, gave us very little to go on. We thought it best to send you with as many supplies as we possibly could as there will be a distinct lack of...umm...how shall I put it?'

'Contact with the civilised world' Dorcas suggested.

'Well, yes, if you like. But there is still the post or carrier pigeon for requests of extra supplies.'

If the convoy only went down twice a year then it was not exactly an efficient postal system Dorcas thought, and carrier pigeons were renowned for losing their way, or worse.

'Surely they have candles in the south?'

'Yes, I'm sure they have, it's just the question of whether they will share, you see.'

Ellen had talked at length about the possible pitfalls and there were many. It appeared that the small town that she was going to was not in total agreement about the procurement of a witch. The General Pagan Council in Masterbridge had been extremely vague about the finer details and even Ellen was struggling to know what was going to happen when she got there.

'You'll have to play it by ear Dorcas, we really don't know very much. Look upon it as an experiment. Practice your basic hedgewitching as and when you can and try to gain their trust. The council have asked that you stay at least a year to give it a chance but after that, well, the choice is yours I'm sure.'

For most people in the northern lands, the south was just somewhere over the Tamalar River and beyond, heathens who worked without the God and Goddess and the beauty of nature. Jokes were made about their indolent lifestyle and apathetic approach to their own destinies leaving it to the male representatives of their harsh and unforgiving church. Seven hundred years earlier, before the Century War, there had been a bridge that spanned the wide, fast-flowing Tamalar River. Trade and commerce had always been a little strained but was ultimately advantageous to both sides. War had broken out over something small and stupid, as many wars do, but had concluded with the fall of the bridge and the end of relations with their neighbours. Two religions divided once and for all by a body of water. People said it was a 'natural divide' and that the north should now keep to themselves and let the heathen southerners 'walk with the devil of their own making'.

In the last hundred years trade had started up again, convoys had ventured down into the southern lands to import and export goods that were mutually beneficial to both sides. The Pagan Council now encouraged these tenuous links and when the call had come in to request the presence of a witch on the southernmost tip of the Lazardian Peninsula they could hardly refuse. The south had long dispensed with their own witches, running them out of town and village, or worse. Dorcas had grown up with stories of what the heathens did to witches during the war. Mother Gertrude had often told the youngsters tales of the poor Porthaveland Witches who were rounded up and driven over cliffs to their deaths on the rocky shores below. That story had stayed with Dorcas for a long time and lately she found herself thinking of it again.

All the way to Mersden she wanted to jump from the cart and make a run for it. It would not have been very difficult. Peterson the driver could only manage to urge his two horses just above walking pace most of the time. The cart was a moving balancing act and it had taken the best part of a morning to load everything on. Pots, pans, chairs, and various other utensils clung onto the sides and rattled against each other noisily as the cart proceeded on its slow journey. Buried underneath the tarpaulin were the parts of a bed and a small, but substantial, kitchen table that was made from the finest Laetham wood. It was a gift from the Mothers and had been commissioned especially for her. A witch needed a good, plain wooden table to work on. The Priestess had gifted her a beautiful chalice that was also made of the same finely grained wood. There were none of the intricate carvings or gaudy stones that were so beloved by Ellen herself. She had obviously chosen with only Dorcas in mind, as the beautiful cup had no other adornment other than the handsome wood it was made of. Trained to look beyond that which was before her eyes Dorcas found that the chalice contained a number of images that changed with the light.

'Thank you, thank you everyone' she said, at what she now termed her last supper. The Mothers and Ellen put on a huge feast on the eve of her going; none of her favourite foods had been left out. Wine, roasted seasonal vegetables, her beloved appleherb sausage and a chocolate pudding that looked suspiciously like one of Maglida's.

'I'm not sure that I deserve all these gifts' she said, inwardly believing that they were really only sympathy gifts. The rest of the students had left with only the equipment and keepsakes that they themselves had bought or acquired during their time at Summerlands.

'We hope that you now have everything that you will need' Mother Elsie said.

'And of course you deserve it,' Ellen added. 'You should be settled before Yule; a good time for anyone to start something new.'

Dorcas hoped so, Yule was six weeks away, and the journey to the south should take no more than three.

'I have heard again from the Council. The general consensus is that the area you are going to is a little more open-minded than its more northern counties.'

That's all very well, but I've got to cross six counties before I get to my destination.'

'They say that the Lazardian Peninsula is very beautiful' Mother Hedda said.

'And that's if I've still got eyes to see it Mother when I get there.'

*

The cart pulled into the market town of Mersden on time. Peterson had been right when he had said they would not miss the convoy, although at times Dorcas had felt that they would be going backwards if they went any slower. The hundred-mile journey had been free of any aggravation and Dorcas had enjoyed soaking up the views of her homeland.

As they entered the market square, Dorcas was amazed to see so many carts, wagons, coaches, and horses. There was a general noisy hubbub of people trying to get things done in a hurry. Sacks of grain were being hefted by lines of burly men, bolts of cloth and crates of brandy stacked as high as they could go on top of long based carts that would be drawn by teams of eight horses. The noise was almost deafening as she made her way to the Market offices to find out where her travelling companions were based. The Council had purchased a place with 'Horton and Sons' who were venturing nearly all the way down with a shipment of wines from the Bressington presses, part of the Masterbridge winery. The return journey would be lighter as they were picking up bales of raw cotton, a natural product of the Lazardian Peninsula.

'Mr Horton I presume' Dorcas said after picking up her messages and making her way back across the square.

'Ah, Miss Fleming, we thought you weren't coming,' said the ruddy-faced man 'We leave in an hour, brought it forward to miss the worst of the bad weather when we cross the Tamalar.'

'Good job we got here when we did then' Dorcas said aware that the Horton sons had stopped what they were doing and had come to have a look at her.

'Don't like this trip much at this time of year, but as a rule the weather improves as you get further down.'

Peterson brought the cart across the square and the Horton sons eyed it suspiciously.

'They didn't say it would be that much Pa' one of the smaller Horton boys said, although none of the six were much smaller than their father.

'No they didn't but that's the council for you. Don't worry Miss we'll squeeze you, and all those belongings, on the cart, somehow.'

Dorcas watched while all her worldly good were transferred to the slightly larger wagon that would be drawn by a single horse. Although her cart was nowhere near as huge as the convoy carts, Dorcas was pleased that Mr Horton himself would take charge of it. His sons were all at that hormonal stage of a boy's life when even a witch looks like a good prospect.

'I'll look after you, don't you worry. Done this many a time Miss Fleming. The south holds no fear for the Hortons.' he said, as they pulled out of Mersden exactly an hour later. About ten of the convoy followed them out of the market town, the rest would catch up when they had finished loading.

'Please call me Dorcas. If we're going to spend three weeks together then I would rather you called me by my given name.'

'That would be fine Dorcas, and you, if you wish that is, can call me Stanley.'

Stanley Horton had a healthy respect and admiration for witches to the extent that he had almost bowed once or twice to the young woman. He had lived in and around Masterbridge all his life, an area that was steeped in the ancient ways. Most northerners held their witches in great esteem and Dorcas proposed to make the most of it while it lasted. She doubted that the same could be said for the population of Pendartha. She had taken a liking to Stanley immediately, he was straightforward when he spoke but generally did not say more to her than he had to. This suited Dorcas; she was not given to verbal diarrhoea herself and found it hard sometimes to join in with the gossip that flew around the kitchen at Summerlands.

The weather worsened as they approached the banks of the great Tamalar River and as they passed through the hills Dorcas spent most of her time hidden under a voluminous oilskin that Stanley provided for her. Her new travelling hat kept the worst of a straight downpour off her face but it could not combat the rain that was as fine as dust, getting into every pore, making her feel soggy from head to foot. The track deteriorated as the rain continued, forcing them to stop every now and again to go back and help a member of the convoy stuck in the quagmire. The tracks that led to the south had been sadly neglected and were full of wide potholes and deep mud-filled trenches. They all worked together to free the stuck animals and carts, allowing the train of vehicles to move on its way again.

Two days later the land dipped sharply away to reveal the body of water that divided the two now separate countries.

'There is no way we are going to cross that' Dorcas thought as she surveyed the swirling brown waters before them. They waited an hour on the sodden bank until out of the misty rain, very slowly, came the ferry that would take them over to southern soil.

'They saw us ages ago, mark my words,' Stanley said 'they always make us wait. Still at war in one way or another I suppose.'

As the ferry drew nearer Dorcas's heart started to pump. She could see the angry waters slopping over the sides of the flat-bottomed ferry and it did not even have a full load on board. She fiddled in the pockets of her cloak and pulled out her talisman, silently repeating an incantation.

'A word of advice,' Stanley said as the ferry started to pull into the bank 'put that away for now and if I were you I'd store that hat under the seat, just until we're away from the ferry you understand.'

The head carter chose his words carefully. He knew what the pointy hat meant to a witch, it was said that they were born and buried with it. The girl was not wearing the usual hat of trade but a witch's hat always seemed to take on that shape no matter how it started off. Dorcas nodded as she complied with his suggestion, she did not want to upset the locals even before she set foot on their land.

The journey across the Tamalar River proved to be just as horrific as Dorcas had imagined. With ten carts aboard, the ferry creaked and groaned against its thick ropes, as if trying to break them and make a bid for freedom that would eventually take it out to sea. The rivers at home, and those around Summerlands, had been meandering, thoughtful rivers that barely changed during the course of the year. Rivers with water as clear as crystal, where you could tickle trout or dangle your hot booted feet in during the warm summer months. This was not a river for tickling anything. The Tamalar was an angry raging torrent that Stanley insisted was much better tempered in the spring.

Dorcas did not know what she was expecting but the five ferrymen looked like fairly decent people and when they eventually reached the other side, they graciously helped her off and helped to guide the distressed horses up the sloping, slippery bank to dry land. She did not realise that the convoy paid a heavy tax to get across the river and the ferrymen were paid extra tips in goods and silver for their safe passage. It was more a case of twenty coins to pay the ferryman rather than just the normal two.

The next hurdle was the pompous little man in the customs office that was situated at the side of the road as they came up from the ferry. In fact, he was not little at all but he had the air of a little man. He strutted out from the brick built office in his too tight uniform and held his hand up for them to stop.

'Let me do the talking, we always have trouble with this one' Stanley whispered.

The officer took out a small notebook that had been wedged tightly in his top pocket; he then licked his pencil two or three times and rocked backwards and forwards on his heels.

'First of the autumn convoy?'

'That's right sir.'

'Carrying?'

'The finest wines from Masterbridge sir, and a variety of goods to trade with the good south.'

'I see no wine in this wagon' the officer said.

'Ah, this stuff belongs to this young lady. The wine is following in the five carts behind us sir. One of me sons in each and two at the back.'

The customs man glared at Dorcas, his eye travelling down her black clothes.

'Widows weeds?'

'Umm, no sir, not exactly sir.'

'I see.'

Dorcas was getting fed up with this game, the man was going to draw this out until after dark and she had no wish to spend her first night in the south on the open road.

'Here are my papers,' she said sharply 'I think you'll find them in order.'

The customs officer snatched them out of her hand and read the first page.

'Happen I might Miss, err, Fleming, but we has to go through the proper procedures.'

He drew out the last word into separate syllables. Then he started to poke at the tarpaulin that covered her worldly goods.

'I think I'm just going to have to ask you to take this lot off so as I can see what you are hiding underneath. We can't have anything illegal coming in, now can we?'

Stanley jumped down off the cart with cap in hand, and started to pull the covering off her things. The carts and wagons were starting to pile up behind them as another part of the convoy was delivered to dry land. The drivers were getting down and starting to make what appeared to be a camp for the night at the side of the road. This officious little twerp would keep them here until tomorrow if he had his way, but that was not going to be the case. Dorcas came around the other side and with a sweet smile, she linked her arm with the tightly uniformed arm of the customs officer.

'I think we should have a cup of tea don't you?' she said, gently propelling him towards the office.

*

An hour later, Stanley was still chuckling into his flagon of beer. Two miles from the ferry lay the first night-stop in southern lands. The owner of this coaching house, aptly named 'The Horse and Cart', was quite used to visitors from all over the south, and occasionally from the north. Money was money after all, and tonight he was going to make more coinage than he had done in the last six months. He looked forward to the twice-yearly visits from the north and would like a lot more if he had his way. Tonight, business was booming. Instead of coming in dribs and drabs, the convoy had arrived all at once and were now making a concerted effort to drink his barrels dry. Very often those who had been held up by that bastard up the road didn't get near the coach house until after closing time and then slept in their carts, losing him valuable revenue. Now the alehouse was packed with the drivers from the convoy and they were all in good spirits. Like Dorcas, they had been grateful to have crossed the river all in one piece and they were also extremely grateful that they were not still waiting at the customs office.

Dorcas and the Hortons found a cosy corner next to the roaring fire. The table was full of flagons and a small fortified wine for Dorcas, a meal of mutton pie was on its way.

'I knew it, I knew it! As soon as you got that snotty witchy look on your face I knew he was done for.'

'I don't know what you mean Mr Horton' Dorcas said snappily.

'I seen it before, when a witch gets that look on, well, you'd best beware. Our Old Mother at home used to get a face on like that when she was riled, you could sour the milk with it.'

'And that is probably what he was worried about Stanley,'

Dorcas said 'now please lower your voice or we'll be thrown out.'

Dorcas had had plenty of warnings about keeping her head down and not drawing too much attention to herself. According to some of her fellow travellers, there were still places in the south where a witch could be tried for her so-called crimes. One of the drivers told her that there was a town in the east where black was strictly forbidden; they even killed black lambs, should one dare to appear. She stayed well back in the corner all night and told herself that her hat and black cloak would travel better at the bottom of one of her crates.

The Horton boys had stopped their awful habit of staring at her and fixed their attentions on a buxom barmaid who looked to Dorcas as if she enjoyed the attentions of many of the opposite sex. The lads took it in turns to vie for her attention and Dorcas enjoyed listening to the many retorts the girl had in her repertoire, making a silent note of the ones she liked.

Stanley continued to snigger all through the meal, stopping every now and again to shake his head and wipe away the tears of mirth that squeezed from the corners of his eyes. Dorcas ignored him and delicately picked her way around the meat. Witches never ate meat but she did not want to jeopardise anything else by making this too obvious. It was said that people in the south ate anything that had legs. Dorcas wondered at the prejudice towards snakes, meat was meat after all.

Once she had finished the meal Dorcas retired to her small, cupboard-like room above the alehouse. They were not used to having paying guests in the upper floors but the sheets were cleanish and there did not appear to be anything living in the mattress. The rest of the convoy would sleep soundly in the bar, tucked in with a few flagons of southern beer, dreaming of the money that they would make in the next few weeks.

Dorcas lay for a long time in her lumpy bed mulling over the events of the day. It had not been a good one. She had only just set one of her sensibly booted feet in this country and already she was on rocky ground. She really had not meant to lose control this early in the game

Hecate, see me in red, and love me
See me in purple, and open mine eyes to spirit
See me in yellow, for happiness
See me in green, and keep me healthy
See me in silver, so I may have the knowing

Chapter four

The weather had improved the next day. The skies were clear and blue, with a stiff, snappy breeze following behind that helped to push the convoy towards its destination. Three of the carts and wagons had broken off already and the next five would be stopping at the first big town that they would encounter on this road. The Hortons would be the only ones to carry on in a straight and direct route to the southernmost counties.

The landscape changed with every hour that passed. They had crossed a moorland a few days before that had been desolate and bleak; miles of open moor without tree nor bush to soften its hardness. The wind had twisted the few sparse trees into the shapes of bent old men, reaching towards the ground in an attempt to protect themselves. In the distance, a few derelict houses still clung to their former shape, the roofs long gone to the harsh elements that blew across this open stretch of land. There were many places in the north that were open to harsh conditions but Dorcas had never seen anywhere so devoid of life. No bird, animal, or living thing was seen as they passed through.

'It is said that there is a ring of stones somewhere around here,' Stanley said, his words snatched from his mouth as soon as they were spoken. 'Nine maidens turned to stone for dancing on the southern Sabbath, so the saying goes.'

'I wouldn't have thought it very sensible to go out dancing in this Goddess forsaken place anyway, 'Dorcas said 'you could turn anything to stone here no matter what day it was.'

As they moved deeper south, their surroundings mellowed considerably. The harsh moorland gave way to soft undulating hills, covering the land like a green patchwork blanket with a couple of large bodies underneath it.

'Looks like my wife' Stanley chuckled, pointing at a pair of buxom hills.

For days, they saw only the empty road and a few tiny villages in the distance. All around these small outposts there were fields that were edged in hedges of grey stone. The southerners certainly grew a lot of crops; the varieties were endless, springing from a fertile soil even at this time of year. They also kept a variety of domesticated livestock and Dorcas noticed that they were not even wearing thick woollen coats in readiness for the winter. The sheep on Ashen Moor nearly lost their faces in the winter with the thick growth, and the memory made a knot in her stomach. She was particularly taken by the herds of doe-eyed cattle that seemed to roam wherever they fancied. The placid creatures held up the convoy on more than one occasion until they decided to move on at their own pace.

A few times, they passed some local traffic but there was none of the social interaction that would have accompanied such an event in the north. Most hurried past with little or no eye contact and only once had someone acknowledged them and asked their destination.

*

Polempter was a busy town nestling in a wide valley in the lower counties of the southern lands and was the biggest settlement that the area had to offer. It seemed to be a crossroads and contained many sights that Dorcas had never seen before. When she went off on her own to browse the open market, Stanley furnished her with a bright red cloak before he took a horse off to the blacksmith for a new shoe.

'Try not to open your mouth too much, it's a dead giveaway, and don't use any of those long words you're so fond of. They don't like it when they can't understand.'

Dorcas promised that she would indeed keep her mouth closed as much as she could but found it difficult when asking the price of anything. The red cloak seemed to be a good cover and she came back with a number of items.

'What's that?' Stanley Horton, the eldest boy, said, pointing to the bundle of plants that were hanging over the edge of her basket

'Comfrey, good for bruises, thromboses, varicose ulcers, and chronic diseases of the joints and bones. Also good for haemorrhoids although care must be taken when applying it, of course.'

Horton the Younger was completely lost after 'bruises' and asked no more as to the contents of her shopping. He had doubted for a while that someone who looked like her was indeed a proper witch but she had the learning, he was sure about that now. As Dorcas stored her new purchases in the cart, she heard a yell from across the square.

'Miss Fleming, Miss Fleming, come quick.'

It was Peter, the youngest son, and he was running at full pelt knocking a few people aside in his haste.

'Come quick, it's Pa.'

Dorcas hurried across the market square and into the smithy.

Stanley was lying on the cobbled floor in a pool of his own making. There was blood everywhere and a horse was trying to back up into the smith's fire pit. Dorcas surveyed the scene quickly and gave her instructions. John went back to the cart for her medicine bag, Stanley went for water, and Peter went in search of a blanket.

'Will you please get that animal under control and get it out of here' she ordered.

The smith did as he was told and vacated the hot dark room with the wild-eyed horse straining at the end of a rope.

The horse, spooked by a log popping right in front of it, had reared in the confined space, and had twisted around, knocking Stanley to the floor. As he went down he had made a grab for something solid and had run his hand down the whole length of the smithy's sharpening blade that was fixed upright into a huge cut log. The hand was open from one side to the other and was still losing an awful lot of blood.

'I need some more light in here.'

One of the locals opened up both of the doors at the front of the building.

'It's not as bad as it looks Stanley,' she said firmly.

Stanley was convinced that he had lost a few fingers but the witch's confident manner and her not-to-be-argued-with tone calmed him down. Dorcas sat him up and held the wound tightly closed until her bag arrived. Over the next ten minutes, she cleaned, mended, and bandaged the wounded hand. A crowd of people had gathered at the entrance to the smithy and were pushing each other aside to get a better look at the disturbance.

'What's all this then?' an authoritative voice demanded.

The small crowd parted and some of them scuttled off. A fair few did not want to miss any of the action so they took up positions in a circle around Dorcas and her patient.

'I said, what is going on here?'

A portly man with a finely cut coat stood in the entrance. The smithy whipped off his hat and bowed his head close to his chest. Dorcas nodded briefly in the newcomer's direction and continued to minister to Stanley's wound.

'This man has cut his hand, I…'

'I'll talk to a man, keep your mouth shut woman.'

The smith took a few steps forward and bowed again.

'Squire, the horse reared and this 'ere fellow fell on my sharpening blade.'

'And the woman, what's she got to do with all this?'

The blacksmith looked at his boots.

'Well'

'She fixed him up. His hand was cut bad.'

'There is the smell of ungodly things in here,' the squire scowled, eyeing Dorcas's bright red cloak, 'I will have the truth of it. Now if you please.'

Stanley struggled to his feet; it had been cold on the cobbled floor, and the chill had set into his aching joints.

'She didn't mean no harm sir.'

The Squire glared.

'Northern?'

'Yes sir, supply convoy on our way down to St Zenno on the Lazardian Peninsula.'

'I know where it is man. And that,' he said pointing at Dorcas 'where is *that* going?'

Stanley the younger appeared at his father's side and offered Dorcas's papers with a low bow. The Squire took them and read them in silence.

'I could clap it in irons if I had a mind,' he said belligerently 'it seems a friend of mine has endorsed these papers, but I would rather have you out of my town the sooner the better. Be gone by midday or I'll have the dogs on you.'

The Squire threw the papers on the floor and Dorcas and the boys helped Stanley back to the carts in the square.

'A close shave,' Stanley said as they cleared the town boundaries

'That squire is a nasty piece of work. Loves the wine we bring but would rather we left it at the edge of town.'

'He needs a lesson in proper manners' Dorcas said, fervently hoping that the inhabitants of her new town were going to be a little more friendly.

Peter drove the cart and they wedged Stanley in between them. His hand would be useless for a few days. Peter was glad of the opportunity to drive the front cart and prove himself to his father; being the youngest meant that he was always at the back with one of his brothers on lookout duty. Dorcas didn't speak for the rest of the day, her head was still in a place that it didn't want to be. When they stopped at the roadside for the night, she ate her supper and went straight to her bed under the cart. The Hortons talked long into the night and drank to the Goddess to deliver their little witch safely to her destination.

Dorcas was pleased with the sight of Stanley's hand the next day, the wound was clean, and there was no sign of infection around the stitching.

'It's a marvel, very neat Dorcas, thank you kindly.'

'You still won't be able to use it for a week or so, you don't want to break those stitches open. I have prepared a small tub of marigold and borage salve for you to use after you have dropped me off. It will keep the inflammation down and there's a tisane of nettle, comfrey and elder for the arthritis.'

'You're an angel Miss Fleming.'

Dorcas raised an eyebrow.

'I don't think the Squire of Polempter thought that somehow.'

Stanley took a deep breath. He had his views on things but had kept his mouth shut, until now.

'I'm sure I don't know all the reasons you've been sent to this heathen land, the council must have their wisdom. But why Dorcas? Why are they sending you here to this Goddess forsaken place?'

'Not sure that I know myself Stanley, the call was put out, and I've been sent to answer it. We cannot question these things.'

Stanley kept the rest of his thoughts to himself; there was no point in upsetting the girl further. She was brave and clever but he had seen some of the things that went on down here and the incident in the smithy had only been a small taste. The southerners were wrapped in the shawl of their religion like a colicky baby, tight and unmoving. They had lost any remnants of the faith that they had once shared with the north, and had abandoned it in favour of a constricting creed that did not allow them to fart in peace, let alone act without the guidance of the church. A cold shiver went up his spine when he thought about abandoning her in this backward land. How she would survive, he just did not know.

*

The journey progressed down towards the very tip of the southern lands and by late morning, the weather had changed again. The biting cold days of the north had been replaced with afternoons that almost felt like a spring day. It was not unusual for the Summerlands College to be cut off from everything for a few weeks around Yule. That was still a while away but Dorcas had sensed the first signs of snow as she was leaving. That cold crispness had been heavy in the air. The winter solstice was approaching, but down here, you could mistake it for the summer solstice.

'Is it always this warm?' Dorcas asked laying her cloak behind her and pulling up her sleeves.

'They get their fair share of foul weather, just a bit milder. The rain is what gets you, no heavy downpours just that awful foggy excuse. They call it mizzle and that is exactly what it is' Stanley said.

Stanley was a true northerner, a spade was always a spade, and he liked his weather to do what it was supposed to do. Rain should come down in straight lines and snow should be expected at exactly the same time every year. He told her that during the summer the roads became a dusty river and that a man could lose his hair in the dry heat if he did not keep his hat on.

'Pa sometimes has to wear just his vest and cap when it gets that hot' Peter remarked.

Dorcas could not imagine Stanley in just his undergarments and it was not a thought she cared to dwell on. All the carters in the convoy wore at least seven layers of clothes and they only ever seemed to peel off a couple of outer coverings when they settled down for the night. She could also not imagine Stanley without his cap on. Whatever the weather, it appeared to be stuck to his head with some kind of glue. In high winds, rain or sun, the cap stayed exactly where it was.

Dorcas was getting used to the pattern of the days that passed in the south. They got up before dawn and she helped to cook a meal that at first she had found hard to swallow so early in the morning. The pottage of beans, salt pork, assorted vegetables, and barley was a rolling meal that was added to every other day with whatever the convoy managed to pick up on the way. Dorcas had emptied her breakfast over the side of the cart a number of times until her stomach became accustomed to the early morning assault but made her own version without the meat. The men did not stop all day unless a town got in the way and even the call of nature was done on the run. Dorcas had found to her dismay sometimes as she had leaped down from the cart that it moved an awful lot quicker than she thought and she had to hitch up her skirts and run to catch up after she had emptied her bladder behind a tree or a hedge.

The gentle hills rolled on for another two days until, far in the distance, Dorcas could see a silvery ribbon shining on the horizon.

'That is the Lazardian Channel, open sea. St Zenno is a few miles down the road. It seems your journey is nearly at an end Miss Fleming. Pendartha is about six or seven miles ahead of us.'

Dorcas had never seen open sea before and was fascinated by the glistening band that changed by the minute. She found herself willing the cart up the gentle hills that stood in their way just to get a better look. When the land started to take its final dip towards the coast the convoy stopped for a rest and Dorcas took a final look at Stanley's injured hand. It was much better, but Peter was still in control of the reins. It would be a few days yet before he would be using it again.

'I have been thinking,' he said as Dorcas wrapped a clean bandage expertly around his hand 'I think you should take this cart on to Pendartha on your own. No good all of us upsetting them before you've set a foot in the place.'

After the reception at Polempter, Dorcas was inclined to agree. She would also arrive in the town at around midday, which would give her time to sort herself out before nightfall.

'You don't want to get this far and then find yourself in gaol now do you? I'll be back in six months, you can let me have the cart back then' Stanley said.

'But your cotton, you'll only have five carts for the return journey.'

Stanley smiled and patted her arm.

'Let's just say that the General Pagan Council have more than made up for the temporary loss of me cart. Don't worry your head about it, just look after the horse, he's a favourite of mine.'

Just outside the town boundary, Dorcas said goodbye to the Hortons. The leave taking was more emotional than she thought it would be. She had grown fond of Stanley and his 'boys' over the last few weeks and she would miss them. The men waited at the crossroads and watched the single cart until it was out of sight. Stanley and his boys rumbled off to their destination with heavy hearts.

Chapter five

The only road down into Pendartha lay before her and the only way back to civilisation was disappearing rapidly into the distance behind her. The road became a rough track about half a mile ahead and then dipped down sharply into a long wooded vale. Dorcas urged the horse on. The trees grew thicker and denser as she went, closing in around her as the track dropped to the bottom of the valley. The sun's rays struggled through the thick foliage, casting shafts of light on the uneven track in front of her. Birdsong announced her arrival and the odd rustle of small animal movement could be heard above the cartwheels and Horton's horse Winston's heavy hooves.

The road twisted and turned until she found she was following the path of a winding river that meandered through the ancient woods. Dorcas stopped for a while to wash her face, dust off her clothes, and gather her thoughts; the icy water revived her a little. She carried on; the woods started to thin and a couple of low granite houses came into sight. One looked deserted and the other had boards across the small windows. The river took a sharp turn curving around a mill; the woods in front opened up and the beginnings of Pendartha itself came into sight. The track became well-worn cobbles as she crossed the bridge found herself at the head of the small valley-bound town. Dorcas took a deep breath.

'Well, here I am, my first placement and let's hope it's not the last. God protect me and Goddess guide me, I am in the wilderness.'

*

Houses grew out of each side of the steep valley walls as far as the eye could see. Before her, in the middle, lay the main part of Pendartha with the small, fast running river cutting the town in half. It wound down between the houses and some of them even straddled the river, with odd-looking extensions held up with water-warped timber.

If she did not know better she would have thought it was a Sunday. The town was completely silent, no dogs barking, no children playing, not a living soul in sight. Dorcas moved the cart further down into the town. The road became very narrow in places, the cart nearly touching the granite walls on either side.

Tiny lanes, only wide enough for walking, led off between the cramped dwellings. Dorcas had never seen houses like these, they were like something out of a fairytale, and 'rickety' was the word that came to mind. The buildings were odd shapes and sizes, as if they had been added as needed and built to fit the available gaps. Some of them leaned out into the street, and in places, it would have been possible to pass a cup of tea from one to the other on the upper floors. She passed an alehouse and a couple of small shops but all were empty of life.

The quiet was unnerving and not what she had expected at all. There were signs that there *were* people here, she could see washing lines high up on the sides of the valley with the trappings of ordinary people blowing out in the wind.

The skies darkened and the rain came. Dorcas tried not to see it as a bad omen. She pulled the oilskin from under her seat, wrapped it tightly around her and carried on through the wet, empty streets.

'Perhaps they have all been stuck with disease, or plague, perhaps I'm too late. But too late for what?'

The horse plodded on until the road widened into a small square with a celtic cross in the middle. At the head of the square was a severe building that shouted its authority over the rest of the town. The structure was some sort of religious place of the like that Dorcas had never seen before. No spire, no nave, and no steeple; it had high windows with small leaded panes and she could see that there were inscriptions painted on them that could only be read if one were on the inside. Outside, the solid grey walls were devoid of the decorative attachments that would have accompanied such a building in the north. High up near the apex of the roof the date of completion had been incorporated into the stone and underneath were the words: 'God alone is the simple truth for a simple people'.

'Oh Goddess!'

As she climbed down from the cart to stretch her legs, the double doors of the huge square building opened to reveal the reason for the empty streets. Six men bore the coffin out on their shoulders followed by, what seemed like the whole of the population of Pendartha and its surrounding area. Dorcas tried to make herself invisible and was ignored for a while as the cortege made its slow way back up through the town in the direction that she had just come. Burial grounds must be some way out of the town, there was surely no room amongst the cramped dwellings to hold a cemetery.

There was a gathering outside the building and Dorcas was suddenly aware of many eyes boring into the back of her neck. She turned and came face to face with a dour looking man who, on closer inspection, needed a good dose of milk thistle to clean his liver out and rid him of the yellow tinge that afflicted his skin. He said something, but the rain drowned out his words.

'What, I'm sorry?'

Dorcas concentrated on his mouth but felt that the man was obviously speaking another language. She cast about looking for someone to interpret. Masterbridge had neglected to tell her that she would have to learn to communicate with the locals before she could help them. He repeated the gobbledegook but she could not understand a word he said even when she watched his lips and strained her ears. The crowd drew nearer and Dorcas fought a feeling of panic that was rising from the pit of her stomach.

'Miss, Miss!'

The crowd parted slightly to let a rotund little man through. Like a child's spinning top, his button-through coat was straining at the equator and there was not much mileage between north and south. Under a peaked hat his white curly hair was making a bid for freedom and Dorcas noticed that his beard showed signs of tobacco staining.

'You are *her,* aren't you?' he said 'I mean, the one we asked for, you have come to us from Masterbridge.'

Dorcas nodded, her brain still deciphering the words of a dialect that was as thick as maple syrup.

'I am Dorcas, Dorcas Fleming, yes from Masterbridge, pleased to meet you.'

Dorcas was so pleased to find she understood, that her words tumbled from her mouth in relief and gratitude.

'I am the Chief Penpol.'

'Chief! Chief? They are a tribe?

Dorcas took the hand that was offered and noticed that the skin was as rough as the bark of a tree and split in a number of places. This man had worked in a harsh environment all his life.

The crowd had become insufferably close and some were jostling for a good position to get a look at her.

'I am thinking t'would be best to get out of this 'ere rain Miss, then us can talk' the Chief said, taking her elbow and directing her into a house on the square. Penpol's cottage was on the opposite side to the building that Dorcas had assumed was some kind of church

He pushed her through the low door that proclaimed above that it was 'Lily Cottage' and closed it firmly behind him shutting out the milling crowd.

'Bit on the skittish side today, funerals always makes them a tad jumpy' the man said, leading her into the building.

'You *are* the Mayor then?' Dorcas inquired as they came into a small hall.

'Amongst other things, Miss Fleming. This is me work down here, I lives upstairs.'

He took her cloak and hung it on a wooden peg on the wall that held a variety of wet weather clothes. He then led the way up a narrow staircase to the first floor and they came out into the most surprising room that she had ever seen.

Gingham covered every surface. Dorcas had nothing against the pattern, but it was in every colour and had taken over the whole room. Red gingham curtains at the small windows, green gingham cushions on the small couch, blue on the table and a deep red runner on the dresser. There were gingham napkins, gingham pelmets and there were even a set of gingham china cats sitting on the windowsill in order of height. It was all a bit overwhelming.

'Cup o' tea then?'

'Oh yes please Mr Chief' Dorcas said relieved that tea was not going to be a problem in this area.

'It's Josiah, Miss Fleming, Josiah Penpol. I am the Mayor of this town and also Chief of the lifeboat amongst other things.'

'Yes, of course' she said removing the cloak, smoothing down her dress and noting her first mistake.

He picked up a small bell and gave it a delicate shake, 'I will just call my wife, but, umm, I must tell you that Violetta is a little nervous of meeting you.'

The bell was answered by a woman who surprisingly only had one piece of gingham on. As short and as plump as her husband, the woman was a vision of failing corsets and was swathed in a heavily-patterned fabric that would have been better suited to a window. Her round face was framed by greying blonde hair that had been teased into ringlets, which fell from a loose bun at the back of her head. At her neck hung a small thin gold cross that sank into an ample cleavage that started just under her chin. The gingham apron around her waist was fussy and frilly and those were the exact two words that Dorcas would have used to sum up

Mrs Violetta Penpol.

'This, my dear, is Miss Fleming from Masterbridge, she is come to us at last.'

Violetta stared at Dorcas and without a word or an acknowledgement she turned and disappeared quickly back to where she had come from. A few awkward minutes later, a tray, covered with gingham cloth, was put before her. Violetta nervously took a seat next to her husband, and arranged and re-arranged the teacups, with shaking hands. With tea as dark as a millpond and a piece of cake that looked as if it would be better off holding up a building, Dorcas waited politely for Mr Penpol to speak. His wife gave her surreptitious glances over the top of her cup.

'So, Miss Fleming, welcome to Pendartha.'

'Thank you.'

'I trust your journey was not too arduous?'

'No, not at all, just very long.'

'I suppose you'll be wanting to see your ... err, accommodation an' all that. When the crowd from the funeral has moved off, I shall give you directions. I must say you're not quite what we was expecting.'

'And this room is not quite what I was expecting!'

'That would be lovely. I was wondering if there would be somebody that would be willing to help me unpack.'

Josiah looked a bit surprised.

'I mean,' Dorcas continued, aware that she may have said something out of turn 'if it's not too much trouble that is.'

'But you are a witch ain't you,' the wife blurted out 'you can do they things, what do you need someone else for?'

Violetta Penpol had been completely thrown by her first sight of the witch. It was her first contact with any of those devil-worshipping, sinful northerners and her mind was all at sixes and sevens. A witch had no business to be that young, that normal looking; it was downright disconcerting to ordinary folk. The Preacher had said that witches carried their evil on them like a vile cloak but this one could pass you in the street and you would not know the difference. If she had the mark of the devil on her then it was certainly not visible.

'My dear, I think Miss Fleming is just trying to fit in, very commendable. I am sure someone would be willing. I'll just go down and see.'

With that, he left the two women alone and Dorcas got the distinct feeling that if Violetta could have opened up a hole in the floor she would have disappeared down it like a rabbit with a ferret after it.

'The weather has been good' she offered.

Violetta stared.

'The journey was very long.'

The staring continued.

'I shall be glad to be ...'

'But you're wearing blue!' the Mayor's wife said as if she had not heard a word that Dorcas had been saying.

Dorcas smiled and could not resist.

'I am sorry to disappoint Mrs Penpol, I only wear black when I fly on my besom.'

That was enough for Violetta. She scooped up the tray and made a dash out of the room. Dorcas could hear her nervously rattling dishes in the kitchen.

Josiah returned with a tall, dark looking man in tow and without saying goodbye to the absent wife, she was taken down to the waiting cart.

'This is second mate Tregonning, he'll help you offload your cart. I shall come down in the morning when you have, umm, settled in.'

It was clear that the second-mate Tregonning was not going to talk to her let alone look at her, so they rode in silence further down into the town. The winding cobbles took them as far as the inner harbour that was now absent of water. Even in the rain Dorcas could see that this was a pretty, if quaint, little town, reminding her of some of the scattered villages in the more remote regions in the north. She doubted that they would be any less welcoming to a stranger who had been thrust amongst them, especially one from the south.

As she looked back up the valley, she could see that there were houses clinging to the cliffs nearly to the top. The whole town looked as if a child had built it, or dropped a pile bricks from a great height letting them fall into a higgledy-piggledy mess. Some of the dwellings looked quite attractive; an attempt had been made to cover the austere grey granite with trailing plants, and with pots at the sides of the low front doors. In the summer, it probably looked quite colourful. The harbour had a few stranded fishing boats and the harbour wall was full of bell shaped pots and lines of nets strung over upright supports. The place gave off a pungent smell that Dorcas recognised as seaweed, a number of types of which were used in her medicine chest.

The cart swung up the cliff on the right hand side of the village passing the harbour that was the mainstay of Pendartha. Two thick walls that nearly met in the middle protected the inner harbour. The outer harbour was formed by the natural cliffs on either side and Dorcas could see the narrow passage that boats would have to take through the rocks that lay just under the surface. They continued out around the small jutting headland, and down onto a long thin beach that wrapped around the coast.

'So they intend to keep me out of the town, I suppose I can't blame them. As long as I have some sort of roof over my head I shall have to be content.'

Dorcas could see no sign of houses. She had been promised a home of her own but there were certainly none along this stretch of the coastline. The chilly wind hit them as they rounded the headland and Dorcas could now see the dark, leaden water being whipped into small white-topped waves that crashed down on the sands. She wondered what it would be like on a really stormy day. The cart rattled on until the track petered out and Tregonning took them onto the fine golden sand. Dorcas was mystified. The cliffs were sheer and came straight down onto the beach; there could not possibly be a cottage along here.

Far in the distance, she could see that the cliffs made a natural ending to the long stretch of sand. Dorcas was starting to feel a little nervous. Were they just going to get rid of her before she had even settled in?

They had gone about half a mile when Tregonning stopped and jumped down from the cart, his feet crunching down on the sodden sand.

'What are you doing? There is nothing here.'

The tall, silent man solemnly pointed to the towering cliffs.

Dorcas followed his finger and could not believe her eyes.

'Oh no. Oh, no, no, no. This really won't do at all!'

Treat them as well as you would your own for they are the meat and the potatoes of the community, one cannot survive without the aid of the other
- Northern saying

Chapter six

'You can just give me papers to allow me safe passage back to the north, Mr Penpol. I don't know who it is you think I am but I will not put up with this treatment.'

Dorcas stood shaking with rage in the gingham palace.

'But...' The Mayor had lost the colour from his round cheeks.

'A cave? A damp wet cave?'

'We thought...'

'You thought what exactly?'

Josiah wrung his hands together and Violetta prayed to whichever heartless God it was that she looked to. Dorcas could see her lips moving in silent prayer. A witch was bad enough, but an angry witch required some serious praying.

'I am now thinking that we have got off to a bad start Miss Fleming,' Josiah said, fiddling with his belt buckle 'I will talk to the committee, I'm sure something can be done.'

Dorcas snorted and Violetta ducked slightly.

'Breathe Dorcas, breathe.'

'Mr Penpol, Josiah, I am a woman of little need but I refuse to live in an open cave. I am not sure what you were expecting but I require a house, bricks, wood and the like. A modest abode will suffice, not large, two rooms will be sufficient for my work. Is that too much to ask?'

'No, no, not at all. It's all bin a bad mistake and I apologise.'

An hour later Dorcas was sat on her cart in the square, huddled under the oilskin cape which was preferable to waiting in that dreadful sitting room with Violetta. The woman looked as if she was going to faint at any minute. In her professional opinion the Mayor's wife needed a course of melissa, an infusion of lavender and a tisane of valerian to calm those jittery nerves. No doubt Violetta Penpol would have said the best cure would be the removal of the witch who had just invaded her sleepy town

The committee was meeting in the severe looking chapel and Dorcas had a long wait before the doors opened. Not many looked her way as Josiah came across the square to give her the news. Half of her had been praying to the Goddess that she be banished back to the north but the other half was screaming to be given a chance. It was an odd feeling and one that Dorcas was not too comfortable with.

Everything in her life up until that moment had been very straightforward. She knew where she was going and what she would be doing when she got there, but that had been in the north where there were simple rules and codes for living that everyone understood. Every community, large or small, needed a witch and the witch herself could not function without the community's support. It was a symbiotic parasitic existence but one in which the witch was held in high esteem. The southerners used the word 'parasite' about witches but in a totally different context.

'The committee have spoken at length on this matter,' Josiah said 'we have come to a resolve if you are willin''

Dorcas listened and then couldn't help smirking at the end of Josiah's long and drawn out explanation as to why she may have to spend a couple of nights in the barn next to the blacksmith's.

'...and the cottage will then be ready for living when we have cleaned it up proper,' he said explaining that Dorcas's new house had been vacated by the recently deceased that she had seen earlier that day.

'That would be fine, Mr Penpol, I have no problem with the dead.'

Josiah's face was a mixture of horror and relief in equal measures. He wiped his fat brow with the bright red hanky that lived in his top pocket. The committee had been hard to persuade because he did not have that many true allies to his cause. Many had gone along with Josiah's mad plan to employ a witch, because of who he was and what he had done for the town over the years. On the subject of accommodation, they had debated for nearly two hours. It had been a long discussion, and the light was starting to fade outside when they finally came to a conclusion.

'What right has the witch to demand a house?' the Preacher Trewidden asked.

He was one of Josiah's main adversaries to this project and he had jumped in at every opportunity with obtuse questions and ridiculous solutions. The witch's presence here was against everything he believed in but for once in his life, he found that he was outnumbered ten to one. He would not forgive them for that for a while to come. He was glad that she had refused the cave; it was one step closer to getting her out of his town.

'The same right as any other human being I would imagine' Telfer Meriadoc continued.

Dorcas would have recognised Telfer as the yellowish man who was in the square at her arrival. Contrary to her first impression of his dour expression, he had been supportive of Penpol's ideas from the very beginning After all, something had to be done about this dreadful situation, nothing else had worked.

'The question is where do we put her if she is so above living in the Barerock Cave on Long Beach?' he added.

'There's always the Richards' cottage,' the Preacher offered, knowing that no one would want to live in a place where a man had recently slipped his mortal coil.

'Would a witch live there though?' Telfer Meriadoc asked.

They rolled around this idea for a few minutes before they decided that they really had no options other than to offer this morbid abode. No Pendarthan in their right mind would take up the offer, but who was to say that the witch would refuse?

'It has timber walls, glass at most of the windows, two rooms, *and* a bedroom in the eaves, more than she said she required. Is everyone agreed that we offer it?' Josiah said.

The committee agreed but knew that the cottage owner had been less than domesticated.

'She can sleep in the barn until we cleans it up,' the blacksmith said 'don't s'pose she'll harm anything in there.'

'I don't want to put a damper on things,' Telfer said, 'but Jubal Sancreed lives but half a garden away from the Richards' cottage. Should we consult him?'

'Jubal will enjoy the novelty of it I expect' Josiah said, desperately brushing aside this last hurdle.

'If he has a problem with it,' said the gruff tones of Grenville Simmons, 'then perhaps he can go back to his wife.'

*

Dorcas spent the night in the barn, tucked up near the rafters in some sweet smelling hay. She lay awake for ages listening to the rain running down the corrugated tin roof, a product that the southerners were apparently very fond of. She was glad that it was not thundering down as she would not have got a wink of sleep. Morning came too soon and she lay stretching her limbs sleepily until the blacksmith came to bring in his first customer of the day.

The horse was limping badly as the smith tried to coax it into a stall. Stanley's horse, who had also spent a pleasantly dry night in the blacksmith's barn, whinnied softly as the newcomer backed into him, disturbing his breakfast.

'Get in there, go on you evil git, get in there.'

'Having problems?' Dorcas called down.

'No, thank you, he has a worn shoe, always bad tempered this one.'

Dorcas wrapped her cloak against the chilly morning air that had found its way through the double doors. She climbed down the wooden ladder into the small barn. The smith kept his customers in here until the fire was hot enough to work. The bad tempered nag was a bane in his life and he dreaded working on it.

The horse tried for a kick at his kneecap as the smith pushed him into the narrow stall and even the temptation of a fresh bag of oats was not enough to calm the agitated beast.

Dorcas wandered over and put her hand on the horse's hindquarters.

'I wouldn't do that if I was you, liable to give you a jab something rotten that one.'

Dorcas laid both hands on the horse and he nickered gently.

'His name is Milligan and he has a thorn wedged deep in his hoof' Dorcas said simply.

'No, no Miss you got that wrong see, he has a loose shoe, nearly threw his rider yesterday up on the Garrards Point.'

'He says he's had it for nearly a year and got it at St Zenno feast day.'

The blacksmith, who went by the name of Jakey Moyle, stood and thought about this for some time. He was a simple man, whose life as the only blacksmith for miles around had been reasonably uncomplicated for most of his forty-six years.

'An' he told you this did he?'

Dorcas did not want to upset the man so she just shrugged her shoulders. There was no point in telling him that a witch could commune with most animals if she wanted to, though only of course, if the animal was willing. This animal was more than willing. Pain and frustration had opened his mind to a human voice, and he was now telling Dorcas the rest of his gripes and woes. The smithies in the north always worked in conjunction with their community witch, whose ability to commune and advice on healing were part of her work in the town she served. These people wanted a witch so a witch they would get, but a watered down version for now.

Jakey took a firm hold on the lame foot of the restless horse and lifted it backwards to his bent knee. After a good amount of picking and prodding, he let the hoof down and leaned against the stall shaking his head.

'Think you 'ad better go,' he said, 'can't get me head round this.'

Dorcas left Jakey holding a large mouldy, bloodied thorn in his hand and went out to explore her new town. Ignorance was going to be her main adversary.

Hunger gnawed at her stomach, she had not eaten properly since having breakfast with the Hortons yesterday. Violetta's 'heavy' cake had filled a gap for a while but she had been too tired to rummage in the cart for her staples after the committee had made their offer. She could smell the aroma of newly baked bread coming from behind the smithy so she followed the trail. The town's bakery had just opened for business and a bap or two would go down just fine. Masterbridge had seen fit to fill her purse with southern money and she had more than enough to buy breakfast, and breakfast for the whole town if she chose. A witch's life was mostly based on a barter system with her community but all eventualities had to be covered and Dorcas knew that she could support herself for many months to come if she had to.

The shop was small, but it held some sights that Dorcas had not seen in a few weeks, and some that she had never seen before. Her mouth watered over the fresh bread and cakes and she changed her mind two or three times before deciding on two plain crusty rolls and a yellow coloured doughy cake with raisins in it.

'Can't serve the likes of you, we's God fearing people 'ere' the thin, bitter-faced woman behind the counter said without looking at her.

The shop had two other customers and they seemed to be finding a loaf of bread very interesting.

'I can pay, in fact I'll pay double' Dorcas offered quietly.

The woman shook her head.

'Can't, 'gainst me principles.'

Dorcas did not want to push the issue but her stomach was

grumbling loudly. The little bell on the door of the bakery tinkled to welcome a new customer. Josiah Penpol took up the rest of the available space in the tiny shop.

'Mornin' to you Mrs Creed, Miss Fleming, ladies. I'll be having me usual meat pie, two bloomers, and a half dozen of they fairy cakes that Mrs P is so fond of. Now Miss Fleming what can I get you?'

Dorcas walked down to the square with her breakfast saviour.

'I think she would rather I starve' she said,

'Now, now, just let 'em get used to you, any problems then come and see me,' Josiah said stuffing half a pie into his already full mouth.

'Thank you, you have been very kind.'

'By the way, Minnie Gembo worked all night last night to get the cottage ready for you, reckon it should be all done by noon and you can move in.'

The sun overhead gave her another two hours before midday. After checking on the contents of the cart and pocketing a few things, she made her way through the town to the harbour. The day had dawned fine and clear and she had plenty of time to explore her new surroundings. On the way, she noticed that a few of the houses had bunches of dried fennel over their doorways, hastily put up and hanging at odd angles. A few even had ostentatious crosses, nailed to the low beams above the front doors.

'It'll take more than that to ward me off.'

The low winter sun shone on the new tide as she took up a position on the harbour wall to watch the comings and goings of the town's main industry. Dorcas thought it best to try to understand how these people worked before she started to work on them herself. There were many towns in the north that were cut off from the larger towns or cities, and they too were steeped in their own superstitions and sub-religions. She would treat Pendartha the same way she would if she had been placed there. One thing at a time, bit by bit. That initial feeling of losing her head on the first day had diminished a little and although she was not feeling safe, at least she was still all in one piece.

The harbour was busy and as Dorcas ate her fresh bread roll, she studied the scene before her and decided that she could have been sent to a worse place. The boats bobbed up and down as men leaped from one to the other across the decks. On the wharf, Dorcas saw men working on nets, mending, repairing, and spreading them out on the ground to inspect them for holes. She watched as a boat came in and was unloaded with the same bell-shaped pots that she had seen the day before, only these were full of something. To get a better look she slid down from the wall and made her way along the quayside. The pots contained creatures with enormous claws at the front and numerous waving tentacles. She hunkered down to get a better look at these strange animals from the sea.

'Don't get too close!'

Dorcas stepped back at the sound of the sharp male voice and fell back against a stack of the basket-like domes behind her. Before she could stop them, a number had tumbled over and were rolling towards the water.

'Bloody Jesus Christ, me pots!'

There was a mad scramble as the man tried to stop the falling bell pots and failed miserably, five plunging into the sea.

'Bloody hell woman, what are you doing?' the man said as he stacked up the rest of the fallen pots.

Dorcas handed him two that were rolling around her feet.

'I'm so sorry, you startled me.'

Dorcas met the dark eyes that were glowering at her. She had seen plenty of those since she had come south, only not on someone so tall. The man must have stood six foot three and he was leaning over her menacingly.

'That's my profit from this trip just gone swimming, you silly cow.'

'That's the witch,' hissed a low voice to the side.

'Told the Chief she'd be trouble,' said another voice coming up behind her. 'Told 'em all. She'll put a hex on the fish and no mistake.'

'Looks like someone got here before me' Dorcas said pointing to the ugly creatures in the pots.

The tall man's face broke into a slight smile and she took this as a signal that she had been let off, this time.

'I will pay for them, of course, come and see me at my cottage when I'm settled. No doubt you all know where it is.'

'So you are the witch then, are you?' he said watching her intently 'I think I was expecting something else.'

His eyes roved up and down.

'Hat? Cloak? Broomstick?' Dorcas asked, feeling brave.

The man eyed her up and down again in a most unnerving manner.

'No, fatter, with warts.'

A crowd had begun to drift in her direction and Dorcas thought it would be a good idea to remove herself from the quayside. She walked back to the smithy as fast as she could without running; it had not been a particularly good start to the morning.

Milligan and her own horse were still tied up in the stalls when she got there but the blacksmith's shop was deserted. She left a pot of burdock and myrrh salve on the anvil for the horse and a note of where and when to apply it. It was nearly noon and Josiah came not long after and helped her hitch up the cart. Tregonning appeared again and silently drove her back down towards the harbour. Instead of taking the right hand side of the harbour, they took the left, which was a lot steeper. Horton's horse, Winston, plodded slowly up the hill, along the top of the cliff and down another short hill into a valley that ran parallel with Pendartha.

'They still managed to keep me well out of town then?'

Tregonning said nothing and they carried on until they turned from the road and onto a rutted track that led to a cottage that was set between a few trees. Neat and tidy, the little house was well kept and she had to admit that it looked more than fit to live in. Small pots of herbs sat beside the neat front door that had its own veranda, she could just imagine sitting out there on a warm evening. It was more than she had hoped for. Dorcas surveyed her new home but Tregonning did not stop as expected, but carried on past the first cottage and further up the lane. They came through some more trees and there it was.

Her new home looked as if it had been made from driftwood with patches of tar and corrugated iron to fill in the bits where it had gone rotten. The chimney leaned like a bent old man and the gutters were full of birds' nests and leaves. The low fence around the front garden was so low that most of it seemed to have sunk into the ground leaving much of the house without a boundary. At some point, there had been a gate, the rusty hinges and catch were still valiantly holding on to the two lonely gateposts. The veranda was missing many of its boards and appeared to have a bit of a slant to the left. A sign above the ill-fitting door proclaimed 'Home

Sweet Home' which Dorcas felt needed shortening somewhat. It was a haphazard house, a house of many different parts and pieces, none of which matched, but Dorcas thought that she was going to like it. In the north, a witch's house was the best a town could offer and was maintained by the community in recompense for services. This house was far removed from those standards but it was hers and she would try her best to make it her very own.

Tregonning pulled around to the side of the cottage and tethered Winston to a convenient post. There was a stable, of sorts, at the back of the house and a privy that had its door hanging off. The back of the house was in no better condition than the front and held somebody's lifetime's worth of rubbish. Dorcas refused to be downhearted at the sight of all the work that was needed, she would make the most of it and try to get on with her job.

Tregonning produced a key to the front door and she let herself into the hallway that in turn led to a small sitting room. Josiah was right, it had been cleaned. The wooden walls had been mostly stripped of their cobwebs, the floor between the faded rugs had been scrubbed, and the chimney had been swept. Everywhere else was a mess. Piles of books and papers were strewn across the mantle and dresser. The three-legged table that sat in the middle of a threadbare rug was covered in bric-a-brac and there were parts of a boat leaning up against the wall. Two bare wooden chairs were the room's only acknowledgement to comfort although Dorcas felt that they would be made more comfortable on the top of a Litha Sabbat bonfire. Its one redeeming feature was a window seat that Dorcas found after moving a few nets, a bell pot and a couple of axes. The hazy windows, which had obviously been cleaned in the middle of the night, gave the promise of a view right down to the sea. This would be a lovely spot eventually and if it wasn't for that other cottage, her view would be completely unimpeded. Tregonning had started to unload the cart so Dorcas had a quick look upstairs. The bedroom floor was built out over the sitting room and most of the railing had gone. To get to it you had to climb up the surprisingly sturdy ladder in the corner. The room upstairs was completely empty and showed no signs that it had ever been used as a bedroom. Her bed would fit up here just nicely and would be very cosy.

The kitchen would require a little work but she was pleased to see that it had the basics and they appeared to be in working order. The range had been dusted but not blackened and the hinges screamed their protest when she tried them.

Tregonning had put her crates on the veranda and was struggling around the corner with the base of the bed. Between them, they emptied the cart and got everything into the house. The silent man put his hand up in her general direction and was gone out of the door before she could say thank you.

'Need to find out about him.'

Dorcas looked around, there was an awful lot to do, but she was here, it was her own house and she had her own community, what more could a simple witch want?

Once she was sure that Tregonning had gone, Dorcas had a go at lighting the black range. After a few blow-backs, the fire took, and she went out the back to look through the pile of rubble that she had spotted beside the privy. The Pendarthan committee had been wrong about a witch not minding taking over the house of a recently deceased occupant; there were things that needed doing before she would feel comfortable. With a brick warming in the ancient oven, Dorcas sorted out a few things from her crates. Her new table fitted nicely into the kitchen and there was just room for her two chairs. Her only gripe about her new table was that the drawer underneath refused to open. She had pushed and pulled and had tried to rub some candle wax on the runners underneath but to no avail. Dorcas put it down to the new wood and decided she would have to keep her working knives and utensils in the cupboard under the sink. She now used her special boline knife to chop up a few leaves and roots of dried angelica and mixed them with three good pinches of salt. When the brick was hot, she took it to what she considered to be the eye of the house, the centre, which in this case was balancing on the rickety three-legged table in the sitting room. She placed the angelica and salt mixture on the brick and sprinkled it with cold water that she had drawn from the well at the back of the house. The water hissed and steam rose in a vaporous cloud.

I call upon the Eye of Horus,
Protect this home, protect this home,
Lay rest to evil,
Begone to none.

Dorcas repeated the chant seven times and then took the brick outside to cool. She would leave it there until she felt that the house was well and truly hers and that there were no ethereal remains of the last tenant. With that done she set about making the house her own, cleaning the things that Minnie Gembo had not touched and finding homes for her possessions. The townsfolk would leave her alone for a while and she would be left in peace to settle in; after that, it would time to find out why they had wanted a hedgewitch so badly.

Whenever ye have need of any thing. . . .

Chapter seven

It had taken over a week to sort everything in its right place and fit all her supplies into the small cottage. Dorcas had forgotten quite how much stuff she had managed to load on the cart. Out the back, up in the top part of the sprawling overgrown garden, she had stored all the things she did not want from the dead man's possessions that were left in the house.

Dorcas was pleased with how the cottage looked, at least on the inside. Once she got rid of the fishing paraphernalia she could fit the dresser in the kitchen and it now housed her few plates, cups, and keepsakes on the shelves. Maghda's little silver pig had pride of place in the middle. In the cupboard underneath she stored all her dried medicines, ingredients for lotions, salves and her precious decoctions of the rarer elements to her craft. There was a shelf above the range that held her salt jar and pans, and the windowsill was now covered with pots that held the beginnings of a new herb collection. Apart from her tins of various tisanes, everything else was stored out of sight of the many visitors that she would not have. Dorcas was having serious doubts that this so-called experiment was ever going to work. If Pendartha's inhabitants had already put up their wards against her then how was she ever going to get them to accept her ministrations to their ailments? That *was* what she was here for, wasn't it?

The sitting room looked neat and tidy but bereft of some of the comforts that she would have liked to make it more homely. In a fit of melancholy, she had hung up a few crystals and charms at the window to hide the fact that the curtains had disintegrated when she tried to wash them. Her new bed upstairs was comfortable if a little bigger than she was used to at the college and she used the empty crates to build herself some storage for her few clothes. She found the distant sound of the sea restful and relaxing but had jumped out of bed in fear the first night that she heard the foghorn blast. The herrrp, herrrp signalled the sailors to beware, Pendartha's rocks were cloaked. She found out later that the foghorn also signalled many other things apart from fog but like any new language, she would take time to learn all its nuances.

The new moon appeared the next day, the thin slither signalling that it was now only nine days until Yule. Assuming the locals would be immersed in their own Sabbath celebrations of one sort or another, Dorcas felt that she would be able to celebrate and spellweave outside, under the fresh, clean orb of the Goddess without upsetting anyone. The journey had prevented any of her usual celebrations of the moon's passage and it would do her spirit good to feel like a proper witch again. Besides, she had some questions that needed answering and the start of the new moon was a good time to bring understanding.

There had been no candlelight or sign that anyone was living in the cottage to the front of her so she decided that the small front garden would serve as her altar that night. She gathered the ingredients she needed and after washing changed into her white muslin gown. White represented purity of heart, cleanliness of mind and spirit and, of course, the moon itself. She had consulted her Book of Shadows, her witch's notebook, and looked up the best spellweave to suit her needs. She decided on vervain, basil, dill and a bunch of dried thyme. Dorcas had never done this on her own before. At the college, she always had the Mothers or the other girls to consult as to the best ingredients for a spell.

'I am a witch alone, in a coven of one, in the Hearth of...oh!'

'I have no name for my Hearth' she said aloud, dismayed at the thought.

She carried her censer, candle, spellworks, and salt pot out into the garden and enjoyed the damp grass under her bare feet. It was not raining but the winter air was chill and sharp under the faint glow from the candles. It was a novelty; a witch could die in the north if she chose to spellweave outside during the deepest winter months. Her heart lurched with homesickness at the thought of Summerlands under a blanket of snow and she absorbed herself in casting a spell ring with the salt. Once she had joined the circle by turning deosil, or clockwise, she set about calling the Elementals to help her. With the dedication to the eternal Goddess done, she burnt the herbs in the censer and set light to the thyme, passing its smokey remains through the air around her. The candle light danced brightly in the darkness and the answer to her first question came quickly and easily. The second required some more preparation. She called to the Lords of the Watchtowers, pointing north, south, east, and west with her athame knife and asked for their blessings and their help. She then sprinkled some water on the charcoal and herbs, lit another candle and gazed into her black mirror.

A witch's mirror could be many things, some liked to use a pool of water, some a crystal ball, some preferred tealeaves and others a black mirror like the one Dorcas was now holding in her hand. All had the same purpose; they were used for individual scrying. Dorcas's was made of the finest and blackest obsidian. It had been a gift when she had done her apprenticeship with Mother Enid on the Lanshire Downs. The old woman came to mind now.

Mother Enid was the oldest witch that Dorcas had ever met and at only twenty-one herself she could hardly imagine getting to that age let alone stomping across those barren hills in all winds and weathers as the old Mother did. Enid was a law unto herself and she had fought against taking on any apprentices from Summerlands for many years. The Pagan Council had eventually demanded that she do her duty as a learned witch and she reluctantly took on Dorcas for a year.

'And if you get on my nerves you're going straight back where you came from young lady.'

Enid was an astute, wise, and clever witch who taught Dorcas a great deal about witching, and about herself. She also made a mean liquorice and fenugreek poultice for applying to arthritic joints. The old Mother had lived alone on the downs for most of her life but as Dorcas quietly un-peeled her hard outer shell she found that the woman was well travelled and worldly.

'Been there and back again twice over Dorcas Fleming' she said as the young woman looked through her immense Book of Shadows. Enid had another forty or so books lining the shelves on the sagging, dark wood dresser. Many of the ingredients of her spellworks were unfamiliar to the apprentice witch. Foreign in name and in nature. Enid had made careful likenesses of all of them. Dorcas hoped that her own Book of Shadows would one day be filled with such exotic information.

Enid had been as testy as a snake when Dorcas first arrived and had refused to impart any of her extensive and valuable knowledge. She grumped and groaned at Dorcas's efforts and picked holes in her preparation of ointments and her lack of knowledge in herbology.

'The mistletoe must be steeped before the others to counteract the poisons, stupid girl, you will end up killing your first patient.'

Enid also had no time for the more spiritual side of witching, she sniffed at help from scrying, divination or any other modern parts of witching that involved what she termed 'hocus-pocus'. She repeatedly told Dorcas 'it was all in the eyes. Look in the eyes and see the illness. People, and animals, are an open book, you only have to learn to read them'.

Dorcas did as any student would when they had no choice, she followed Enid around and watched her every move, it was enough just to watch an experienced hedgewitch doing her work. Her patient nature paid off, and after a while, the old Mother relented a little. She let her mix a few basic salves and help with a few of the locals' more minor ailments but never any of the more serious stuff that Dorcas wanted to experience. She feared she would return to college and the others would spend the evenings reminiscing about their apprenticeships and all the things they did and saw, whilst she herself would have nothing to share.

All the theory and practice at college could never make up for some 'hands on' experience and Enid was not going to let her get her hands near anything interesting. Dorcas was sure that Enid used much more than her 'looking' theory when treating her patients. She had witnessed the old woman rise from a snoring sleep, dress, and make her way to an isolated farmhouse that was miles away to treat a sick child or animal. She also displayed some signs of travelling on the astral plane to find a suitable remedy for this or that but the old witch had got annoyed with Dorcas when she had asked. Enid gave nothing away willingly and Dorcas felt she would be going back to Summerlands with not much more than she came with. Just after Imbolg Sabbat, Enid took to her bed with an ailment that even she herself could not understand. Sweating profusely and with a cough that hacked at her lungs night and day, the old woman lay in her bed muttering incoherently. Enid's stone cottage was miles from the nearest village and they were completely on their own. Dorcas tried numerous syrups and decoctions but to no avail, the cough refused to budge and the sweats were getting worse. Coltsfoot, white horehound, and elecampane root helped a little for a few days but they were not strong enough to loosen the grip that the disease had on the old Mother. Dorcas was getting desperate. Enid's heart was showing signs of not being able to withstand such an onslaught and she was getting weaker by the day. Dorcas had the makings of an idea, a dangerous idea, but she needed help and advice to try to assess the outcome of such a risk. Time was of the essence and there was no one else to ask.

In a spare room at the back of the house, she searched through Enid's many chests for something to divine with. The rusty-hinged trunks were filled with oddities, collectables from different places that Enid had visited over the years. To her relief, in amongst all the tat, Dorcas found a bag of ancient runes that she could use to scry. She prepared her circle and tipped out the runes in front of her only to find that their markings were completely illegible and made no sense to her at all.

Back in the spare room she searched through the rest of the bags, boxes, and tin trunks until she came to the last one. At the bottom, wrapped in a threadbare piece of faded velvet was an ancient witch's mirror. Made of black volcanic obsidian, it had been polished to a sheen that reflected everything in its glossy smooth surface. Later, with the flames from the hearth reflected in the mirror, Dorcas concentrated her mind on seeking out what she needed to know.

'So you cured me with the most lethal of herbs' Enid said a few days later.

Dorcas nodded.

'Jimsonweed for your lungs, ruta for the sweats, and lily of the valley for your heart. I decocted and decocted until I thought I had the right potency.'

'You take risks when you have to, I like that. You will make a good hedgewitch and more Dorcas Fleming. The brain in that noggin of yours is a good 'un, use it wisely.'

Once Enid recovered, Dorcas found that she was gradually allowed into the whole of the old woman's life as a witch of the downs. When she returned to Summerlands six months later, she was able to share her knowledge and experiences. A parcel arrived for her just before Yule. There was a simple note inside which read; 'You have more use for this than I.'

Under the darkness of the new moon Dorcas held up the polished obsidian stone and asked her question.

'Goddess smile upon me, bless me with your guidance, show me the path I must take to answer mine questions.'

She threw some more water on the censer and passed the mirror through the steam.

'Goddess and God I bid thee show me my path and set me on it good and true. Show me the way into these people's lives.'

There was a slight flicker in the mirror, a shadow of a cloud or vapour from the spell, but then nothing. The mirror refused her invocations. Dorcas prepared the spell again, taking care with each part but still the mirror remained blank, refusing any of her persuasions. A damp coldness started to creep up through her ankles to her knees making the lone witch shiver in her thin gown. It was time to go back into the cottage and warm up. She closed the spell and set it free burying the contents of the thurible in a corner of the garden.

Later, over a tisane of ginger and mallow, she pondered her lack of success with the mirror, it was usually so reliable. She put it down to her being a little tired and the fact that she was still feeling upset at the dramatic move from the north. Dorcas was not given to bouts of self-pity but she put her head in her hands and wept.

'*Too full of negative emotion to cast a good spell, that's the answer.'*

She resolved to try again at Yule, the God would be reunited with the Goddess and the spirits strengthened, it would be a better time. At least there had been nothing negative in answer to her question.

Dorcas had put her biggest pot on the range whilst she was out in the garden and the water was just coming to boiling point. She had not had a proper bath since she left Summerlands and she dragged the tin bath from the back store and set it to warm in front of the fire. A sprinkle of lavender, a few drops of rose oil, and a handful of jasmine would relax her before bed and clear her of any spell leavings.

The bathtub had been one of her purchases in Polempter. Ellen and the Mothers had supplied her with as many things as they could and the Council had given her a considerable amount of money to set herself up in the foreign land. She was more than well off at the moment but the money would not last forever. She had been frugal so far, but the bath had been a bargain. There were many things that Dorcas had on her list of 'wants' but for the present she would keep to the 'absolutely musts' in order to live. A witch usually lived in a town that helped to support her, she was very rarely paid in hard cash and people gave what they could, when they could. Help was never refused to anyone, regardless of rank or privilege. It was a basic law to give aid where one could. Enid had a regular supply of firewood and seasonal vegetables delivered each week and was forever finding small gifts on her doorstep in thanks for one or other of her ministrations. It was unheard of in the north for a witch to starve to death and it was said that a fat witch was a tempting prospect for any male suitor. In the larger towns and cities, there were many witches who often lived together in a coven, helping each other with this problem or that. For the apprentice witch there was comfort in numbers, you always knew you would be safe, fed and clothed in times of need. If a witch was over-indulged then she gave the money to colleges or schools of witchcraft to help those coming behind her. There was no one coming behind Dorcas and the nearest coven was three weeks travel away. She was alone.

She had brought with her the bare essentials, although Stanley the younger would have argued that fact when he was trying to find a space for the bath on the already overloaded cart. He had eventually tied it on the back and used it to store the rest of the things that she had bought in the market.

'Seems an awful lot of gubbins for just one person' he said.

'Everything in the cart is necessary. I don't know if I'll be able to buy anything from the inhabitants.'

The cart contained all the usual household goods that she would require to set up a home and all the things essential to her trade. Some of the crates contained flasks of carrier oils, essential oils, and soap bases. It was not unheard of for a witch who had fallen on hard times to sell soaps and creams for a few pennies.

Dorcas thought over these things as she wallowed in the hot water. The answer to her first question under the moon had been as clear as a mountain pool. Her hearth had been named, but the question she asked herself now was how she could win over the inhabitants of Pendartha. With no help from the scrying mirror, she would have to come to her own conclusions. She swished her hand through the pungent scented water, taking in the relaxing aromas. An idea came to her.

'Women! That was it, the women.'

If she could win over the female inhabitants then the men would surely follow, that was a natural law in a witch's book. The people of Pendartha would not buy anything from her at present, there was distrust everywhere, but they may just take a small gift. It was worth a try.

Dorcas's new, excited thoughts were interrupted by a scratching sound. She lay still and listened. The scratching came again.

'If you're a mouse, go away, I'm a witch!'

The scratching persisted and Dorcas heaved herself out of the soporific water to investigate. She had not seen sight nor sign that the house had mice when she was cleaning although there had been enough mouldy scraps under the sink to keep a family of small rodents going for a number of years. She padded around and tried to detect where the noise was coming from and ended up at the front door. She opened it slowly and peeped through the crack. A mangy ginger cat sat on the doorstep looking very sorry for itself.

'You don't live here cat' she said opening the door a little wider.

The cat did not seem to hear and pushed his way past her and into the kitchen. Dorcas scooped him up and tried to communicate. The cat struggled, leaped to the floor and started sniffing at the cupboards.

'I'm not feeding you, you'll only want to stay and you are the wrong colour for me.'

She picked the cat up again and put him outside. The scratching carried on for an hour or so and then he gave up and went off into the night.

*

Dorcas felt much happier the next morning. She got out of bed earlier than the sun and put her plan into action. The range was full of pans that were simmering gently with scented ingredients bubbling in their depths. The kitchen got far too hot and she opened a window to let some fresh air in. The cat came in with it.

'You again!'

The cat jumped onto the floor and meowed pitifully, rubbing around her legs and purring. He was not a thin cat, in fact he was possibly the fattest cat that Dorcas had ever seen. His long orange fur was matted and dirty, and he smelled like a stagnant pool.

'Out! Out! You will foul my work with your smell.'

The cat did not look as if it intended to go anywhere and some of the preparations in the pans were ready to decant.

'Well, you'll have to get out of my kitchen, I've got work to do,' she said putting a foot under his bottom and pushing him gently into the sitting room. 'You can stay until I've finished here and then you're out.'

When her concoctions were cool, Dorcas wrapped them carefully and put them in her basket. She was just about to set off for town when she remembered the stray cat. She found him on her bed, sprawled out and fast asleep looking very at home.

'You can just get off there, you stinky thing.'

He rolled over and Dorcas caught a glimpse of a collar underneath all the stinking fur. On the collar, there was a small wooden disc into which had been carved 'GINGER'.

'Very original.'

Ginger did not want to move but Dorcas was firm. She took him out and shut the door behind them both.

'Go home, you don't belong here.'

The cat was closed to her persistent attempts at communication and sat down to wash his bottom.

'Are all animals in this place as blind and deaf as you?'

Dorcas thought about the cat as she started on the long hill that would take her back to town. He certainly did not seem able to talk to her. Mother Enid had told her that an animal has to *want* to talk to you but she secretly thought that all the animals and birds that she had encountered so far down here were as deaf as posts. A few days ago, she had taken a stroll down to the beach and had seen some gulls up above. She had called to them but they ignored her. The day before yesterday she had met a fox crossing her garden at dusk. The vixen at least had the decency to stop when she had acknowledged her but skittered off when Dorcas had spoken further. Milligan, the horse in the blacksmith's, had been able to talk to her, but perhaps that was because he was in pain. It was a mystery.

It was a cold afternoon; the wind whipped her face as she rounded the headland and headed down towards the harbour. This was the first time that she had returned to Pendartha and she hoped to make some headway. The harbour was nearly empty of life with only a few boats in, and half a dozen men on the quay. She hurried past, not wanting to encounter that tall man again and took the road into the main town. Dorcas slowed down and took in more of her surroundings. The houses were really quite neat and she noticed that they all had a little wooden sign above the door telling the visitor what the house was called.

Lily Cottage, the Penpol's house, looked deserted as Dorcas knocked on the door. She had wanted to catch Josiah alone and prayed that Violetta was not in, but now it appeared that neither of them was at home. Josiah was to be the starting point of the plan, she had to find him.

'Who is it? Who is it?' a voice from above called.

'I'm looking for Mr Penpol' she answered.

'Is that you Lizzy Mims? He's gone to the harbour master's office, it's his day' the old woman shouted down.

'I'm not Lizzy, my name is Dorcas Fleming.'

'You be that witch then,' the voice said. 'Door's open, come on up.'

Dorcas made her way up to the gingham sitting room and found a sprightly old lady sitting in a cushioned chair by the window.

'Violetta's gone to St Zenno on the cart, can't walk too far these days so I has a bit of peace and quiet while she's gone, don't suppose you wanted her anyhow. I'm Morwenna Penpol, Josiah is me son.'

'Merrymeet and pleased to meet you' Dorcas said holding out her hand.

Morwenna took the proffered hand and held it for some time.

'Can't see much with these old eyes but I does detect things and I detect that Josiah may be right.'

'About what?'

'You. Now make us a cuppa tea dear and let's have a chat here by the fire.'

'Violetta would have a fit if she knew that I was here in her kitchen.'

She filled the pot and joined Josiah's mother by the roaring fire. The old lady had pulled up her skirts and was rubbing at her thick woollen stockings.

'My son, bless him, has always been a little compulsive, or is it impulsive, anyway he does things from his heart. Do you get my meaning Dorcas Fleming?'

'I think I do Mrs Penpol.'

'That's it you see, you youngsters think you have rights over a first name, call me Morwenna, or you'll get me mixed up with the gingham princess.'

Dorcas stifled a grin.

'Don't mind me, I loves me daughter-in-law in me own way but she do get on my nerves somehow, could do with a good dose of salts I've always said. Listen to me gabbling on, tell me about yourself Miss Fleming, how did you become a witch?'

Dorcas found the old woman endearing and told her in brief how she had come to her calling.

'You don't seem bothered by my, err, I mean about the witching.'

'Bothered dear? Of course I'm not bothered, seen too much in this long life o' mine. Far worse things to be scared about than a young girl with knowledge of the herbs. Seems this place needs a person like you.'

Dorcas sipped at her tea and took in the various ailments that were plaguing the body of Morwenna Penpol.

'I have noticed, if you don't mind me saying so, that you have some nasty looking boils on your leg. I could give you something for them if you like.'

'That would be grand Dorcas, they play me up something rotten, but I'm thinking that that's not the only reason that you came here today.'

Dorcas decided to take another one of her risks.

'I need your son's help.'

'Oh?'

'I need him to help me win over the women of Pendartha.'

'And once you have got the women the men will follow eh,' Morwenna cackled 'clever girl.'

'I have made some things that I think that the women would like, I just need someone to promote them for me.'

The old girl had a nefarious glint in her eye.

'And what's wrong with me then?'

'You'd help me?'

'Listen my girl I may have lived in Pendartha all me life but I know that they witches up north are not *all* disciples of the devil and now that I've seen you I've proved me own point. Now, let's have a look at what you've got in that basket of yours.'

Half an hour later Morwenna had relieved Dorcas of the whole contents of her basket.

'Lizzy Mims will be here in a minute and if you want something to spread around Pendartha then Lizzy's your woman. Now off you go and leave this with me and if you don't mind, come back tomorrow with that potion for me boils.'

Dorcas left Morwenna smelling her homemade goods. What a surprise, another ally. She left the square feeling pleased with herself and made her way down to the quay. The harbourmaster's office was easy to find and Josiah rose from his chair as she entered.

'Miss Fleming, I was wonderin' how you was getting on over there. I saw you come into town a while ago, not much luck with the shopping then?' he said, pointing at her empty basket.

'Umm, well...'

'I'll get Tregonning to drop you up some bread and I'll 'ave a quiet word with Mrs Creed whilst I'm about it. She don't mean no harm.'

'That would be lovely Mr Penpol but I have another problem.'

'What can I do to help?'

'I seem to have acquired a cat, or rather the cat had acquired me. I need a bit of fish.'

'I think I know who you are referring to' Josiah grinned.

'Oh?'

'Fat?'

'Understatement.'

'That would be Ginger then, he used to live in that cottage. He's sat over there on the wall at the bottom of the hill. I guess he's waiting for you Miss Fleming.'

Chapter eight

The day before Yule Dorcas checked over the things she had prepared. It was so much harder to arrange everything yourself. At Summerlands, everyone had a role to play in all the Sabbats and festivals and they all mucked in. This was her first one down here and she was alone with no one else to celebrate with. It was a daunting challenge but one that she was determined to overcome.

Dorcas had taken a walk that morning to gather holly, mistletoe, and evergreens to decorate her hearth. It was a very long walk as the things that were found so commonly in the north were not to be found so easily here. The woods behind the house were full of oak, beech and the smaller silver birch. The walk had been pleasant in the mild winter climate but she had to forego the mistletoe, and the holly was nearly bereft of seasonal berries. She had cut some very pretty ferns, a small branch of oak and had found a modest log to use for her Yule candles. Her walk had taken her up the long thin valley for about a mile until she had come to a waterfall spilling over a low crag. She had sat for ages meditating quietly in the peace of the woods. There was a softer beauty to the south and she should really take more time to enjoy the gentle natural world around her.

By the end of the afternoon, the kitchen looked as if a storm had hit it. There were pots and pans everywhere and she was covered in syrup and flour. She was pleased with the steeped plums but the mulled wine was lacking something that she could not put her finger on.

'I'm sure I don't know' she said to Ginger who was stretched out like an orange rug on the floor. She had trodden on him a few times but he did not seem to mind. He had enjoyed the fish that Josiah had procured, had gobbled it up, and come looking for more. She doubted that she was going to get rid of her ginger intruder but the thought did not displease her. A cat was a cat after all and he was company, of a sort.

Dorcas returned to the town the following day and bought some more fish from the quayside and although the fisherman had been very terse, he had handed over a very fat mackerel and two herring for a penny each. The main purpose of her visit had been to see Morwenna Penpol and she had taken a prepared salve of burdock, goosegrass, and coneflower for her boils. As an afterthought, she included a tisane of valerian and lavender for Violetta. She had a feeling that the old woman would get her to try it.

'I can't say as I will take it' Violetta declared as predicted.

'You'd cut off your brain to spite your noggin you would' Morwenna said as Dorcas sipped another cup of strong tea.

Violetta had been horrified to discover that the two had met before; she did not like to have things going on she did not know about, especially in her own house. She would have to have words with Mr Penpol about this. His mother was mad enough as it was without that witch woman influencing her. Everyone said what a saint she was for putting up with her for so long. Now the old woman was positively encouraging that daughter of Satan to keep coming back, something would have to be done. Lizzy Mims had told her only that morning that she had seen her talking to gulls up on the cliffs and she would not have somebody like that in her house, it was not right. The witch was just as likely to try to poison them all one by one.

'I suppose you's thinking that the girl is trying to poison you Violetta' Morwenna said taking the words out of her head.

Violetta tittered nervously and brushed off her mother-in-law's comments by making up the tisane there and then. She would not be shown up by a daft old woman even though her hands shook as she took the first sip.

'Needs a bit of sugar I dare say, and tastes like grass but tis palatable' she declared reluctantly.

'I have something for you' Morwenna said as Dorcas was leaving.

She pulled out a basket with a cloth draped over it.

'Mrs Creed loved the rose petal hand lotion and asked if she could possibly have some more, she'll pay you a loaf a week. Rosie Trevennen had two bars of that rosemary and lemon balm soap and has put a pat of butter in for you. The Moyle girls had some of that bath stuff. They will get their dad to shoe the horse when needs be and there's some veggies from the Jenkin girl, picked fresh this morning in payment for the face cream. All the goods has gone, some paid, some didn't, some will, and some won't. It's a start.'

Dorcas was delighted they had taken the bait.

The thought pleased her later as she worked in the kitchen on some more of the rosemary soap. The day after tomorrow she would make up the next batch of beauty products and take them down to Morwenna.

'I could add some Neroli this time and a dash of thyme into the soaps.'

This could be the start of something; the female population of Pendartha was starved of womanly goods and she would use this to her best advantage. In the meantime, she got on with the task in hand and was so lost in her recipes and cooking that she nearly missed the thump that was followed by swearing and a harsh knock at the door.

'Nearly broke my foot on that bloody brick.'

'Oh it's you!' Dorcas said dismayed at the sight of the tall man from the quay, hopping about on her veranda. She really had not wanted to meet him again, especially on her own. He stood there staring at her.

'You're busy then?' he asked, not taking his eyes off her face.

'Yes I am, can I help you?'

'I've come for me payment.'

'Sorry?'

'The pots, on the quay.'

'Oh Goddess, I had forgotten, please come in a moment.'

Dorcas ushered him into the sitting room, and went upstairs to the bedroom for her purse.

'How much?' she called down.

She could see him but he could not see her. He really was very tall and looked a lot different out of the oilskins he had been wearing on the day she met him. Apart from the dark brows that seemed to be fixed in a permanent glare he was not bad looking. Dorcas judged him to be a little older than her but it was hard to tell as his face was weather-beaten from salt and sun.

'I have a deal to offer' he said as she came slowly down the ladder from her bedroom.

'And what might that be Mr...err?'

'Sancreed, Jubal Sancreed.'

'Merrymeet to you then Mr Sancreed, and the deal?'

'Seems you can cook, although it looks as if you are going to try to feed an army' he said gesturing towards the open kitchen door.

'Umm, yes, I mean, yes I can cook' Dorcas said well aware that she had far too much food for one person. It had been so hard to calculate what she would need. She was used to cooking for thirteen at feast times and although she had not prepared *that* much there was certainly going to be a lot of waste.

'Well here's the deal then. I haven't had a woman's cooking for a long while now, I'll forego payment on the pots in exchange for that decent meal that you are making. I'm home for a few days now.'

'It is one of my feast days tomorrow, I'm not sure that you would want to join me then.'

The words were out of her mouth before she had thought them through.

'The food smells good, and as long as you are not going to add 'essence of man' to any of the dishes I'll join you. What are you cooking anyhow?'

Jubal made his way to the kitchen and lifted a few lids taking a deep sniff at each.

'Mulled wine?'

'Yes, but I can't seem to get it just right. It needs…'

'Root ginger and a bit more sugar,' he said dipping his finger into the hot liquid and licking it.

'Do you think?'

'Mother made it every year for Christmas, I know what goes in.'

The deal was struck, Jubal Sancreed would come for supper the following evening. She saw him to the door.

'Two more conditions before we spit on it, I mean agree on it.'

'Yes?'

'I likes a pudding, not fussy what it is but I've got a bit of a sweet tooth.'

'And the second?' Dorcas asked already panicking at the thought of having to rustle up a sweet course.

'You're not going to dance about in the garden in your nightie are you, and if you are could you do it when I've gone home? Still not sure I'm comfortable with all this witch business.'

Dorcas promised that she wouldn't and shut the door on his departing back. The door knocked again.

'Forgot to say, put a candle in the window when you're ready for me. You can go and wash your face now.'

Dorcas looked out of the kitchen window to check that he really had gone this time.

'The cheek of it!' she thought as she rummaged for her hand mirror in the dresser drawer but smiled when she saw the sight that greeted her. Her face was covered in refined talcum powder and palm oil; she looked like a spirit of the night.

'And what was he doing skulking around in the middle of the night. If he had witnessed my new moon rituals then it was his own fault. He should be more careful where he skulks.'

She washed her face with rosewater, made some tea, and pondered her dinner guest. The man was a mixture of politeness on the one hand and complete rudeness on the other and the matter of the pudding had rattled her. She could fool the folk of Pendartha with her salves, lotions and creams though none were as finely made as Gwenna's or Eliza's, but a pudding was a different matter. Dorcas was an average cook, Joan had often told her so, but she got by and the coven ate. Sweets were off the menu, she was no Maghda. She would have to think on it.

*

Yule dawned brightly but soon descended into a cold, grey drizzly day. Dorcas had risen at daybreak to drum in the coming sun and welcome the God to his winter solstice. Today was the shortest day, from now on, the sun would be seen for longer, it was a time of celebration and a time of laughter. She tried to brush off the feelings of sadness of being on her own.

'I shall have company tonight but I'm not sure it would be the type I would choose at this time of year. The man seems so grumpy.'

With her rituals done, Dorcas wrapped herself up in her oilskin cloak and walked into Pendartha with some preparations stored in her basket. She tried not to think of her home in the north and her coven and concentrated her thoughts on being positive. Another milestone in her Sabbat calendar and she was still walking on the solid earth. She knew that she had a long way to go to gain the trust of these southerners but she had made good progress. The mizzle continued and the wind caught her again at the turn of the headland. By the time she got to the square she was half frozen.

She had been into town twice since the new moon and each time she had picked up a few gifts from Morwenna and had left some things in their place. The second time she picked up a couple of new orders and requests for additional items It seemed that the womenfolk of Pendartha were completely starved of feminine products and were flocking to her agent's house in their droves. She just hoped that they did not ask for anything too complicated, her skills had their limits in that department.

'Telfer Meriadoc asks if you can pop in to see him in the store,' Morwenna had said as she took the tissue wrapped soaps and creams.

'Does he want some of the hand cream that Mr Penpol had?'

'I dare say he might but he don't like talking to me, just go and see him girl, he don't bite hard.'

Dorcas pushed open the door of the general store and was faced with a shop full of people. She could smell the tea chests and a variety of familiar smells that brought back memories of Brexham market. The shop was overcrowded with goods all vying for position on the sagging shelves. The customers hushed their chatter as she made her way to the counter. Some of the people in the shop left with a few loud 'tuts' and some rude mutterings. A young girl who was waiting for her ham to be sliced winked.

'I'm Rosie Trevennen, the soap is gorgeous, me husband loved it' she whispered although all ears in the shop heard her words. 'My sister Lily would like some as well, could I come up and buy some off you?'

'Of course, you know where I am.'

Dorcas waited her turn and then asked the young girl at the counter if she could speak to Mr Meriadoc. The girl glared but went through a door behind and yelled up the stairs.

'Dad, that witch is here, she's asking for you.'

There were nudges and whispers all around her and a voice called that she should come through to the back.

Telfer Meriadoc met her in his kitchen and Dorcas recognised the yellowish, dour face from her first day in Pendartha. He offered tea and she accepted, sitting down at the untidy table.

'Sorry about the mess, Mags does her best. Since her mother died four years ago she's had to help me in the shop an' we don't get much time for the housework side o' things.'

Telfer's thick accent was difficult to decipher but she could understand more than she had done on her arrival.

'Morwenna said you asked for me' she said when he had shut the kitchen door against the prying ears. The man blushed, making a very unpleasant combination of colours.

'I….perhaps this was a stupid idea, you look a lot younger than I thought you were'.

'Please Mr Meriadoc, if I can help then I will, just tell me.'

Dorcas tried to put as much reassurance in her voice as she could, this was a chance, and she recognised it immediately. Telfer

Meriadoc slumped in his chair. He started to talk two or three times and then stopped. Dorcas waited patiently, the man would speak when he was ready.

'I think I'm dying,' he said at last 'Mags is worried sick. I need to know iffen I'm going to meet my maker. You witches can look into the future so they say. Can you look for me and see when I'm going?'

While she was waiting for Telfer to speak, she had looked around, keeping her ears open.

'Mr Meriadoc,' she said softly 'do you want to die?'

Telfer Meriadoc raised his yellowing eyes to her.

'No, no I don't, she needs me. It's been bad enough since her mother went. I've tried to be a good father but it ain't the same.'

'Good, that's a good place to start but you need to give up the drink. It is affecting your liver, making your skin yellow and giving you that metal taste in your mouth.'

The man looked at her, denial was in his eyes, but he knew the truth of her words. The witch seemed to know everything about him. The doctor in St Zenno had been useless and had cost him a week's money for the privilege.

'I can help you to live Mr Meriadoc, your daughter has had enough sadness don't you think And come to that, so have you.'

'I, I…'

'I will make you up a tonic as a replacement for the brandy that you're drinking and give you some milk thistle to clean the liver. Then we'll start you on a course of valerian to take away the pain.'

'The pain? I'm not in pain, as such.'

'The pain of your grief,' Dorcas said gently 'I didn't mean bodily pain. It seems to me that you have spent all this time making sure that your Mags is all right and you have completely forgotten about yourself Mr Meriadoc, is that so?'

Telfer nodded miserably and a tear escaped from the yellow eye and trickled down his cheek.

'I miss her' he said.

'I know,' Dorcas said putting her hand on his. 'It will get better, especially if you're not looking at the world from the bottom of a bottle.'

'How did you know?' Telfer asked as she made for the door.

'No second sight or hocus-pocus I'm afraid. Your bottles are rolling around under the sink and poking out from under the sideboard. Your skin tells me the rest.'

*

Today Dorcas returned with the tonic and a supply of milk thistle and found Telfer behind the counter as she entered the shop. His stern face broke into a near smile when he saw her. The shop was empty, so they could do their business in peace.

'I want to thank you, I needed your words. I have cut the drinking in half and I only have a couple in the evenings.'

'That's the spirit, or not the spirit in your case,' Dorcas said with a slight smile. 'Here are the things I promised, the dosages are on the bottles. I have also made up a tisane of agrimony, chamomile and red sage to take in the evenings.'

'Thank you, you helped a lot the other day, I think I needed someone to speak the truth and you did that right enough, even if you are a bit young.'

'Well, that's what I'm here for Mr Meriadoc, you may not like what comes out of my mouth, but it can help to listen sometimes. I'll come back to see you next week to see how you are doing Don't expect a huge change, *my* miracles take a little longer!'

Telfer was glad that the Preacher Trewidden was not around to hear her blasphemous statement but he was grateful. Josiah Penpol was right; she could do this community some good, even if it was only in the doctoring way.

'I'd like to pay you for the medicines,' he said 'Morwenna told me you don't take kindly to money, so have your pick from the shop. Fill your basket.'

'That is very kind Mr Meriadoc, I don't think that will be necessary, but there are a few things that I need.'

Dorcas returned home and filled the pans and kettles for her bath. The damp cold had invaded her bones, she needed to purify herself for the Sabbat celebrations, and for the little bit of work she had to do in order to prepare the meal.

Merrymeet, and merrypart, and merrymeet again,
Cernunnos returns in love and life,
To heal Cerridwen's pain,
The Yule Sabbat we celebrate, the sun returns to earth,
The Gods come cloaked in finery,
Rejoice in life's re-birth.
- Northern Yule song

Chapter nine

The issue of the 'pudding' haunted Dorcas all night. She had picked up a few things in Meriadoc's store but she still had no idea as to what it would be. After her bath, she changed into her best dark green velvet dress and tied up her apron. She placed her hands either side of her Book of Shadows and asked for help; after a small incantation they took on a life of their own. Flour, sugar, and fat were beaten into submission and the eggs folded in expertly. She was surprised at the addition of dried plums and brandy but let the process go unhindered. Maghda's clever hands made a perfect candle cake, with iced symbols on the top to represent the season.

'Well Ginger, what do you think of that?'

The fat cat purred and rolled over in front of the range. Dorcas had given up trying to get rid of him and he had become her main companion. She consulted him on all her dilemmas but he kept his mouth shut tight.

She put the cake in the 'cold cupboard' out of reach of the greedy animal. Twice she had forgotten to put food away and had lost part of a dinner. The cat would eat anything, which she was pleased about as it meant she did not have to go into Pendartha for a supply of fish every day.

The little clock on the mantel said it was nearly seven and all was prepared. With a few touches to the sitting room, Dorcas felt she was ready. She did not know how the man was going to see the candle from the road but she lit it anyway. She smoothed down her dress and patted the tight bun at the back of her head. A minute or two later there was a knock at the door; Dorcas was nearly caught off guard.

'Merrymeet Mr Sancreed, that was quick, were you waiting in the lane?'

'Merry whatever to you as well, and no I was waiting in me bedroom.'

Dorcas's head worked everything out in the blink of an eye and it all made sense apart from the fact that this man didn't look like the type to own such a neat cottage as the one in front of hers.

'The spelling's wrong.'

'Excuse me?'

'The spelling on your house sign. Nice thought, but Denzell is all one word not Den Zell.'

There was no way that Dorcas could explain how this mistake came about, she was so sure that the vision in the smoke on the new moon night had been right. When she had asked for the name of her hearth, it had quite clearly said 'Den Zell's Cottage'. She had taken it to have some mystical meaning and had dutifully carved it into a piece of driftwood she had found on the beach. She smiled.

'I should leave it as it is, if I were you, Denzell Richards would just be pleased that the old place is looking so nice.'

Dorcas took his jacket and noticed that he had put on his good set of clothes. He looked quite handsome in a rugged sort of way, but he could do with some of that marigold cream that she made for Josiah Penpol; his hands were split and rough. The men all seemed to suffer with what she had dubbed 'fisherman's hand'. A good dollop of the salve twice a day would clean and heal the wounds inflicted by salt and rope. His index finger and thumb were also stained, surprisingly with the blue-black of writing ink. He was literate, a skill that was rarely developed amongst those with a trade such as his. A vision of Amberlynne jumped into her mind. How her eyes would be popping out of their sockets at such a masculine sight, rough hands or no. She would be proud to think that Dorcas had actually made an effort with her appearance and had noticed how someone else was looking.

The old chairs had gone on the fire after one of them had fallen to bits. They sat in the sitting room on the window seat, with Dorcas in one side of the bay and her guest in the other. She would purchase a couch or a couple of armchairs in the spring and then with the addition of a homemade rug the room would be very cosy.

'See, it's improved' he said sipping the warmed wine.

'I followed your advice, a little more ginger and a spoon of sugar.'

Jubal looked around the decorated room.

'What's with the greenery?'

'Part of...'

'One of your heathen celebrations?'

'Mr Sancreed, if we are going to spend an evening together shall we make some ground rules? If I don't talk about my heathen beliefs then we won't talk about yours.'

He glowered at her for a while and then smiled.

'The name is Jubal and you are Dorcas I understand. I get to talk as much as I like and about what I choose. I'm only pulling your leg about the decorations; it looks very nice if you like your outside on the inside.'

'Jubal then, I...'

'So this is one of your Pagan festivals.'

'Yes, but the true....'

'So you do agree that you have heathen beliefs.'

'To you yes, just as much as yours are to me, but...'

'I personally don't have any heathen beliefs of any sort. God deserted me a long time ago.'

'I'm not surprised, you probably never let him finish a sentence. Shall we eat?'

Jubal laughed and they went into the kitchen where Dorcas had set the table with a green cloth and placed coloured candles on the dresser and on the table. She served up the first course of roasted lamb with a lavender and rosemary jelly, carefully watching his reaction.

'Is this poisoned with witchbane?' he asked as he took his first bite.

'Of course not.'

'Then why are you watching me like a hawk and why aren't you having any lamb?'

'I don't eat meat and we agreed not to talk about my religion.'

'I didn't agree. I want to know more about the vegetable-eating, devil-worshipper from the north. Pendartha is waiting or rather, Lizzy Mims is waiting.'

Dorcas smiled, it was nice to find someone she could banter with.

'You look better with a smile on your face, you should let your hair down once in a while as well, that severe style don't suit your face.'

'It is really none of your business how I dress my hair but if you must know I wear it this way to keep it out of my work.'

She looked younger now than on that day she first appeared and Jubal found himself wondering what she would look like with her hair down. Her small features would be softened considerably by that thick chestnut hair framing her face. It was hard to tell exactly what colour her eyes were in this light but he remembered from the first time he had seen her that they were a very deep blue.

The first course went well and Jubal cleared his plate. As he pushed the roasted meat and vegetables into his mouth, he grilled Dorcas about her journey and her first week in Pendartha. He had definitely not had a home-cooked meal for a while and was enjoying the experience as if it was his first. He was in company, so he refrained from licking his plate.

'This place is so different from home' she said after a few more glasses of mulled wine.

'I think the people of Pendartha have overlooked the fact that you are just as scared as they are.'

'I am not!'

'Do not lie to me witch, I know women, and I know their wily ways. You *are* scared and even if your tongue is as sharp as a knife, you use it to cover your nerves, and those dark clothes just serve to make you look older than you are. How old are you anyway?'

'You are very rude Jubal Sancreed; it is not polite to ask how old a lady is.'

'You aren't a lady, you're a witch, there's a difference.'

'I'm twenty-three, twenty-four just before Imbolg.'

Dorcas had no idea why she was telling him so much about herself, the wine must have loosened her tongue somewhat. She removed the plates and took the candle cake out of the cold-cupboard.

'I'm twenty-seven, twenty-eight in January,' he said 'which is just before February, in *our* calendar, which doesn't contain any of your heathen months or whatever Imbolg is' he smiled.

Dorcas returned his smile and fished out a knife from the dresser drawer.

'We witches like to have the best of both worlds, we incorporated your calendar into our own hundreds of years ago. We don't like to feel we're missing out on anything. Imbolg is the second of the new year festivals.'

'The second? Isn't one enough?'

'If something is good then why not have it a couple of times?'

she laughed.

Dorcas lit the candles on the cake and brought it to the table. He commended her on her efforts and after the first bite, he stopped talking and closed his eyes to the taste of the light cake with its creamy filling. The steeped plums gave a more than pleasant bite to the sweetness.

'Lovely' he said after the last mouthful.

'If only you knew.'

Dorcas put the dirty dishes in the sink and they retired to the sitting room with more wine. The window seat appeared to have shrunk, Jubal was now closer than she felt comfortable with. She wriggled around and faced him, letting her knees become a barrier between them.

'So, these festivals, what do they celebrate, or is that too mystical for the likes of me to understand?'

'No not at all. Today is Yule, the Goddess gives birth to the God. It is the winter solstice and we celebrate the rebirth of the sun. The daylight gets longer from now on as you know. Then comes Imbolg which is a time of renewal, then Oestara, the spring equinox, when life springs back to the land. Beltane is May Day and the land is fertile again. In June, we have Litha Sabbat, the summer solstice, a time of healing and health. Lammas is harvest time and Madron is Thanksgiving and also the autumn equinox. Samhain at the end of October is the most important as the door to the otherworld is open, and then we are back to Yule.'

'Interesting, the calendar follows the pattern of the year and some of our festivals are the same as yours, Oestara for instance.'

'Easter and Oestara are the same festival for different reasons. At one time the two calendars ran along side each other, Pagan and Christian together, the war pulled us apart, dividing north and south but we are the same people from the same earth you know, underneath it all.'

Jubal nodded. 'I know an awful lot of people who would never agree to that statement, the Preacher Trewidden springs to mind.'

'He could not possibly accept me and what I stand for; it would also be against everything he believes in. But enough about me,' Dorcas said. 'Tell me about Pendartha.'

By the time Jubal had finished Dorcas felt as if she had been introduced to the whole population of the town.

'So Mr Penpol is 'Chief' of the lifeboat. I see now.'

'There are ten of us. If I'm on duty then I sleep on the quay in the Harbourmaster's office so as I don't miss the alarm. The rest of the crew live within spitting distance of the quay.'

'And the mysterious Tregonning is second mate of the lifeboat. It all makes sense now.'

Jubal told her that Tregonning had been silent for fifteen years. His two sons had been drowned at sea and he had never spoken since.

'His wife threw herself off the Lazard Head after the boys had gone, just about finished him off. He wouldn't go near the sea for months.'

'Poor man, what tragedy in his life.'

'There's a lot of that around here and folk tend to try and blame, well, anything else but just plain bad luck. If you are working with the sea then you have to expect that sort of thing every now and again, don't you?'

'There is bad luck everywhere but it is always balanced by the good. Now tell me more about Violetta and Morwenna Penpol.'

Jubal told her what he knew. Josiah had once been a captain of a merchant vessel that traded between Port Morgan, the capital of the south, and the Lazardian Peninsula. He met Violetta in Port Morgan and they married and settled in Josiah's home town of Pendartha.

'That's where she gets those airy fairy ways of hers, thinks she's a cut above the rest of us.'

'Not sure that I would call an abundance of gingham a sign that one was a cut above.'

And Morwenna?'

'Josiah's mother, mad as a March hare since her husband died.'

'More bad luck?'

'I think he was lost at sea during a storm. It was about twenty-five years ago.'

'Like you said, these things happen.'

Jubal told her more titbits about the people of his town.

'And you Jubal Sancreed, are you going to tell me anything about yourself?'

'You'll hear all about me in time and none of it will be good I can guarantee.'

Dorcas did not want to think of Pendartha any more tonight, she got up and lit one candle on the Yule log.

'What is that for?' Jubal asked looking at the hefty, ivy-wound log in the grate. On the underside, Dorcas had scraped it flat so that it would not roll over. On the top side, she had gouged out two holes to accommodate the candles. She lit one of them and closed her eyes for a moment.

'You're not going to turn me into a toad or anything are you?' he said when she returned to the seat.

'No, not tonight. The candles are wishing candles, you get one wish for good at Yule.'

'So what's the other candle for?'

'You, if you want it.'

Jubal knelt down at the hearth but was interrupted by a flying ball of orange fluff.

'Ginger!' he cried, stroking the purring animal who was rubbing himself against the fisherman's legs 'I thought he'd gone when Denzell died. You've cleaned him up, I hardly recognised him. He looks good.

'He has been ignoring me since I gave him a bath and a comb. He was in a bit of a state, tangled fur and a large colony of fleas but he washed up well and he seems to have adopted me.'

'Not much of a witch's cat eh? I believe they should be black?'

'He is a complete embarrassment to a witch, I agree, but he is good company. I longed for a cat all through my days at college and now I've ended up with that poor excuse.'

Ginger meowed loudly and pitifully and Jubal laughed

'A witch's un-familiar then.'

Dorcas asked about Denzell and how he had died.

'He died at sea, plain and simple and once again, don't let anyone tell you any different' Jubal said sharply.

'I'm sorry, I only wanted to know what kind of person lived in this house before me. This is the first house I've ever lived in on my own.'

'Do you miss your home badly?'

With more wine on board than she should have, Dorcas found herself telling him about Summerlands and Brexham, the Ninnis Stones, and Grindle Point. 'Ashen Moor was my favourite place; I loved the peace, and the sounds and the smell of wet bracken in the Autumn.'

She told him of a place called Brexland Scarp, where massive lumps of granite were piled on top of each other as if a giant had stacked them up carefully. When the wind was in the right direction it whistled through the gaps in the stone making the granite sing and hum.

'I have a place like that,' he said 'I'll show you sometime when the time is right.'

Dorcas said she would like that and they finished the evening with Jubal lighting his candle. She was not sure if he made a wish or not but it was a very polite thing to do.

'Thank you for a nice evening, my stomach thanks you as well' he said patting his mid section.

'So I'm off the hook then, I've paid off your fishing pots?' Dorcas said as he made his way down the path.

'I wouldn't say you're off the hook but yes the pots are paid for. They weren't mine anyway!' he called over his shoulder.

Dorcas was still laughing when she went to bed. It would be good to keep Jubal Sancreed as a friend. Her first Sabbat in the heathen lands had not been as bad as she thought it was going to be and it looked as if the locals might just be won over.

Chapter ten

Ellen pushed open the double doors and made her way along the Long Hall, her feet click-clacking across the highly polished wooden floors. She took in the ancient dark paintings hanging on the walls and the familiar smells of beeswax, incense and burnt toast. It was good to be back in Masterbridge, good to be home again. At the end of the hall, she turned right and took the main staircase up to the next floor. The High Council chambers took up the whole of this wing and there was another long walk before she reached the last office on this floor. As usual, the door was slightly ajar. Ellen had often thought that this particular door had forgotten how to close completely. Although she knew that the occupant of the room would have felt her presence long before she got here, she still paused to take a breath before pushing the door open.

The room was shot with shafts of light from the high windows and a man with long gunmetal grey hair sat in between them. A pair of ink stained hands lay on top of an ancient document and the stain was echoed on the bridge of his nose where he had absently pushed up his metal-rimmed glasses. The desk at which he sat was at odds with the rest of the room, piled high with leaning stacks of papers and surrounded by enough books to fill a library. The rest of the room was neat and tidy and bereft of any other comfortable furniture. One stiff armchair sat beside the hearth, as pristine as the day it had been commissioned for the high Councillor's office. The walls were lined with books from floor to ceiling, many of them safely kept behind glass to preserve the ancient paper and the mysteries that they contained.

He lifted his head and took a long look into the face of one of his favourite High Priestesses.

'Ellen, you are come back to us!'

The High Druid Elshalamane rose from his heavy oak chair to greet her, kissing her on both cheeks and bidding her to take the chair in front of him. It had been nearly three years since she had last sat in this chair and conversed with the High Druid. It felt good to be back in the fold and good to be once more looking at the man who had been such an influence on her life.

'I am here and eager for news,' she said.

'First things first, Ellen my dear. Is all well at Summerlands?'

'High Priestess Freya has taken over as planned; she will serve the college well. The Mothers are happy with the new intake this year and one looks promising as an elemental.'

'Good, good.'

The High Druid rang for tea with the silver bell at his side.

'I'm just sorry that this had taken you away from your work for so long. I expect you'll want to get back to it as soon as possible.'

'I would like to take this through to the end if you don't mind,' Ellen said.

'Commendable.'

'You know I hate starting something and not seeing it through.'

The tea arrived and Ellen had the distinct impression that the High Druid was stalling for time. He asked after many of the mothers at Summerlands and rattled on about the ambience in the hearth building telling her that he felt it was one of his finest works.

'The design is so right for nurturing the students, don't you think?

Ellen nodded, sipped her tea, and waited for him to get to the point of her visit.

Those who worked within the hallowed halls of Masterbridge held their High Druid in great esteem but an interview with the great man could take hours out of a working day and night. Elshalamane therefore startled her with his next words.

'So, we shall see what happens then. You have faith in this girl?'

'Yes, yes, the evidence showed itself as soon as I arrived, she will prevail as I said in my letters.'

'You are very confident.'

'And you are not, High Druid?' Ellen asked, surprised.

'Not until she completes the set task.'

Ellen fiddled with her bracelets.

'Is there word from the convoy?'

'She has arrived, that much we know. Horton left her at St Zenno. He said she was nervous and didn't know what to expect.'

'No more news?'

'Ellen, we must be patient, if she is what we think she is then she will prove herself.'

Ellen discovered a long time ago that patience was not one of her virtues. This was her first major undertaking since she had become a High Priestess and she wanted to make a success of it. She knew what rested on her shoulders. The Mothers at Summerlands had done their job, recognised the signs and called for help. Masterbridge had been waiting.

'Do we know any more of the task?'

'No, Pendartha has a need and she must fill it. That is as it stands.'

Ellen watched the dust motes dance through the shafts of light.

'I just want to know if she is safe.'

'The lower workrooms have been busy here, they have been scrying, morning, noon and night but there is no sign. A blackness seeps into any image as soon as it is formed and they don't seem to know what it is. Meredith Spooner has had more success with her chalice but the results are inconclusive.'

'I am sorry,' Ellen said 'I have become far more involved than I should have done. I knew the risks.'

'Yes, if she fails she will take a piece of all those that were involved with her. I note in your report that her coven have been cleansed, especially Ginnifer Belle.'

'That was a minor oversight on my part. We had no idea that the blocks we were using between the two girls had failed and they were getting closer. Mother Elsie picked up on it and it would have strengthened during the final ritual. We took Ginnifer out as soon as possible. She is now working, as we always thought she would, in her father's community as a hedgewitch, and she is apparently very settled.'

Ellen neglected to say that all this had happened on the last day. There was no need for the High Druid to know that she had made a potentially fatal mistake. It had been corrected without affecting any of their plans. Ginnifer had been shocked and dismayed to find out the truth but was not unduly harmed by the incident. A witch should always be prepared for anything, even news as shocking as that. The coven obviously knew that Dorcas was going to Pendartha but none of them knew the real reasons and it was best to keep them in the dark. If she had been suspected then her coven would have turned her out and she would not have finished her training, which was vital. Joan Barton had been the only student who had suspicions about her and she was now safely ensconced in a teaching post here in Masterbridge. Joan had been ecstatic to get Masterbridge but somewhere deep inside she knew that she was always going to be second best to the girl who had been unceremoniously shunted off to a place at the ends of the earth.

Ellen remembered the day of Samhain clearly. Dorcas had already shown the kind of self-control that Ellen herself would like to possess. On receipt of the placement, she quickly pulled herself together and comforted her coven, who had been shocked and dismayed at the decision. Control was high on the list of attributes of Miss Dorcas Fleming, and Ellen had never met anyone with such steely command over their body and mind. The High Priestess had been sent to Summerlands College because of her natural ability to 'spiritually read' a person's true intent. Dorcas had given her a violent headache on a number of occasions and she was forced to delve deep into her skills to unpeel the natural guards that the girl had placed around herself. The only solid thing that Ellen had come up with was that Dorcas was hiding a vivid scar on her cheek. Mother Lylas had been the only other one to see it and that had been in a fleeting moment when the girl was in her care. That incident had prompted Lylas to bring her to the college to seek help. She knew what significance the mark held but did not know how to help her. Masterbridge had been informed but they had to wait until Dorcas matured before they could make any assumptions about her true status.

All Masterbridge had to go on was a suspicion. If they turned out to be wrong then an awful lot of effort would have come to nothing. Ellen herself was a true believer; she had faith that her protégé had what they were looking for. All the evidence pointed this way, but then again, they could be wrong. This had happened a number of times before, a student with potential had been sent on a task and had either never returned or had failed to recognise what she must do. It all hung on an athame edge and Ellen was more than anxious about the whole thing.

Many had doubted that she should have taken on the role of High Priestess at Summerlands and she knew that there were those who doubted her ability to manage and control such a situation. Elshalamane, above all, had a deep and trusting faith in her but did she have enough faith in herself?

Ellen first heard the whispers about the girl seven years earlier. Anyone with a hint of potential was watched from a number of angles and by a number of experts. It was not good for the general hedgewitch population to know that there was one more powerful among them; even an elemental witch was kept hidden by her mentors until the time was right. Many students with this potential chose not to use it for one reason or another but someone with the talents of Dorcas Fleming had to come to their own conclusions and make their own decisions.

Witches were separated into many levels, some were born with it, and others acquired more skill as they went along. Most of the colleges turned out good, hardworking hedgewitches year after year, supplying their communities with an esteemed commodity that was needed and wanted. Some of their number would be elementals, witches with a natural talent for working with the elements of nature itself. Others may be spiritwitches, communing with the dead and the living, and able to cross the veil between this life and the otherworld as easily as blinking. Every so often, maybe once in fifty years, something else came along, something deeper, a mix of all these and more, a lot more. The last one was sitting at the desk in front of her but even Elshalamane had denied some of his legacy in order to function in Masterbridge. Was this what they now had on their hands? Was Dorcas Fleming a truewitch? Only time would tell.

Witch, I charge thee,

To serve, to help, to heal,

Blessed or cursed,

Thy gifts to be used,

Witch, I charge thee.

- First book of the Elandine Grimoire

Chapter eleven

Dorcas avoided the town in the first few days after Yule. They had their own festival of Christmas to celebrate and she did not want to upset them with her presence. On Candlemas, the eve of the new year, she walked into the town with a heavily loaded basket. Five pots of marigold salve for the fishermen, a jar of calendula ointment for Mrs Creed's niece, ten sachets of a tisane for those afflicted with the common cold and some more valerian for Violetta. Things were going quite well although Dorcas did not get her hopes up.

She noticed, as she walked through the town, that some of the cottages were absent of their fennel wards and some people did not even cross the road to avoid her.

'They will even acknowledge me soon.'

The square was bereft of people with only an old man that she hadn't seen before, sitting on the low wall outside the chapel.

'Storm's coming witch, but I s'pose you know that.'

Dorcas looked over at the man who was wrapped in three overcoats, with a tattered scarf wound around his head. His white whiskers were stained yellow in places from the pipe that was held precariously between the only two teeth in his head. Mother Elsie, her coven Mother, had smoked a pipe in the evenings that the girls suspected contained a large amount of hemp. Dorcas had tried it once but had nearly heaved. The man rattled the pipe on the brown teeth and pointed a yellow finger in her direction.

'Storm on New Year's Day. Bad. Bad. Badder than bad.'

'Foggy Isaacs, keep your daft predictions to yourself and stop harassing the poor girl.'

Morwenna leaned out of the upstairs window and beckoned her up.

'He don't mean no harm, he's a bit mad these days,' Morwenna said as Dorcas looked over her boils. Violetta was at choir practice so they sat in comfort in the sitting room.

'Not madness, Morwenna, the man has an affinity with the weather doesn't he?'

'He lives up the west cliffs, keeps a look out for weather and wrecks. Sounds the fog horn and the like,' Morwenna said.

'In the north he would be called an 'elemental' of sorts, a person who works with the forces of nature.'

'...and he would not be in that state' she failed to add.

Morwenna looked down at her and stared into her eyes.

'And you, Dorcas Fleming, what do they call you?'

'A plain and simple hedgewitch,' Dorcas said crisply 'using the gifts from the land to heal and help others and speaking of which, can I leave you these remedies?'

Morwenna laughed.

'Good answer, and the one that you should supply to everyone you meet.'

Dorcas unpacked her basket.

'Well, you certainly know your trade, hedgewitch, me boils are looking 'andsome and now that you've done with me you need to go and see Morley Trewidden's wife.'

'The Preacher?' Dorcas asked, astounded that the man would want her anywhere near him or his wife.

'No, no, Morley is the brother of our dear Preacher. The wife is pregnant, she's been having a bit of trouble. She came to see me yesterday.'

Morwenna said that she could go any time in the next two weeks and that the girl would be in every day but only well after noon.

'I'll go today, it will be nice to help usher a new life into this world.'

'...but I hope the poor girl doesn't realise that this will be my first attempts at midwifery on my own.'

Dorcas left Lily Cottage with directions to the Trewiddens. She stopped off at the store on the way to see how Telfer Meriadoc was doing. Mags was behind the counter cutting some ham off a large knuckle joint.

'Dad is in Polempter getting stock, he'll be back tomorrow' Mags said without looking up.

Dorcas looked around the shop and picked out a jar of homemade chutney and a pot of apple jelly. She could make them herself, but it was a kind of test. They sat on the counter for a good minute until a hand reached out and wrapped them efficiently in brown paper. Dorcas handed the money over and Mags looked at her for the first time.

'He's better you know, not right yet, but he's better.'

'That's good.'

'I suppose it's thanks to you?'

'If you like, but the healing is within him Miss Meriadoc, he just needed showing.'

'Couldn't lose him as well you know.'
Dorcas nodded and turned to go.
'Miss Fleming.'
'Yes?'
'You don't look like a witch.'
'The absence of a pointed hat and a broomstick fools everyone.'
Dorcas smiled and Mags smiled back.

Dorcas thought about her hat all the way up the steep hill to the Trewiddens' cottage. She had been advised to leave it in its box until the time was right. Dorcas could not ever imagine a time when she could wear her hat of trade freely. All through their training, her coven discussed the day that they would swap their black caps for a true witch's hat; large in the brim to shield against wind and rain and offering shade in the hot summer sun. It was an acknowledgement of their intensive thirteen years in training, a recognition of their expert status. How did these southerners ever become so ignorant and insular? The Pagan Council acknowledged all forms of worship to whichever God or Gods you fancied and were happy to include celebrations and rituals into their own festival heavy calendar. The northerners had many strange customs and weird superstitions, especially in the more remote areas, but generally, they blamed their bad fortune on just plain bad fortune. Mother Enid had been consulted a number of times with suspicions of hexes on sheep, or curses on this person or that. She handled them a little roughly sometimes Dorcas had thought, but Enid knew her people and that was what a witch was supposed to do.
    'Will I ever know these people, will they ever know me, and when, oh when, can I wear my hat again?'
    Dorcas had thought to ask these questions at full moon, which had been the day after Christmas. Full moon was the time in the lunar month when thoughts or ideas could be enlarged and increased. It was a good time to augment the power of a spell and imbue the ingredients of a spellweave with extra potency. Dorcas had chosen the latter, she needed the people of Pendartha to believe in her cosmetic aids and come back for more, and then they would hopefully allow her to treat some of their ailments. That was what she had come here for after all.
    Dorcas took the main road out of Pendartha, past the mill and turned up an almost hidden track that snaked up through the woods. The Trewidden cottage was nestled prettily at the foot of

an old quarry, long since abandoned and covered in climbing greenery. The neat garden had the promise of beauty in the summer and a rich harvest of vegetables all year round. The house looked well cared for. The door opened as she arrived and a grey face peeped out.

'Merrymeet,' she said to the young girl. 'I'm looking for Sarah Trewidden, Morwenna Penpol sent me.'

'I am Sarah, you can come in.'

Dorcas was taken aback, the girl looked no more than fourteen or fifteen, but the young face was grey, with hollow, sunken eyes.

The house was as neat on the inside as it was on the outside, clean and sparkling with not a thing out of place.

'What a lovely home,' Dorcas said, trying to break the ice.

The girl had that frightened rabbit look that all the women of Pendartha seemed to adopt when they first met her. Dorcas resisted the urge to utter an incantation of protection on entering the house; this one would probably drop dead on the spot. Sarah offered tea and went into the kitchen whilst Dorcas sat on a very hard couch. This room was certainly the young woman's pride and joy, Dorcas could smell the blacking drying on the grate. Many poor homes lacked the knick-knacks that you often found in a front room but this one was bereft of everything. Apart from the fire, which had been laid in for the evening and the two cups of tea, now sitting on a small table, there was nothing else to suggest that a young couple lived here. Even the poorest of the sheep farmers on the downs had one or two heirlooms passed down from generations past.

'You can tell a lot from the way a woman keeps her house, always keep your eyes open and notice things,' Enid had said.

There was not an awful lot to notice in this room and from the tiny glimpse as she passed, Dorcas could see that the kitchen was much the same. She turned her attention to Mrs Trewidden. The girl did look very young, far too young to be having her first child. Lank mousey hair dripped around a pale face that was too thin and gaunt and Dorcas noticed that her hands were reddened and rough and were bleeding around her knuckles. She waited for the girl to speak but after sitting for what seemed an age, she decided to speak first herself.

'What is it that I can do for you?'

Like Telfer, the girl seemed to find it hard to put her ailments into words.

'It's the baby,' she said at length 'I'm sick all the time.'

'How far on are you?' Dorcas asked gently, thinking that by the look of her she was still in the first three months.

'Nearly six months.'

Enid had also once explained that young girls often did not show until they were five or six months.

'Stomachs like over-tight drums,' she would say, referring to those pregnancies that were not really wanted. This one was wanted; the girl was legally married even though she looked so young.

Dorcas explained to Sarah that some women suffered with sickness all the way through and the girl let out a soft moan.

'I'll make you up a tisane to calm your stomach and it would help to chew a little bit of ginger in the mornings, if you can stomach it.'

Sarah looked horrified.

'Can't take nothing, he won't agree to it, thinks it will harm it.'

'Your husband?'

The girl nodded and fiddled with her skirt.

'Well he doesn't have to go through it does he?'

'It would help,' Dorcas said aloud. 'Is there anyone who would keep the ginger for you?'

Sarah thought for a while and then suggested Mary Moyle.

'Her father is Jakey, the blacksmith, I goes there a couple times a week, more if he's at sea.'

'Is that where your husband is today?'

Sarah nodded

'He wouldn't want to know that you are here today' Sarah said quietly.

'That's fine Sarah, he doesn't have to know. I don't like going behind people's backs but I really think that the tisane would help. Now, can I take a look at your stomach, I'll check that the baby is growing and the like.'

Dorcas got up from the couch to let the girl lie down. She seemed embarrassed as she undid the lower buttons on her blouse and let out the drawstring that held her skirt. Dorcas felt around and judged that Sarah was at the stage that she said she was. Her stomach really was as tight as a drum but she relaxed a little under Dorcas's gentle ministrations.

'Movement?'

'Yes, a little.'

'That's good, everything seems to be in order. We can work out the exact dates at another time but the baby is due sometime in April, a good time, the weather will be better.'

Sarah buttoned up her blouse and Dorcas noticed marks on her legs as she straightened her stockings.

'Those bruises look nasty.'

'I fell against the range' Sarah said putting her hand against the injuries.

'Then I'll leave some witch hazel at Mary Moyle's as well, we can't use arnica as it may harm the baby. I'll come back to see you in another couple of weeks.'

'I'll come to you,' Sarah said quickly. 'It will be easier.'

The weather had changed during her visit to the Trewidden girl. The sky was darkening and the wind had strengthened, blowing Dorcas's cloak up around her face. Foggy Isaacs was right, there was a storm on the way, and it would be here before nightfall. As Dorcas hurried home, she noticed a lot more boats in the harbour.

'They're running for home,' Josiah said as she stopped for a moment at the quay.

The Mayor was helping to secure the smaller boats to the larger ones and had called to her from the deck of a boat called the 'Mary Lou'. Dorcas could see a few luggers battling the growing waves to reach safety.

'Storm's coming Miss Fleming.'

'So Foggy Isaacs told me.'

'Best get home and batten down the hatches, this one's going to blow all night.'

Dorcas arrived home just as the first drops of rain hit the roof. She was surprised to see she had acquired a gate whilst she was out; no fence, but a substantial new gate. On the doorstep was a basket, which she picked up as she hurried inside out of the weather. She put the basket on the table, stoked the range, and set the kettle to boil. Pendarthans loved their strong tea, Sarah Trewidden was no exception, but it left her tongue feeling thick and rough. It was a wonder that they did not all suffer from chronic arthritis as tea was a known culprit.

'No dancing in the garden tonight for Candlemas then, Ginger,' Dorcas said observing the rain that was beating hard against the window. The cat purred, indifferent to the ritual that would have taken place in Summerlands. He was glad of the fire that had just been lit and he took up his customary place in front of the hearth. Dorcas made a warming tisane of lemon balm, ginger, and cinnamon and had a look in the basket that had been left outside. It contained what Dorcas had suspected, gifts from a number of people. A loaf of bread and a selection of those heavy cakes with currants in them from Mrs Creed, half a dozen large brown eggs from the Trevennen girls and a bag of fish heads from the quay. There was also a large jar of preserved plums with a gingham cover, no doubt as to who they were from.

'I'm just like a proper hedgewitch, payment for services, and everything'

There was a note inside the basket and Dorcas opened it to see that it was from Jubal Sancreed who had surprisingly neat handwriting.

Witch,
You cook well, you can do it
again some time. Hope you
like the gate, I owe you a fence
 when you've fed me once more
that is. JS

Dorcas laughed. The man was incorrigible.

*

Late in the afternoon, the rain abated and Dorcas took a walk down to the beach to blow out the cobwebs. The wind was still gusting and it reminded her of the blustery, wind-swept top of Ashen Moor. Dorcas missed the rugged beauty of the fells around Summerlands College but she was becoming increasingly fond of the wild waters and beaches of the south. Never having lived anywhere near the sea before, she found it fascinating and loved its ever-changing moods. Looking at it from the beach was one thing but being out on it was another matter. She could not understand how those fishermen spent days or weeks out there without fear or dread. On some days, the sun sparkled off its surface creating a crystalline reflection on the rocks. Dorcas loved those days when the blue of the water changed from turquoise at the shoreline, through ultramarine, and then to deep cobalt further out. She sometimes sat on the rocks, watching the boats round the headland and make for the open water, following them until they became tiny dots on the horizon. On other days, the sea was grey and dark and looked menacing and angry. Today it was neither, today it was a heaving, boiling cauldron of white-tipped waves that smashed down on the beach like a hammer on an anvil. The storm had pushed the water right up to the tide line and beyond. There was no beach to walk across so Dorcas walked along the road a while and watched the rolling waves attack the land. Spray filled the air, stinging her eyes and face, and the wind whipped loose tendrils of hair into strings and flattened them to her head. Dorcas stood and watched its measure for a while and then gave up and went home. Fresh air was one thing, getting drenched to the underwear was another.

Dorcas filled the sitting room with candles and settled down to eat a hearty vegetable stew. Ginger gobbled up the fish heads and then begged for some of her food. By the time she had finished eating, the rain had started again and was hammering down on the roof like a thousand nails being dropped into a tin pail. The wind increased its velocity, shaking the windows and blowing the hanging charms. Dorcas felt uneasy. Candlemas should be a celebration of the coming New Year, a time for positive reflection and hope for the future. The wind howled at the chimney and squeezed itself through invisible gaps. It blew out some of the candles and made the rest struggle to stay alight. The cottage became cold as the warmth from the fire was stolen away. Dorcas wrapped herself in a thick woollen blanket from the bed and hugged it close. She moved to the kitchen closely followed by her ginger shadow but the wind was whining in the closed flue of the range shutting off all her attempts at quiet contemplation. Dorcas gave up, went to bed, and tried to block her ears from the sounds of the raging tempest outside. She prayed madly that the cottage did not disappear around her.

*

In the middle of the night, she woke with a start. She was sweating from head to foot and could not get a grip, or a trace, of the dream that was quickly fading from her mind. The only thing that was left from the nightmare was a taste of terror in her mouth and a searing pain in her side. The storm was still blowing outside but had abated a little. Its forces would be spent by dawn, but that was a long way off. Dorcas held her cramped side, stemming the pain with focussed breathing as she paced the cold wooden boards.

'What is this, what is going on?'

'Breathe, Dorcas, breathe.'

It was a mantra she often used to get things under control, but tonight she did not feel she was winning. The storm was responsible for this mare of the night and a tempest was still raging inside her. Wild half-visions flashed past her inner eye, changing, swirling, making her dizzy and nauseous.

She willed her mind to stop racing and to focus on those first few moments after she had woken. Something was there, something was calling, something had happened.

'You need to go to the quay, Dorcas Fleming.'

Ginger sat on the bed, his head tilted to one side, and his eyes locked on hers.

'Ah, so now you speak,' she said looking at the cat.

'And we will speak later,' the cat said 'now go to the quay, you are needed.'

Dorcas dressed quickly, wrapped her two cloaks around her, and lit her hurricane lantern.

'Take the path that leads from the back lane, it is quicker.'

The feeling of foreboding rose as she fought against the wind but Dorcas forced her feet to go faster until she was nearly running. Snatches of the dream surfaced in her mind showing chaotic scenes that she struggled to understand. Branches caught her in the darkness, catching on her cloak and tearing at her hastily scraped-back hair. The unlit path was full of tree roots and disguised rocks that she tripped and stumbled on. She had no idea if she was on the right track until she came out at the top of the cliffs overlooking the harbour. The cat was right, this path was much quicker than coming around the headland.

The scene below her made her stop and take a calming breath. In the dim light that shone from the houses, and from the lamps that had been brought to the quay, Dorcas could make out a hundred or more people scurrying around on the wharf. She heard shouting above the residue of the storm and there was a group of folk on the end of the quay waiting for a single boat to come in. This was a dangerous place to be, as the waves were smashing into the wharf and throwing water over the top. Dorcas could just make out the bobbing lifeboat in the shallow light; it was struggling to get through the narrow opening between the cliffs and into the safety of the harbour. She hurried down the rocky path and onto the quay.

Dorcas flicked her eye over the chaos. Boats had been smashed together causing irreparable damage and one had sunk completely, its mast just visible every now and again above the inky black water. Although the storm had died down, the waves still had strength and were washing over the wall in places. She found Violetta with her head in her hands sitting on the steps that led down to the lower quay. She looked up as Dorcas put her hand on her arm.

'Josiah?'

'There,' Violetta said, pointing to the incoming lifeboat. 'They were out trying to save the crew of a merchant frigate gone aground on the point. Been trying to get in for an hour. It'll get them you know, it'll get them all.'

'Now stop that, Violetta, Josiah has survived worse than this, have faith in that God of yours' Morwenna said coming up behind them. She had been waiting for news at home but decided to hobble down as the night had worn on.

Dorcas left the two women and moved to where the townspeople had taken up vigil at the end of the quayside. The boat rose and fell with the massive waves, in sight one minute and gone the next.

'They'll be exhausted, they get a bit further in and then wind and tide knock them back. They can't keep this up for much longer,' Grenville Simmons said.

Dorcas watched the boat, willing it to move forward. She sent prayers to the Goddess pleading and entreating her to bring them home safely. She thought of every relevant incantation that she could and repeated them over and over again.

'It's coming, it's coming in!' someone shouted.

Dorcas shut her eyes tight and mouthed more prayers. She opened them to the hard eyes of the Preacher Trewidden.

'Some would think that you are trying to keep them out there, Dorcas Fleming. I pray to God that you are not that callous.'

Dorcas's reply would have to wait, the lifeboat was nearly at the quay, and a mass of hands reached in the air to grab the ropes that were being hurled from the deck. A loose boat rammed into it, knocking Josiah's boat sideways with a massive jolt. Dorcas saw the crew lurch to the side from the impact and one of them nearly lost his footing. Tregonning, leaning dangerously out over the swirling water, caught a flailing rope, and tied it down quickly. The men on the quay acted as one and pulled. As the boat came in, more ropes were thrown and caught and the lifeboat was pulled to safety and lashed securely to the quay.

Josiah ensured the rescued crewmembers from the frigate were taken off his boat and into the helping hands of the Pendarthans, before signalling for his own injured to be moved off. Joshua Small had a broken arm and Billy Mims had blood all over his face from a nasty gash on his forehead. They would live. What concerned Dorcas most was the makeshift stretcher that they were now bringing off the boat. Violetta pushed her way through the crowd to get to her husband who was last off the vessel. Josiah looked beyond exhaustion and on the verge of collapse. His voice was cracked as he turned to his wife.

'It's Jubal. Got crushed between the boats. Took on a lot of water. He's near dead.'

Violetta put her hand to her mouth and then turned, her eyes searching wildly for Dorcas in the watching crowd.

'Do something,' she screamed at the witch. 'Do something!'

Everyone turned to look at her as she walked to the man who was now lying on the cold stone of the quay. Josiah shook his head but Dorcas knelt beside the inert body of the man who had been so full of life only a few short days ago. She put her hand on his neck to check for the feel of the heart. It was there; faint and fading, she could detect just a weak beat against her fingertips. No breath left his body or entered. He had stopped breathing, and his face was as white as parchment under the lanterns held above her head.

'When did he take his last breath?' she cried.

'As we came in, we were nearly here' Josiah said.

Dorcas bent close to his face, put her mouth against his and held his nose closed. She forced her air into his mouth and down into the sodden lungs.

'She is taking 'is soul,' someone cried and the crowd moved forward a little.

'Wait!' Josiah said holding up his hand 'Wait a moment, give her a chance.'

Dorcas gave him another breath and listened to his chest. The thump of his heart was slow and very faint so she breathed again, pushing the air deeper. His chest heaved slightly and the crowd gasped. She drew back a little, looked at his colour, and felt for the pulse again. Dorcas gave another dose of air and he spluttered back into the land of the living. The men helped turn him on his side as the lungs ridded themselves of the brine, retching over and over again until they were clear. When he had finished, Dorcas was aware of voices behind and around her where there had been silence before. She bent low to listen to his breath again, checking that it had a rhythm and that the beat of his heart had improved.

'This is no place for our first kiss,' he croaked in her ear so that no one else heard.

Jubal Sancreed opened his eyes and a roar went up from the crowd.

Chapter twelve

An hour later Jakey Moyle and Tregonning lifted Jubal into his own bed. Dorcas had gone back to her cottage to fetch some extra blankets, a pot of stew for later, and a number of ingredients from her dresser.

'Seems to be sleeping now,' Jakey said as she entered the bedroom.

Dorcas nodded.

'His body will be exhausted from its fight for life, he'll sleep for hours. You go home, both of you; I'll keep an eye on him tonight. You need to get to your own beds.'

'We always sees our own to safety,' Jakey said as they left the room, 'He fought long and hard for they men tonight. He'll never lose that death wish of his though; he takes far too many risks that one.'

Dorcas saw them to the door. Tregonning turned and nodded to her, which was as good as a spoken 'thank you' in his book. She returned to the bedroom and checked on her patient again, and once satisfied with his breathing, she settled down in the rocking chair to keep vigil and see him through the night.

'I like this one, I'm glad you saved him.'

'Ginger, how did you get in?'

'A cat knows the way, Dorcas Fleming.'

Ginger jumped onto the end of the bed and started licking his damp fur.

'Why has it taken you so long to talk to me? I was beginning to think I had lost my touch.'

'It has been a long time since my ancestors have communed with a human. I was not sure that I wanted to.'

Dorcas smiled. Typical of a cat, fickle creatures who would never lower themselves to do anything they found distasteful. They were also dreadful snobs and Ginger would not have wanted to lose 'face' if he was out of practice.

'If we are now communicating, would you honour me and lend me your proper name, if you please?'

Most humans named their cats what they considered a catlike name and were completely unaware that they were sent into the world with a title of their own. It was said that Bast herself, the daughter of Ra, named all cats before their birth and they were certainly named for royalty.

'My true name is . . . .' Ginger paused for dramatic effect. 'Zebulonus.'

Dorcas bowed her head.

Then I am pleased to make your acquaintance, Zebulonus, and I'm sorry for all the curses and the rudeness. I thought that all the animals in the south were ignorant and dumb.

'You cleaned me and fed me, I am grateful, all is forgotten. Now sleep, the new day will bring work for you.'

Dorcas slept a lot longer than she had intended and woke as Jubal stirred in his bed. She hurried down the narrow staircase and lit the range in the kitchen that was a lot bigger than hers. Jubal's house was as neat on the inside as it was on the outside. While she waited for the kettle, Dorcas had a quick look around. The sitting room, that was also slightly larger than hers, was as tidy and clean as the kitchen. There were some pictures on the whitewashed walls and an ornament or two on the mantelpiece. On closer inspection of the seascapes, Dorcas realised that Jubal himself was the painter. There was an easel in the corner beside a box that contained oils, brushes, and watercolours. The man had depths it seemed. A massive sea chest took up most of the centre of the living room. It was old and rusty in places and had a white cloth on the top with a spray of ferns in a jar. Dorcas acknowledged the fact that he had made an effort to make it look like a home. The view from the front of the house was better than hers was and took in the whole of the cove that the little valley emptied into. On a side table sat a large leather bound book, which, at first glance, Dorcas took to be a bible. The pages inside revealed a different story. It was a journal, much like her own Book of Shadows, filled with lines and lines of neat writing in the hand of the man in the bedroom upstairs. Dorcas would not have been so rude as to read these private words but she took note of the dates that passed before her eyes and saw that Jubal Sancreed had been recording his life for quite some time. Interesting. She returned to the kitchen, made the tea, and boiled some of the eggs that she had found in his cold cupboard.

'You're awake then?'

'I ache from head to foot, feel as if I've been run over by a cart.'

'By all accounts that would have been preferable, Mr Sancreed, seems you saved a lot of people last night.'

Dorcas set the tray on the side table by the bed and drew back the curtains. Jubal winced as he eased himself to a sitting position.

'Not a good idea' he said breathing in sharply.

'Eat your eggs. I'll have a look at you in a minute.'

She studied his face and his demeanour as he ate his breakfast. The man was in some pain and discomfort and there was still a greyness to his skin that showed the traces of his fight for breath the night before. He would be tired for a good few days to come, and if she was right about her diagnosis, he would be confined to his resting place for a week or so.

'Are you always this bossy?'

'I'm working, I'm allowed to be bossy.'

'Does your work mean that you always sleep with your patients?'

'I'm not even going to answer that. Now eat.'

Jubal finished the eggs and stroked the ginger ball that had also shared his room the night before.

'I dreamed that you were talking to the cat.'

'I often talk to the cat,' Dorcas said smoothly. 'There is no one else around to talk to.'

'He was answering you in my dream' Jubal said.

Dorcas took the tray and snorted at such silliness.

With a five-minute examination, she told Jubal that her initial thoughts about his injuries were correct.

'You have snapped at least two ribs, a bone is broken in your finger and you have a mild concussion. I think you have been lucky, Jubal Sancreed, although I'm sure it doesn't feel like it. I will bind the ribs and put a poultice on them to help them heal. The finger can be strapped and you won't notice the concussion at all because you won't be getting out of bed for a few days.'

Jubal glowered.

'I'll get up when I want to witch, and none of your hocus-pocus will keep me here. I've got me pots to see to; some of us have to work for a living.'

'We'll see about that. Ribs need time to heal, you cannot splint them because of their shape and position, so unless you want more trouble you will just have to do what I suggest.'

'Have you finished?'

'Yes thank you, I'm going downstairs to have my breakfast now. You can shout if you want anything and I'll ignore you whilst I'm eating but I'll be back up with bandages and the poultice in a while.'

Dorcas left him before he could say anything else.

*

It was nearly a month before Jubal could work again. For the first couple of weeks he found that he was almost completely helpless and dependent on the witch to look after his every need. Two days after the rescue, he developed a fever and once again had to fight for his survival. Although Dorcas felt that it was not going to be fatal she stayed with him night and day listening to his incoherent ramblings.

'Lies all lies, don't listen to them, us knows the truth.'

His lungs had developed an infection from the saturation they had received and his body was racked with a violent cough that forced the healing ribs apart making the pain unbearable. She gave him Balm of Gilead infused into brandy, it acted as an expectorant, the buds of the plant also contained a powerful antiseptic. Elderflower and hyssop helped quell the fever and she kept an inhalation of thyme and aniseed bubbling beside the bed. He fought her when she tried to undo his shirt to place a warmed poultice of bladderwrack seaweed on his chest.

'Curse it, curse it, curse them all and their lies,' he shouted, his flailing arms catching her more than once.

On the second night, Dorcas gave him a decoction of opium poppy to give his body a break and let him have some restful sleep; it also allowed her to have a look at his ribs without the fight. While he was sleeping peacefully, she pulled open his shirt and used a preparation of witch hazel to sooth the bruising. His smooth chest was still coated in sweat so she changed the shirt, carefully pushing his arms through the sleeves to prevent any further damage to his broken bones.

'Why are you fighting against this so hard? Why?'

Dorcas had heard many stories of patients who were in the midst of a fever, throwing their witch across the room or breaking fingers. Fever often addled the mind and loosened the tongue. She could remember Mother Lylas telling her coven about fevers.

'Alcohol loosens the tongue and expands a lie. Fever loosens the mind, lets out the truth, and is sometimes worth listening to. You can gauge a lot about a person when they are in the throes of delirium'.

Jubal's truths were a mish-mash of images that flashed across his delirious brain. Meandering snatches of his life, his work and the night of the storm all mixed up together.

'She leaves. She leaves. Said she would. They don't know. Don't know the truth. The water. Can't breathe. Must breathe. She's gone. Gone on the ninth.'

'He's remembering that night and the frigate when she sank.' Josiah said as he sat beside the bed. 'We had to leave two on board, couldn't get them off in time. The ninth he's talking about is the ninth wave, always the worst and the biggest.'

'An omen, Josiah? I've noticed that folk seem to live their lives around their superstitions. Surely your God is responsible for good or bad fortune?' Dorcas asked.

'Mmm, I see the irony, Miss Fleming, but that is the south for you.'

'And I am beginning to see that the south has not totally forgotten the Pagan way. They have just twisted good things around and made them bad.'

Josiah had come twice in the last week to visit his crewman, and to bring food. The basket was full of staples; bread, potatoes and the like all wrapped in a blue gingham cloth..

'There's not that much but a few people added to the things that Violetta and I put in. A lot of people don't see eye to eye with Jubal Sancreed but they won't see one of their own starve,' he said.

'Oh?'

Josiah looked out to sea.

'He was a bit wild in his youth, you know, folk take a long time to forgive some things,' he explained.

Josiah had also brought news that the Pendarthans were blaming Dorcas for the storm, saying that she called it up in order to save Jubal Sancreed and gain recognition for her good deeds.

'And do you believe this?'

'Not at all, we always have at least one bad storm during the winter months. Last year we lost three men trying to save a trader off Zenno Bay. You must give them time. Mother says that people are buying your creams and things and the fishermen have taken my lead and are using that salve for the hands. I dare say Violetta has noticed the difference,' he winked, showing Dorcas a much-improved palm.

'I think giving breath to Mr Sancreed may have put them off, don't you? They will not accept my medicines now,' Dorcas sighed.

'Little by little, Miss Fleming, take it slowly. Two steps forward but only one step back,' he said pulling a long list out of his top pocket.

'Keep goin' along as you are and very soon they'll be coming to you for all their aches and pains. Here's a list and it has a few new names on it. I hear Telfer is having help for his drinking.'

Dorcas was beginning to realise just how much this town gossiped. People in the north were not exempt from this pastime but at least they got all their facts right before imparting a juicy titbit to a neighbour.

'Chief Penpol. I realise that this is good if news of my healing skills is getting about but please realise that I cannot, and will not, be part of it. My patients' ailments are their own and I will not share them with anyone else.'

Dorcas knew that this would be spread around as well in Josiah's well-intentioned way and he had taken no offence from her little tirade.

There were other visitors to the cottage and not all of them for Jubal. Sarah Trewidden came on the day of the full moon.

'You said to come,' she said with a worried frown on her pinched face.

'Of course. You are looking a little better, Sarah.'

Like the rest of the population of Pendartha, Sarah knew that Dorcas was at Jubal's place most of the time. She had called first at the fisherman's cottage. He was a lot stronger but had given up trying to fight her advice after he had fallen over getting out of bed on his own.

Jubal was now the model patient so Dorcas took Sarah to her own house and made some tea. She was glad to see that the young girl sipped slowly and managed to eat a small piece of the heavy cake that Violetta had sent up.

'That herbal tea has calmed me guts and although I don't care for the ginger, it has done the trick.'

Dorcas had not forgotten the Trewidden girl even in the midst of Jubal's fever. She had sent a package down with Josiah and he had dropped it off at the Moyles'.

'Shall we have a look at you?'

Sarah nodded nervously and pulled up her dress. Dorcas ran her hands over the protruding stomach

'The baby is doing well Sarah, but you seem to have some more of those bruises.'

Dorcas had had her suspicions the first time she examined Sarah. Now the truth was staring her in the face. Sarah's thighs were marked with bruises that could only have been caused by somebody squeezing, and squeezing hard, leaving five-finger bruises behind. Dorcas also saw red marks on her wrists.

'Do you want to talk about this?' she said gently.

'I, I….fell,' she stammered, her eyes filling with tears.

'Who is doing this to you, Sarah, is it your husband?'

The young girl shook her head vigorously but under Dorcas's watchful gaze she changed her mind, nodded slowly and burst into tears. Dorcas let the tears run their course and then handed her a handkerchief to wipe her reddened eyes.

'I don't do nothing right, he's older than me, knows more. I'm just a stupid girl. Me mum says I should be grateful to have made such a match.'

'Grateful that he beats you?'

'He don't mean it, he's sorry after. I just make him so mad with my stupidness.'

Dorcas was aware that fingernails were digging into her palm.

'Sarah, how old are you?'

'I'll be sixteen next month.'

Dorcas sighed inwardly. She would like to give this bully of a man a good piece of her mind, and some other things, but that would not help the young girl.

'Things will be better once the baby comes. I know he really wants it. His first wife didn't give him no children, she couldn't hang on to the baby.'

Dorcas tried to find a solution. There was no point in suggesting that she should leave him because Sarah would be turned out with nothing, and it did not appear that this community would support her. That was one thing that would never happen to a witch. If marriage, or placement, went wrong, then the community came down on the witch's side. However, a witch's marriage very rarely went awry as she took great lengths to choose the right husband in the first place.

'Your husband's brother is the Preacher, isn't he?' Dorcas asked.

'Could you seek help there?'

Sarah's expression said it all and Dorcas did not pursue that line of thought again.

'Just give me more of that cream and I'll be all right.'

'I will give you more but there must be something else we can do. Could you get Mary Moyle to give you a hand with the housework?'

'Maybe,' Sarah said thoughtfully. 'When he's away she could come, Mary is a good friend.'

'Good, well that's one step. You *must* look after yourself for the baby's sake.'

'Perhaps he'll stop when the baby comes, he's worried about it as it's the first,' Sarah said.

'I doubt that, if he's doing it now when the baby is inside you he's not likely to stop when it's born.'

Dorcas laid her hands on Sarah's stomach.

'The baby is growing fine, small, but growing. Would you like to know what sex it is?'

Sarah brightened.

'You can tell?'

'Only if you want me to.'

Sarah nodded and Dorcas told her it was a girl child.

'Don't say nothing to nobody though, will you? This'll be my secret. A girl, I can't believe it. I hoped it was.'

'Well I didn't, I expect the poor little soul will be subjected to the same treatment as you before long.'

Dorcas told her to come back in another couple of weeks when she would give her a raspberry tisane to help her muscles get ready for birthing. Sarah went away happier than she had come but Dorcas was far from happy. When the girl was out of earshot, she kicked the door of the range and bruised her toes in the process.

'There's nothing to be done, you can't educate pork,' the haughty voice of her cat said from the windowsill.

'When I want advice from you I'll ask for it,' Dorcas snapped.

'Well, excuse me for breathing, witch.'

Dorcas calmed herself. From his perch next to the range, the cat watched her smooth down her black dress and fuss with an invisible strand of hair. He would have to watch this one, she had hidden depths.

'I'm sorry, I was rude,' Dorcas said.

'You can't change everything you know, you must work on the

little things.'

'Oh, that I could change things, Zebulonus my friend, I would start with that girl. There's nothing good going to come out of that pregnancy.'

'Then that is the way of it, you know the rules.'

'Only heal and help, I know the rules, Zebulonus. I also know that a witch can manipulate a little when she has to. Down here these people are so wrapped up in their righteousness that they forget about the plain and simple truth.'

Sarah did not leave her mind all day and neither did her temper.

'Steady!' Jubal cried when she changed the bandages on his ribs later that day.

'I'm sorry, I have other things on my mind.'

'That wouldn't be Sarah Trewidden would it?'

Jubal had two windows in his bedroom; one looked through the trees and out to sea and the other faced towards her front door.

'Nothing gets by you does it?' Dorcas said.

'Not much.'

'Do you know her?'

'Not well, she comes from Port Ruas. They married hastily last spring. I think he bought her.'

'What?' Dorcas said aghast. 'You can't buy a human being, not in this day and age.'

'It still happens sometimes. When a family falls on hard times, they sell off the only goods they have. '

Dorcas's head was spinning; this was something that she had not learnt at Summerlands.

'But he's the Preacher's brother, didn't he have something to say.'

'The Trewiddens are a law unto themselves. Morley Trewidden lost one wife, I suppose he didn't fancy making the effort to court another.'

'And you agree to this way of doing things?'

'There are worse things, Miss Fleming, probably suited them all. At least he's got a wife that will stay with him.'

'These people don't care about each other, they don't care about anything at all. Have they really forgotten the natural order of things?'

Dorcas made her excuses and spent the first night in nearly two weeks in her own house. She was still agitated the next morning when she returned from giving Jubal his breakfast. On her doorstep stood the tallest woman she had ever seen.

'Merrymeet to you, can I help you?'

'I need a husband,' said a deep, mannish voice.

Dorcas looked at the woman and judged her to be about thirty-five. She was dressed in the apron that Dorcas recognised as denoting the trade of fishwife. The dark maroon material was soaked in blood and stank of fish guts. Dorcas opened the door and ushered her in. She was glad to see that the woman left the offending apron outside. She put the kettle back on to boil and stoked the fire while the woman pulled out a chair and sat down heavily. Dorcas sensed no nerves in her guest but she did have something on her mind.

'I am Dorcas.'

'Name's Avergila Pengelly and I needs a husband.'

'So you said and how do you think I can help you?'

'You're a witch aincha? Mary Moyle says you can see things. I want you to see if there's a husband in the offing for I.'

Marriage had obviously passed Avergila by in her younger days and a tiny bit of Dorcas could understand why. If Avergila dressed in men's clothes, it would be very hard to tell the difference. Not that she was ugly or disfigured, she had good bone structure, high cheekbones, and a mass of deep brown hair, but she had the forearms of a miner and a tone to match.

'Runes, tea or mirror?' Dorcas asked after weighing up her customer and deciding that she could tune into her.

'I don't know what else you just said but I'll have a cuppa tea, black and sweet.'

Dorcas explained that she could scry for a husband with the other objects but with no promise that it would show what Avergila wanted to see.

'I have the tea leavings then, I knows what that is.'

After downing a very strong cup of tea from one of Dorcas's fine china cups, Avergila turned the cup three times on the saucer nearly grinding away the rim. She watched the witch intently as she studied the leaves at the bottom.

'I has to have one see, I don't want to spend me last years on me own.'

'That's understandable,' Dorcas said as she turned the cup to the light.

The results were astounding.

'Well?'

'Avergila, is there a market of some sort that you go to sometimes?'

'Aye, the fishfest in Polgarras, comes up on the second day of February.'

'That is a festival for me also, but you need to go to this one, there are three men waiting for you.'

'Three?'

'That's what it says, you'll have to pick.'

'If this is true I'll tell 'em all that you're a good un but I think that the witching is just a sharp mind and a way with the herbs, am I right?'

Dorcas nodded. Hedgewitchery was all about using your brain, assessing your patient or client and giving them what they wanted. If Avergila wanted a husband that much then she herself would do the finding and the Goddess would bless the match. It was as simple as that but you still could not argue with the signs when they were as clear as these were.

Avergila left the cottage an hour later. Dorcas had warmed to the rough and ready woman and Jubal teased her about it.

'Most men are frightened of that one, wouldn't go near her with a dogfish in each hand.'

'I seem to be back in that category myself. Avergila said that they are certain that I caused the storm.'

'And did you?'

'If you make comments like that I'll just have to break some more of your ribs.'

Jubal looked thoughtful.

'But you could if you wanted to?'

'I thought you were on my side.'

'Only so you won't curse me' Jubal smiled wickedly.

'You are impossible, but let me tell you this and you can pass it on to the rest of the heathen idiots in this town. I cannot curse anybody; I am bound by the Threefold vow. If I use evil against anyone it will come back on me three times as bad as I gave it and not only on me but on those I love and those who have dealings with me. Cursing is not the way if you wish to keep yourself healthy and alive.'

Jubal Sancreed went quiet and turned his face to the window away from her as she tended to him. This was not what he, or the townsfolk of Pendartha, wanted to hear. This was not why she had been brought here and he would have to tell the committee that she was just what she said she was, a plain and simple hedgewitch with an educated knowledge of herbs and the like.

There are limits to your power
There are limits to your sway,
Loosen your grip, lose your thrall,
Influence falls away,
Even now your power is gone,
Leave her life, your day is done.
- Banishing spell to be done on the waning moon

Chapter thirteen

Jubal left on the day of Imbolg and was gone on the evening tide. Dorcas watched his small lugger depart from her viewpoint on the top of the cliffs. His pots had been calling and Dorcas gave him a half-hearted blessing to return to his trade. He was nowhere near ready to take on full responsibility and he had reluctantly agreed to take Samuel Creed with him on his first trip out. With his ribs still bound, Jubal had loaded the boat, answered the call of the sea, and gone back to where he belonged.

With her neighbour out of the way for a few days, Dorcas was free to celebrate the Imbolg Sabbat in relative peace. No citizen of Pendartha had so far ventured out this way after dark and she was grateful for it. Dorcas observed the rituals of the renewal of the land and the Goddess's recovery from birth. Imbolg was a gentle time, the earth was awakening from its winter sleep, and fragile shoots poked through the weather-hardened earth. It was a time for rejuvenation and Dorcas thought back to the last one at Summerlands. Her coven had sought to enhance their emotional and spiritual regeneration and Dorcas took herself back to that time in her mind and went through the spell again, only this time alone. It was hard, much harder than she had thought. She missed the coven and often wished she had made attempts to be friendlier to them. She also often wondered how Ginny was and whether her abrupt leaving had worked out for her. Dorcas thought how typical it had been for Ginnifer Belle to do something like that. Her family seemed to be unaware that their daughter was one of the spiritually strongest people that Dorcas had ever encountered. She would love to have even a little of the resolve that Ginny had. To throw away a whole thirteen years' training was powerful in Dorcas's eyes, and she just hoped that it had all been worth it; assuming it was true. For a while now Dorcas had gone back over her last few months at Summerlands and there were one or two things that didn't quite make sense to her. There was no point in worrying about it now, what was done was done and the clock could not be altered.

Imbolg also fell on the waning phase of the moon and Dorcas used its powers of reduction to her full advantage. She cast a spell in a ring of white candles, calling to the elementals to help and protect. She would not openly curse Morley Trewidden but would seek to lessen his power over his wife. If she had more strength in that young mind then Sarah could possibly find her own way to deal with her domineering husband. It was no wonder a lot of witches never married, they saw and heard too much of other people's lives to want to enter into it themselves. Dorcas had long since come to the conclusion that a husband was not on her list of priorities, she got on well with men, and this was probably why. She gave off no hints that she was looking for a mate and talked to them as equals. Jubal was on the verge of being promoted to the status of 'friend', she had used him as much as he had depended on her in the last few weeks. There was something inside Jubal Sancreed that was as closed to her as a locked door with a lost key and she had no real wish to find it. They shared humour and a love of the natural world but that was as far as it went. It was enough. Friends were important, lovers were not. Here in the south it was not deemed correct or proper for anyone to take a lover; you married or remained a spinster. Under God's law, intercourse did not take place outside the sanctity of marriage. She had not been told that before she was sent, but had learnt quickly. Witches were by their very nature sexual creatures who communed with the elements and celebrated the raw power of bodily want and need. Dorcas's last encounter had been the previous year at Litha Fair in Brexham. A young man had followed her for an hour before he had finally approached her. Ginny had teased her until she herself had given in to the gentle pleading of a burly thatcher from Illkingham. Dorcas often wondered if this was the lover that her friend had run off with to avoid working on her father's lands. Ginny had always been free with her favours.

'You shouldn't keep it to yourself Dorcas, it is there for the giving and the taking. Free yourself, just this once, and give in to the call of nature.'

Dorcas *had* given in and had spent a very enjoyable night with the travelling actor who had finally come up to her as she stood in the queue for a hot toddy. A witch was often seen as a great coup for a common man, a feather in his cap so to speak and on the night of the summer solstice Dorcas knew she had just given him something special to take away with him. That had been the last time and pleasant though it was Dorcas had sworn to herself that it would not happen again There was too much at stake.

A week after Imbolg, Dorcas woke to a banging on her door.

'All right, all right I'm coming' she shouted hurrying down the new oak staircase that Josiah had commissioned for her.

The door was going to give way at any moment with the pounding it was taking. Dorcas opened it to a raised fist that was just about to pummel the wood again.

'Avergila Pengelly, good morning.'

'Mornin' witch,' Avergila smiled, showing a rotten tooth. 'Put the kettle on I've got some news for ee.'

Over a large mug of tea, Avergila imparted her important news.

'So I want you to come, the nuptials is to be held at the chapel next Sunday with a shindig at Jakey Moyle's after.'

'That was quick work.'

'No point in hanging around at my time of life and he can hardly wait until then, if you get my meanin'.'

Avergila followed this statement with the lewdest wink that Dorcas had ever seen.

'So you chose then?'

'You was right, absolutely right, three of 'em, lining up like pilchy's on a tray, couldn't put a foot wrong I couldn't.'

Dorcas said how pleased she was but politely declined the offer to attend the wedding.

'But you must, I have spoken to the Preacher and he has agreed. He owed me a favour anyhow so I just called it in. Unless you has a problem with me God then you're comin' whether you want to or not. You brung us together and I want you to see me happy.'

Dorcas made no argument, she would rather have avoided the chapel for other reasons, but Avergila was persistent and would not be deterred. Things had been running smoothly with the townsfolk lately and she had no wish to rock the proverbial boat. There were more and more orders coming in from folk who needed creams, salves and the like and she had even gone as far as treating Violetta Penpol and Bargus Smith with medicinal tinctures to cure bronchial coughs. She was far from being accepted but it was looking more hopeful.

'I *will* be there Avergila, I wouldn't miss if for the world.'

*

The wedding day dawned bright and blustery. Dorcas smoothed down her best green dress and fiddled with the tiny mother of pearl buttons. She tidied up her hair and shoved a few more pins in to secure the twisted bun to her head.

'You have taken off that flowery head thing' Zebulonus said lazily from his warm patch on the bed

'I forgot that this is no handfasting, greenery wouldn't be acceptable. Do I look all right?'

'As far as a body ever does when it is clothed from head to foot. It isn't natural of course, but you will do'

'Why do I bother asking a cat, what would you know?'

'I know that it is a good day Dorcas Fleming, things will happen.'

'And I know that there is no point in asking you exactly what is going to happen so don't tease' Dorcas said adjusting her hair.

She grabbed her velvet purse and her basket from the table and hurried out of the house. She planned to arrive early so that she could take a seat right at the back. As she made her way up the path to the top of the cliff, she heard footsteps behind her. Jubal caught up as she got to the summit.

'Thought you were away.'

'I thought so too, but I'd like to see Avergila married, our mothers were good friends, so I came back in last night.'

Jubal admired her dress, she admired his Sunday best suit, and he helped to carry her heavy basket.

The chapel was already filling up as they got to the square. The Preacher was standing outside the chapel doors, welcoming his flock and a few extras. Dorcas hesitated as she approached.

'Miss Fleming, Miss Fleming!'

Dorcas turned to see Josiah hurrying across the road followed by a confection of gingham and lace.

'A walking meringue' Jubal murmured in her ear.

Dorcas smothered a snigger and greeted the Lifeboat Chief and his decorous wife.

'Mother will join us afterwards; she's not been too grand since the storm.' Josiah said.

The Preacher Trewidden was obviously under the impression that if he did not make eye contact with the witch then he could pretend that she was not infecting his house of worship. Dorcas aided his secret plan by ignoring him as well. She nodded in his general direction as she passed by and took her seat just inside the chapel. Jubal surprised her by following her into the hard wooden pew.

'I thought you would sit with your own family.'

'None here,' he said.

'It looks as if the whole town is here though.'

'They like a good knees-up, makes things seem normal, besides a wedding is a lot more fun than a funeral.'

Dorcas had no chance to ask what 'normal' he was talking about because the Preacher swept by in a waft of mothballs as the last guests seated themselves.

As Dorcas looked around the austere building, she realised that she knew nothing about the man who was sitting beside her and he really knew nothing about her. That could still be said about most of the people she had met and Dorcas wondered if she should look to herself to find the answers, but she was not in the habit of letting people get too close to her.

The chapel was a cold, damp building that housed a number of stiff looking icons and religious artefacts.

'The Preacher would have a fit if he ever got a look inside the Hearth building at Summerlands.'

The Pagan coven had a love of all things bright and shiny, colour was important to all rituals and festivals; it helped the mood and the focus. Although Dorcas had always sneered a little at High Priestess Ellen's penchant for purple velvet and silver amulets, it was definitely preferable to this. A witch accepted all forms of worship to any and every God, but this was dreary and boring, and more like a punishment than a celebration. If Dorcas did not know better then she would have sworn that she was attending a funeral instead of a wedding and she hoped that the celebrations afterwards would be a little more light-hearted.

The groom waited at the front of the rows of prim pews but tall hats and concoctions of feathers and flowers impeded Dorcas's view. The first dreadful notes from the organ that announced the arrival of the bride cut off any further thoughts of her surroundings. Avergila had stepped into the chapel and all eyes turned towards her. She looked lovely in an awkward, tall kind of way but her face said it all. This was her day, a day she going to enjoy and it showed on her beaming face.

Dorcas got her first look at the groom as the newlyweds left the chapel and climbed into a cart that had been decorated with white ribbons. He was a little taller than his wife, but they shared certain features and both looked incredibly happy. There was a lot to be said for finding Mr Right later in life.

The cart started up the hill towards Jakey Moyle's house. The guests were puffing and panting by the time they got to the top of the steep hill. Although small, the property had an enormous yard at the back and some effort had gone into decorating it for the occasion. A table had been put up against one wall and laid with a white cloth. The guests were offloading their contributions of food to the wedding feast but Dorcas led Jubal and her basket to another table that held the drinks. A number of barrels of ale had been placed there and Dorcas added her own offering.

'Wine, Miss Fleming, and not nettle or figwort I see?' Trewidden said coming up behind her.

'Or hemlock or nightshade, I have a nice recipe at home for despatching your enemies overnight.'

'Only the very best Preacher, from Masterbridge's own winery and made from the finest grapes that the north has to offer.'

Stanley Horton had gifted her ten bottles of the capital's finest when she had left him at St Zenno.

'That'll get you in with the locals' Stanley had told her.

Dorcas grabbed a couple of the glasses that had been placed on the table along with a number of pint pots. Jubal opened the first bottle. The Preacher held his hand out to receive the glass but Dorcas turned and found the bride and groom.

'Your health, wealth, and happiness Mr and Mrs Boslowek.'

'Glad you came' said Avergila taking the wine and downing it in one.

'Never met a witch before; you aren't as ugly as I was led to believe' said John Boslowek in a voice only slightly deeper than his wife's.

Everyone in the yard went silent and held their breath until Dorcas smiled and the party began.

The day wore on and as evening came, the dancing started. Although it was still early in the year, the night was bearable, especially as a substantial amount of alcohol was consumed. Dorcas had been the object of fascination for a few of the townsfolk who had not seen her before. Some even came to stand right in front of her to get a better look. Dorcas saw many faces that she did know, some acknowledged her and some did not. Mostly she kept to the sidelines and with a glass of wine in hand she observed Pendartha with its guard lowered.

Sarah Trewidden was there and Dorcas got her first look at the husband. He was as sour-looking as his brother and kept his wife close to his side for most of the evening. Telfer came to ask her for a dance and she was glad to see that he had a glass of lemonade in his hand.

'Took the advice,' he said 'and I'm getting better.'

'He's doing well' Mags confirmed from over his shoulder.

The music was provided by a band that did not have an awful lot of control over their instruments but Dorcas let Telfer lead her in a very conservative waltz. She was aware that the Preacher was watching her every move.

'He's looking for a pointy tail' Telfer said as he guided her around the cobbled yard.

'I have it tucked out of sight tonight,' she whispered 'and have pushed my horns back into my head.'

It took Telfer a few seconds to smile, but smile he did for the rest of the dance. Dorcas had another ally.

A little later Jubal relieved her of another glass of wine and whisked her around the yard in a breezy polka. The band were now playing with gay abandon, strumming, blowing, and drumming where the fancy took them. Dorcas had noticed that many of the band members swapped in and out all night, as one drifted off to get another drink so another took their place. The music was unadventurous and leaned towards a religious tone, with a hymn or two thrown in to please the present company. The polka had been the only nod towards something that was a little lighter for the feet.

Despite the music, Dorcas was enjoying herself and was reluctant to leave. The bride and groom had long since departed to their wedding bed in the alehouse.

'Here try some of this' Josiah said handing her a bottle of brandy.

'Contraband?' Dorcas asked trying to focus on the foreign label.

'We calls it 'acquired goods' Miss Fleming, try some, it'll warm the cockles.'

Dorcas sipped the strong liquor and looked around the yard. Violetta was slumped in a corner, her mass of ringletted hair now falling over to one side. Her mouth was open, a small trail of spittle escaping from the corner.

'One really shouldn't lose control like that.'

A number of other guests had given up and gone home or had found a place for the night against a wall. Morwenna Penpol was one who had left earlier. Unable to keep up with the party spirit she was escorted home by the widower Penberthy, a relative of Avergila's. The Preacher and his brother had left soon after and there was immediately a certain lightening of the mood in the remaining guests. The band had stopped playing an hour before and there was just the low murmur of people engaged in drunken conversation. Jakey Moyle signalled to his daughters and a couple of other men that Dorcas knew from the quay. They picked up instruments from behind a table. With flat, wide drums and a reedy pipe, they played a lilting tune that was embellished by the feminine harmonies of Jakey's girls. Dorcas swayed to the rhythm, the low beat ran through her bones conjuring pictures of the sea.

'The old songs are the best,' Jubal whispered 'Trewidden frowns on anything that isn't a hymn.'

Dorcas could understand, this was her kind of music. This was Pagan, through and through, and it brought tears to her eyes to hear melodies and rhythms that reminded her so much of home. She let her mind go, lost her body to the call of the earthy music and danced as a body should dance to such music.

*

She woke the next morning with a head as heavy as lead. As her mind caught up with her opening eyes, Dorcas groaned as the memories of the night before became clearer.

'Oh Goddess.'

There was a smell of cooking coming from her kitchen and Jubal appeared at the top of the stairs with a tray.

'Oh Goddess, Goddess!'

'How did you get in?'

'I never left, stayed the night on the floor seeing as you don't have anything else to sleep on. You were in a bit of a state, thought you were going to break me ribs all over again at one point.'

Dorcas put her hand to her head and flopped back on the pillow.

'I danced, didn't I?'

Jubal grinned.

'Oh yes, you danced all right'

Dorcas groaned.

'I have to get down to the quay, I'll come back later. You should take it easy today; you drank nearly the whole of Josiah's brandy store.'

Jubal left and she tried to eat some of the poached eggs and toast that he had made for her. Her stomach and mouth were not in agreement about this but she needed to eat to clear her head. With fork poised in front of her mouth, Dorcas suddenly realised that she was naked under her sheets. It was another hour before she tried to eat again.

*

Jubal took the long way round to get to the quay. Apart from walking off his own consumption of alcoholic beverages from the night before, he had some serious thinking to do. He walked across the beach and back again, trying to order his thoughts and banish the uncomfortable feeling that was hanging around his loins.

No woman, witch or not, had the right to invade his mind as much as she had done last night. He was angry. Angry that a dance could have affected his resolve, but what a dance it was. She had hypnotised all those left at the wedding party, losing herself to the drumming of Jakey and his band. Her body took on a life of its own, weaving a spell that was completely contrary to the persona that she normally displayed. Jubal liked and admired the Dorcas he thought he knew. She was sensible, educated and no threat to his masculinity. Jubal Sancreed had done with women; the one that he had allowed into his life had almost lost him everything. Now this witch, with her two personalities, had wormed her way in and he was not happy about it. She had played her role well so far, helping folk and seeing to their needs but there was something else, something dark lurking below the surface and he had seen it last night.

On the way home from the wedding party Jubal had all but carried her until they got to the cliffs. They had been making up stupid ditties about Pendartha's more eccentric inhabitants and she was laughing and giggling at his description of the Preacher wearing a dress. In the dim light of the waxing moon, she had turned her face away from him to steady herself by a tree. He had seen it.

In the cold light of day, he tried to reason that it had been a shadow or a strand of hair, but it wasn't. Somehow, and in some way, the witch had managed to disguise a vivid scar on her right cheek that ran from ear to mouth. If she could do this then what else was she capable of?

By the time they had reached the cottage Dorcas had been falling all over the place, muttering about people and things that Jubal had never heard of. He carried her up the stairs with the sole intention of just leaving her on her bed. A part of him that he did not care to dwell on today, was spurred on by curiosity and need and he carefully stripped her of every stitch of clothing. There was no sexual desire there, too much brandy had been consumed that night, but there was a need to see, and a need to know.

And today, here on the beach, he knew. Stones flew from the end of his boot, bouncing across the sand and splashing into the turning tide. He had defiled a woman in her own house. He was ashamed. Dorcas Fleming was a woman, and a woman all over, of that much now he was certain. The scar on her face had disappeared again by the time they had arrived home and there were no other marks on her creamy skin. When he was finished, he had carefully covered her naked body with the bedclothes and fallen into a restless sleep on the floor, only vaguely aware that the ginger cat had watched the whole thing.

Chapter fourteen

By the time Dorcas got her thoughts in place, the day was half over. She was glad that she had made a huge pot of stew that would see her through the next few days. There would be no cooking today. The vegetables had come from some of the Pendarthans who kept gardens on the slopes of the valley. The stew, and the weekly bread, provided by Mrs Creed, would suffice for a tasty supper. She spent the morning tending to her aching head with a massage of lavender gently rubbed into her temples. With a mixture of tisanes and a few large cups of tea, Dorcas started to feel a little better. She came back slowly into the land of the living, swearing never to touch Josiah's contraband liquor again.

Just after noon, she opened her door to a trio of giggling girls, one of whom was clothed in a floor-length brown cloak. She recognised two of them as Jakey Moyle's daughters, Mary and Anne, but the third was a mystery.

'Tis the feast of St Valentine and if it is convenient we would like to see who we are going to marry?' Anne asked.

'You did it for Avergila, we have money, and you did promise last night' Mary added.

'I did?' Dorcas said, trying to recall what else she had promised.

'This is Rachael, Rachael Trewidden the Preacher's cousin, so you mustn't say we were here.' Anne said pulling the third member of the trio forward.

Rachael held out a pale hand but refused to let her hood down until they were safely inside the cottage. Dorcas sat them down at the table in the kitchen and fetched her scrying equipment from the dresser. No harm could be done allowing young girls to see their intended, it was natural. Dorcas lit a small piece of charcoal and placed it in her thurible. When it was smouldering she added a mix of red rose petals, a slither of oak bark, a sprinkling of rosemary and a sprig of dried heather. The pungent smoke wafted across the room. Dorcas gave each of them a length of red cotton and instructed them to pass it through the smoke while asking in their minds for a true picture of their future husbands. They then wrapped the thread around a finger and placed their hands over their hearts. On the table she laid out her mirror, the crystal ball and the chalice, filled with clean water from the stream.

'Anne, which will you have?' she asked.

'I'll have the ball' Anne said, setting the others off in a fit of giggles.

Blessed spirits bring to me
Near or far, o'er land or sea
Send a picture true to me
Give me a sign that my love will be
Always true and good to me.

Anne chanted the given spell six times and passed her piece of cotton over the crystal. Dorcas waited for an image to come. It did not take long.

'Your husband will be from a distant place. He is tall and dark-haired with a distinctive mole on his left cheek. He will make himself known in the next six months.'

More giggling followed as Mary took her turn, requesting the cup.

'The name of your husband is already on your lips but he has something he must do before he can marry you.'

'I knew it, I knew,' Anne cried 'it's Johnny isn't it? He has to take that apprenticeship in Polempter, you thought it was going to be him.'

Mary smiled sheepishly.

'Now you Rachael.'

Rachael pointed to the mirror. Dorcas led her through the spell and waited for the sign but nothing came. The mirror remained obstinately black and solid.

'Is there something wrong?' Rachael asked.

'Not at all' Dorcas said, struggling for an answer.

'Try the ball, it worked for me' Anne said.

Dorcas cleared the crystal and tried again but still there was nothing.

'Rachael don't be alarmed, sometimes these things don't work. It doesn't mean that there isn't a husband for you it just means that it is the wrong time. Perhaps you have something else on your mind. Come another day, you will be welcome.'

Rachael accepted the explanation and Dorcas saw the girls to the door.

'You won't tell anyone will you?' Rachael said earnestly.

Dorcas promised that she would not, but after they had gone she wished fervently that she did have someone else to talk to. A witch could always rely on the aid of her coven and it was never considered to be breaking a confidence. The spell should have worked and Dorcas was worried. The mirror had done the same thing it did on the night of the new moon, only this time she had caught a glimpse of the blackness beyond the mirror's depths. It had flickered briefly across the smooth surface blocking the vision that was trying to push through. Dorcas wished there was someone she could go to for advice. There were many reasons for the darkness in the mirror and the clouding in the crystal. Rachael herself could be blocking the spell, Dorcas could be failing to connect with her, or there could be something more sinister going on. The latter was almost instantly dismissed in her mind, as the southerners did not use witchcraft for good or for evil. She would have to keep her ears and eyes open.

*

February melted into March as Dorcas busied herself in the kitchen. The daylight was getting longer and it would be spring equinox at the end of the month. She had not seen much of Jubal Sancreed, he had been out on his boat almost continually since Avergila's wedding.

'Perhaps he is avoiding you.'

'Don't be silly Zebulonus, humans don't take offence as easily as you cats do, besides I haven't done anything to upset him that I can think of.'

Zebulonus had taken refuge on top of the dresser, as there was no other workspace available in the crowded kitchen. Dorcas had soaps drying on the windowsill, a poultice simmering on the range and strands of wick lined up on the table ready to dip in the wax bath.

Dorcas was busy from morning to night and now had many regular clients. She saw Morwenna on Thursdays for her arthritis, Grandad Creed on Mondays for his gout and held an open house on Fridays for walking ailments. Mrs Creed was acting as her agent in the town and gave her a weekly list of needs.

Sarah Trewidden had become too big to visit Dorcas at her home so they arranged to meet at the Moyles's. Dorcas had been down that morning and had waited in the square until she got the signal that it was safe to come up. Sarah still did not want anyone to know that she was seeing the witch apart from her closest friends.

'The baby is doing well Sarah.'

'Morley is pleased,' she said 'he's laid off me a bit lately.'

Dorcas knew he had, the bruises were less, and Sarah looked a lot better. Over her last two visits, Sarah had lost that haunted look and even started to appear as if she was enjoying the pregnancy. The banishing spell had done some good but Dorcas doubted that it would hold its potency after the birth.

'I have made you an oil to massage into your stomach. It will help the skin to stretch and aid the contractions. It will also calm you down and help with the pain.'

'I shall have to wear two pairs of drawers to hide the smell of this stuff' she laughed but took it all the same.

Morley Trewidden was away for at least two weeks; he had taken his boat and a crew of five to catch the cod that were moving through the western sea. It would give Sarah some respite from the wife-beating husband and add to the strength that Dorcas felt was growing inside the frightened young girl. Sarah was still worried about the birth itself. She would like Dorcas to have delivered the baby but knew this was going to be impossible. Granny Jenks, from up the valley, would come when the time was right; she was the only one that Morley trusted.

Dorcas left the house and went down the hill to the square to take some salve to Telfer's sister, she had caught her arm on the range and had suffered some deep wounds to her forearm. A few minutes later Sarah and Mary left the house and saw the Preacher standing in the middle of the lane. Sarah nodded to her brother-in-law as they passed but she missed the glower that followed her down the road.

Dorcas felt good. Oestara was approaching and the change in the land was tangible. New growth was everywhere and Dorcas took joy in seeing the daffodils and bluebells in all their glory in the little valley behind her house. She took many walks with her larger basket to replenish her dwindling stocks. Many familiar herbs grew in and around the cottage, but she had to improvise to replace some of the less common ones that did not seem to grow in this part of the southern lands. In the north, it was easy to pick up new stock from travelling herbmongers; their very job was to carry the goods of the lands to where they were needed. Some covens specialised in growing a certain herb or root and then stocked everyone else. The Gretnor Mountains, where Amberlynne had been placed, supplied everyone from the largest source of white heather in the land. Some herbs were imported from foreign parts and Dorcas knew that these would be unavailable to her once she was in the south. Oils and resins she used in minute quantities knowing it would be a long time until she could get them again. The favoured tea-tree was replaced with a strong decoction of thyme, but acacia resin could not be replaced with anything. The southerners were plagued with arthritis in older age, the damp climate affecting the joints making them warped and painful. Stanley Horton would return in June and she planned to have a long list for him to take back to the north.

Bunches of drying herbs, roots, and stems, hung from her veranda and from the eaves of her newly repaired roof. Dorcas had recently treated the son of the local carpenter for nettlepox and he had come through unscathed by scars or deafness. Mordecai Leven was more than grateful; his son had been a long time coming, and he and his wife did not want to lose their little boy to the virulent, destructive disease. Mordecai wanted to repair the whole of Dorcas's house but she had trimmed the deal down to just the veranda and the roof, which she still thought was too much. In passing conversation, as he nailed down the boards, Dorcas found out that he was related to Foggy Isaacs and that at present Foggy was bed-bound with an infection in the hip.

Dorcas took an 'Enid' poultice of fenugreek and liquorice, with the added ingredient of feverfew, which grew in abundance around her cottage. The flowers were just budding and this would make the poultice more effective. Foggy lived high up on the opposite side of the valley in a small white-washed cottage that looked as if it was sinking into the ground. It was a one-roomed house and Foggy's bed looked over the cliffs and out to sea. It was a perfect spot for weather watching.

'Tis you witch, come to take me 'ave you? I'll not go quietly, no I won't. You won't get Foggy Isaacs that easily'

Dorcas resisted the urge to tease him, the man was in a lot of pain, and his brains were addled enough as it was. Apart from that, Dorcas wanted to spend as little time as possible in the home of Foggy Isaacs. The morbid stench was overpowering her nostrils and threatening her stomach. Foggy was a blend of smells that had built up over the years culminating in an unidentifiable reek that almost had a life of its own.

'I've brought you something for your leg. Your relative, Mordecai, said it would be all right to come. I've also brought you some lamb stew from his wife.'

Foggy's face was grey with pain; he had been suffering for some time. He lay beneath a mountain of ragged blankets and a threadbare eiderdown. Dorcas built a small fire in the grate, it had not been lit for some time, and mould had added itself to the rest of the smells. She set the stew pot on the hook over the fire and found a plate under the bed.

'Are you going to let me have a look at your leg then Mr Isaacs?' Dorcas asked.

'Let you look, let you look, then you'll see' Foggy cackled.

Dorcas removed some of the layers and breathed through her mouth. The leg was reddened around the joint and Dorcas put on the poultice and withdrew quickly.

'Now you see, I saw, now you see. Saw I did. Saw 'em do it, out at Aggstone. You'll know.'

Dorcas could not detect a fever and let Foggy ramble on for a while on his own until the stew was warmed.

'I'll get someone to come up and help you' she said.

'Help! Help? They need that, stuck in their ways. I see the weather, I see all, saw it then, see it now.'

Dorcas made a mental note to include some vetiveria in the next poultice and some large supplies of mint to spread on the floors. Vetiveria was known as the 'oil of tranquillity' it would help his wandering mind, calm his thoughts, and give him some peace. The old man had probably lived up here, alone, for most of his days, his life's work to see to the safety of the town from his vantage point on the cliffs.

'And what a view it is,' Dorcas thought as she stood outside the little house. The panorama was beautiful and she could see for miles and miles up and down the coast. Foggy would see all the comings and goings from the harbour as well as the impending weather that blew in from the southwest. Dorcas could see from the jagged tip of Lazard head cutting into the choppy sea right across to The Mengels, a series of sharp pinnacles that rose from the water to catch ships that had been blown off course. The large foghorn was housed in its own little house and with an ingenious design in mechanics that meant it could be used in all winds and

weathers. Dorcas had only ever seen sirens and alarms that were driven by steam; this one was stimulated by a wind-up mechanism and sent a loud, shrill warning to the town.

When Foggy had finished his first hot meal for days, Dorcas washed the plate and stoked the fire up. Foggy had a good supply of firewood out the back, no doubt from a kindly donor, as there were no sources up here on the barren cliffs. Dorcas promised to come back the following day.

'They likes to forget about me until I'm needed, they remember I sees all.'

'I'm sure you do Mr Isaacs but you need to rest for a few days, the weather will wait.'

She could hear Foggy's loud ramblings as she made her way down the narrow, stony path to town. There were things to pick up in the store that Telfer had promised to try to get for her and then it was time to prepare for the next festival.

Oestara was a good and positive time of year. Dorcas had already started on the task of cleaning out the cupboards in her cottage and scrubbing every scrubbable surface. It was not only a celebration of the fertility and cleansing of the land, but a time when you could put out emotional and spiritual clutter along with the dirty water. It was a hopeful time of year where you could wipe the slate clean of the past and start out with new ideas. Dorcas had to remind herself daily that things were getting better and although slow, she *had* made progress. She had already started to write a letter that would go back with the Horton convoy telling the council what had happened and what she hoped for the future. They had sent her here with a job to do and although she would have liked more contact with home, she felt that she had done the council proud, so far.

Apart from Zebulonus, there were no other animals that she had encountered that she could commune with, so the suggestion of getting a message back earlier was not to be.

'Birds have small brains, they have forgotten,' Zebulonus said 'not worth bothering about really in a cat's eyes, unless a fish fails to appear on your plate that is.'

Dorcas had snorted at her cat's snobbery, but that was cats for you. They really only thought about how the world affected them as individuals. Zebulonus was right, birds did forget things very easily, their wandering minds were hard to get a grip on, and they could only transmit a message in the form of a single picture or image. Carrier pigeons were the best developed for taking a message; they usually knew where they were going, but a beautiful sunset, or the sight of an attractive female could obliterate the message hidden in their minds before it got to its destination. Wolves and foxes were a different matter. It depended on your relationship with them as to whether they would deign to deliver the communication you required. Foxes were useful for local information, they were dreadful gossips and carried the history of their area around in their heads. Dorcas had tried many times to speak to the vixen that crossed her garden at night; if she could get her to understand then she may possibly fill in some of the history of Pendartha. Dorcas knew that there was more than met the eye about her new home but no person was willing to share that information and the animal population had long since dispensed with communing with humans.

The list of provisions that she needed, and would need, was growing daily but Telfer had provided an excellent substitute for the yellow ochre that a witch used to colour her yellow candles for Oestara and other rituals. Saffron was an excellent colourant derived from the wild crocus; it imbued a deep, sunset yellow to the wax that did not fade over time. The southerners, or rather those that lived in and around the Lazardian Peninsula used it to colour a bread-like raisin cake that Dorcas was now rather partial to.

She was in the middle of another batch of candles when a cart drew up outside. Tregonning appeared at the door, a worried look on his face.

'Come!'

It was not so much a request as an order and in the first word that the man had spoken aloud for years he managed to convey a need for speed and urgency.

'Sarah? Is the baby coming?'

Tregonning nodded and Dorcas grabbed all the things she thought would be needed and a few extras.

'Why are they calling me, Granny Jenks was supposed to be dealing with this and it's much too soon, the baby isn't due for over a month?'

Tregonning rushed the cart through the town and out the other side and she hung on tight as it bounced over the uneven ground.

As they drew up to the Trewidden cottage Dorcas saw a crowd of people waiting outside the door. Josiah helped her down and guided her in through the low front door.

'You have to help, she's in a bad way' he said in a low voice.

People drew back to let her through. An old woman, who she presumed was the midwife, was holding the girl's hand and shaking her head. There were numerous bloodied rags on the floor.

A woman in the throes of labour could be bad enough but Dorcas was not prepared for the sight that greeted her. She had witnessed, and helped, with a birthing when she had apprenticed with Enid and was aware of the pain and suffering that a woman could go through in order to bring a new life into the world. The bloodied rags were not from the birthing; by the looks of it, Sarah had only just started to contract.

The poor girl's face was a mess; blood oozed from a gaping gash under her left eye and her jaw was pushed to one side, indicating that it was dislocated and broken. The right eye was closed completely with swelling and there was still fresh blood coming from her nose.

'Out! Out!' Dorcas shouted. 'If I don't give you a job now, then get out and make yourselves useful elsewhere. We need some room and some privacy.'

Dorcas issued orders to those she recognised, sending them for water, bowls, clean rags and anything else that she could think of to get them out of the way. The room emptied and Dorcas was left with Granny Jenks, who did not look as if she was going to be any help at all. The older woman had been crying but Dorcas left her where she was, doubting that she would let go the iron grip that she had on Sarah's hand. She washed her hands thoroughly with the soapwort she had brought with her and rinsed with the clean water that had just come in from the well outside. More water was set to boil on the range in a variety of pans and kettles.

Sarah moaned as the next contraction came and Dorcas tried to clear her mouth and nose of blood and waited for the pain to subside before sitting her up further in the bed. Dorcas took off her lower clothing and put her ear against Sarah's blackened stomach to listen for life. There was none. The baby was not moving.

Dorcas knew that babies often went quiet just before a birth, almost as if they were trying to conserve their energy but there should have been some hint of a heart beat.

Sarah's body heaved with a huge shudder and the contractions started to come a lot quicker. The poor girl was a broken mess.

The eye that was still open told Dorcas everything, the hurt, the heartbreak, and the pleading for her to do something about it. She soothed Sarah with gentle words and breathed alongside her as each pain took hold. Sarah could hardly get air in through her mouth and when the time came she was going to have to bear down against those injuries, the pain would be awful. It was too late to administer anything that was gong to take effect quickly so Dorcas arranged her as comfortably as she could and encouraged her to start to push.

In between contractions, Dorcas wiped her face and tried to listen for the baby's heart again through her swollen stomach. All across Sarah's waistline were horrific bruises one of which bore the outline and stud marks of a hob-nailed boot.

'Oh my Lordy Lord, the poor wee thing.' Granny gasped.

'We have to look past this Mrs Jenks and help her get the baby out. We will lose both of them if we don't focus.'

She moved Granny Jenks and positioned her so that Sarah could dig her feet into both of her midwife's hips. An hour went by and there was still no sign of the baby. Sarah had little strength to push, as she would have done if she was uninjured. With each contraction, Dorcas placed her hands upon Sarah's abdomen and helped the baby down into the birth canal. It was a long slow process and in between the pains Sarah lapsed into a faint like state, only coming to when the next contraction washed through her broken body.

'What makes someone do this?' Dorcas asked out loud.

'The Preacher told her husband that she had been consulting you,' Granny said 'he saw you leave the Moyle house.'

'Oh Goddess.'

As the last contractions rode through her body, Sarah had gone beyond tears or moaning and was now silent. Only one sound escaped her lips as her daughter passed the threshold into the world.

'Bastard!' she hissed through her broken teeth and a gush of blood followed.

Dorcas could see what was coming long before Sarah gave her last push. The baby's skin was blackened, the little girl had been dead for some time. As soon as the cord was cut, Dorcas wrapped her in a shawl and gave her to Granny who took her out into the kitchen and away from Sarah's sight.

Dorcas delivered the afterbirth, then slowly, and carefully, started to administer to the wounds of the girl before her. Sarah was going to have to fight for her own life now.

She was bleeding heavily and lapsed into unconsciousness as soon as her daughter was taken from her. The effort had been too much for her frail body to cope with and she was fading like a waning candle.

Josiah appeared at the door and she shook her head in answer to his question about the baby. There was nothing anyone could do now for the little soul but there was still hope for the mother.

'I need things from my cottage if she's to live. Someone will have to go, I'll not leave her.'

Josiah nodded and relayed the list to the waiting crowd outside. He returned to see if there was anything else he could do.

'Where is the husband?' Dorcas asked.

'The Preacher took him.'

'He must not come back, she will need time and she can not be moved.'

Josiah went off with a list of instructions and she went back into the bedroom to take care of her patient. Women sometimes gave up when all was lost to them and she would not blame the girl for letting herself slip into the next world, but Dorcas had hope. In amongst all the blood and the loss and the carnage, Sarah Trewidden was angry, angry enough to want to live, for now.

Pain and fear be the destructors, let not the two affect the mind. Be gone, away from this place and let the witch do her best for thy body
- Second book of the Elandine Grimoire

Chapter fifteen

Dorcas sat on a chair in the middle of her cell, her hands folded neatly in her lap, waiting. She dabbed at her filthy dress with some of the meagre water supply and tried to make herself look a little more presentable. Her greasy hair was scraped into a tight bun and fixed in place with the two pins that she had left. They had taken the rest along with her amulet and the contents of her pockets.

'Could take someone's eye out with one of those' the guard had said.

Dorcas had resisted the urge to say that she could take someone's eye out with the spoon that she ate her foul dinner with, if she had a mind. It would be more effective than a hairpin, but there was no point in antagonising them. They needed little enough excuse to abuse her, verbally, and physically. The sun squeezed through the bars on the high window for the first time that day and as dawn broke, the bell sounded to announce the day of her trial.

In the first week of her incarceration, she was put in a holding pen with other prisoners who were either waiting for their trial like her, or simply waiting to be transported to another larger gaol to serve their time. She was moved to a solitary cell when word got round that she was a witch. Royston Carleen, the guard, would rather have seen her torn to pieces by her fellow inmates, but the Governor of Polempter Gaol had decided to keep her alive for the trial. A case like this would bring the town some much-needed revenue. A good hanging with a story behind it had not happened in these parts for quite a few years and this one would draw a large crowd that would need feeding and housing.

'Won't be long now witch, hear they're forging an iron rope for your scrawny neck an' it's going to take a little longer to make. Still, worth the wait in my book and you can't do much spell makin' in there, can ee?'

Dorcas ignored Royston Carleen as much as she could without provoking him. He was made for this job, born to it. He took joy in other people's pain and Dorcas had already witnessed him break a man's fingers with the length of polished oak that he carried around under his arm. She had no wish to add to his twisted pleasures.

Here in her cell, when the guards left her alone, Dorcas had time to spare in which to ponder her predicament. In the last three weeks, she had explored every emotion she had inside her, working her way through them methodically. She had started with the absolute outrage at being arrested the week after the baby was born. It had been spring solstice and Sarah had turned a corner.

In the few days after the birth, Sarah had been visiting another plane most of the time. She dipped in and out of this world, preferring to stay where her mind, or her body, could not hurt her. Dorcas aided this with minute doses of opium poppy as she had done for Jubal Sancreed. It was better to let the body heal unhindered for the first few days and Sarah's distress would not help her to knit the broken bones and skin. Dorcas and Granny had washed her, put a clean nightdress on, and stayed with the young girl night and day. Although Granny had very little understanding of the medicinal properties of the herbs that Dorcas was using, she bowed to the witch's greater knowledge. She helped where she could, applying poultices and ointments, changing bandages and boiling up the soiled ones to use again. After learning the mysteries of infection, the old woman turned out to be more of a help than Dorcas had first thought.

'Don't think she want to be here.'

'I don't think she does at the moment Granny, but she is young and she has her whole life in front of her. We cannot stand back and let her throw it away, we have a duty. If she chooses that route later on, then so be it, that is her decision. Witches are charged with saving life and healing and that is what we will do for the present.'

The old midwife had nodded. The younger woman was wise beyond her years and Granny Jenks had learnt more in the last few days than she had in the whole of her life. She had, however, with more luck than judgement, delivered most of the babies in this area for the last fifty years, and she had also delivered the man who had done this.

'Can you not put a curse on him?' Granny said tentatively. 'He don't deserve to be walking on this earth after what he has done?'

Dorcas told Granny that she was not that sort of witch. 'You have it all wrong you know. We northerners are no different to people in the south we just believe that everyone is entitled to their own god and their own way of doing things.'

'But witches is everywhere, up there I mean?'

'Yes they are and they are similar to the doctors that you use down here, except they are cheaper. There are some areas up north that don't hold with witching but they are few and far between.'

'And you all walk about free as you like?'

'Of course, I'm no different to you Granny except that I went to college to learn how to heal people.'

Granny was like a dog with a rather tasty bone.

'And the magick?'

'The magick is in the healing. The rest is in knowing how people work and what their need is.'

'So you couldn't turn me into a frog or something?'

'No, I couldn't, no more than you could turn me to stone.'

Granny Jenks nodded and sucked on her gums. She had the measure of this witch now but still crossed herself surreptitiously when entering or leaving Sarah Trewidden's house.

When Sarah started to pull herself out of the stupor, Dorcas withdrew the poppy and allowed her to come to her senses slowly. She cried for hours and Dorcas and Granny held her in their arms and rocked her as if she herself was a baby.

'Where is he?'

'The Preacher has taken him away somewhere. I don't think he will be back.'

Sarah sank back into the bed and relaxed a little. She was not strong enough to see anyone but a few select people and even then only for a few minutes. Baskets of food and little comforts arrived on the doorstep daily but only Josiah Penpol and Mary Moyle made it through the door. Dorcas and Granny fended off the other well-meaning visitors and gave Sarah the peace she needed to heal her mind and her body.

'Violetta has sent some more books up for you' Josiah said one morning.

Sarah was enjoying the novels that Dorcas read to her in the evenings and had expressed an interest in learning to read herself when she was better. Dorcas was pleased, as this was the first sign that Sarah was looking ahead. Her only complaint about this was that Violetta's taste in reading material was worlds away from what Dorcas liked to read. The bawdy love stories would probably be best read in the sanctuary of one's own mind, but at the moment, Sarah was enjoying them. Granny was also not very literate and she often stayed on later than she intended in order to listen to the next chapter.

A week had passed since the birth and just after daybreak on a fine spring morning Dorcas went to fill the kettle from the well. Unable to sleep any longer she spent the first hour of the day out in the small garden clearing away debris to make room for the new shoots. She heard the boots on the path before the two men came into sight. Josiah came running up the track with Jubal following close behind. The man was red-faced and out of breath when he turned into the cottage.

'You've got to go Dorcas, they're coming for you' he panted.

'We have just heard from Lizzy Mims, she saw the Preacher come into Pendartha' Jubal added.

'Please calm down. The Preacher doesn't bother me; we can keep him away as long as Morley is not with him.'

'He's got the southern guard with him Dorcas, it don't look good' Josiah said, dabbing at his forehead with his faithful red hanky.

Dorcas put the kettle on, the act of lighting the fire and waiting for the water to come to temperature always calmed her thoughts and focussed her mind on a problem.

'What makes you think they are coming for me?'

'Lizzy Mims heard your name and they have a warrant.'

'A warrant?'

'For your arrest, please Dorcas, go now while you can' Jubal pleaded.

Dorcas carried on making the tea.

'Jubal Sancreed I have never run away from anything in my life especially when I haven't done anything wrong. Let them come.'

'Josiah, tell her!'

'Dorcas, the southern guard are run by the church, they are powerful. Trewidden has probably been waiting for something like this to happen so that he can blame you. You must leave Pendartha.'

Dorcas would not be swayed.

'They cannot blame me; there were too many witnesses to Sarah's injuries. What have I done except saved the life of a young girl who was nearly beaten to death by her own husband? Please stop worrying.'

'But you don't understand Miss Fleming' Josiah panted.

'This is as it must be, I will not run.'

The men gave up and waited for the sound of the posse arriving and it was not long in coming. They hammered on the door and Dorcas, against the wishes of her protectors, answered it and stood at the door with her arms folded. There were ten or more guards standing in the front garden; they looked uncomfortable in their bright red uniforms, the Preacher was at the back.

'Dorcas Fleming?' the officer asked.

Dorcas nodded.

'Sarah Trewidden has been accused of being in league with the devil and using evil to influence her husband into unnatural acts. You will stand trial for the death of Morley Trewidden's baby.'

Dorcas felt bile rising in her throat but the officer continued.

'As a known witch and one who worships the horned one you will stand in her place and answer the laws of this land. Sarah Trewidden will be tried when she is able to stand.'

'Breathe, breathe.'

So that was it, the Trewiddens were out to get not just her, but both of them. All of this would die down a lot faster if both of the women were hanged from the gallows.

Jubal and Josiah were at her shoulder and Granny was crying behind them, but there was nothing they could do. Dorcas was dragged forward, shackled, and led to the waiting cart.

As they pulled away from the cottage, Dorcas looked back at the Preacher who was standing in the middle of the road. A smile spread across his face and Dorcas knew that she had just witnessed true evil in a man who dedicated his life to his God.

*

Dorcas had no word from the outside, she was not allowed visitors, and she very much doubted that anyone would come anyway. If she thought that the Pendarthans were suspicious and wary of her then they were positively friendly compared to the inhabitants of the prison. The first night she was there, she had been beaten with a cat-o-nine tails that made bright red welts all over her body. The second night she was subject to a lesson with four heavy boots to make sure she did not forget who was in charge. The guards did not need an excuse to beat her, their fear of her was apparent. Dorcas realised just how much progress she had made in Pendartha; such a shame it was all going to come to a finish so abruptly, at the end of a rope.

She had long since given up hope of leaving this prison alive. The talk she gleaned from the other prisoners and the loose words from the guards gave her no encouragement that all would be well. The Trewidden influence would not be broken; the man had connections all over the Lazardian peninsula and had used them to whisk his brother away into hiding. The word in Polempter was that he had saved his brother just in time from the evil of his young wife and her lover, the witch.

Dorcas thought long and hard about her life, she had no regrets about how it had ended up and felt that she had done the best that she could. High Priestess Ellen had been right, there were not many other students who could have contemplated coming to the south. The only other one she knew would have been Joan and she had won the place at Masterbridge that Dorcas had secretly longed for. She could admit that now but at Summerlands she would have bitten off her tongue rather than say she deserved the elusive place at the capital.

Masterbridge was the centre of the universe as far as covens go. The brightest and the best were housed within its ancient walls. A student could gain a place there for life and Dorcas had thought she had done enough to get inside. No one had studied longer or harder than she had and she felt cheated when the names were called out. Now she realised that the Goddess had another path for her, but at the moment it was hard to fathom what it could be.

All that seemed so very long ago, although it was only four months since she had left. What would the council think and how was Stanley going to get his horse back?

One night she awoke and found mother Lylas standing at the end of her bed. In an eerie glow, the mother smiled and repeated her words from the night of the last ritual at Summerlands.

'Your path is drawn, you will know what to do when the time comes.'

'It's a bit late for all that now.'

'It is never too late Dorcas, look into your own records and see the truth of it.'

The old mother faded away and Dorcas was left with a strange feeling in her bones. She realised that her relationship with Lylas at Summerlands was a lot deeper than she had ever thought.

*

As she sat in the middle of the cell, Dorcas was once again racked with the deep cough that had invaded her lungs. The damp cell that was freezing at night and too hot during the day was an ideal breeding ground for diseases of the chest and Dorcas saw the irony of longing for a good dose of elecampane root. Having a cough would not be as stressful to her body as having a noose around her neck.

The guards came as the noon bell struck, and a gloating Royston Carleen led out her. The two men with him looked nervous and tightened the shackles more than they could have. Both refused to look her in the eye but Carleen more than made up for it. His foul breath hit her face as he leaned into her.

'No more hexin' for you then witch. Today is the day and the rope is waitin''

Dorcas longed to stick something sharp and pointed into his triumphant face but she kept herself under control, focussing on remaining calm and collected. All the time in her cell she had given no encouragement to his taunting comments and that was worse for him than if she had let loose a tirade of insults.

She was taken from the lower cells and out into the sunlight, across a yard and into a long building that had 'COURTHOUSE, JUSTICE FOR ONE AND ALL' written across the top of its double doors. Dorcas revelled in the few minutes she had in the quiet courtyard; the only sound that broke the silence was a dog barking in the distance. The day was warm and bright, spring had well and truly arrived and she had missed celebrating it formally. Alone in her cell she had acknowledged the day and wished the God and Goddess well in the coming months of fertility. At a time when it was good to cast out old fears and worries Dorcas struggled to rise above her own predicament but she had hope for Sarah and she would do her best to keep her from the gallows.

The courtroom was a sterile place that held the memories of misplaced justice and assumed guilt. She was taken through the empty room into a holding cell at the back.

'Now we wait for your audience, witch' Carleen said as he pushed her roughly into the dark room.

No natural light ever got to this room and it stank of the physical remains of human fear. There was no chair provided so Dorcas stood in the middle and waited patiently.

She heard the crowd long before they burst through the doors of the courtroom. It sounded like a Litha Sabbat with singing and laughter getting louder as they approached. If Dorcas could have looked outside, she would have seen the families with large and small children making their way up the hill to their entertainment. They carried baskets of food and kegs of beer and rugs and blankets to sit on when the time for the hanging came. The first flashes of fear ran through Dorcas's mind and she squashed them as soon as they appeared. Fear would get her nowhere.

'At least I will have a number of people to witness my going to the otherworld, nothing is worse than dying alone.'

The crowd quietened as they entered the courthouse, a natural reaction for those who had ever had dealings with the law. They were soon settled and comfortable on the hard wooden benches and the trial would get underway with the appearance of the heathen witch. Dorcas's shackles were replaced with heavier ones that linked hand and foot together making walking nearly impossible. Royston Carleen took great pleasure in placing a metal gag in her mouth and tightening the leather band at the back of her head so that it cut into her face.

'So as you can't curse no one' he grinned.

She was taken out and greeted by a riotous cheer from the crowd. The entertainment had arrived. The room was full to bursting with standing room only at the back. She hobbled to the stand and the crowd went quiet, all trying to get a good look at the condemned. The stand was at the side of the room and the judge's chair faced square on to crowd who were now as quiet as mice. The chair was filled a few minutes later by a face that Dorcas had no trouble at all in recollecting. It was the Squire from the day in Polempter when Stanley had cut his hand in the blacksmith's shop. Dorcas did not even allow her heart to drop at the sight of the man, there was not one person in this room who would see her innocent, and the best that could happen was that it was over quickly. The horde were also praying for a speedy conviction, this was just all part of the process to get to the interesting bit outside where the hangman was already preparing his rope.

Squire Flench took his seat of office and surveyed the assembly. This trial would not take long but he would draw it out as much as he could. People liked to get their money's worth and he was not going to deny them. There was no opposition to the case, it was cut and dried. The bitch from the north was guilty before she set foot in his court. He remembered her from the day that the convoy had been in town and he looked forward, with alacrity, to despatching her somewhere other than a local village in his domain.

The Preacher Trewidden had positioned himself so that he could see every emotion that passed across his nemesis's calm face. His was the first person that Dorcas had seen as she was brought in and she met his eye and nodded. She would not give him the satisfaction of knowing that he had beaten her; he would never beat her.

The charges were read out and each one was accompanied by a gasp from the crowd. They had already whipped themselves into a death frenzy and were baying, silently and impatiently, for blood. There would be hours before it was too dark to hang her so the Squire took his time and relished every moment. Apart from the main charge of her foul liaison with Sarah Trewidden, the list went on, and Dorcas stifled a need to smile at the ridiculousness of the accusations.

'...putting a hex on the older women of Pendartha and making them believe themselves to be attractive to the opposite sex. Putting a thorn in the hoof of a horse and then claiming that the horse told her it was there. Giving an old woman boils that were supposedly cured by placing a poultice of grass upon them. Dancing lewdly in public...'

The list was endless. The Preacher had done his homework and then embroidered it to his own needs. Not one Pendarthan was present to disclaim the outlandish indictments but Dorcas had no blame in her. They would be up against the two most powerful men in this area and their words would never be heard. It was best that Pendartha just forgot about their dreadful mistake.

'...calling up the worst storm in years and then claiming to have saved the lives of men, women, and children. In league with the devil and known criminals. Instilling madness in the old and the decrepit....'

The Squire paused for effect before launching on a well-rehearsed speech about the true nature of northerners and what should be done about any further contact with them.

'As I am a fair-minded man I give the accused the chance to answer to these charges. Witch, what say you?'

No one came forward to undo the gag. If Dorcas could have laughed then she would have, loud and clear just to let them know the absurdity of their beliefs and ways. She had heard of a time when witches were tried for their sins and ducked in a pool on the end of a long pole. If they drowned, they were innocent. Another method was burning them at the stake; if they endured unscathed then their virtue was proved. An idiotic system thought up by idiots and carried out by idiots and here in this room were some survivors from those times.

'If you are what you say you are then you would answer regardless of the restraints that have been placed on your body. Answer now and save your own soul.'

Dorcas, of course, stood immobile unable to answer.

'I say again, speak now witch and save thyself.'

The doors at the back of the courtroom opened and a loud voice said 'I will answer for her.'

The veil between the worlds is thin to a witch, her cloven feet stand betwixt the two, but wary be those who would assume that she would go willing if the time be not at rights.

- extract from the diary of Samuel Henwood (Witchfinder)

Chapter sixteen

Mayor Penpol made his way forward and by the looks of it the whole of Pendartha was trying to squeeze into the courthouse behind him. Both Trewidden and Squire Flench looked momentarily shocked. They had not been expecting this. Dorcas saw it pass across both their faces as it must have passed across hers. What in the Goddess's name were they all doing here?

Josiah was flanked by Morwenna and Violetta, with Telfer, Mags and Jubal right behind them. The rest of the population made do with filling the aisles or waiting patiently outside in the courtyard.

'We feel it is our duty to the county and to our country to come forward and say our piece about the witch that has been living in our community.'

'The trial is nearly over Mayor Penpol,' the Squire said calmly 'I do not think there is anything that you could say that would make a difference.'

The appearance and demeanour of the Mayor, that had reminded Dorcas of a picture she had once seen of St Nicholas, now changed in the blink of an eye. He retained a smile on his jolly round face but his jaw hardened and his eyes had the sharpness of flint.

'By law, she belongs to Pendartha, we has the papers to prove it. There are many that have a story to tell about her and by the law they can relate these testimonials to the court, if you please.'

The Mayor and the Squire exchanged stares and eventually the Squire spoke. There was no need to antagonise these idiots, let them have their say, this trial was done and dusted.

'Then speak and we will listen. Let it be known that this court always adheres to the law, unlike so many.'

Josiah stepped up and told the court his point of view about the witch. He told of his worries and his misgivings that he had made the right decision. He explained about the salves that she had made for his hands but openly admitted that he did not know what was in them. He rambled on for half an hour about this and that, and then Violetta took his place. She also started at the beginning and informed the court of her distrust and disgust when Dorcas first arrived in Pendartha.

Dorcas was confused. What did they think they were going to achieve? These two testimonies had certainly not put her in the best of lights and had even agreed with some of the things she was accused of. Morwenna stood next and was more positive than her son and daughter-in-law. She told the court about her boils and went into minute detail about the ingredients that Dorcas had used. She finished by lifting her skirt a little so that the court could see the faint scars that the ulcers had left and some people got to their feet to have a better look.

The Squire was getting a little twitchy but as soon as Morwenna left the stand, another took her place. Telfer Meriadoc and Mags, then Jakey Moyle and his daughters; even Foggy Isaacs got up and told the now fidgeting crowd about the weather and its effect on the sea. One after the other the inhabitants of Pendartha came forward and said their piece.

The afternoon wore on and some people started to leave. They had come a long way and it did not look as if they were going to get what they wanted. Dorcas, who had been standing all this long while, now leaned on the barrier that separated her from the rest of the court. Her mouth had gone beyond dryness and it occurred to her that the Pendarthans were trying to save her from the rope by letting her die of dehydration.

The Squire was now visibly distracted and kept looking to the high windows of the courthouse. The Preacher Trewidden had a look on his face that would turn the milk. He too glanced from time to time at the windows or consulted the large fob watch that lurked beneath his robes. The Squire tried two or three times to stop the endless trail of souls that tramped to his stand but there was no let up. After hours and hours of speeches that were unrehearsed and stumbling, Jubal Sancreed eventually took his turn. He passed Dorcas and gave a hint of a wink as he took his place. He brought a candle with him and placed it on the bench. The last light of the day was just about to sink below the horizon.

'I don't have much to say, so I will be as brief as I can. I have only known Miss Fleming for a short while but that is a good woman if ever I met one. It seems we have all done a great injustice to her....'

The Squire rose to his feet, banging his gavel on the table.

'That is enough, you have all said your piece, now we get on with it, she is …'

Jubal lit the candle and held it up 'Shall we have some light on the proceedings' he smiled.

The Squire scowled at him and tried to speak again but Jubal interrupted.

'I think you are forgetting something Squire, if you will excuse my presumption, the day is done, is it not?'

With a glance to the window, the Squire threw his gavel on the floor, got up and walked out of the room. A low cheer went up from the Pendarthans.

Dorcas was as confused now as she had been at the beginning. The guards took off her shackles and gag and she was, unbelievably, released into the care of Josiah Penpol. Someone handed her a flask of water and she drank gratefully.

The Preacher had followed the Squire out of the door and the disgruntled crowd dispersed as fast as it had come.

'What happened?' Dorcas croaked.

'Southern law is what happened,' Josiah said 'didn't think we were going to pull it off.'

Jubal took her arm and explained.

'Southern law states that the accused witch must be sentenced before sunset on the day of her trial' he said.

'How did you know?' Dorcas asked.

'Started my training to be a lawyer a long time ago, must have picked up a few things.'

'We didn't think people would testify as such, so we just asked them to talk' Josiah added smiling broadly.

'And talk they did!'

Dorcas gave them both a hug but was suddenly aware of bad breath invading her nostrils.

'You won't get away with this witch, they'll have you the moment you set a foot wrong, and then I'll be waiting for you.'

Dorcas turned to look at the bitter face of her guard.

'Mr Carleen' Dorcas said sweetly, putting her hand on his arm 'I hope that we can both just get with our lives now, forgive and forget, that's my motto.'

Dorcas took her hand off his arm and Royston Carleen spent many weeks trying to work out exactly what she had said to him. The words that had come out of her mouth were at odds with the ones that were now implanted in his head. He had no wish to meet that witch again for reasons that he had yet to fathom, but those reasons were somehow cloaked in fear, and cold dread.

Tregonning and the cart were waiting outside and they helped her in and wrapped her in blankets against the damp evening air. Morwenna, Violetta, and Josiah rode up front and Dorcas was in the back with Jubal. The road was crowded with Pendarthans making their way home. Some had walked all the way and the road was lit by bobbing torches as they all made their way back to the coast.

'He'll never forgive you, any of you' Dorcas said as they left Polempter.

'We have done nothing wrong in the eyes of the law. If you weren't accused and hung by sunset then you are innocent. He will leave you alone for the time being' Jubal said.

'And what of Sarah?'

'They cannot accuse her now if you have been set free. She is doing well and has gone back to her family in Port Ruas. She left you something at the cottage.'

Dorcas's head felt like lead and she laid it against Jubal's arm. Tiredness was gnawing at every bone and sinew in her body.

'Did you feed my cat while I was away?'

'Zebulonus knew where to come when his food supply was cut off.'

'Good, that's my boy' Dorcas said and drifted into a peaceful sleep that took her all the way back to Pendartha.

*

She woke in her own bed but had no recollection of getting there. The bed had unfamiliar clean sheets on it and there was a tray with a gingham cloth laying beside her.

'I have been Violetta'd' she said to the sleeping cat.

'I'm here Miss Fleming' Violetta said panting up the stairs 'we couldn't let you spend the night alone so Josiah and I took it upon ourselves to be your protectors.'

Violetta bustled in with a large frilly apron on, that appeared to have each and every pleat starched to perfection. She scooted Zebulonus off the bed and straightened the covers.

'Thank you Violetta, that was very kind of you both.'

The cat jumped right back on again.

'Now, there are a number of things in your kitchen that I don't quite recognise but I have given them all a good scrub and Minnie Gembo is coming over this morning to help me clean the rest of the house. We didn't do it sooner because, well, we didn't know if you would be coming back, so to speak.'

Dorcas nodded. The woman drove her mad but her heart was in the right place and she wasn't to know that a lot of the pots and pans were only ever used for spellweaving and should not be washed.

'I have made you some nice beef cobbler for your supper and it should see you through the next few days. You need to rest and take it easy, I'm surprised that *I'm* even awake this morning after the trouble that we went to.'

'I am very grateful Violetta, you have been exceptionally kind to me, and I will not forget it.'

Dorcas laid it on as thick as she could and Violetta puffed a little.

'Yes, well, you have helped a few people, never let it be said that we aren't Christian in our ways.'

'But not at all Christian to cats' Zebulonus said as he found his warm patch and began to clean every place on his body that Violetta had touched.

'You really shouldn't let animals on the bed, filthy creatures.'

Violetta left a while later and Dorcas made her way down to the kitchen. She felt as if she could have slept some more but it was nice to be back in her own home, surrounded by familiar things. She worked hard to banish the images of that Goddess forsaken gaol and after sitting in the window seat for a while, she found that she needed to check on the whole of her small house and reacquaint herself with everything. A cup of tea would start her off nicely.

In the kitchen, there was a neat package on the dresser for her from Sarah Trewidden. She cut the string and revealed the small gift and a brief letter.

Dear Miss Fleming,
No words can express my thanks for your help and care of me. I will never forget you, Sarah.

She took a while to decipher the poorly scripted words but Sarah

Trewidden had very cleverly chosen a gift that was most suitable to a witch. Dorcas wondered who had told her that a round stone with a hole in the middle was a witch stone. She put it on the top shelf along with her other little mementoes and keepsakes. She would write to Sarah in the coming days and wish her luck for the rest of her life. They had both escaped, but Dorcas wondered how much luck was going to follow her, things had changed and they had to be addressed.

*

It was three days before Beltane, May Day, and the second most important Sabbat after Samhain.

'And I have done nothing at all to prepare.'

'It will all be taken care of.'

Dorcas was pleased to see the cat, and he looked fatter than ever. She gave him half of the beef cobbler that Violetta had made for her and put the other half out in the garden for the fox. Violetta would never understand the concept that a witch never ate meat and considered it to be eating family.

'I see you haven't missed a meal in my absence' Dorcas said eyeing his protruding belly.

'A cat does what a cat must do.'

'Thought you would have been raiding the cupboards by now.'

'I didn't, but the harbour man and his wife did. They had a look at everything the day after you went.'

'Violetta I can understand, but Josiah?'

'And it took me half a day to get her smell from my fur.'

Dorcas did not feel badly towards the couple, they had their reasons and they and the rest of the town had just saved her neck. If they had gone through everything then they would have read her Book of Shadows and it would serve them right if they read anything about themselves. A witch's book was her own property, a mixture of recipes, advice, gossip, and daily diary. Dorcas was meticulous about recording remedies and events and her thoughts about them. She was now on her fifth book. Inside each cover, she had written an index for easy referencing. The one book that she did worry about was her book of Akashic Records. If Violetta had got her hands on it then there would not be much to worry about unless she had damaged it in some way. Dorcas had not used the book for some time and it was right at the back of the dresser, its silver inlaid cover appeared to be undamaged.

'What were they looking for?'

Dorcas opened the heavy leather-bound book and perused her last entry. She felt the call to search for a new entry but it would have to wait, her body and soul were tired from the long incarceration in Polempter Gaol and she had sworn that she would give herself time to heal and regenerate. Floating on the astral plane and searching the Akashic Records took energy and a certain amount of deep concentration that she did not possess at present. The information you received from the otherworld was documented and used when the time was right. Some things that Dorcas had written down over the years had never made any sense at all and some had been as clear as a mountain stream. Violetta would not understand anything that was in this book, the language of the ether was often different to ordinary words and even Dorcas sometimes had trouble interpreting the meaning at times.

Minnie Gembo and the mayor's wife must have come back at some point but Dorcas did not hear them and continued to sleep through most of the next two days. There was nothing to be done about Beltane, she would have to miss it this year, she did not feel particularly enamoured with celebrating fertility at this time anyway.

On May Day itself, Dorcas took a long walk and tried to put her thoughts in order, in between sleeping she had tried to figure out what to do next. This was the first time that she felt like giving up and going home with Stanley Horton when he came in June. It was only another month away and who would blame her for leaving Pendartha after all that she had been through?

She walked up through the valley behind the cottage and was gone for most of the afternoon. The woods showed definite signs of spring, a carpet of lush bluebells lined the path and spread between the thick trees.

'I can hedgewitch anywhere, I know that now. Pendartha would not miss me and most would be glad to see the back of me. Goddess only knows why they wanted a witch, there doesn't seem to be any rhyme or reason to it?'

Dorcas picked an armful of the heady blue flowers and sat down on a tree stump to think about her problem.

The council had asked that she stay for a year but surely they were not so unfeeling that they would send her back again? She had tried and had certainly made some headway but she would never be accepted. There was something here, something not quite right, but she doubted that she would ever get to the bottom of it. The Pendarthans had only just started to accept the things they could understand. Her beliefs were too far removed from their suffocating church and she just could not spend the rest of her time here hiding her rituals and celebrations to keep them happy. Besides which, she was now a hunted woman, a day would not go by without her having to look over her shoulder and see how close her enemies were.

By the time she started to walk back to the cottage, Dorcas had convinced herself that leaving was her only option. She never liked to give up on anything but there was no point in flogging a dead horse and this horse was dead, buried and residing happily in the otherworld. She would prove to the council that the south was still immersed in its choking ways and that there was no place for her or anything associated with the north. Trade, by the likes of the Hortons, was the only way forward.

She heard the music long before she broke out of the woods. Pipes and drums were playing a merry tune that was nearly familiar to her ears. Ta-pum-ta-ta, ta- pum tiddly-ta. She caught sight of yellow and green streamers flying in the breeze and found a decorated cart parked in the lane beside the cottage.

'We have been waiting for you,' Jakey cried 'it's May Day, come on, there's a party to be had in the square.'

On the road into town, Mary Moyle explained why they were having a May Day shindig. 'The Preacher is not here to put the stoppers on it. May Day was always celebrated years ago but Trewidden frowned on it. We have always remembered the first day of May, it's a very old festival you know, and everybody is there.'

'Must be a left over from before the war, I wonder how many other festivals are celebrated in secrecy, observed in silence.'

Dorcas had not been anywhere near the town since she had come back from Polempter; she was a little nervous as they drew up but soon found she had nothing to worry about.

'Miss Fleming!' Josiah shouted beckoning her over to the drinks table 'You have come at last. We thought you had run away, Tregonning has been up three times for you.'

Just as Dorcas was about to answer, Pendartha's band struck up a chord and the square came to life. Couples joined other couples in a sort of square and they all paraded around, stopping to do a hop and a skip before dancing off again.

'Shall we?'

Dorcas took Jubal's outstretched hand, the dance did not look too hard to master, and she was whipped along by a happy throng of people. The bonfire was missing but the men were dressed as the 'Green Man' and the women were decked from head to foot in spring flowers; just like a Beltane festival. Dorcas doubted that sweethearts, young and old, would be love-making in the woods that night, but the intention was the same as in the north. They were glad to see the back of winter, celebrating survival and welcoming the warmer and longer days that the coming spring would bring.

The Pendarthans could enjoy themselves when they wanted to and although Dorcas tried to keep an eye on how much she drank, she did manage a few more dances with some of her supporters. There was an air of freedom about the place, a lightness, and even some of Trewidden's staunchest followers were letting their hair down for once.

'We missed you' Telfer said as he polka-ed her around the cobbled square.

'You missed my remedies.'

'No, we missed you; you have brought, um, a zing to this place.'

'A zing?'

'Made us think about a lot of things, woke us up a bit.'

Dorcas did not see Jubal for most of the evening, she caught a glimpse of him talking closely with Hannah Trenery, but she did not dance with him again. Josiah plied her with more of his 'acquired' brandy and the evening slowed down into a singsong accompanied by Jakey and the girls. Josiah's deep and surprisingly rich baritone led them all in a couple of sea shanties that ended with a good slurp of liquor After that Foggy Isaacs got up and danced a complicated jig and Dorcas couldn't work out if it was genuine or fuelled by alcohol.

'Glad to see his hip is better' she said to Morwenna who had managed to keep going.

'He said you told him that he would be needed and that he had to get better.'

'I did?'

Dorcas was interrupted by a tune that was as familiar to her as a child's nursery rhyme and before anyone started to sing along, she jumped in and sang it for them.

In Tuatha de Danaan this night,
Beltane fire burning bright,
Cailleac Bhuer, winter crone,
Cast your staff and turn to stone,
May Day comes in joyful gladness,
Hawthorn banish winter sadness,
With the crone throw out thy sin,
And let the fertile summer in.

Everyone joined in, learning the new words that fitted their tune.

'What was that all about then, they words to that song I mean?' Garfield Prinner asked. Dorcas recognised him as one of the lifeboat crew and one that had ignored her completely up until today.

'It's about the crone of winter turning to stone for another year and we welcome the fertile land and the better weather. It is a May Day song' Dorcas explained.

'Can't be doing with all that heathen rubbish, the Preacher may be gone but we still hold true our Christian values. May Day is just a bit of fun.'

'I....'

'Now, now Garfield,' Josiah said, coming alongside her and taking the arm of the witch. 'We promised to enjoy our May Day didn't we? The Preacher is in Porthaveland and a new one will arrive soon. Let's make the most of this day shall we and no harm done to no one.'

'Porthaveland?' Dorcas asked with a shiver, calling to mind those stories that she had heard as a young child.

Josiah drew Dorcas to one side and offered her a swig from his private supply.

'To be sure, and there he will stay if I've got anything to do with it. He's staying with family at the moment until the church decides what to do with him. Don't get me wrong Dorcas Fleming, the man was a good preacher. He served this community well but he let his private life affect his work and you and I both know that the two don't mix.'

'He has family there, in Porthaveland I mean?' Dorcas asked ignoring most of what Josiah was saying.

'Oh yes, three of his aunts still live there, it is about twenty miles away so he won't be bothering us. The old aunts all lived in Pendartha at one time or another. Anyway enough about him, are you glad to be back Dorcas Fleming?'

Dorcas said she was, but this was not the time to impart her news. There would be plenty of time for that. She felt that Josiah Penpol would take it the worst. For his own reasons the poor man had dragged her here and worked hard to promote her cause, and now, it seemed that all that time and effort was to be wasted.

And I looked,
It was there and I beheld it. More ancient than time it was,
a web of souls, eyeless and helpless. The calling came and I
had to answer -
- Akashic records.

Chapter seventeen

Her conversation with Josiah had put a dampener on her party spirit. Thoughts of those poor Porthaveland witches invaded her mind and blotted out the festivities around her. She had no wish to hurt these people after they had so kindly, and so unexpectedly, rescued her. But it wasn't enough; it was time to go. They might miss her medications as more and more of them were turning up at her door each week, but they would soon forget and go back to using the quack in St Zenno. She would take a placement like Enid, as far away from the hustle and bustle of city life as she could. She doubted that the Pagan Council would have much sympathy when she deserted her post so soon after arriving. A witch was supposed to do her best wherever she was placed, but at present, the only place that she wanted to be was north of the Tamalar River.

As soon as was socially acceptable Dorcas made her excuses and took the shortcut back to her cottage. Once inside she made herself a good strong cup of tea and smiled to herself. Some of the southern habits were already seeping into her and she was developing a taste for the dark liquid and had also become partial to some of their confectionery.

'Tea and saffron bun were meant to be together like sand and sea' Violetta had said.

Dorcas thumbed through her current Book of Shadows as she drank. The last entry had been a recipe for a new poultice for headaches that she had developed. Some of the plants that she found in the woods had been unfamiliar but she found that they contained properties similar to some of her northern herbs, barks and spices. She had made a note to find the names and had drawn likenesses of the plants to take to Josiah.

'They will have to find their own remedies from now on, I'm finished here.'

For a long time she listened to the sea in the distance before finally dropping into a deep dream-filled sleep.

*

The voice had urgency in it but she could sense no fear. It called again, repeating her name over and over again and dragged her from a half remembered dream that was weighing heavily on her chest.

'Dorcas! Dorcas! Wake up!'

She tried to block out the invading shouts and return to the sleep that she needed.

'Please wake up before I am forced to tear his eyes out with my claws. He has been calling for a while now so will you please answer him.'

Zebulonus was balanced on her chest and stomach, his fishy breath invading her sleepy nostrils. Dorcas rallied herself.

'Who?'

'The fisherman, he's in the garden throwing things at the house. It seems he wants you to go outside with him.'

'Dorcas, Dorcas Fleming!'

Dorcas heaved herself out of bed and struggled to the window. It was still very dark; dawn was still some hours away. The waning moon shone brightly, casting a glow in her garden to reveal Jubal Sancreed with a stone in his hand,

'Don't throw it! I am awake. What on earth do you want?'

'I said I had something to show you. I'll show you now, only hurry up. I've been here for an hour. It was like trying to wake the dead.'

'Hardly.'

Dorcas pulled on her boots, hastily wrapped a shawl over her nightgown and joined him outside.

'This had better be good Jubal Sancreed, good enough to drag me out of bed in the middle of the night.'

'It is, come on, quick, it will all be over by the time we get there.'

He grabbed her hand and pulled her down the lane towards the beach.

'Where are we going?'

'You'll see, trust me.'

In the clear light of the moon, Dorcas could see that the tide was nearly out. Jubal led her across the beach to the far headland where they picked their way carefully across the huge boulders and around the corner to a place that Dorcas had not known existed. In front of the sheer cliff was a flat stretch of rock that poured down into the sea like a dollop of melted treacle, smooth and bereft of the jagged rocks that peppered the coastline. He dragged her over to a rock at the side and sat her down.

'It looks lovely in the moonlight' Dorcas offered.

'Not that, wait, you'll see, the tide is turning.'

Jubal sat close and she was glad of the warmth from his leg to keep her warm. She would have picked up her cloak if she thought they were going to sit out here by the sea for any length of time. She watched the moon dance upon the calm water, its shimmer running from the horizon to the shore. Many times, she had come to watch the moon on the beach, perhaps Jubal thought that she had not witnessed this sight before.

'I'm cold.'

'Shh, just wait, it's nearly here.'

Dorcas was just about to desert her post and make a break for freedom and the warm bed that she had left behind but a noise stopped her. It was a soft noise like a bubble rising up through melted toffee.

Werrpluump!

'What was that?'

'There!' Jubal shouted 'it has begun, I knew it was the right kind of night.'

Werrraaplooomp!

'Yes, but what is it?'

'Look, over there.'

Dorcas followed the pointing finger. Water started shooting out of hidden holes in the rock and sprayed up two or three feet into the air. As soon as one finished another one started, like a contagious disease.

Waaaaplooomp, werrplooomp, weeeraapluump!

'What is making it behave like that?' Dorcas asked rising to her feet.

'Blowholes. When the sea, the moon, and the tide are in a certain arrangement this is what happens. The water is forced up from below Wait, it gets better.'

Water shot upwards like mad fountains, some of them in neat rows as if they had been placed just so, others randomly shooting towards the night sky. They were steadily growing in height and some reached ten feet or more, crashing down onto the rocks and disappearing down the holes again, or spreading out to be scooped up by another blow. The noise was like music.

'Like a symphony of the sea' Dorcas shouted above the cacophony, running towards the spraying water.

'I knew you would like it.'

Jubal stood back as Dorcas threw off her shawl and her boots and danced in amongst the spurting columns of water. Some she managed to avoid but others caught her and soaked her to the skin. Her hair blew out as the up-draught took the loose strands and whipped them above her head. Dorcas pulled out the pins that held the remainder of the bun and shook her head to let the long chestnut stream blow with the wind. This was the first time for a very long time that she had let go completely and communed with nature. It was beautiful and she spun in circles, arms out to the side, revelling in this strange phenomenon. The blowholes whoomped about her causing tiny cyclonic winds between them and Dorcas let her body go where it wanted, celebrating the rawness of nature.

He had seen her dance in her nightie before; that night in her garden, he was unable to tear his eyes away, but that had been controlled. This was completely different. Under the luminosity of a bright moon on a clear night, she looked so different than she did in the daytime. Free and unbound, this was a witch at her best and Jubal joined her, catching the infection that had taken her over. They skittered and danced in and out of the fountains until they were exhausted and collapsed on a large boulder. The blowholes finished their song and disappeared under the rock quicker than they had come. The natural magick had finished, but Dorcas was still lit from within. Water dripped down her face and she was still laughing. Jubal picked up her shawl, it had managed to escape the worst of the salt water and wrapped it gently around her shoulders.

'Come, we must go home and get dry, you'll catch your death and I don't want to be responsible for that, especially as we have just got you back.'

Dorcas was still elated and had no intention of leaving just then. She made her way to the end of the smooth rocks where they met the sea.

'I must thank the Goddess, she does not give us these gifts everyday.'

With her feet still bare, Dorcas balanced on the edge and looked out across the calm sea. The water lapped at her toes; she giggled as it tickled and pulled her gently as she stood on the slippery rocks. Jubal again stood back and watched as her mouth whispered a monologue of thanks. He was beginning to understand where her beliefs came from. Apart from all the rituals and mystery, there was a rock solid faith underneath that was centred on the elements and he likened it to his own knowledge of the sea and the weather. These northerners were not so very different.

'The moon is very special to you isn't it?' he asked, coming alongside her.

'The moon has influence over much more than you can comprehend, its pull affects the sea but it also affects the water in our own bodies. Full moon is the most powerful time when a coven comes together. It is called an Esbat, many spells and rituals depend on the state of the moon. The New Moon is for gaining understanding, a waxing moon is to add to something or for attraction. A full moon is for increasing or enlarging something and a waning moon is used to reduce or take away something.'

'So that night, in the garden...'

'I was asking to be shown my path.'

'And the moon can do this?'

Dorcas nodded, trying to gauge his seriousness. 'Fishermen observe the power of the moon every day, it is no different. You just forget to thank her.'

Jubal was thoughtful, her words made perfect sense. 'We have many superstitions about the sea and I can see that some of them come from the old ways.'

'Really?'

'And I'll have you know that a fisherman always thanks Neptune for the catch, and we make an offering before we get into harbour.'

'And no one has hung you for this?' Dorcas said smiling.

'A lot of superstitions are based in truth, once out at sea a fisherman relies on them to bring him safely back to shore; that and the stars and sun.'

'Hah, our faiths are not so removed from each other. Moon, stars, and sun play a huge part in the Pagan way.'

So, that night, did the moon tell you why you are here?'

'No, there wa....'

Dorcas stopped and fixed her eyes on the sea. Something dark had just passed in front of her, just below the surface.

'What was that?'

'What?'

'There, under the sea. Do larger sea creatures come in this far?' Dorcas asked stepping back a little.

Jubal strained his eyes. It was not unheard of for a basking shark to be in this close to the shore but it was usually only in the hotter summer months when they came in to feed on the algae rich coastal waters.

'It may have been a seal.'

'I have seen the seals, this was much bigger.'

Jubal had no answers and Dorcas stepped forward again to get a better look. It was still there, hanging just below the surface like a submerged cloud. Her toes touched the lapping waves and she felt it, a tingle at first and then a prodding at her mind. She tried to pull her foot from the water but it resisted her request and tried to sink deeper into the dark water. A coldness crept up her ankles and she found herself unable to move. The presence drew her mind and enveloped her free thoughts.

Jubal was aware that something had happened. Dorcas stood like a statue beside him, staring at the seemingly calm sea. Her eyes were wide and shining with fear.

'What is it?'

Dorcas could not answer, her mouth refused to open. Something was dragging her mind to a place it did not want to go, a black place that was as cold as marble and as deadly as nightshade. Voices whispered to her but she could not make out what they were saying, only their intent.

The coldness reached her chest and was starting to constrict her breathing. It was trying to force her body into the water and Dorcas started to fight with everything she had. The voices took on an urgency and she could make out some of the whispered gibberish.

'Come, come to us, be with us.'

Dorcas felt many unseen hands pulling at her, tugging her soul, tearing at her life.

'Come, come. We are the answer you seek.'

Jubal was unnerved and confused. Under the moonlight, the witch looked as if she was turning to stone and he could get no sense from her. He reached out and touched her arm.

Inside, Dorcas was pleading with him to pick her up, move her somewhere else, but her mouth still refused to open and her silent pleas went unheard. She tried to breathe but there was something else rising within her, something that should not be set free. It started at her heart and rapidly moved out across her whole body.

'*Breathe, breathe.*'

Dorcas was now trying to contain the two conflicting feelings that were consuming her inside. The dark coldness was calling, luring her weakening mind, urging her to step off the rocks and join with the water. The other feeling was expanding, gaining power and was ready and willing to be used. Dorcas had no choice, the power had grown from fear. She needed it now, wanted it now, but a tiny piece of sanity was holding it back and she was more fearful of it than the creeping death that was now up to her neck.

Jubal was confused and helpless. The hand that he had placed on her arm was now stuck to her frozen skin and he was being drawn in with her.

'*Two for the price of one*' the voices whispered.

Dorcas was vaguely aware that Jubal was now inside her mind and was being sucked downwards towards the cold entity. She could not let this happen, would not let this happen. The power erupted, unbidden, and out of her control. Her arms flung themselves forward, fingers pointing at the sea; she opened her mouth as an unearthly wail vomited from her core. It rose, unleashed from its cage, battling the cold, flooding it with warmth and light. The force repelled them both back across the rocks and away from the sea. The link was broken and both were freed from their unseen shackles.

Dorcas gathered her wits quickly enough to observe the dark shape leave the shoreline and slowly make its way out to sea.

'*Soon, soon Dorcas Fleming....*'

They made their way home, supporting each other across the beach with no words passing between them. Dorcas lit the range and set the kettle to boil.

'What was it?' Jubal asked, wrapping his hands around the steaming cup. This was his third cup of tea and the first time that he had managed to put a sentence together.

'I don't know, you're the seafarer, I thought you would be able to tell me.'

Jubal shook his head. He had worked in and around the sea for many years and he had never witnessed anything similar, or heard tell of its like from other sailors. Men of the sea had plenty of tales to tell about sirens that lured you to the rocks and giant creatures that could swallow a boat whole. This was different, this had been trying to lure them into the water, calling, tempting. Jubal knew that they had both been on the verge of leaping into the dark water.

She had given in and used the latent power that slept within her, something that she swore she would never do, but she also knew that she had not killed the thing she had only shocked it into releasing its grip.

'You did something' Jubal said 'I felt, something?'

'It went on its own' Dorcas said quickly.

Jubal decided not to pursue that line of questioning, the tone of her voice had warned him off, but he had seen. As she stood on the edge, she had suddenly been lit from within like a flash of lightning and the dark cold thing had let them both go.

There was scratching at the window.

'I felt it, what was it?'

Dorcas did not answer the cat and carried on sipping her tea.

'There was something out there, by the water.'

'We don't know what it was Zebulonus.'

Dorcas spun round and stared at Jubal.

'You spoke to him.'

'You are not the only one who can communicate with the animals' Jubal said with a slight smile. 'When you were in gaol Zebulonus asked me what had happened to you. I nearly fell of my chair when I realised it was him talking and it took me a while to learn to speak my words in my head but he was very patient.'

'You spoke to him?' she said to the cat who was sitting in front of the warm range.

'He can hear me, and I keep telling you, a cat does what a cat must do. I needed to know where you had gone and who was going to keep my belly full.'

Dorcas snorted and Jubal laughed.

'Mercenary creature, and I stupidly thought you might have been worried about me.'

'There is more to you than meets the eye Dorcas Fleming, do all witches talk to animals' Jubal asked.

'Most. Anyone can do it after a little training. Other than that, it just depends on the intelligence of the animal.'

'And cats are the most adept. Am I right witch?'

'You can just be quiet now, I've got more important things on my mind that communing with a ginger ball.'

'The ginger ball was more than helpful when you were away, he helped me find the answers I needed,' Jubal said 'he really is quite remarkable.'

'I'm sorry to both of you and I am very grateful to both of you, but we do have to think about what has just happened.'

Jubal tried desperately to obliterate the events of the last two hours from his mind but neither he nor Dorcas could let it go. Dorcas was still shaking and Jubal made more tea. This was the first time that she had felt truly scared since she had come here. Even the imminent hanging at Polempter Gaol had not held the same fear that was now attacking the very core of her being. A witch understood the process of dying and was safe in the knowledge that her spirit flew home when the body gave up, that was tangible. This thing under the sea was a completely different matter and she did not want to fathom it by herself. Now, more than ever, Dorcas longed for the refuge of her coven, or of any coven, at least they would understand. There was always a certain safety in numbers but down here in the south, people shared so very little, living their lives in isolation without the Goddess to look after them. Dorcas was lonely and homesick and the words came out of her mouth before her mind had a say in it.

'Will you stay with me tonight?' she asked quietly 'I shall quite understand if you say no.'

Jubal looked shocked.

'I'm sorry, I forget how wrapped you southerners are in proper relationships, I just don't want to be alone. You have already seen me sky clad, naked I mean. I don't want anything from you, just your company.'

'Yes,' he said, after a pause, 'if you want me to'

Later, in Dorcas's bed, both of them stared into the darkness separated by their own thoughts. Dorcas was running through her memories and trying to think if she had ever come across or heard of anything like this before. She had heard of malevolent creatures that lived under the seas but most of them were flesh and bone and had an official name. Some of the creatures that fishermen brought in could be large and ugly but no one had ever heard of fish that whispered. The darkness, she realised now, had been there once before, she could taste its likeness. Jubal had reminded her of the night of the full moon when she could get no response from the scrying mirror. That tinge of blackness that had flicked across the obsidian surface had shown her a hint of it.

That 'thing' in the sea tonight was old, that much she knew. She had seen into it, felt its intent and knew now there was a task for her here in Pendartha. This was why she had been sent here. She just hoped that the God and Goddess would show her the way and give her the strength to deal with it.

Jubal was also trying to put his thoughts together. Nothing in his experience had ever happened like this before. There was something there, something evil; something he did not understand. The Pendarthans had been whispering for years about a curse on the town and he knew that Dorcas had been brought here to try to find out about it. Death was sitting on Pendartha's doorstep; men, women and children had lost their lives, but not all of them at sea. Nothing had changed since the witch had come to the town but his mind let a thought flitter through.

'Did she bring it with her?'

He dismissed the thought as soon as it emerged into his conscious mind, bad things had happened in Pendartha for as long as he could remember. She had not been responsible for his own troubles, or that of the others in this God-forsaken town. The Pendarthans blamed and complained about anything and anyone who crossed their path, it was the way of things in a small remote fishing village like this. Jubal secretly thought that Dorcas had been brought here to act as a scapegoat, but this was surely locking the door after the horse had bolted and he really did not think that the Mayor would suggest such a thing. Josiah Penpol was as straight as a die and he had no reason to suspect him of securing a witch only to blame her for their unexplainable troubles.

*

Dawn pushed the first rays of light through the curtains. Sleep had not happened for either of them. Dorcas grew cold and turned to the warmth of the man's body. His arms wrapped themselves around her unbidden, and pulled her close to him.

'I want you' he whispered.

'I'm here.'

'I'm married.'

Dorcas answered him with a soft kiss.

'We both have secrets,' she said 'let's put them to one side for a while, too much has happened tonight.'

As the cockerel crowed two people found solace in the warmth of another's intimacy, both would think about the consequences at another time.

Chapter eighteen

Ellen was awake long before she heard the footsteps hurrying down the corridor outside her room. The night had been filled with worry, fuelled by something that she could not get a grip of. She waited patiently for the feet to stop outside her room. The tap at her door was quietly urgent and Ellen rose to find an anxious face staring at her with wide frightened eyes. The High Priestess recognised her as an assistant from the lower workrooms but the name escaped her.

'What is it?'

'I am June Partridge, I work for Meredith Spooner. She asks for your counsel and makes apology for the time of day. Please come with me High Priestess.'

Ellen had no doubt that the apology came from June herself. Scryers lived in their own space and time in the depths of Masterbridge and Meredith Spooner would no more know the time of day, than what year it was.

'Wait one minute, I'll need something warm down there.'

Ellen pulled on a cloak over her nightgown and joined the assistant who was waiting patiently in the corridor. They could hear the residual sounds of the May Day celebrations in the Grand Square outside, and the noises of low female giggles were audible all along the corridors as the two women hurried by.

She had left her own May Day celebration in her bed. The pretty herbologist had not stirred as she left the room and she would keep the bed warm for Ellen's return. That was if she managed to get back to her own room tonight. Ellen had a feeling in her bones that this was going to take a lot longer.

Masterbridge Hearth was built in the shape of a pentagram. The lower workrooms were situated under the Great Hearth itself but the entrance was a little known staircase at the tip of the northern apex. It was a long way between the accommodation block where Ellen resided and the stairs to the underground rooms. Masterbridge was riddled with corridors and tunnels and even the eldest resident didn't know where all of them were situated. One could spend a lifetime trying to map the complicated building and all the offshoots above the ground, let alone what lay beneath the streets. Masterbridge had grown considerably over the last hundred years, already a huge estate it now housed over five thousand people, all of whom were integral to the workings of the country's most important coven. The city had grown like all cities, starting at a central point and spreading like wild ivy. It had gobbled up villages and hamlets, vineyards and orchards, and claimed them as its own. It was the capital of the north and had been the capital of the whole country before the Century War. Situated more towards the south of the northern lands it would have been in a strategic position to serve both north and south before the divide. On its eastern side lay the port that, like the rest of the city, had grown immensely over the last half century. Masterbridge welcomed the world with open arms and the city was often filled with more creeds and colours than one could name.

Masterbridge was a spiritual nerve centre as well as a thriving, busy city. Many common folk came here at least once in their lives and considered it to be a form of pilgrimage. Samhain Sabbat saw the city full to bursting point with alehouses and lodges filled with accents from all over the northern lands. You could not move in the squares and parks for shrines and gatherings and many of Masterbridge's residents took flight to the country for a few days to celebrate in peace. Ellen had first come here from the Temple of Arianrhod, a less prestigious college in the western provinces. The mountainous region had produced some of the most revered council members over the years, who were celebrated for their wisdom and foresight. Ellen herself had shown great potential as a student and had been rewarded with her placement at the centre of the Pagan world.

Her first seven years had been dedicated to shifting paperwork around as an assistant to an assistant on the Great Council. She had been stuck behind a mountain of reports and documents from the lesser councils around the country, filing and sorting through the complaints and moans that all governments had to deal with. Ellen had worked hard, and worked even harder to make herself noticed for her work rather than her appearance. With long flowing blonde hair and a taste in clothes that did not match her peers' idea of a good witch, she struggled for years to be taken seriously. She was the youngest woman to make High Priestess in over three hundred years and still applied her stringent work ethic to everything she did. The High Druid had recognised her talents and she was brought to work in the main offices of Masterbridge's elite.

Ellen had come a long way from her humble beginnings in Caerllithy and she had no wish to throw it all away after she had been given a chance. She worked hard, taking on the less savoury jobs that many under-druids or priestesses would baulk at.

Ellen was a spiritwitch and had acknowledged the potential of the student at Summerlands as soon as she took up the post. Lylas was right; the girl was hiding a scar on her cheek, a vivid red mark that she concealed from everyone night and day. Ellen had only found it with the help of a coven of Mothers. In a midnight gathering, She had performed a 'Drawing down of the moon' ceremony and had crossed the bridge into the Spiritworld. Her guides had shown her the truth but she had needed the support of twelve others to confirm it. Even in sleep, Dorcas Fleming had placed safeguards around herself and Ellen realised with growing fascination that this was as natural to her as breathing. In a following letter to the Council, she had stated that although this was the only sign that she found it was to be taken seriously and acted upon immediately.

Ellen had tried to keep a distance between her and the girl she was sent to observe but she found herself being drawn in and involved in the student's basic welfare. Dorcas was not unpopular but found it difficult to bond with her own coven. Small in height, Dorcas hid herself behind traditional clothes and scraped her hair into a tight bun that made her small features look older than they were. She was not unattractive but she never made the best of herself. It was a definite attempt to blend in and make herself disappear in a crowd. Next to Ginnifer Belle, Dorcas looked positively dowdy and Ellen had been surprised to learn of Dorcas's nocturnal affairs at the Sabbat celebrations in Brexham, wondering how the girl managed to let go of that cast-iron control that she had over her body.

Apart from the obvious differences in their looks and demeanour, there were many similarities in Ellen and Dorcas's upbringings. Ellen had spent her formative years in a home for abandoned girls and like Dorcas, a kindly witch had rescued her, spotting the talents that could be used elsewhere.

Summerlands was renowned for its nurturing of a strong talent, but unlike many of the other colleges, sat and watched for a long time before acting. Lylas had brought the girl when she was ten and the reports had said that the old witch had her suspicions even then. The High Priestess Margarite Fellows had waited a further time, watching, listening, and recording the girl's every move. Ellen had read some of the reports that had come in but they did not make interesting reading. If Dorcas Fleming was a true witch then she was already hiding her talents under a cob wall. Ellen was all too aware that some other colleges and establishments were sometimes a little too keen to announce the arrival of someone with talent. It raised the profile and improved the kudos of the school just to have it known that there was a possibility of a strong talent among them. Margarite was cautious, and waited for Dorcas to come to maturity before approaching Masterbridge with serious questions. The council had advised that the student should take up her last placement with Mother Enid on the Lanshire Downs.

'Enid Sowden?' Ellen had asked 'she has been on the Downs for sixty years or more, curing sheep of the bellyache, what would she know?'

Elshalamane smiled and patted her hand.

'Ellen, just remember that we don't always know everything, Enid Sowden is a truewitch. We have invested a lot of energy in getting her to agree to take the girl.'

Ellen was still in shock from the news that a real live truewitch lived only twenty miles from the capital. A thousand questions ran through her head.

'Don't look so worried Ellen, there are no records of her, and you didn't miss this one in your research. Enid took herself off the register.'

'But?'

'She failed her task and went to foreign lands. We thought she was lost to us until she returned and settled on the Lanshire Downs. If anyone can get through those natural boundaries then Enid can. Like recognises like where they find it.'

Ellen had taken over at Summerlands a year before the students took up their last apprentice placements. She was thorough in her studies of all the girls and no one had suspected the true nature of her move to the college. High Priestess Margarite had taken a sabbatical to the North Erinburgh coast and Ellen would stay at Summerlands until the girls graduated. She had waited with bated breath for the girl's return but Enid's report had been gruff and to the point.

"She has the makings."

The old witch had set her a number of tasks and the girl had shown something far deeper than a simple talent for managing herbs and remedies.

"I gave meself a dyin' disease, one that could not be got from no book. She cured me. Look after this one".

Ellen had no intention of not 'looking after' Dorcas Fleming but then Samhain had come and the Goddess had seen fit to take it all out of her hands.

Ellen followed June down the steep winding steps that took them into the bowels of Masterbridge. The assistant skipped down the wet, slippery staircase with the confidence of one who has used it for a long time. Ellen came along behind holding onto the wooden rail, struggling to find her footing in the areas with no torch to light the way. The High Priestess had been down here before a few times but it was not a place where she would want to spend the rest of her days. Those that inhabited the deep dark caverns under the city were those who were happy to be amongst the very stones that the city was built around.

Under the central Hearth lay the core of Masterbridge, a huge ring of sarsen columns and pillars that was built by the first Pagans. All the ley lines converged at this monument and it was the holiest and most powerful site in the land. Masterbridge was built around it and had grown over the top of it to preserve the stones.

Ellen felt the hairs on her arms rise up in reaction to the power that emanated from these most ancient of stones. The Scryers who worked down here were said to be the most far-seeing and accurate, using the lines to reach out across the world and bring back information to the Council. Elshalamane had once described it as the most useful spy organisation that a High Druid has at his disposal and during his office, he had nurtured his scryers, giving them anything they wanted, within reason.

Tucked away in a small cavern to the west side of the stone circle was Meredith Spooner. Ellen had secretly thought that she was born to this work. The woman was a witch incarnate according to the heathen ideas of what a witch should look like. Bent and thin, she had sparse white hair and eyes that had not seen a visible image for decades. Her face was enough to frighten the most hardened of souls, long beaked nose, and a mouth that had forgotten what it was to have teeth. As they made their way towards Meredith's workroom Ellen heard the sounds of other scryers at work. There was no night or day down here and the people worked as and when the fancy took them. All were free to come and go as they wished but most of the older ones now lived down here, unable to adapt to the light and weather that changed silently above them.

'Who is it?'

'It is I, June. I have brought Ellen with me.'

June lit a few more lamps and torches to reveal the scryer in the midst of her work. Three rings, balanced on top of each other, were spinning in opposite directions. Meredith lost her concentration and the silver rings tinkled onto the floor.

'Why?'

'You wish to show her something mistress.'

'I do?'

Ellen stepped forward and let the old woman run her fingers down her face. Meredith's fingertips had taken over where her eyes left off.

'Oh yes, 'tis you, I remember. What do you want?'

'You want to show me what you have found, Meredith.'

'Yes, yes that's right. Some tea, June would you make us some tea?'

June slipped out of the doorway and Ellen sat in the one other chair that was not occupied by Meredith. She had been in this room once before on a very fleeting visit to deliver some papers and it had not changed at all. Meredith had no need for the visual comforts of home and her workroom and bedroom were all within easy finding distance of each other. The walls had countless mirrors on them all showing the bent form of the person who used them. In the corner was an ugly cupboard that contained bags and bags of runes, stones, crystals, and cards that spilled out over the stone floor. June had made some sort of effort to label the bags but they were still stored in heaps rather than neat rows. In the centre of the room lay Meredith's table and next to that was her chalice. All witches used a chalice for scrying at one time or another but Meredith's differed in the fact that it sat on the floor and was over two feet high. It had been fashioned from a single piece of serpentine and in the dim light Ellen could make out the flecks of white and black that ran through the dark green stone. The water inside looked murky and dead, but scryers were superstitious and never changed anything unless they absolutely had to. There was a smell down here that was not only confined to this room but permeated the whole area. Unlike the spellweaving rooms in the main building, you could never put a name to this smell. The rooms upstairs smelt of the smokiness of spell leavings, incense and charcoal; this smell was different. Now that it had invaded her nose again, Ellen thought of it as 'ancient'. It was the aroma of the primeval bluestone that held Masterbridge together.

Meredith rambled off again and lost her train of thought until June returned to the room. The young assistant was like a focus to the old woman, keeping a little piece of her mind in the real world whilst the rest of it seemed to have been left somewhere else.

'You wanted to tell Ellen of Dorcas Fleming' June prompted.

'Yes, yes I know, the witch in the heathen lands, I saw her first you know.'

'You did Meredith,' Ellen smoothed 'and for that we are all grateful. It was just a case of waiting after that.'

Although an adept scryer at her own level, Ellen knew that you had to give the professionals time to gather their thoughts and give you the information. She sipped her tea and waited for an hour while Meredith went round the houses and back again.

'We have heard you know. We have news'

Ellen snapped out of her own thoughts as Meredith Spooner focused on her subject; she nodded encouragingly.

'The blackness hides nearly everything but we have seen, yes, we have seen. The chalice doesn't like it, comes from the same place you see. Serpentine from the South.'

The Scryer wandered off again but June gently brought her back to the subject.

'She showed herself' Meredith cackled.

'Showed herself?'

Ellen panicked, if Dorcas had 'shown' her true self then was it all over.

'Too early to tell whether she has landed on the right side of the coin, so to speak' Meredith added as if reading her questions 'have no idea if she'll go one way or the other, do you want to see?'

A Scryer of Meredith's talent could hold an image that had been caught with her equipment and she could bring it back at will. This was not always reliable as the information was often scrambled with pieces from other sessions but Ellen willed it to work this time. Dorcas Fleming had not left her thoughts since the day she departed for Mersden and the heathen southern lands.

'I would very much like to see what you have Miss Spooner, if you please.'

June extinguished the torches and apart from a weak candle in the corner the room was in near darkness. Meredith noticed no difference in the light, finding her way around the room to where the chalice sat. She stood over the inky water and prepared her mind to focus on the task. When she was ready, she beckoned Ellen and June to the chalice and they all peered in. Nothing happened for a minute or two; Meredith Spooner searched her addled brains to get a start. She dipped a long, yellowed fingernail into the inky water and swirled until she caused a minor cyclone. As the water calmed, the black surface changed imperceptibly, to a deeper shade of black.

'There, do you see?'

Ellen could not see anything except a faint ripple on the surface. She was beginning to think that maybe all this was a figment of Meredith's scrambled brain.

'See, see, here it comes.'

The black faded, melted and changed, leaving a faint impression of two figures, a man, and a woman in white, standing beside the sea. Ellen sharpened up and concentrated on the image to support what Meredith was holding. She was vaguely aware of a sudden coldness creeping up her ankles. The cold became penetrating and fixed her feet firmly to the flagstones beneath.

Ellen was just starting to feel a mild panic when there was a low flash of something and the picture faded. The bleak coldness left her feet.

'Was that it?' Ellen said without thinking, she had been hoping for so much more.

'Patience, patience, the black gets into everything, she was there, we saw didn't we?'

Ellen could not be sure that the figure was indeed Dorcas Fleming, with hair down and her back to her, it was hard for Ellen to pick anything out that would be recognisable as the girl.

'I'm sorry Meredith, I thought it would be clearer. Isn't there any way to get rid of the blackness or is that just because they are so far away?'

'My dear girl,' Meredith said in a moment of complete clarity 'I can scry across the dimensions if I wish, the south is but a few hundred miles away. The blackness belongs to her, it wants her, this is the task.'

Ellen sat down on the chair that June had hastily placed behind her. It was some time before she could speak.

'I felt it, the blackness I mean, coming up my legs. What is it Meredith?'

'Who can tell? It is strong, strong enough to block even me from seeing it for what it is. She repelled it though, not enough to kill it or use the full power that lies asleep within her, but enough for us to see. She is aware of it now, the good, and the bad; the rest is up to her. The battle commences'

'And if she turns away from the Goddess?'

'Then we are all at risk, she will have a way to get to all of those who have touched her life. And I'll be first, oh yes I will, I'll be the first, won't be long, she'll know I'm here, watching, always watching.'

'Why do they have to go through this?' Ellen asked aloud.

Meredith patted her hand absently.

'To know, of course, can't have a gift like that without the task. Got to land on the right side of the fence, can't go walking around in broad daylight with that amount of witchpower inside you. They are the yin and the yang, the keepers of the black and the white. Can't have one without the other now can we? She chooses. No earthly involvement. Chooses for herself, yes she does.'

Ellen hurriedly crossed the Great Courtyard just as dawn was breaking and she tapped on the private chambers of the High Druid a few minutes later. Elshalamane took one look at her face and rang for some hot sweet tea to be sent up.

'She is there, she has found something, found it, the task. Oh sweet Goddess!'

'Tell me everything.'

The Druid listened and then sent Ellen off for a hot bath and some sleep, there was nothing more for her to do.

For the next two nights, he also got no sleep. In a little known room at the back of the West library, Elshalamane ploughed his way through long forgotten documents and papers that were kept under lock and key and away from the general population of Masterbridge. This room contained the most ancient Grimoires and the most infamous Book of Shadows and he leafed methodically through them all to find some answers.

Whatever Dorcas Fleming was up against had never been documented before and whatever it was, it was now growing stronger and gaining momentum, of that he was certain. There were reports in the antique documents of sea creatures and evil sprites that had once inhabited the darker depths but nothing that explained a black leviathan that had made its home under the southern seas. This task was too great for one so young and so inexperienced and the High Druid found himself asking if the Goddess knew what exactly she was doing.

Call on my name and I shall answer truthfully. Ask, and the answers shall be yours. Above all, remember the truthfulness of thine own truth
– Akashic records

Chapter nineteen

It was four weeks since Jubal lay in her bed; it was three weeks since he lost his livelihood. It was two weeks since Grenville Simmons died and it was a week since Josiah came and asked her to leave. Dorcas was in turmoil. Her mind ran over the events of the last few weeks, trying to put them all together and make some sense of it all.

The week following May Day was a haze of jumbled pictures and half-remembered events. She had woken every morning since drenched in a cold sweat, trying to push the blackness from the mare of the night out of her mind. There was no peace, and the night terrors had started to encroach on her during the daylight. Each day she was plagued with invasive thoughts that dominated her spirit and dragged it down. Every night was the same, visions of death all around her and a longing deep inside of wanting to die herself. Death was calling, calling loudly, and Dorcas was terrified.

On the night of Beltane, something had stirred in Dorcas, a thing that she had kept pushed down in the core of her being. When her toes had touched the blackness under the sea it had woken and demanded that she take notice. Dorcas did not want it to wake up; she had spent her life keeping that part of herself under cover, and away from the prying eyes and minds of those around her. She knew it was there, that something that made her different from the other girls in the coven. She had used it every now and again, dipping just below the surface to tap into it. Most of the time she ignored it, pushing it down deep inside, hoping that it would go away. Other times she felt that it was like a silent volcano, waiting to erupt, and she dreaded the time when it would. Her lessons in college had never touched on this subject so Dorcas had done what she had always done, kept it under tight control. Occasionally it leaked out and she knew that it was somehow responsible for hiding the scar on her cheek but other than that, she knew nothing of this happening to anybody else.

'You are special' Mother Lylas had often told her, but the last thing that Dorcas Fleming had wanted to be was special. For the most part, she could keep the thing inside her under control but now the leviathan had found it, touched it, wanted it, and now neither would leave her alone. Dorcas felt as if she was being torn in two by opposing forces that she had no understanding of. The last month had been an ever-decreasing circle of one disaster after another and she was not sure where it was all going to end.

In the first few days after May Day, Dorcas tried to analyse what had happened but nothing made any sense to her. Jubal seemed content to put it out of his mind and was far more bothered by the fact that he had slept in her bed. Dorcas was too wrapped up in her own thoughts to care much about his problems and had not seen much of him the following week.

Dorcas had not seen anyone at all that week, and she felt no great urge to go into the town. All she wanted was peace and quiet and time to sort things out. One minute she made up her mind to leave and the next she knew that she had been sent here for a reason and had no choice but to stay. With the moon waning quickly it was no time to ask for help but her attempts at scrying had been stopped abruptly when the blackness once again clouded her obsidian mirror and tried to enter her mind. Dorcas had thrown it from her like a hot brick and shoved it back in its velvet bag. She felt hopeless and lost and there was no one to answer her questions or to sooth her troubled and tangled mind.

Jubal said that the townsfolk thought there was a curse on Pendartha; as many had died on the land as they had in the sea. Dorcas knew also from the night she first saw the thing in the sea that she was here because of it but had no clues as to what to do about it. She was tired and irritable from lack of good sleep and could not think straight most of the time. As each day passed, she found it harder and harder to think and she barely managed to fulfil the duties she had to complete every day in order to survive.

As she returned from an afternoon walk up through her valley, she found Tregonning's cart tied up outside Jubal's cottage. Both men were carrying out boxes and throwing them into the back.

'Jubal?'

'Leave me alone' he snapped.

'What has happened, where are you going?'

Jubal threw the last box on and jumped up beside the waiting driver.

'Listen witch, get out of here while you can before they destroy your life as well. Curse them, curse me, and curse the bloody town as well.'

'Where are you going?'

'Anywhere but here.'

The cart drove off leaving Dorcas standing in the middle of the lane. She stared after it for a long time watching it make its way up the hill towards town.

'They made him leave' Zebulonus said from the wall.

'Why?'

'I don't know everything Dorcas Fleming, I am only a cat. He has no bells left to catch the ugly ones, they took them away.'

'Lobster pots' Dorcas said absently.

Dorcas went inside, grabbed her cloak, and then thought twice about it. There was no point in going into town to make a fuss or to ask awkward questions. She would find out all in good time. If she had done anything to upset people then no doubt Josiah Penpol would beat a path to her door very soon and what did she care? Jubal Sancreed was a grown man he could make his own decisions. She really did not care about any of them any more.

The days went by and Dorcas trudged through each one. The nightmares plagued her the moment she put her head on the pillow and she was now barely eating. Irrational thoughts passed through her head, whispered thoughts that consumed her and blocked out everything else.

'They will want more of the potions and salves soon, are you going to make some?'

'None of your business cat, please don't talk to me anymore, I'm fed up with your whingeing and whining.'

Zebulonus leapt onto the kitchen windowsill.

'I suggest that you look in the mirror Dorcas Fleming, I think you will see that the person looking back at you is not the person who you thought.'

Dorcas threw a cup at him as he dived out of the window.

In a haze of annoyance and anger at the stupid animal Dorcas found a hand mirror in the dresser drawer and studied her reflection. When she finally put the mirror down on the table, she found that the cat was right.

'Who are you?'

There was someone else looking back at her, a shadow of her own self, a stranger. Something in the back of Dorcas's mind pushed and struggled to get to the place where it would be recognised. There was a battle going on inside as Dorcas fought herself for control. Something had been trying to take over, to squeeze her out and it was written all over the face looking out from the mirror. Dull eyes with dark rings around them looked out from a face that was wizened, grey, and lifeless. Dank hair that looked as if it had not been washed in years hung limply around her gaunt features

'No! No!'

With the little energy that she had in reserve Dorcas pushed the fog that surrounded her brain and it shifted a little.

'Get out, get out of my mind.'

The fog started to drift away reluctantly, unwilling to let go of the firm grip it had on her. Dorcas let loose the feeling that was welling inside, she let it go, and the fog went instantly. The force of the last effort sent her stumbling into the kitchen table and she slumped onto the floor.

'I have been possessed, that thing had me.'

Disgust and horror washed over her in equal measures, making her sick to her stomach. It had wanted her dead, one way, or another. It could not tempt her into the water on the night of Beltane so it had crept into her mind and had started to take over from inside.

'Oh for Goddess sake, what is it?'

Dorcas stood and held the table, shaking like a leaf. As she looked down she noticed that the drawer that had been stuck in the table had opened when she had fallen and there was something inside. With her head still thumping Dorcas put the kettle on the range and sat down to look at the contents of the drawer. Before she opened the letter she knew exactly who it was from, the smell gave it away.

'Ellen.'

The mix of roses and patchouli oil was unmistakeable and she opened it with shaking hands.

Merrymeet dear Dorcas,

If you have been able to open the drawer then I know that your time of trouble is coming. I was not allowed to help or give

you any advice and the fact of the matter is that I have no advice.
You have a task, I do not know what it is, but it will mean that you
will have to make some choices. You are supposed to be there, that
much is certain and you must know that Masterbridge is behind
you. We cannot tell you any more, you will unfortunately have to
find the answers yourself. The Goddess has chosen you Dorcas,
walk this path with steadfast and cautious boots and know who
you are,
    Ellen.

Dorcas could almost hear the tinkle of Ellen's bracelets and she
found it comforting. She read, and re-read the letter and an ache
worked its way from deep down in her stomach until it burst forth
from her mouth in a wave of grief. She cried for a long time, long
racking sobs that cleared her vision from the residue of the miasma
that had enveloped it. Her mind ran over the things that had been
obliterated by the greyness and a confusion of thoughts came in at
once. Jubal had gone and she did not know where he had gone and
she had some kind of task that Masterbridge knew about. There
was the thing in the sea that was trying to possess her but now she
was completely alone, and she cared. For the last few weeks, she
had not cared about anything, anything at all. Now she felt as if
she cared about everything and it all hurt.

*

Dorcas wanted to keep an eye on herself for another few days so
she went about her daily routine until she felt a little more normal.
She busied herself with making scented candles and sachets of
tisanes that she had been experimenting with. The work took her
mind off things that she was not well enough to deal with yet.
When she was certain that the fog had left her for good she took a
basket and filled it with the remedies she would need for the
people in town. It was time for a serious talk with Josiah and she
felt strong enough to make sure that she got some answers this
time.

She found the Chief at home in bed with a chest infection.
    'Why did you not call for me?' she asked Violetta as they
climbed the narrow stairs to the first floor.
    'He's not been well since May Day, half the town has got it and

you have not been around.'

Dorcas caught the hint of sharpness in her voice and decided to wait until she had spoken to Josiah.

He was wrapped in a mountain of eiderdowns, his red nose just poking above the sweating hill.

'If you are well enough I would like to ask you some questions, Chief Penpol.'

'Can't say as I can answer them but fire away' he spluttered, coughing wetly into a large red handkerchief...

'Why did you want me here? It seems we have skirted this question for a long time Josiah, I need some answers.'

'He can't answer that' Violetta said from the doorway.

'Violetta, please, I need to know' Dorcas said.

'Don't say a word Josiah Penpol, you know what the town council said, not a word.'

The Chief's wife stood with her hands on her hips defying the witch to stir up trouble.

'What did they say Violetta' Dorcas said quietly, fixing Violetta with a look that would have stopped a herd of stampeding bulls.

'They said you have to find it yourself, there will be no help from us or anyone. If it is a curse then you shall have to find out about it on your own, no one shall give you any help.'

Violetta clapped her hand over her mouth; she had not meant to say anything.

'You made me say that' she accused.

'I did not get you to say anything that you did not really want to tell me Violetta.'

Josiah coughed from the bed and the hedgewitch in Dorcas took over.

After making him more comfortable, with slightly less weight bearing down on his chest, Dorcas asked another question.

'Why has Jubal Sancreed left?'

This was met by silence, Josiah looked at his wife.

'He left by his own means, no one ran him out' she said a little too quickly.

Josiah started coughing again and Dorcas had no wish to make him feel any worse than he did. She left them and made her way slowly back down through the town. As she rounded the corner just before the harbour, Morwenna came out of a cottage that Dorcas thought belonged to Lizzy Mims.

'Dorcas, we have not seen you for a while. I need some more of that stuff for me arthritis. I have been asking Josiah to bring me up to you.'

Dorcas nodded and said that she would drop some in the next day along with a cough syrup for her son.

'Morwenna, can I ask you something? Why did Jubal lose his pots?'

The old woman caught her breath.

'You had best ask Grenville Simmons, Jubal worked for his father.'

'I don't understand.'

Morwenna looked uncomfortable.

'Grenville is his brother-in-law. Jubal was, *is,* married to Elizabeth Simmons If you want to know any more then you had best ask him yourself, not my place to go spreading stuff about. He's down on the quay, saw him go past half an hour ago.'

'Thank you Morwenna.'

'Dorcas' Morwenna said as she turned to go 'it's a bad business, careful what you say to him.'

'Can't be any worse than any of the other things that are going on in this Goddess forsaken place' Dorcas thought as she crossed the bridge just before the quay. If she were to find the underlying cause of the curse theory then she would have to do a little digging that may cause a bit of discomfort to everyone.

She saw a group of men at the end of the wharf and one of them looked to be about the right height and look of Grenville. On the horizon a storm was brewing, the black clouds were making their way swiftly towards the land pushing a smell that Dorcas had now come to recognise as approaching bad weather. The water in the enclosed harbour was still quite calm as Dorcas passed, the boats bobbing in the undulating swell. A few men looked up and acknowledged her but the same amount turned their backs and got on with mending their nets. She could see Grenville Simmons in the distance, he was arguing with Jakey Moyle about some pots that were lined up against the inner wall. Jakey stomped past her and spat into the harbour.

'Weasel' she heard under his breath.

Dorcas approached.

'I got no argument with you, Dorcas Fleming, don't come looking for one' Grenville cried, throwing lobster pots left and right.

'I did not come to have an argument, I can't think what we would argue about.'

Grenville gave her an odd look.

'It's about Jubal, I…'

'Thought you didn't want an argument'

'I don't Mr Simmons, I just want to know where he has gone.'

'You took him into your bed witch, you should know.'

Dorcas stopped in her tracks, gossip was faster than the tide in this place. Grenville moved to a pile of pots that had been left on the end of the quay. The wind had picked up and Dorcas moved closer so that he could hear what she was saying.

'I'm not sure that is anybody's business other than mine. Do you know where he is, I heard he had lost his living?'

'He should have thought about that before he started asking about a divorce,' Grenville spat, 'he wronged her before and now he wants to bring shame on the whole family.'

As Grenville got more irate Dorcas drew on the inner calm that had been instilled in her during her training.

'I am sorry, I don't know anything about his marriage, or the dishonour it brought. If I….'

'He left her you know, left her when she was in labour with their first child, kicked her out of her own house. Even then, my father never took back what was rightly his' he said, pointing at the pots.

'I'm sorry,' Dorcas said 'I knew nothing of this.'

'He's a bad 'un, through and through. My sister was forced to take up lodgings near Porthaveland for the shame he brought to her, the shame he brought on all of us.'

Grenville was waving his pot-filled arms about and a small crowd started to gather behind them. Dorcas did not want to cause a scene so she stepped back a little and turned to go.

With his back to the sea, he never saw the wave coming. Huge, and fast, it rolled up the end of the quay and knocked him off his feet. Like an arm it curled around him pulling him backwards in its retreat and in the blink of an eye Grenville Simmons was gone. Dorcas ran forward, arms outstretched futilely in front of her.

'No!'

Men passed her with heavy ropes grabbed from the numerous piles on the quay, threw them over the end, and tied them off. There was nothing to save, the dark rolling sea had dragged him under, and Grenville Simmons never came up. Dorcas stumbled back along the quay that was now filling with screaming people, aware that accusing eyes were watching her.

'I didn't do anything' she shouted back.

She ran all the way home, tears tearing at her eyes at the horror she had just witnessed. She lay hopelessly on her bed with visions of that freak wave sweeping the man to his death and in her mind's eye the water had been tinged with an inky blackness.

*

Nothing anyone could have said or done would have made her feel any better about the events of the last month. When Josiah arrived to tell her that it was time for her to go she met the news with a resignation of one who had already given up.

'The town council do not,' he emphasised 'hold you responsible for Grenville's death. A freak wave did that. They happen from time to time, but we know now that you can do nothing for us and it is best that you leave us.'

Dorcas nodded and looked out of the window. They did not hold her responsible but they thought it all the same.

'I am the one who feels responsible,' Josiah continued 'I was the one who brought you here, we expected too much of one person.'

Dorcas turned her gaze to the round little man.

'What exactly did you expect Josiah?'

The Chief came and sat on the window seat, his hat turning in his hands. He fumbled for the right set of words.

'The curse had been over us for many years and it has got a lot worse over the last two years. Many have died with no apparent reasoning behind it, so much, so much bad luck. We wanted answers and we, I, thought that the north would hold the answers being as they are, well, umm, in that line of business so to speak'

Dorcas looked at him. He meant well but his words were way off course.

'You were expecting some sort of fire-wielding witch who could blast this thing from the town in a shower of Sabbat fireworks, weren't you?'

Josiah nodded.

'Then you were mistaken. Magick is not like that Josiah, it comes from the world around us. We call it earth magick, the ability to understand the world around us.'

'Like the knowledge of plants that you possess.'

'Exactly. Very occasionally we can summon up something that

looks like magick.'

'Like talking to the animals?'

'Yes, but that is only like learning another language and it's open for all to learn not just witchkind. We are in tune with nature Josiah, that is all.'

The Chief looked at his lap and rubbed his face with his faithful hanky.

'I have been a fool and I am sorry Miss Fleming. We were desperate. The church could not help and Trewidden thinks that God has forsaken this part of the world anyway. He and his brother were the only ones left from his family, the rest had moved away. We thought you could do it, we thought you could somehow break this curse of ours.'

Dorcas sat beside him and put her hand on his.

'Cursing can only be done by one who knows how to do it and no one person can curse a whole town. If you want my opinion Josiah, there is something here and it is more than a curse. It is centred on Pendartha of that I am sure.'

Josiah looked up and met her eyes

'How do you know that Miss Fleming?'

Dorcas took a deep breath and a shiver ran through her from the top of her head to the tips of her solid northern boots.

'I have seen it Josiah, but that doesn't really matter now, does it?'

Chapter twenty

Dorcas was trapped. She could not leave Pendartha for another two weeks, as Stanley Horton and the convoy were not due in St Zenno until three days after the Litha Sabbat. This coming Sabbat was the liveliest and the noisiest in the whole year and she was going to spend it here waiting to return home.

She had already started sorting out her belongings and had packed some of her things that would go near the bottom of the cart. The dresser had been emptied of the supplies of herbs and oils, and they were waiting to be put into the straw lined tea chests that she had retrieved from the shed. Even the dregs in the bottom of the canister, that contained her precious Neroli oil, would have to be taken back.

'*No good leaving it for this lot,*' she said to the watching cat '*they wouldn't know what to do with a Mistress Oil if it bit them on the backside.*'

There was going to be a lot more to take home with her than she had thought. The small shed by the back door contained gifts from the townspeople that she had not known what to do with. The latest were two bolts of cloth that Sally Cribbin had given her for curing the warts that had plagued her son's hands.

'The girls don't want to hold his hand at Sunday school' she had said.

Warts were easy. Dorcas had made up a strong tincture of greater celandine and dandelion and the warts melted away over the course of the next month. The two bright bolts of cloth had been wrapped up and stored away. Dorcas could never see a time when she would make anything to wear that involved yellow or orange.

The cloth lay on the kitchen table and she ran her hand over the fine lawn cotton. The sun was now nearly at its hottest and in the dark colours that she preferred for her work Dorcas struggled every day to keep cool. The temperatures down here were much higher than at the edge of the Ashen Fells at Summerlands. Even in the height of the season there was always a cool breeze blowing off the moor and the abundance of woods and thick forests that were absent in the south, gave shade to anyone who sought it. In the last few weeks, the heat had grown during the day to a point where she had filled the tin bath with water and sat in it in the garden. Jubal was gone and there was no one else around so she had dipped sky clad in the cooling water. During the day, she walked around with her sleeves pushed up past her elbows and a straw hat, which she had found in the back of the dresser when she had arrived, jammed down on her sweating brow. Both gave little respite to the searing daytime heat.

She unravelled the bolts of cotton and had a look at them.

'Well, there is no work now' she said 'and I would be a lot less conspicuous on the journey home and an awful lot cooler.'

She set about making a new travelling dress, choosing the slightly less garish yellow that was trimmed with small white daisies. The Pendarthans had a penchant for the brighter side of the colour spectrum and aside from Violetta's love of gingham she had noticed that an awful lot of the women wore highly patterned fabrics especially as the season had progressed. Dorcas completed her new outfit in a couple of days and spent the evening sewing the last few buttons to the bodice. With no frills, flounces or any other kind of embellishment, the yellow dress was rather attractive. Dorcas had, by habit, added two large pockets to the skirt. A dress could not be a witch's dress unless it had somewhere to store all your bits and pieces. The skirt was also slightly fuller than the plain ones that she usually wore and it reminded her of Ginnifer Belle decked out in her Sabbat best.

She often thought about her coven, how they were getting on, safe and secure in their northern placements. Some, who were close enough in miles, would have reunited for May Day and Dorcas was sorry that she could not have been there. Many times, she had wondered what would have happened if she had refused her placement. Did the balance of the universe depend on a witch doing what she was supposed to do? It was too late for this kind of speculation; she would soon be trudging back to Masterbridge with her tail between her legs.

*

Josiah came three days before she was due to leave. The garden was strewn with boxes and furniture ready to load onto the cart. Stanley's horse, Winston, had arrived back from his home in Jakey's barn and the nearly silent Tregonning was going to help her with the heavy things.

'Miss Fleming,' the Mayor panted 'I see you are almost packed.'

Dorcas nodded at the obvious statement.

'Umm, we are having a picnic up on the Lazard cliffs tomorrow to celebrate the longest day of the year. I hear that it is a festival day for you too. We, that is the committee, thought that you might like to join us.'

'Josiah, I really don't think that it would be a good idea.'

'But we insist.'

Dorcas thought for a moment. It would a good time to say goodbye properly to those people that she had become fond of over the last six or seven months. It really would not matter what they thought now anyway, she would be gone in a few days. She would miss some of them more than others, Jubal Sancreed for one, but he would not be at the picnic.

'Me Uncle thinks he has gone back to Port Morgan,' Mary Moyle had told her 'he heard it from a cousin of Jubal's in St Zenno. He lived there for a while, in the capital I mean, before he got married, or so I've heard.'

Dorcas did not dwell on this information, but she was relieved to hear that the man still had some sort of family.

Mary Moyle had come to see her a couple of times and Dorcas had taught her how to make the soap that she loved. With the two women immersed in their task, Dorcas had wheedled tiny bits of information from the blacksmith's daughter. She also found that Mary had a natural talent for mixing perfumes and in time, she would have made a fine apprentice for soap making and the like. Avergila Boslowek had also come.

'I wants a baby.'

Dorcas smiled inside. The rough and ready fishwife had approached her in the same way as she had asked about acquiring a husband.

'I cannot make a baby for you Avergila, that is something you will have to do on your own, or rather with that husband of yours.'

Avergila let out a barking laugh.

'Very good witch, see you haven't lost that sense of humour of yours even through all your troubles. I like you and I shall be missing you when you've gone no matter what they all say about you, so there.'

Dorcas smiled. Avergila must have honest, open northern blood in her somewhere.

'So what can you do? John says that you'll be telling me that there are three babies waiting under a bush somewhere. Hah!'

'I'm afraid it's not as easy as that Avergila. To be honest with you, your age is against you.'

'I feel younger now than I did years ago, but a baby will not start and it's not from lack of trying.'

Dorcas had to agree, Avergila did look younger. Marriage obviously suited the fishwife, her features had softened, and she seemed a little more feminine. She could but try.

'I have packed most of my things but I am sure I can dig out what I need.'

'That's the spirit, don't give up, never give up.'

Avergila watched while Dorcas took a hen's egg and made a tiny hole in the top and bottom. Over a bowl, she gently blew the contents out until the egg was empty. Taking her boline knife she expertly cut the eggshell in half and placed some Lady's Mantle and an oak leaf inside one half. The fishwife watched with interest.

'When you get home you will need to place a lock of your hair and a lock of John's inside with the leaves. I will write you the spell that must then be said under the crescent moon.'

Avergila nodded.

'When you have done this put the egg shells back together and tie them with a ribbon to hold them in place and leave it near your bed, or wherever you make love.'

Dorcas carefully wrapped the pieces of egg in moss and put them in a small basket for Avergila to take home.

'Don't break it before you get there, and umm, try making love when the tide is in.'

Avergila looked puzzled.

'Tide and moon are at one with each other right now, it will be a good time' Dorcas explained.

Avergila set off down the lane, walking so slowly that Dorcas thought that she would not get home before dark.

'I'm sorry if it doesn't work' she called after the retreating woman 'it just means it wasn't meant to be. The Goddess always knows best. Merrypart Avergila.'

'Merrypart Dorcas Fleming' she heard from the lane.

Dorcas was pleased that some people had made the effort to come and see her; it meant that they had not lost faith in her witching as much as she had. She was starting to worry about her return to the north, and her immediate future. Where would they put her now? A failed placement was worse than no placement at all but at least she would not be answerable to the Mothers at Summerlands. They had done their job as well as they could, she was the one who had messed it all up. No doubt, she would be dragged before the Pagan Council to answer their questions and Dorcas had now blown it up to the proportions of her trial in Polempter, only without the rescue committee.

Those dwelling thoughts brought Jubal back to her mind and she pushed them out again, there was no need to go over all that again. She had really thought they might have got somewhere, shared something. It had been too early to talk about love but Dorcas had toyed with a similar word a couple of times.

'And what a waste of time that was!'

'I wouldn't know' Zebulonus said lazily from the porch 'humans have such complicated lives if you ask me.'

'Well, I didn't ask you, you were eavesdropping.'

'But you liked him and so did I.'

Dorcas would have liked to have seen him just once more before she left, to tell him that marriage and divorce meant nothing to her. He must have had his reasons for abandoning his wife although it seemed that most of Pendartha would disagree with her. Dorcas felt that there was more to the fisherman than met the eye. The night that they had shared had been special, at least to her, and then he had left, perhaps they were right about him.

*

Tregonning picked her up on the morning of the picnic and she rode into town to meet the rest of the revellers in the square. Carts had been decorated with ribbons and flags and there was a general atmosphere of merrymaking that Dorcas had not experienced while the Preacher Trewidden was still around.

There were many admiring comments about her dress and Violetta in particular made a great fuss about it.

'Suits you much better than those dull dresses that you prefer, brings out your colour. You can be quite pretty when you make the effort.'

Dorcas had been unsure as to whether she should wear it. She knew from her visitors that there were no ill feelings about the death of Grenville Simmons, but she still had to deal with the rest of the population. She felt that she stuck out like a sore thumb but she was very cool, especially with the straw hat stuck on top of her head to shade her eyes.

Once out of Pendartha, on the road to St Zenno, they turned off at the crossroads and took a long winding dirt track that would have been impassable a few months ago. Dust hung in the air and made the cart riders cough and splutter. It was not long before they were taking draughts from the flagons of cider and ale that had been brought along. The Lazard Point was no more than a mile or two from Pendartha as the crow flies but they had to take a very long inland route to get to it.

Despite the dust, Dorcas enjoyed the ride. This was the first time she had been out of the town, apart from her detainment in gaol. The convoy of carts turned back towards the coast and they rode along the heather-laden cliffs until they came to a wide-open grassy area. To her left, Dorcas could see the bite out of the land where the entrance to Pendartha harbour started and to her right was the long, narrow peninsula of Lazard Point. The children spilled out of the carts and ran across the rolling, cliff-top downs. They were a few shouted warnings to the smaller children to keep away from the sheer cliffs that dropped straight down to the sea. The young Pendarthans had brought brightly coloured kites, that immediately took flight in the stiff breeze that was blowing off the turquoise seas.

It was a beautiful day. The picnickers set up their cloths, and blankets, in a rough circle and pegged them down with small iron forks to stop them blowing away. Dorcas had brought her own supplies but Josiah and Violetta beckoned her over to join them at their pitch. Dorcas got the distinct impression that Violetta was being extra friendly now that she knew the witch was going.

'It is a beautiful spot' she said.

'We used to come here as children' Josiah said 'and we sneaks up here on this day every year to honour the longest day of daylight.'

'We would light a bonfire sometimes in the old days' Morwenna added.

Dorcas smiled; there were truly some similarities between their cultures, but the southerners interpreted them in different ways. It must have all been rooted in the same beliefs at one time or another; the southerners had just kept the ones that did not interfere with their righteous, stifling God. Litha Sabbat was all about bonfires and Dorcas took her mind back to the celebrations in Brexham the year before. If only she had known what was in store for her.

Dorcas looked around at all the people she had come to know.

Avergila was there with her large husband, and Jakey and his girls. Mary caught her eye, winked and pointed at Anne and the dark-haired boy sat next to her. Dorcas did not recognise him from around Pendartha but he had a very distinct mole on his left cheek. Dorcas winked back.

Mrs Creed was there with a year's supply of fresh bread and Telfer and Mags were sat with Minnie Gembo and her brood of eight noisy offspring. Minnie was ignoring her many children in favour of picking up the latest piece of gossip from Lizzy Mims, who was mouthing something important to her at close range. Dorcas was also pleased, a little later on, to see that Telfer took a long walk with the widow, Siddie Jose, who lived next door to the Penpols. Foggy Isaacs was swigging noisily on a flagon of beer and would content himself with liquid refreshment until he could no longer stand.

'Should have a word with him about his drinking, that will not do his arthritic hip any good.'

Dorcas noticed that a number of people had left a little pile of food for him on his small, dirty blanket. Life would carry on without her and they would no doubt manage quite happily in her absence, but at least she knew that she had brought some small changes to their lives. Foggy Isaacs had been ignored for most of his muddled life but now the town was starting to recognise his worth. A bit of care was being dropped at his door every now and again.

There were others too, Telfer looked happier than when she had first come here. His skin had only the vaguest hint of yellowness to it and she knew that Sarah Trewidden was starting to make a new life for herself. Dorcas was suddenly overcome with misery. She excused herself from the Penpols' hospitality and took a walk by herself.

The Lazard Downs rolled on for mile after mile, covered in a blanket of hazy purple heather and yellow gorse that smelled like coconut oil. Away from the others, Dorcas lost herself in the sound of the wind and the sea crashing on the rocks far below. She sat on a large granite lump just off the path and let the warm wind blow her hair around her face. With her hand protecting her eyes from the bright sun, Dorcas took in the wonderful scenery. The Lazard Point was spectacular, dropping into the water as if a giant had stepped on the end and forced it below the water line. Dorcas realised that she had not explored very much of her new home; the valley and cove surrounding her cottage were the exceptions. The south was really rather beautiful, with a wild, rugged coastline and rolling hills behind. The summer heat had taken some getting used to but the milder winters were far more preferable to the cold ones of the frozen north. Up here away from the grey little town of Pendartha, it was breathtaking, nature at its finest. On the next hill, just before the Point, Dorcas could see some sort of monument staring out to sea. No one would miss her for a while and it would be ages before the picnickers went home. Dorcas set off to explore a bit further.

*

It was nearly dark before they found her.

Lanterns bobbed all along the cliffs and the sound of her name being called could be heard for miles. Telfer Meriadoc saw her first and thought she had been turned to stone. He ran as fast as he could to get to the monument on the summit of Rundle Hill and found her with her hands pressed against the old granite ring. She was staring ahead with wild un-seeing eyes, cold and shaking and in another world that Telfer could not get in to, no matter how loudly he shouted. He prised her hands gently away from the granite and sat her down on the grass. More lanterns caught up and they carried her limp body back to the picnic area. By the time Violetta had wrapped a thick woollen blanket around her Dorcas started to come back to consciousness. She sat up and gazed around her, re-focussing her eyes on the worried, puzzled faces.

'I know, I know now, some of it anyway.'

'She's raving. The cold has got to her' Telfer said worriedly.

'I'm not raving, I need to talk to Foggy Isaacs about the curse, is he still here.'

Dorcas was still freezing cold despite being near a bonfire that had been lit in her absence. Her teeth chattered audibly and Josiah handed her his hip flask that was half-full of something very strong. In the light of the dancing flames, Foggy was brought through the small crowd that had gathered around her. Not all the Pendarthans had been concerned for her welfare, some would have gladly held on to the idea that she had thrown herself off the cliffs.

Foggy was very drunk. He lolled to one side and was propped up by Telfer and Jakey Moyle.

'Foggy, listen to me,' Dorcas said shuffling a little closer 'what did you say to me the day I came and saw to your hip?'

Foggy looked completely confused at the expectant faces.

'No good asking old Foggy, he can't remember what he had for lunch Miss Fleming, let alone what happened weeks ago.'

A few people laughed and Dorcas moved close enough to the old weatherman to put her hand firmly on his arm. As if it were a signal to his brain to reach back a few weeks Foggy shivered and closed his eyes.

'I need to know, something happened and you told me a bit of it' Dorcas said quietly.

'Yes, yes. Saw them do it didn't I?'

'Yes, you did Foggy. What did you see them do?'

The crowd had fallen silently and were hanging on every word that was said. Foggy rolled again and Dorcas added her other hand to his arm.

'The Hag stone' she encouraged.

'Aggstone, Aggstone. Saw them do it. They didn't see me, but I saw. I saw.'

'Yes Foggy.'

'Lots of them, gathered round it. Church won't like it, up there in the middle of the night. Did something they did, something they shouldn't have.'

Foggy gave out a great moan and Dorcas let go of his arm.

'What was all that then?' Josiah asked.

'I need to put it all together. Would you mind taking me home now?'

*

As she lay in the spare bed in Josiah's house, Dorcas ran her mind back to the moment she had first touched it. She had been amazed to discover the Hag Stone as she walked along the cliffs. She remembered coming up in front of it and finding that it was not a monument at all, but a good, old-fashioned ring stone, one piece of circular granite with a large hole carved out of the middle. They were dotted all around the north and there was a prime example of one on Ashen Moor, but it was only half the size of the one on the Lazard Point. Known as Hag stones, Witch stones or Holey stones, they were places of strong magick and were often the focus for rituals or Esbats of the full moon. Dorcas had walked around this one two or three times, touching the rough stone with her fingertips, glad to see something that reminded her of her home in the north. She had then reached out with both hands to take in the feel of the familiar stone. The rest was a blur until she had come to her senses beside the bonfire. In her mind, she knew that it was connected with the so-called curse and that Foggy Isaacs had a clue to it. She would have to sleep on it and hope that everything was clearer in the morning.

Lengthen thine inner eye to recognise the signs that have been set before thee. Seek out those who would reluctantly help and bind thyself to a number of safety
- Akashic records

Chapter twenty-one

When Violetta knocked on the door, Dorcas had already been awake for hours, nursing a headache that was threatening to split her head open.

'Gave people a bit of a fright last night' Violetta said as she placed a tray down beside the bed. She drew back the curtains and let the early morning sun flood the room. Dorcas pulled the patchwork quilt up over her head to protect her aching brain.

'When you are ready you can come down for some breakfast with me and Mr Penpol before he goes down to the quay for the day. He has some questions for you.'

'I bet he does.'

Dorcas drank her strong tea and washed her face in the bowl on the chest of drawers. Violetta's towels had V and J intertwined in blue embroidery in the corner, which Dorcas fingered idly.

'Details, I need details' she said.

Josiah came up from his office on the ground floor just as Violetta was serving a morning meal. This was breakfast, lunch, and tea as far as Dorcas was concerned, with eggs that sat on top of eggs that in turn squatted on huge slices of bacon with a hunk of fried bread on the side.

'Ah, breakfast, best meal of the day' he said tucking a good forkful into his mouth.

Violetta chewed delicately on a small piece of bacon rind and they both waited for Dorcas to speak. When breakfast was nearly over and nothing was forthcoming, Josiah broke the silence.

'Is there anything you need to tell us, Miss Fleming, I mean about yesterday?'

Dorcas placed her knife and fork down on the table and clasped her hands together. This was going to be difficult, more than difficult.

'I am not sure if you are going to like what I am going to say. I cannot do this on my own; you will need to get a few people together to find the answers.'

'To what?'

'Your curse.'

'My curse?' Josiah asked looking horrified.

'Not yours, somebody here in Pendartha called it to life many years ago but …'

Dorcas was interrupted by an urgent knock at the door.

'Josiah, Josiah come quick!'

'What's all the fuss about young Creed, I'm just having me breakfast.'

'Boat's over, in the harbour.'

Three chairs scraped away from the table in unison, breakfast forgotten as they all made their way down to the door to see what was going on. Dorcas could see people starting to run towards the quay. Josiah followed Simon Creed and soon they were all making their way swiftly through Pendartha, doors left swinging in their going. The younger Creed boy still had the youthful ability to run and speak at the same time.

'It's Joe and Petey Gribble, they went without me, we was going crabbing off end of the quay, they decided to use their Dad's rower.'

A mass of people all turned up on the wharf at the same time and joined the few that had arrived first. Josiah, who was quite sprightly for a man of his stature, just reached the end of the wharf as the boys' father dived off the end and started to swim towards the small up-turned boat. He was already making progress towards the boat when an arm appeared from under it and the frightened face of the elder Gribble struggled out from the watery trap. Just as Vic Gribble got to the boy, he was dragged under as if by an unseen hand and both disappeared under the water again. A shriek went up from the quay and John Gembo launched himself off the quay. Josiah, and a number of other men, had jumped into the small rowing boats that were moored in the harbour and were making haste to the scene of the accident. The rest watched helplessly from the quay and let down ropes into the calm waters in case they were needed. Violetta hung onto Dorcas's arm, her nails making crescents in the witch's skin.

''Tis the devil's work again, he has got Pendartha around the neck.'

Vic appeared spluttering; the men with boat hooks plunged them into the water and the two men who were already in the water kept diving down and resurfacing for what seemed an age to those who watched helplessly.

One boy came up and then the other, bobbing helplessly like wine corks and both were simultaneously dragged onto the waiting dinghies. The waves seemed to reach out to them as they left the water and Dorcas felt a shiver run up and down her spine.

When they arrived at the steps, the boys were pale and shocked but they were alive. Dorcas heard the elder boy tell his father that a hand had come out of the water and had turned the boat over.

Something new took Dorcas's eye, a figure on the harbour wall was jumping up and down, shouting and pointing. When the boys were safely on dry land, she directed Josiah's attention to the excited man. It was Foggy Isaacs and he was now yelling.

'Come, see, come!'

People started to follow him to see what all the fuss was about and as soon as they got near Foggy danced off up the path that led up the cliffs towards his cliff top residence.

'See it, see it now. I told ee'

Halfway up the path Foggy stopped and pointed back down to the outer harbour. Dorcas could see it as plain as day and she soon realised that the others could see it as well. Like an inky stain from an octopus, it lay just under the surface of the water. Josiah came alongside her and she heard his intake of breath.

'There! There! Do you see?' Foggy yelled.

It stretched out to touch the cliffs on either side of the Pendarthan inlet, like a slick of oily cloud it undulated in the clear waters. It surrounded the little boat that the Gribble boys had been in only a few minutes earlier and there was a communal shiver as the townsfolk realised that it was pulling the boat out to sea even though the tide was on its way in.

They watched for a while until the blackness lost its depth and seemed to disappear before their eyes. Many had sat down on the path in horror and fascination and when it finally went, it was as if a spell had been broken. Chatter broke out through the ranks and all eyes turned to the witch.

By nightfall, the whole of Pendartha knew what had taken place and they all gathered at the meeting hall beside the chapel to find out what the committee had to say about it. Josiah had decided on an open meeting, there was no point in trying to keep things quiet now.

It was a balmy night outside, and in the hall it was hot, stuffy, and airless. All the bodies were packed tightly together, jostling for space, and the hall, that had appeared quite large when she first walked in, now seemed small and oppressive. Along with the rest of the town committee, or the 'curse committee' as she had dubbed it, Dorcas was sat at a table at the front, raised up on a small dais. Josiah, in his role as Mayor, called the meeting to order. The low murmuring stopped and all ears tuned in to his clear southern tones

'You knows why we are here. We all saw something this morning that we can't explain.'

'The devil has come to Pendartha, we should bring back the Preacher' someone yelled out.

'*That* devil has been here for years, what good would that do, bringing him back?' a voice quipped from the back.

'Now, now, let's not get too excited. We are expecting a new man of the church any day now. God has not forgotten Pendartha, but there is someone amongst us who may be able to help.'

Dorcas smoothed her dress down and fiddled with a loose strand of hair. She was aware that there was still an awful lot of hostility towards her presence in the town.

'Miss Fleming has been trained to deal with these things and she may have some suggestions for us' Josiah continued 'I know a lot of you questioned the wisdom of bringing a witch from the north to help us, but these are desperate times.'

'Don't see that a dollop of hand cream is going to get rid of a curse' Ivan Wesley said.

Dorcas got up and put her hands on the table to steady her.

'I know that many of you here tonight have used some of my remedies and it is true I am a hedgewitch, trained to work with nature, to heal and to help people. When I first came, I heard the whispers about a curse and many towns and villages in the north feel the same way when bad things happen. I need to know everything that has gone on in order to understand what you have been through. Now that we can speak aloud of this curse that you believe you are under, I would ask people to come forward and tell me about their experiences. I need to know as much as I can, if I am to help.'

Dorcas's request was met with silence. No one was willing to stand up and say their piece. Josiah cast about the room trying to encourage someone to break the ice. Dorcas was just about to speak again when Tregonning got up.

'The sea took me boys and then me wife' he said quietly 'they were all good souls.'

There was a gulf of silence again when he sat down and Dorcas felt it was more in shock of the silent man finally speaking. She spoke again.

'I am due to leave Pendartha tomorrow morning, if I am to offer any advice then you will need to open up, please do not be afraid to speak.'

'My Grandfather died in the harbour' Billy Mims said.

'And mine, on the same calm night, no reason for it we always said' Joshua Small agreed.

More people stood up and by the time they had finished Dorcas was aware that there was not one family in Pendartha who had not lost someone to the sea.

'Foggy Isaacs knows something, we have heard him rambling on for years. Is it madness, or is it truth' Mrs Creed asked.

Dorcas took a breath. Her head was still spinning. There had been many more lives lost in this small town than she had ever come across. This was no natural bad luck, this was an on-going disaster.

'Foggy Isaacs witnessed something many years ago at the Hag Stone, or Aggstone as you call it, near the Lazard Point, but I can get no more from him.' Dorcas said 'Does anyone know anything, anything at all.'

Dorcas had indeed tried. All that day she had spent time with the old man and tried to put his strange words into something that made sense. He just repeated the same things over and over again and Dorcas had come to the conclusion that there was only one thing to do. She was reluctant to say anything as it would mean that she would miss her ride to the north but now she could see that the Pendarthans had suffered more than any one town ought to.

'I have not spoken to Josiah Penpol of this but there is something I can do to try to understand what is happening here. Once we understand then I may be able to help you.'

'I'm sure we will give you all the help you need' Josiah said confidently.

'And I'm sure that you won't even entertain it once you hear what it is'

Dorcas had no wish to leave these people without offering them some sort of aid. It was in a witch's nature to help but even she seriously doubted she could do anything, and she certainly would not be able to do it alone. She took a deep breath.

'If you do wish to help then it will mean that I will have to stay for a while longer and I'm not sure that the committee will agree to that. I will give you a chance to make up your minds when I have told you of my proposal.'

Josiah nodded for her to continue.

'I will need twelve people with strong and open minds to take part in something called Pathworking. In the north, when we have a problem, we get together and form a, umm, group. This group links their minds together and very often can resolve an issue, or a mystery, for instance. There are things that we need to know and this is the only way of doing it but the volunteers who take part will need to be trained. I cannot say that it is not without its risks and I do not even know if it will work. There is something here, something that has been casting a blight on your town and if we work together, we may be able to find out what it is. I will wait outside until you have made a decision.'

Dorcas could hear the raised voices as she walked around the square. After a while, the doors opened and people started to spill out into the warm night air. Many refused to look at her and scuttled by, or took an alternative route home to avoid her. Some nodded and thanked her for her services and wished her well.

Josiah stood at the door and beckoned her in. The hall was empty apart from the Mayor and Jakey Moyle. On the table was a piece of paper and Josiah handed it to her.

'There are many who want no part in this and we has to accept that fact, but there are a small number who would help.'

Dorcas looked at the paper. Fourteen names had been listed.

'The committee has asked that you stay' Josiah continued 'but only to try and sort this matter out. '

Dorcas's thoughts raced ahead of her. If this was her task then was she up to it? Could she train these people to do something that would be alien to them and if she could, would they then be able to utilise that skill? There were so many questions that she could not answer. She now had a coven and suddenly Dorcas was not sure at all that she wanted one.

*

The next day, just after dawn, Dorcas met with Tregonning and Jakey Moyle. Both the men had added their names to the list and had volunteered to go with her to St Zenno to return Stanley's horse and cart. Jakey had kindly offered to bring them back in his own cart and he followed behind on the dusty road.

Stanley was late, and pulled into the town just as it was getting dark

'Didn't recognise you there Miss Fleming what with the clothes and all.'

'I'm blending in' she said of her yellow dress.

Stanley gave her a warm hug and Dorcas responded with tears welling up in her eyes. It would be so easy just to leave them all to it and go back to the north with or without her belongings. Dorcas pulled herself together and introduced Jakey and Tregonning to the members of the convoy.

'You look loaded up Stanley.'

'Wine down, cotton out, same old same old' he smiled.

'And an extra cart, the Goddess is smiling on you' Dorcas said acknowledging the brand new addition to the convoy.

'No, that one is for you, had to get me sister's boy to bring it down. Council have supplied you with your own nag as well and I must say I will be glad to have Winston back when we swap. Missed the old git, he don't get the jitters down here like some of the others. Begging your pardon, no offence meant' he said, nodding to Tregonning and Jakey.

'None taken, think I would get the jitters in the north meself' the blacksmith replied.

Stanley did not understand a word that Jakey said but he smiled and nodded. How on the Goddess's earth did the witch converse with these people, the blacksmith fellow almost spoke a dialect of his very own.

With a precious cargo of Masterbridge wine on board, Stanley's sons settled in for the night under their carts as they had done so many times when Dorcas had travelled with them. Jakey took Dorcas, Stanley, and Tregonning off to his cousin's alehouse where the two Pendarthans settled in for a session at the gloomy bar. Dorcas and Stanley found a snug at the back and sat down with a pint of bitter apiece. Dorcas told him of her first few months in the south.

'Didn't think we would see you again. I said to the lads on the way here that we could be taking your stuff right back with us. We kept our fingers crossed.'

'I have survived but it has not been easy, things are so different down here Stanley. I have a letter for the Council, could you see that they get it.'

'I have a letter for you as well, from Elshalamane no less, gave it to me in person.'

Dorcas looked suitable impressed and took the letter that Stanley produced from his coat pocket. It smelled of incense and the north.

'So you are staying then?'

'Seems I have to. I was all ready to come back with you, but something has happened.'

Stanley knew better than to ask a witch her business but he knew that it must be serious, the High Druid had come to see him himself.

After spending a restless night in a flea-infested bed in the alehouse, Dorcas said goodbye to the convoy early the next morning with great reluctance. Stanley hugged her for a long time and wished her well. He would be returning in the autumn as they were now running two extra trips a year. Dorcas smiled, and just for a while, the north didn't seem quite so far away.

The new cart was full to the brim and Tregonning, once again, helped her to unload the new supplies. Dorcas was in a festive mood. The council had thought of everything, and more, there was even a small couch. Two carefully protected crates contained things that she knew were used in strong magick. She had only read about them at college and hoped that the letter would give her some clues. Dorcas waited with anticipation to read the message from the High Druid, leaving it propped up on the dresser until she was alone. The letter did not contain comforting words of support; instead, it contained a quote from an ancient and revered Book of Shadows.

The power inside the Hexenbanner was tangible, there as it always had been. She called and it had answered her, somehow. As I watched, helpless and bound in certain death, the witch turned widdershins calling the name of Morrigan, Morrigan the death bringer. The Hag battled the Maiden and I thought all was surely lost. She drew animus and anima from all around, male and female spirit coming to her like trained, slathering dogs and the resulting

maleficium was truly ghastly to the watching eye. No enemy was left standing in the cold light of day to tell this great tale, rent limb from limb in her furious blast.
And I? That night I witnessed the birth and death of a true witch and lived to tell the tale'.

- Grimorium Pentaculum.

Chapter twenty-two

The fourteen faces in the meeting hall looked pale and twitchy. Josiah and Tregonning had placed some chairs in a circle and everyone quickly took a seat.

'Thank you all for coming,' Dorcas said soothingly 'we will only need twelve of you, and me, for the actual Pathworking but I think it is best if we all practice together. We can then get the mix right.'

There was a nervous shuffling of feet and Telfer Meriadoc put voice to the concerns of the new coven.

'There are some here who are wondering if we are denouncing our own God in favour of your, umm, beliefs, Miss Fleming.'

Dorcas turned and smiled. She had been waiting for this.

'If you try and think of it as a 'communal think' then perhaps we can dispense with any talk of religion in this, we are just trying to solve a problem. Humans have always been able to do this; there is no great magick involved.'

'Well, not much anyway!'

Dorcas took a long look at her candidates. She had healed or helped all of them and she knew, that despite their misgivings, they were keen to help, and to try to relieve the town of this thing that weighed on their shoulders like a millstone.

Dorcas had never taught her craft to anyone before. At college, she had helped her classmates to understand a law, or a ritual, but she had never taken responsibility for a whole coven before. A Priestess trained for a further five years and was skilled in guiding a coven through a Pathworking. Dorcas was not nervous, she knew what had to be done and that she had little time to do it, her choices were limited. The main problem was where to start. These people were not like the ordinary folk in the north who grew up with an understanding of the Pagan craft and believed whole-heartedly in the Goddess and the Natural Law. A nervous mind amongst them would keep them all from seeing anything.

Dorcas felt the first thing to do would be to try to get the group to learn to relax but looking around the seats she wondered if even that was going to be possible, Siddie Jose looked as if she was going to run out at any minute. In giving each member, a candle Dorcas hoped that they would be able to focus their inner eye and clear their conscious minds. Words like that were alien to these people so she tried to explain in as simple terms as she could.

'So it is like having a daydream, only all together' Avergila said.

'Exactly. Your minds should be empty of everything but the question that we wish to ask. Now, if we are ready we shall start.'

Dorcas asked them to place their candles on the floor and hold hands. Even this was difficult for some, and there was awkwardness between some of the men and women. Finally, they were ready.

Goddess,
Bind this circle, bind it tight
Bless our eyes and give them sight,
Bless our hearts, true and open
Bless our minds, words unspoken,
Grant us vision true and whole
Link together body and soul.

'I'm sorry Miss Fleming, I can't do this, it just don't feel right.' Louise Creed stood up. 'God don't want me to do this. I wanted to help, we have all been touched by this curse, but I can't do this. It goes against.'

'It's all right, please don't feel bad,' Dorcas said calmly 'I would rather you pulled out now, than later.'

Mrs Creed made her way quickly to the door, apologising to everyone on the way out.

'Anyone else, before we go any further?' Dorcas asked.

'I think it would be better if you spoke up now' Josiah added, but no one else moved.

The circle linked again and Dorcas led them into some deep breathing. She could sense straight away that it was going to take some time for the group to function as one; they had so many knots inside them. By the end of the first evening, surprisingly, Dorcas felt as if they were getting somewhere. They had the advantage of wanting to rid the town of its unwelcome visitor, but could they overcome their fears in this room?

In ideal circumstances, Lammas Sabbat would be the best time to try to find the answers they were looking for but that was six weeks away and Dorcas did not have that much time. She had given herself two weeks to try to get them working together and then they would try for real at the new moon.

'We know that time is short so we thought we could meet every night if you are willing' Telfer said.

'I quite enjoyed it,' Minnie Gembo said, taking a cake from the plate that Violetta was handing around 'it's a bit of a social event.'

For the next week, they met in the meeting hall every night at seven, only one night was disrupted when Mordecai Leven had an upset stomach. Each time they got together Dorcas felt that the link between them was getting deeper and although they did not realise it, the coven was bonding. By the middle of the second week, Dorcas stopped the meditation half way through.

'I'm afraid we have to stop' she said quietly,

The coven slowly opened their eyes.

'There is someone here who will have to leave our circle. We have reached a depth where I can link with each and every one of you and I'm afraid there is one who cannot continue with this.'

The coven looked confused but the witch did not look upset about anything, she was smiling.

'What is it?' John Boslowek asked 'have we done something wrong?'

'No not at all, seems *you* have done it all right' Dorcas said looking directly at Avergila.

'What?'

'I think your wish has come true' she said tactfully.

The light dawned on Avergila Boslowek.

'I am?' she asked, a half-formed smile playing on her lips.

'Yes, you are.'

Avergila shot out of her chair and wrapped her thick arms around Dorcas's neck.

'Thank you, thank you, I knew you could do it' she cried

The rest of the group now looked very confused.

'What is it?' Siddie Jose said, she had just begun to enjoy these gatherings and she did not want to stop at all.

'I'm having a baby, apparently' Avergila said slowly 'that's right innit?'

'For sure' Dorcas confirmed, laughing.

Her husband's eyes were as round as full moons and he gave his wife a kiss on the cheek.

'And before you ask Josiah Penpol, this child was conceived in the natural way, the witch just gave us a helping hand with a few bits of old egg shell and the like' she smirked.

Congratulations went around the room.

'I'm afraid you will have to stop the Pathworking Avergila' Dorcas said.

'But, I wanted to help?'

'It wouldn't be good for the baby, and it would increase our number to fourteen overall, so no. I'm sorry, but I'm also very glad for you.'

The tea and cakes came out early that night and there was a feeling of lightness in the room.

'I know this is going to sound silly' Morwenna said 'but I think I knew about the baby somehow. Is that how it works Dorcas, are we getting there?'

Dorcas was very surprised at Morwenna's statement but made a mental note that Josiah's mother would be on the final list. She desperately hoped that no one else cried off. A coven was at its strongest when there were thirteen, more or less than that number just confused everything and took the power away, and they would need every bit to make this work.

The last hiccup happened on the day of the new moon. Dorcas was working in the garden when she heard a cart coming up the lane. Billy Mims was driving and Josiah was at his side.

'The Preacher has arrived' the Chief said 'scuppered our plans good and proper.'

'The Preacher?' Dorcas said horrified.

'The new one, not Trewidden,' Billy said 'but we can't go using his meeting hall for, well, what we're doing, can we?'

'We don't want any awkward questions' Josiah said 'seems like a nice man but…'

'We can't let him know that we are performing heathen practices in the hall' Dorcas said.

'Exactly.'

'We shall have to meet here then. Can you let everyone know?'

Josiah assured her that he could and as the dark moon rose, the coven gathered in Dorcas's small sitting room. Tregonning had brought up chairs that belonged to the various members of the coven and they all squeezed in. They were very nervous and Dorcas gave them all a tisane that she had made especially for that evening. Many had never set foot in her house before and they glanced around, eyes darting at some of her more witchy artefacts. As they sipped their chamomile and lavender flower teas, Dorcas looked at the final twelve. Telfer and Mags worked well together, their bond had deepened since he had stopped drinking and they complimented each other mentally. Violetta was a bit of a wild card, her emotions were all over the place, and Dorcas had been surprised that she had kept coming when she had found it so hard to let go of her prejudices. Minnie Gembo was a natural seeker and Siddie Jose had a strong talent for drawing power into the group and linking them together. Siddie was a latent witch, of that Dorcas was certain. Morwenna too, would no doubt have had a calling in the north and Dorcas resisted a few times in referring to her as 'Mother'. The old woman had no trouble in meditating to a very deep level and would have been good in the scrying department had she had the training at an earlier age. They were all unaware of Dorcas's summations of their innate talents. She kept them to herself, there was no point in frightening them more than was necessary. It was a shock that they had gone this far already.

When she felt they were ready Dorcas called them to the chairs and they began.

'We are bound in the safety of thirteen, do not be afraid. Remember what you see and don't try to make sense of it. I will do that for you.'

The circle became quiet and one by one, they closed their eyes and focussed on getting the question that was on their lips to form itself clearly in their minds. Dorcas called on the Goddess for help and linked herself in with the circle.

'We are too tense' Dorcas said quietly 'let go of your bodies and let your minds go free. There is nothing to fear'

This time Dorcas felt the familiar, gentle free fall of thirteen minds uniting and letting their thoughts blend together. Unbeknown to the coven she had set a circle of safety around the room and had said many rituals before they came. It was still difficult to keep the black taint from trying to invade but the Pendarthans did what they had been taught to do and kept their minds firmly fixed on the task.

Dorcas guided their thoughts as they drifted together on the astral plane collecting small pieces of knowledge and understanding. She had warned them that they would be distracted and confused but they all kept on the straight and narrow path that Dorcas was treading on.

Time passed and they opened their eyes. Dorcas was the last to come back into the circle, gathering and collating everything that had passed between the group. As she opened her eyes, it was like a signal for the others to start to talk.

'Stone' said Siddie Jose 'I saw it as clear as day.'

'Aggstone' Telfer confirmed.

'There were thirteen of them' Morwenna added.

'There was a full moon' Josiah said.

'And they cursed something' Violetta said bursting into tears 'and there was pain, lots of pain and it goes on. Ohh!'

Dorcas put it all together. The coven had done well but it was still not a full picture.

'Something happened that drove them to curse the sea' she said incredulously.

'Can you curse the sea?' Jakey asked after a while 'I mean, is it possible?'

Dorcas had no answers to that, in theory, you should not be able to curse an element, but somehow they had, but why, when, and how? These were the answers that they did not have.

Their silent thoughts were broken by the sound of a thump that was followed by loud swearing and a bang on the door.

'He has come back,' Zebulonus informed her from the doorway.

Dorcas got up to open the door and left the coven staring at the cat who they had definitely heard speak to the witch. Their horror and fascination was only broken by the words that drifted in from the door.

'I have been to Port Morgan and have obtained a divorce. Will you marry me now witch?'

Jubal left Dorcas at the door with her mouth open and came past her and into the candle lit sitting room. The sight that greeted him nearly made him turn and go out again.

'What's all this then?'

'We have been Pathworking Jubal, we are trying to find out what happened here in Pendartha' Josiah said in answer to his astounded expression.

The rest of the coven filled him in on everything that had happened since he had left the town.

'Well, I have some news for you as well only I had to go two-hundred miles to find it. Is there any tea?'

Violetta and Minnie fussed around in Dorcas's kitchen whilst Jubal found another chair in the already crowded room. It seemed that everyone wanted to talk at once and the only two people who were silent were the ones with the answers. Dorcas found his mind.

'You have got a divorce?'

Jubal looked at her, his mind engaging with hers as if he had been doing it all his life.

'So as I can marry you.'

'Who says that I want to marry you?'

'You did, when you were asleep when we were, err, together.'

'Who says I want to now, you left me and I'm just about to leave myself.'

'Not now you're not, we've got work to do.'

The rest of the room quietened and Jubal told them what had happened in Port Morgan.

The church in the south kept a watch over its inhabitants and recorded every birth, marriage, and death in its parishes. Every year these records were sent to the capital along with anything else that their Preacher thought to be important. In order to obtain a divorce Jubal had to prove that his marriage had been legal in the first place, so this was where he started. Posing as a lawyer, his records had been easy to find, but he had also found some very interesting facts about Pendartha's recent and past, history.

'I think you all know of my hatred for the Trewiddens, and you all think that he took my wife in out of the goodness of his church-going heart. The truth is that his cousin was having an affair with my wife and the baby was not mine.'

This statement brought forth a few gasps but Jubal continued, it was not easy for him to wear his heart on his sleeve or to air his dirty washing in public. Jubal's eyes did not leave Dorcas's face as he spilled out his heartbreak.

'That is why I kicked her out. Trewidden was only covering the tracks of one of his own when he kindly spread the word around that I had beaten her and thrown her out as she went into labour. Morley Trewidden beat his wife and the Preacher did the same thing as before, covering up the family shame and trying to put the blame on others not able to defend themselves.'

There were a few awkward shuffles, many people here tonight had gossiped about the story.

'I believe you Jubal Sancreed, never did quite get me head around the story that the Preacher gave us, but I believed him as he was a man of God. And this was all in the Parish records was it?' Josiah asked.

'Not as such, but he has signed all the paperwork for the

movements of either his victims, or his family. He has also reported on a lot of Pendarthans for the bad luck that has befallen this town and I now know that the man is an out and out liar.'

There was silence for a few minutes as the circle soaked in this information.

'But he *is* a man of God' Jakey said 'he can't go around doing things like that.'

'I have some other news,' Jubal said 'but I don't think it is connected. The Trewiddens are descendents of the original Porthaveland witches. They moved to Pendartha when they were all run out of town. They were all in Pendartha at one time or another.'

'And now they have all returned to where they belong and good riddance to them all' Josiah said.

'They have, but the aunts all moved back at once and it said that they had special dispensation to go home but must never return to Pendartha. It was signed by Augustus Trewidden, our dear Preacher.'

'But they are his kin, what does it mean' Jakey said looking to Dorcas.

'I don't know but I think it is all linked and that we had better find out.'

*

It was late when the coven piled into Tregonning's cart and set off for town. They had talked for hours but had come up with no solutions to their problems. It was a mystery and Dorcas mulled it over as Jubal made yet another cup of tea.

'How on earth did you persuade them?'

'To Pathwork? I didn't, the curse did that all by itself.'

Dorcas told him of the Gribble accident in the harbour and the blackness in the sea afterwards. Jubal nodded.

'I felt that blackness and it affected me somehow, ate into my head, and twisted things around.'

Dorcas knew what he was saying. It had taken days for her to shake off the shroud that hung around her but she did not stop to think that Jubal had been affected in the same way.

'I was not myself until I was three days away from Pendartha and even then I had dreadful nightmares that plagued me day and night. I'm sorry I left like I did, I had to get away and if I am honest I did wonder if you had done it.'

Dorcas sympathised and told him of her own feelings.

'I could not understand why you were going and at that time I didn't really care. It was only a week later when I realised the enormity of what had happened and then I was swept up in other things.'

'Enormity?' he asked.

'I didn't want you to go and I longed to have you back.'

Jubal took her in his arms and held her for a long time. She had missed his company and his presence in her life and it would not be untrue to admit that her feelings for Jubal Sancreed ran deeper than merely friendship.

'I don't suppose I could stay with you tonight. All my belongings are still outside.'

'We are not man and wife yet you know' Dorcas laughed

'Is that a yes then, will you marry me, you heathen witch?'

'I don't know' she said seriously, 'there is a lot to be done here and not much time to do it in. We still don't know where this curse came from but I am forming an idea that I don't like very much.'

'Then we should sleep on it, it may not seem so bad in the morning.'

Dorcas doubted that very much but there were not many ways she could tell this man that her very life and soul would be in danger if she continued with this task. The words from Elshalamane had shocked and upset her but they also put a light on things that had been dark.

All her life Dorcas had fought against herself. There was something inside her that was trying to push her own self out, to obliterate the person she thought she was. In the depths of the night, she realised that this final battle was coming. There would be no hiding from it and it would mean that she would return to the earth in the Cycle of Natural Being. As a witch, Dorcas had no fear of her body dying but Jubal Sancreed still stood in the light and she had no wish to drag him to that place that she was surely going.

Darkness has its own set of rules,
cowering behind the blessed light.
- First book of the Elandine Grimoire

Chapter twenty-three

Three men, and a witch in a yellow dress, rumbled out of Pendartha and took the road that led west, out past the Lazard Point. Wheat and cotton waved feebly in the parched dry air, and although still very early in the morning, the heat rose from the fields in a shimmering haze. A month of relentless sun had bleached the once lush landscape around Pendartha and dried the roads to a reddish brown powder.

The travellers were silent, saving their energies for the task, which lay twenty miles ahead of them. The journey was difficult along the narrow, little used tracks and lanes and the cartwheels complained at the hardened potholes.

Dorcas looked at her protection squad, they were all as nervous as she was, but at least she had their physical presence, and that would count for something. Tregonning was a man built like a mountain and Jakey had huge strength in his upper body from working at the anvil all day long. Josiah, although the shape of a child's ball, was sturdy and would stand his ground if he had to.

The uncomfortable ride in the cart took them nearly four hours. The hot dry wind parched their mouths, and they stopped frequently to water the horse and wipe the dust that had caked their noses. It never got this hot in the north and although Dorcas had adapted to the summer heat, Josiah told her that it was not always like this.

'We will be due for a rotten winter if this keeps up into August. Storms always follow a parching summer.'

Dorcas asked if they ever had snow.

'Only once in my lifetime, to my knowledge. Many years ago, Pendartha was hit by every kind of weather that God could throw at it. We lost over fifty people that winter, it was awful.'

Dorcas dreamed of snow, not just a scattering, but the deep snow that they had every year in the north. Whole towns were cut off for weeks but it was expected and they were always prepared. She could see how much of a shock really bad weather would be to the southerners. Life would stop.

Unlike Pendartha in its shady valley, Porthaveland sat on top of the cliffs and surveyed the countryside around it like a king on a granite throne. There was nothing pretty or endearing about this town and even in the heat, it gave the impression of being cold and windswept all year round. As they passed the first few cottages on the outskirts, Dorcas could see that their gardens were all hidden from the relentless wind that blew off the sea. The few trees that managed to grow in the harsh landscape leaned inland.

Dorcas shivered as she caught her first sight of the infamous Porthaveland cliffs that dropped a hundred and fifty feet to the jagged, sea-washed rocks below. She tried to stop her imagination forming any more pictures and looked away to the barren, desolate moorland that surrounded the town. There was nothing comforting there either. The town was empty; a few people walked the narrow streets and dogs barked in the distance. It was Sunday, the day of rest and worship in the south, so most townsfolk were going about their business inside their own homes, escaping the sun that was now beating down above their heads.

The church stood out above everything else and the cart made its way to the square where the house of the southern God was situated. Like all Pagans, Dorcas had no problem with Gods and Goddesses of other religions. Her own deities took many forms from many different sources, and they were quite happy to include any that they found favourable or attractive. The southern God was different; the church demanded complete obedience and at least a once-weekly observance inside its chapel. Pagans worshipped wherever they fancied, taking delight in the open air and the elements, they needed no one place to focus their prayers to the Goddess. In the Pagan religion, rituals were observed in a light-hearted fashion, music and singing played a big part in any gathering held in the Goddess's name. Here it was all doom and gloom, fire and brimstone, hell and damnation. Dorcas found it all a bit miserable.

'The church would be a good place to start, the Preacher here will know everything that is going on in his town' Josiah had said.

As in Pendartha, the house beside the chapel belonged to the Preacher in residence. Jakey and Josiah knocked on the door. The Preacher Menkes had been taking a nap but proved to be very helpful. The Trewiddens lived on the road that led out the other side of the town and the man they sought was sure to be in today as he had attended morning service. He had left about an hour ago and had returned to eat Sunday lunch with his elderly aunts.

'His brother lives in the square,' Preacher Menkes said 'I could give him a knock if you like.'

Jakey politely declined.

Tregonning guided the cart through the town and onto the rocky coastal path. Dorcas could see the house in the distance and a wave of nerves flooded her body. She wished desperately that Jubal could have been with her but that would only have served to antagonise Trewidden further. In truth, they did not expect to get any answers from him but they were short of options. They needed to know why and how the Trewiddens were involved in all this.

As she had promised, Dorcas sat in the cart and waited for the men to knock on the door.

'We don't want to upset him before we have even crossed the threshold, especially if you are going to use that, what did you call it?'

'Fascination.'

'Yes, if you are going to fascinate him then we at least need to be inside the house.'

Josiah was right. Trewidden would probably take one look at her and slam the door in their faces and she needed to be face to face with him to achieve her objective.

Dorcas had used fascination on the pompous little customs officer at the border and he had been putty in her hands. Stanley would have given his right arm to have that skill but a witch trained hard to do it, and it was frowned on if it was abused. You could be held before the Council if it was deemed that you had used it to further your own ends. Dorcas had never found that particular skill difficult, she could reach into a mind and sway it to her will if she so desired but it was another thing that she kept hidden, even from herself. At a very young age, she had discovered that her coven sisters at Summerlands found it nearly impossible to take over the mind of even the smallest creature. When no one was looking, Dorcas had the white mice that they were practising on, nibbling pieces of bread from her fingers and rolling over onto their backs on the table begging for more.

'Then why did you not use this at your trial' Jubal had asked when she explained what her plan was. They had been sitting in the shade on her veranda discussing their next move and how they were going to persuade Augustus Trewidden to see them.

'I cannot fight against a mindset like theirs. When used on an individual it is effective, for the most part. I could not change the minds of a hundred or more people, it is not possible.'

'Can you not just reach in and take the information from him?' Jakey had asked.

'Robbery' Tregonning said gruffly.

'Exactly, I can persuade a mind to cooperate but I cannot steal from it.'

This was not strictly true. Deep inside Dorcas felt as if she was capable of doing just that, but as Tregonning had so succinctly put it, it would be like a kind of rape.

The large house in front of her was like a fortress, tall granite walls surrounded a barren, weed-infested garden and the only way in was through the iron spike topped gate. The Trewidden family home must have once been quite impressive, standing tall and proud over the surrounding countryside, it was the largest residence that Dorcas had seen in these parts. It was not a patch on some of the magnificent buildings in Masterbridge; they were all fussy turrets, carved gables, and rounded windows, but it spoke of old, established money. The once expansive roof was in disrepair, slates lay on the ground where they had fallen, and the windows looked as if a hard push would send them tumbling to join the tiles in the unkempt garden.

The door opened with creaky hinges. Dorcas held her breath; she was just close enough to hear what was being said, but was out of sight behind the boundary wall. The old woman who answered must have been one of the aunts, but she looked to be about a hundred years old, her voice was crackled and rough. Dorcas answered the call to the door and she joined the men on the doorstep.

'We have come all the way from Pendartha' Josiah repeated.

The hearing loss that afflicted the arthritic old woman was almost total and Josiah had to enunciate each word loudly.

'Pen-dar-tha.'

'Come in, come in. Augustus is not here but I am sure he will want to see you, he speaks often of his people.'

The reception hall was dark and dismal and in the same repair as the outside of the building. The expensive wallpaper was tired, discoloured, and hung off the walls in faded curls. They were shown into the parlour where a young woman appeared from another room and offered them tea.

'I am Eleanora Trewidden, Augustus is my nephew. My sisters will be down in a minute' the old woman said, offering them a seat on the tatty, threadbare velvet couches.

It was cool in the house and a draught whistled under the door and shot straight up the chimney as if it did not want to stay for long. Dorcas felt the same. The house had an air of derelict despondency about it, which was not surprising considering its occupants. Eleanora was as old and decrepit as the house and left a trail of mothballs and rancid cologne in her wake.

The parlour, in which they now sat, was a florid example of how a room should not be dressed. Ghastly ornaments jostled for space on the dark, marble mantelpiece and fussy, filthy chandeliers hung above their heads. There was a multitude of floral rugs on the floor that covered the stained and dirty floors and there was a dead plant on every other surface.

There were a few bumps and shuffles from overhead and Eleanora explained that Tatiana, her elder sister was mostly bed-bound but would be down to greet them presently.

'And Elvira is just making herself presentable; we don't get many visitors these days. Augustus will be so pleased that you have made the effort. All that trouble with that witch girl has made him quite ill you know, not himself at all.'

'Oh Goddess.'

The tea and the sisters arrived at the same time and they all moved seats to accommodate the fragile ladies. Dorcas could see straight away that they were not going to get any information from the elder Trewidden aunt. Her mind was already in the next world and nothing that came out of her mouth made any sense. Tatiana seemed content to sit and smile through everything, nodding and laughing at inappropriate moments and hitting Tregonning on the knee with her shabby fan.

Jakey Moyle looked horror-struck at the sight of Elvira, the youngest aunt. She had hastily applied some make-up to her paper-thin skin and half of it was running down her face. Rouge smeared her cheeks and stained her lips in a vicious red and her hair had been dyed to a shade of orange that would normally have been associated with ladies of the night. A pink bow sat askew in the hair and both clashed with the girlish green satin dress that hung from her bony body. Elvira, who had now sat down next to Jakey, was running her fingers up and down his arm, smiling coquettishly and leaning her head to one side in a very flirtatious manner. The blacksmith looked a little more than uncomfortable and had broken out into a sweat.

Josiah scratched his chin, something was not right here but he could not put his finger on it. He started the investigation with some gentle inquiries into their time in Pendartha. He was nervous and kept looking towards the door. Eleanora had already informed them that Augustus was walking his dogs and could be back at any minute. Josiah got on to his subject.

'I cannot answer any of your questions my dear man,' Eleanora said sweetly 'I'm afraid my nephew has given us strict instructions never to speak of that time. It is best forgotten, is it not sisters?'

'We think something happened at the Aggstone that resulted in a curse on the town. Would you know anything about that?' Jakey asked.

'No, no, no, you have got that all wrong, no harm was done, no harm was done at all. Augustus told us.'

The three sisters giggled childishly.

'That wasn't us; you have got it all wrong. Wait until Augustus gets here, he will tell you, we didn't do anything that night.'

'No, we didn't, nothing at all' Elvira cackled.

Tatiana nodded, laughed raucously, spilled her tea down her white lace dress, and dabbed at it with a stained antimacassar that she had pulled from behind her.

'Oh Goddess, give me strength.'

'No good calling the Goddess in this house. She has long been forgotten here.'

Dorcas looked around and found a sleek black cat stretched out on a rocking chair in the corner. With her eyes closed, the beautiful glossy feline gave no hint that she had even acknowledged their presence. Dorcas leapt at what looked like their last and best hope.

'Good afternoon beautiful lady, my name is Dorcas, would you, very kindly if you please, lend me yours?'

The cat purred, still refusing to open her eyes but Dorcas had her attention. The cat's ears swivelled as if to pick up the inner voice that was being directed at her.

'I am Jezabella, descendant of Aurelius and Zephonicus from the line of Carmenellanius, a true daughter of Bast.'

Dorcas was suitably impressed. Not only did this cat of the south remember how to talk to humans but announced her lineage proudly.

'Never have I seen a cat of such beauty and refinement and your parentage is truly remarkable.'

Jezabella preened and opened her eyes a fraction. Dorcas was not surprised to find that they were the colour of the deepest, purest serpentine.

'If I were to ask you some questions would you do me the honour of answering them truthfully?'

The tip of Jezabella's tail flicked slightly.

'I would never lie witch, it is not in my nature, and it is a pleasure to make your acquaintance, if you don't mind me saying. For so long I have been completely surrounded by imbeciles, it will be nice to talk to something with half a brain.'

Dorcas buttered the queen up as quickly as she could, males were so much more prone to flattery, but this one had been starved of anything for years and was lapping up every syrupy word that Dorcas said; and was craving more

'I would call on the generations of your esteemed family to help me solve a problem.'

'You wish to know of the sisters here and their curse, do you?'

'Yes?'

'It is no use asking them, they are as mad as dogs now, you will get no sense from them. I know what they did. My father knew of this and has gifted the knowledge to me.'

'And you would share it?'

'I will share it with you Dorcas Fleming, you have a smell about you, a smell of power, but you are walking the edge of a knife.'

As if sensing Dorcas's growing impatience the cat rolled over, stretched, and licked her paw. She was enjoying this exchange, it had been a long time since anyone had addressed her properly and she was going to draw it out for as long as possible.

'You are right, there is danger and that is why I need as much information as possible in order to combat this curse.'

Jezabella spread her toes and showed a fine set of hunting knives. She fixed her deep green eyes on the witch and drove them deep inside her mind, showing the pictures that were stored there.

'There was a storm, a fierce storm that took their men. They had the power you see, locked away inside from times gone by and that night they used it. Can you see it witch?'

Dorcas could hear the wind screaming.

'They called the power of the earth and cursed the sea with the power of the coven, and as you know witch, that it is not the natural order of things. They brought it to life with the power of thirteen, gave it an identity and a purpose.'

Dorcas was drawn deeply into the vision inside the cat's mind and was oblivious to the rest of the room. The sisters were still chatting amongst themselves but Jakey realised that the witch was in a kind of trance. The cat on the rocking chair sat up and stared straight at her through narrowed slits.

'It lives and grows and the Pendarthans feed it with their souls. You will feed it as well' the cat whispered cruelly in her mind. 'It will pull you in and take you to the other side. You can't kill it, it has grown strong over the years, nothing can stop it now.'

Dorcas felt a creeping in her mind and recognised it for what it was.

'No!'

Jezabella jumped down from the chair and stood at Dorcas's feet. Its demeanour had changed and it now appeared quite menacing.

'Never!' Dorcas cried aloud, jumping to her feet.

'It touches us all Dorcas Fleming and it knows your name.'

Dorcas snapped out of the spell that cat had woven and she threw it out of her system

'You are its servant, be gone from my mind, get out!'

The cat yowled as Dorcas aimed her boot at it.

'You are a disgrace to have turned so!'

'And you will turn too, I know it. Light and dark, they are both inside you but only one will win. Only one will win Dorcas Fleming.'

Dorcas kicked out again but the cat jumped at her, unsheathing the set of sharp daggers and aiming them at her face before leaping at the open door.

As Dorcas looked around, she realised that the men in the room were staring at her. The sisters were still prattling on about their beauty and their youth, oblivious to what was going on around them. Josiah handed her his handkerchief and she pushed it against the damage that the cat had managed to inflict on her neck.

'I probably don't want to know what just happened there but I think it is time to leave. These women are not going to tell us anything' Josiah said.

'We must get out of here now, the blackness taints everything and everyone here' Dorcas said quietly

Jakey and Josiah looked despondent. This was their last hope and if the answers were not here then where would they find them?

Pendartha could not go on as it was and Josiah once again let the notion of moving back to Port Morgan scuttle through his head. He had no wish to leave the place of his birth just when his wife was beginning to feel settled. It had only taken her twenty years and she would not be happy to be dragged away now. Josiah Penpol was a frightened man. Every day that he went to work for the sea was a day too long. For a man who had spent his entire life around the sea it was unthinkable that he should now be terrified of getting in the water or even being on top of it.

They left the house of the three mad sisters just as Augustus Trewidden was coming into sight along the cliff path. They saw him before he spotted them, Tregonning turned the cart around on a sixpence and they made haste along the rough track ignoring the two hunting dogs who were straining on their leashes.

'Used my own weapon against me,' Dorcas said tetchily when they were safely away from Porthaveland 'I cannot believe that I let a cat fascinate me. Me!'

'Do not worry yourself Miss Fleming, we will get our answers somewhere. I'm just glad that you are all in one piece, that animal had a nasty streak right enough.'

'That animal was, a servant of the dark side' Dorcas shivered 'but it told me what we need to know.'

'It did?' Jakey cried.

'It did,' said Tregonning 'I heard every spiteful word it said to Miss Fleming here. Seems that those mad bitches cursed the sea when they lost their husbands in a bad storm.'

Josiah and Jakey stared at their driver. Tregonning had not made a speech like that for years and the content of his words showed a deeper side to the man who lived amongst them.

For the rest of the journey home the three Pendarthans remained silent, mulling over the newest piece of their complicated puzzle. The witch also sat in silence, staring across the southern landscape with a scowl on her face. Dorcas was livid.

'A cat, a mere cat!'

Chapter twenty-four

Maghda wiped her muddy hands down her trousers and returned the fork to its resting place by the gate of the sty

'Another day done Bessie girl.'

The Tamhill sow looked at her with intelligent piggy eyes and then returned to the pile of scraps that Maghda had just delivered to her trough.

'An interesting mix' the huge pig observed sticking her nose into the large heap.

'Nothing but the best for my girl.'

The sun was sinking over the hill as Maghda stomped through the eternal sticky mud that surrounded the animal pens. She let herself out through the five bar gate that would take her over the lower paddocks and up to the path that led to her cottage. A bath was the order of the day and she had been looking forward to a good soak, her nose had been complaining of her own stink for days.

Sallington suited Maghda more than she could have anticipated. Working with the livestock was more than just a job and she had recently taken on a promotion that had delighted her. To be in charge of the piggery at her age was almost unheard of, especially in a place like this. Sallington was famous, and animals from all over the northern lands were brought here to breed with the best or to receive medical care from experts. Ideally placed in the loam-rich lowlands, the farm was really five or six massive farms joined together. Apart from the livestock, Sallington was the largest producer of wheat and corn in the north.

Maghda was one of thirty witches who served the Sallington community, dealing with animals and humans alike. Her morning had consisted of soothing Mavis Lamprey's inflamed bunions and then treating one of big Bessie's many daughters for itchmite. Her days were varied and fulfilling and her spirit was definitely where it should be, the Goddess could not have placed her anywhere better. Maghda was born to be at Sallington. All through the long years of training, she had never been truly happy. The others girls had complained constantly about her, berating her for moaning and groaning about her lot. Here she was happy, here she had come home.

In recent weeks, she had caught the attention of a hand in the equine quarters and had been seeing him on a regular basis. Maghda hoped that after her longed for bath he would make his customary visit to her small cottage; the thought put a smile on her face. Her ample proportions had not put him off, or her obsessive love of all things pig-related. Maghda thought herself lucky to have landed anyone, let alone someone who shared her obsessions. They had met over a pen of new piglets that she had just helped to deliver. The prim little saddleback had mated with a wild peccary and had produced ten hairy piglets that were already showing signs of their father's build and their mother's temperament.

'Wondered what all that noise was about, could hear it from the stables.'

'Ursula likes to let it be known when she is bringing new life into the world' Maghda had laughed.

'I heard.'

The sandy-haired boy had introduced himself as Jamie Parkhurst. He had just started working for Nevin, the horsemaster, but since that day, he tried to spend as much time as he could in the piggery. Maghda wasn't sure for a long time whether he was just interested in her charges or whether he was making a play for her.

Maghda whistled a ditty as she let herself into her house and pushed the kettle onto the already warming range. This was another bonus. When she had first come to Sallington she had been sharing with two other girls in a loft. Being head of the piggery had definite perquisites. Although small, barely more than one up and one down, Maghda loved her place and filled it with all the things that she had kept hidden away in a box under her bed at the college. As a naturally untidy person, she had suffered for years at Summerlands where things were put away as soon as you got them out. It was not much fun sharing with twelve other girls and Maghda's moods had reflected this. She had missed them all at first, even bossy Joan and vain Amberlynne, but Sallington was hers.

She had received letters from Joan, Maegwyn and Nancy; they said they were settled and doing well. Joan's letter was typically terse and to the point, only giving Maghda the barest facts about her placement in the capital. Maghda did not envy any of them but she did miss the times when they all got together to solve a problem. All the coven seemed to have been sent to the right places, all except one.

She hummed as she filled the bath and added the last of the rose oil that Amber had made her as a parting gift. The door knocked with a familiar tap-tap-tappity-tap as she put her left foot in the water. The door opened.

'Ah ha! Just waiting for me' Jamie said, his eyes taking in her nearly naked flesh.

'You are disgusting Mr Parkhurst, you can wait upstairs for me.'

'I have brought sustenance for our long night together' he grinned.

'Put the basket on the side and go! I need this bath, on my own' she added.

They had already tried squeezing into the bath together and it simply did not work. Jamie took another long lusty look and made his way slowly up the stairs. He would wait as long as it took.

*

Maghda stretched and yawned loudly, taking her time to open her eyes. It was a restday so there was no need to get up at the crack of dawn. The space beside her was empty and cold. It appeared that Jamie had gone, but when she eventually went downstairs, she found him sitting at the kitchen table. There was a pile of plates and cups in front of him.

'Couldn't sleep in? I know, I usually find it hard on a restday.'

'Got nothing to do with that' Jamie said grumpily.

'Oh?'

In the time, that Maghda had known Jamie she had not come across a mood before, that was her prerogative usually, and she did not take kindly to others who displayed the same symptoms.

'You sang all night and kept me awake.' Jamie grumbled 'I hope this isn't going to become a habit.'

Maghda was puzzled, no one had ever complained of her singing at night before and she questioned it.

'Same song, all night, over and over again until I nearly smothered you with a pillow.'

'Well, you can never accuse me of being boring, perhaps I didn't get enough of my own entertainment last night' she smirked.

Jamie's scowl softened into a smile, he could not be cross with Maghda for long, but she had driven him out of her bed last night with that daft tune.

She made a huge breakfast, one that included meat for her lover, and they made plans for the day. Maghda suggested that they take a walk along the canal and then on into Sallington town. Lammas

Sabbat was drawing near and the town would already have its decorations up. Maghda was looking forward to Lammas; everyone had told her that it was the most important Sabbat in this part of the world. Bringing in the harvest took them a whole week to celebrate and there was already an excited air about the place. The brewery produced a special apple ale called Cantago.

'Because you can't-a-go anywhere after a couple of pints of that stuff' Jamie had laughed.

He had come to Sallington a year before Maghda and had already experienced his first Lammas here. He could not remember much about it as his co-workers had introduced him to the lethal brew and he had been unconscious for two days. Everyone had told him that he had been the life and soul of the party.

Maghda, as all the workers on the huge farm, could buy essentials from its stores. Sallington was three miles away and provided anything else that she needed. As Masterbridge was only fifty miles away, the town was well stocked with surplus from the city.

'I need new drawers' she stated.

'And I will help you pick them' Jamie said with a naughty glint in his eye.

The walk along the canal was peaceful and quiet. The warm summer sun sparkled on the still water that was only disturbed by the odd longboat making its lazy way into the town with a cargo of coal, or cloth. The main industry of the town was the farm that almost entirely encircled it. Sallington dabbled with a few factories but most of it was made up of abattoirs and processing plants. Maghda had never had a problem with her witching and her job although mostly she was employed to preserve and extend animal life rather than eat it. She was not adverse to the odd bit of chicken when the fancy took her, chickens were not known for their intelligence and you could barely hold a sensible conversation with one anyway. Pigs on the other hand were highly intelligent and conversed smartly. Maghda would compare them with cats for humour and sarcasm.

'You are doing it again.'

'What?'

'Humming and singing' Jamie said.

She had been completely unaware of even opening her mouth but Jamie looked very grumpy. Maghda was not known for her fine singing voice; she could hold her own in a group but was not inclined to serenade anyone for fear of driving them away.

'I'm sorry, I was immersed in a problem I'm having with a piebald Wychester. He is suffering from some sort of scale and nothing I have tried has worked.'

Jamie offered a number of solutions that he had seen work with horses and while Maghda listened she pondered the humming problem.

She made her purchases and they had lunch by the canal. Jamie was still a bit grumpy and ate in silence and when she spoke he snapped back at her.

By the evening, he'd had enough and was ready to leave. Every time Maghda stopped talking to him directly, she started to whistle, or hum or worse. Now she was singing at the top of her voice.

'If you can't stop that infernal racket then I'm off, I can't stand it any more.'

'What is it, what am I singing?'

'Maghda please, you have tortured me all night and all day surely you know what you are singing.'

'I don't, there is no trace of it in my mind.'

'It's like a children's rhyme, you just repeat it. Na na, na na, na na, n....'

'The words, what are the words?'

'Come my sisters gather here...'

'Yes, yes of course I know it.'

The song was a witch's nursery rhyme, harmless, fun, and used by children everywhere.

Come my sisters gather here,
Let me know that you are near
Safe in light I call to thee,
Answer my prayer and come to me,
Come my sisters gather here,
Under a moon, that holds no fear.

Maghda had not thought of it for years, she remembered the clapping songs that her coven practised when they had first started at Summerlands. She had no idea why it should be stuck in her mind now.

'What does it mean? Is it a witchy thing?' Jamie said, a little more gently.

Jamie had been very blasé about Maghda's status. He had not had much to do with witches other than the one who had taken a rotten tooth out of his head when he was ten. To the general population witches were almost a different breed and they let them go about their business unhindered. Jamie did not have an opinion about witches in general but if he were pushed, he would have said that he would not willingly have got tangled up with one. Maghda was not like a witch; her cottage was normal, untidy, but normal. She also did not tend to wear the pointy hat very much, preferring a flat cap that kept her hair out of the pig muck. She was as down to earth as her job was and although he was aware that she used some of her skills when she needed to, she did not make it that obvious.

Maghda was silent and Jamie was expecting another rendition at any moment. He left her to her thoughts and said he would return on Thursday when he was on the early shift. Maghda kissed him distractedly on the cheek and sank into her armchair to ponder the spellweave that had been placed on her.

Maghda was, by nature, a very practical woman. With the job she had, it would not do to have hysterics when she had a problem, the pigs would not respond to her. Something, or someone, had felt the need to plant this tune in her head and there had to be a reason for it. When she looked at it objectively, she could see no reason for anyone to spellweave out of spite. Maghda had never attracted that kind of attention and she dismissed any jealousy about Jamie Parkhurst. No, there was no one here that would do this to her.

'Na, na, na, na, na….Shut up, I'm thinking!'

Now that it had been recognised, the tune became audible and kept playing in her mind repeatedly, the words rolling over and over in a never-ending loop. Tomorrow she could get a coven together and let them work it out, but at this rate, she might well be as mad as a snake by the morning. She relaxed her mind and reluctantly let it open up.

'All right I'm listening, who are you?'

There was a pause as if something was listening back.

'Come my sisters….'

Maghda concentrated.

'I'm here, you have got my attention, now who, or what are you?'

Maghda felt a slight change in the air like an indrawn breath.

'Come on then, I don't fear you, let me know what you want and

then leave me alone.'

She closed her eyes and let the feelings wash over her. There was no voice, just a hint, a sense of ....sea ...cotton ...sun...sea ... salt...south ...fear ...sea.

Maghda reached deeper than she had ever had too, focussing her mind to the sharpness of a needle and the answer came.

'Dorcas!'

The song stopped and there was a silence in her head that Maghda now realised had not been there for a while. It was replaced by a need inside her that she knew would be as relentless as the song unless she answered its call. Jamie Parkhurst was going to have to wait longer than Thursday.

Chapter twenty-five

It was just downright disconcerting to walk in on such a thing in the middle of the day. A person had no right to do those things and frighten innocent bystanders.

Anyone watching would have seen Minnie Gembo fleeing from the scene with her skirts hitched up around her knees. She had seen many things in her life that her mind could not explain but they had always been out of the corner of her eye, a fleeting shadow. This was odd, odder that odd, but she had seen it with her own eyes and it was real. Even though she had had plenty of dealings with the witch over the previous few months the vision before her made her take two steps backwards and fall over the low fence into a bramble thicket. She would still be picking the thorns from her bottom in the weeks to come.

'Serves you right for poking your nose in where it shouldn't be' she heard Lizzy saying to her when she told her friend what she had seen.

Minerva Alissa Gembo attracted gossip like a dog attracted fleas and Lizzy Mims ran her a close second. Hearsay and rumour were meat and potatoes to them and they gathered tittle-tattle as if was going out of fashion. They had been friends for years, sharing the goings-on in their town behind twitching curtains and cupped hands. Nothing happened in Pendartha that the two women did not know about and they were always first on the scene when disaster struck down some poor soul. Lizzy scoffed loudly when Minnie confided that she had joined the Pathworking group.

'Only so as you don't miss any titbits.'

Lizzy, infuriatingly, was right. Minnie couldn't argue with that particular statement. Dorcas Fleming had frightened the undergarments off her when she first came to town. Minnie's theory was that if she kept a close eye on her then she would be safe from the curses and hexes, as she would always know what was coming. It was an unsound theory, but Minnie felt better about the whole thing. Peggy Penberthy, in a fit of temper, once told her that she thrived on other people's misfortune, taking joy from their sadness, and making her own life seem better. Minnie, privately agreed; a bit of juicy gossip, or a tasty morsel of scandal always put her right. The Gembos were blighted with the same misfortunes as their neighbours, but it still did not stop her prying, and spying, on anyone she wanted to. She had watched the witch for a long time and often sneaked out late at night to see what she was up to. Her family got used to her little forays and Minnie made no excuses for them. She saw it as part of her job, imparting news to those that should know, like newspapers did in the big cities.

That morning, Minnie felt the need. She had not seen Dorcas Fleming since the last meeting when she told them more about the curse, and with Jubal Sancreed now back on the quay she could not do any more of her surreptitious probing. There was nothing for it but to take a walk up the coastal path, through the woods and take up her customary position behind the large oak tree to the side of Denzell's old cottage.

The witch was already up and about despite the hour, and Minnie found her sitting on her veranda as if she did not have a thing to do.

'Shameful. A woman with nothing to do in broad daylight.'

The witch was doing something but it had taken Minnie over an hour to realise what it was and even then, she did not believe what her own eyes were telling her. She was sitting, in a most un-ladylike manner with her legs crossed in front of her and her hands clasping something in her lap. As Minnie could not get a good look, she crept a little closer when she saw that Dorcas had her eyes shut tight. From her new vantage point behind a bush, Minnie saw that the witch was moving her lips. She was repeating the same thing over and over again. In her bent position, Minnie became uncomfortable and retreated to stretch her legs by walking up and down for a while in the thick woods that surrounded the cottage. When she returned things had changed and Minnie had to sit down and take a breath.

At first sight the witch appeared to be in exactly the same position but when Minnie, whose expert eye missed nothing, lowered her gaze to the floor she realised with horror that Dorcas Fleming was floating about ten inches off the wooden boards.

Minnie Gembo could have stayed there all day and found that nothing else changed but after her realisation, she made haste to the safety of her home. When Lizzy appeared for her customary cup of afternoon tea, she found her friend staring at the walls of her kitchen and could get no sense out of her for an hour.

Dorcas broke the connection and made herself a strong tisane of vervain, betony, and damiana known for their restorative properties. She drank two full cups before she felt back in the world once again.

'A tough nut to crack, this one.'

'You will find a way' Zebulonus said.

He was sitting on the kitchen table and had observed his witch as well as Pendartha's prime gossip. He eyed the small silver pig on the table.

'Perhaps she is not the one.'

Dorcas picked up the small amulet and put it against her forehead.

'No, she is the one but she is just not listening.'

'Will you try again?'

'I have to Zebulonus, there is no one else that I could connect to easily. I will try again and keep going until my pig-headed friend eventually hears my voice.'

The cat licked his paw and fastidiously cleaned the side of his face.

'You were watched you know, the monger of gossip was here again.'

Dorcas had been aware of the presence of Minnie Gembo, as she had been aware of her many times before. It was Minnie who had spread the rumours about her bedding with Jubal and the woman was responsible for many of her troubles in Pendartha. Dorcas had thought to shut her mouth once and for all, a small hex to alter the mind would do the trick and a lot of people would thank her but she could not be bothered. The world was full of Minnie Gembo's and if she quietened this one, then another two would surely take her place.

In the cool of the evening Dorcas tried again. Jubal was still out with his pots so she knew she would be on her own until it was fully dark. The smell of bread filled her nostrils threatening to overtake her concentration but that would have to wait until tomorrow when she had promised herself a break and time to celebrate the Lammas festival.

The crickets quietened as she brought the image of Maghda Cotton into clarity. With every ounce of power she could summon Dorcas gave one final push to the destination. There was nothing else she could do, she had given it her all, and it was now in the hands of the Goddess.

*

Since the trip to Porthaveland, many things had happened and Dorcas had not had much time to herself. It was time to stop, take stock, and observe some long ignored rituals in readiness for the Lammas Sabbat.

'I'm hungry' the cat said as she came in from the veranda.

'Jubal will be home soon, he promised to bring a pilchard.'

'Are you not meeting with the coven tonight?'

'No, we are all having a rest.'

It was more than a rest. They had worked so very hard but had come to a standstill, unable to go any further with their initial plan. When Dorcas had recovered from the indignity of being fascinated by the Trewidden cat, Josiah had called the coven together and Dorcas told them what had happened.

'But why would they curse the sea? Many lives are lost around here, we live by the sea and die by the sea' John Boslowek asked.

'Something happened a long time ago, there was a great storm. I thought some of you might remember.'

'There is at least one bad storm every year' Telfer said.

'The pieces of the jigsaw are all here, of that I am sure. We just need to put it all together. There are mysteries surrounding this and I don't understand it all.'

'Like the aunts. They should be in their sixties but they looked older than that, much older' Josiah said.

'That would be the curse.' Dorcas explained 'There is a rule called the threefold law. When you use magick to curse someone, or something, it comes back to you three times worse or more. Without the proper protections the sisters are living proof what un-shielded magick can do to people....'

Dorcas broke off. Something was coming this way and her senses were twitching like a branch in a thunderstorm.

'But how did they do this magick?' Siddie Jose asked.

'With a blasphemous book that had been passed down through the generations of mine own family.'

All eyes turned to the back of the meeting hall. Augustus Trewidden stood in the entrance. As he walked towards the circle of chairs they could all see the vivid scratches on his face and the eye patch that covered his left eye. He wore a floor-length coat that in better light would have revealed rust coloured stains.

'I will speak to Penpol, alone' he said.

There was a shuffling of chairs but Josiah put his hand up.

'These people have gathered together for the sake of Pendartha, they will stay and listen if you have anything to say.'

Trewidden looked as if he was going to argue and then thought the better of it.

'The new Preacher informed me that you get together in here and that he doesn't know what for. After you visited the Aunts I assumed it would be something like this.'

There was nothing humble about Augustus Trewidden's demeanour but Dorcas got the distinct impression that he had come here to help in some way. She kept her mouth shut until he addressed her.

'And you witch, still communing with those in league with the devil himself?'

'You spoke to the animal then?'

'Yes, and then I killed it' he said, matter of factly.

'It held your aunts under a spellweave; it was a servant of the curse.'

Trewidden nodded.

'Twenty-six years ago my mother and her sisters lost their husbands over the course of one winter. They turned to a book my family had hidden from the authorities many, many years ago. The curse was done at the Aggstone, by thirteen stupid women who had also lost souls to the sea. They cursed a creature of the sea and threw it off the cliffs. That is all I know.'

'We know most of that. Now we need to know how to get rid of it' Jubal said.

Dorcas could tell by his tone that Jubal was spoiling for a fight but by the looks of it, there was no fight left in Augustus Trewidden

'And the book?' Dorcas said hopefully.

'Destroyed, but it has made no difference. I have protected my family for long enough.'

'Your protection has destroyed lives' Jubal said and Dorcas noticed his fists were curled by his sides.

'Yes. I have no excuses. I thought I could keep it all under control until that witch came here.'

'I was sent. You called, I answered. You knew you were getting a witch.'

'A hedgewitch yes, but you are more, are you not?'

Dorcas shrugged and Trewidden turned to go.

'I am the last of the Trewiddens, they are all dead now, and I will join them soon. It must end now. I pray to God for your release but

I think that he has forsaken us. God help you all, but I fear you are beyond it now.'

*

They found the body of Preacher Trewidden in the harbour the next morning. There was a small service in the chapel that a few people attended and he was buried on consecrated ground out of town. The aunts were buried in Porthaveland and it was said that the graves were robbed the following day and the bones thrown over the cliffs.

*

'At least he tried to make some sort of peace' Josiah said.

'I wish he had kept the book, it must have been some sort of Grimoire' Dorcas muttered.

'Have you still no ideas about how to rid us of this thing?'

'Without the book to give us the clues? No, not at the moment although I have some ideas but I need time to work on them. I will need the coven and any other people who you think will be sympathetic to our cause.'

Dorcas had already driven the coven way beyond their capabilities, squashing years of training into a few weeks. Although fairly adept at Pathworking they had really only scratched the surface and she needed them to go much deeper.

'I don't understand' Jubal had moaned.

Dorcas had asked Jubal to join the coven in case any others should drop out. He had worked hard but his head was splitting and his eyes felt like two glass balls. Dorcas worked them hard and now she took a restorative with her for the end of each session.

'You are taking us somewhere aren't you?'

'I need to reach the deepest levels of Pathworking so that you can support me when I cross over into the other world. We cannot rely on abstract messages now. We have to get it from the horse's mouth, so to speak. We need answers and we need them now.'

Jubal did not like the sound of her words. As far as he understood, when Dorcas spoke of the otherworld, she was referring to the place that Pagans believed they went when they died.

'I must drink fully from the cup of Akasha at the next full moon before the Lammas Sabbat. The coven have to be strong enough to pull me back and bring me home again.'

'Are we there yet?' Jubal asked, knowing that the full moon was only a week away.

'You will have to be. The curse grows stronger every day and I do not know why.'

Dorcas did not want to tell Jubal that he was going to be her lynch-pin. Love was what bound the worlds together and his love would hopefully give her a reason to come back. Jubal Sancreed had a heavy weight upon his shoulders and one that he was, blessedly, unaware of for the most part.

The night of the full moon came all too quickly and once again, they gathered in Dorcas's sitting room. There were more of them this time so they took up positions on the floor to make more space. Dorcas sat in the middle and they began.

When they had practised at college Dorcas had never imagined that she would one day have to do this for real. It was all very well using your coven to look for a cure to an unknown illness but this was different. At Summerlands, deep Pathworking had always been done under the guidance of two or three Mothers or the High Priestess herself and although they had all experienced drinking from the Akashic cup they only did it in a sort of second-hand way. The Mother took them with her, guiding them through the pitfalls and making sure that they took the right turnings. It was a different thing to have to rely on a coven of heathens who did not know the God from the Goddess.

Within the invisible pentagram, Dorcas sat at the Akashic point and drifted with the tide of souls that were holding her up. She saved her strength for later and let them take her deeper and deeper into the veil. She could feel all of them and they all had their own signature. Josiah was red and solid; Telfer was greeny-white, steadfast and trustworthy. Tregonning was surprisingly strong and was represented by a bull. Minnie, Mags and Violetta were joined together, she could tell them apart but they were stronger as a whole. Jubal was her light, his strength of character showed itself as a red stag, a fitting totem. Others were around her supporting her and willing her on.

She left them and spun out on her own into the darkness. No light, no sound, no sensation of touch or feel.

'Goddess, hear me, bless me. God, hear me, bless me. Bless me with the sight to see and the knowledge to hear your words. We ask humbly for your counsel to deal with the coming darkness.'

Seconds passed and Dorcas opened her eyes to the pure white light that she was now bathed in. The Goddess and God had heard her words, they were going to listen to her pleas.

'Dorcas, Dorcas!'

She blinked a few times and Jubal came into focus, he was kneeling on the floor beside her.

'Are you all right?'

'Too soon. Too soon. Why did you pull me back?'

'You were gone from us for three hours' Jubal said gently.

Dorcas sat up and was aware of people stretching their stiff limbs and tea-making noises coming from the kitchen.

'I don't understand. There was nothing there.'

'There, there' Josiah said patting her on the arm 'you tried.'

'No. no, it was right, everything was in place. I reached it, touched it, drank from it.'

'Damn them. I was a fool to believe that they could do it.'

Violetta bustled in with a tray of tea.

'I made one of those teas for you. I wasn't sure which ones to use so I put a bit of each in.'

Dorcas did not care as long as it was hot and wet. Her mouth felt as if it had swallowed a desert.

'I, I…'

Dorcas felt a gurgle in her stomach. The gurgle grew to a rolling sickness that made beads of sweat form on her brow. The witch clutched at her stomach. Something was in there and it was trying to get out.

'Are you all right' Jubal asked.

Dorcas had gone a strange shade of green.

'It must be the tea, I always said it was a bit funny' Violetta said.

Dorcas could not speak; she was trying to talk her stomach into waiting until she got outside. She staggered to her feet but it was too late, the ball inside her was rising to the surface, filling her throat, and threatening to choke her air supply. The coven gathered around her, fearing for her safety as she dropped to her knees and gagged wretchedly. The vomit of words came tumbling out of her mouth and shocked them all into silence.

'Tulpa - demon - coven - thirteen there - Hagstone - twenty - six - years - Tulpa - grows - in - strength. Thirteen - times - thirteen -

to - mend - what - has - been - torn. High one - Wise one - Hag - and - True -witch - all - must - come …. Bledarrh - Maleficium - Grimoire - gathering … here - as - one.'

After wiping her mouth, she spoke again before collapsing into Jubal's arms. 'I have the knowledge.'

And it comes to pass that the weight of this knowledge is a burden to the heathen crone. Then is the time to loosen her grip, then is the time to strike as best ye may
- diary of Samuel Henwood, (witch finder.)

Chapter twenty-six

The Preacher Rowe shook his head in disbelief. It was one thing to realise that his parishioners were supporting a witch in their midst but a totally different thing to understand that they were all completely and utterly raving mad. The Mayor, a man of some considerable standing, related to one of the most esteemed families in Port Morgan, had stood here and proclaimed that the town was under the spell of a Tulpa.

'An ele-mental demon' Josiah had pronounced.

And this demon had been brought to life by the family of the previous Preacher with a forbidden book and that they themselves were descendants of the cursed Porthaveland witches. It was unthinkable. Now they were saying that a spell, a heathen ritual, had to be performed to rid the place of a supposed curse and that half the population were in on it.

Dorcas had stayed in the background, lurking towards the back of the chapel. A deputation consisting of the Mayor, Jakey Moyle, Telfer Meriadoc, and Tregonning had approached him after Dorcas had explained the meaning of the words she had spewed forth on the night of the Pathworking.

'Thirteen times thirteen means that one hundred and sixty nine souls will be needed Josiah, no more, no less, to rid the town of this evil. It has doubled in strength because it is now twenty-six years since the curse was invoked, and it will never stop. It will only grow.'

Dorcas had fervently wished that she could have called on the whole of Summerlands. There was always a number of power there, trained and willing. Once again, she let herself wallow in the misery of homesickness.

'And you can do it?' Josiah interrupted.

'It is my task. It is why you called and why I was sent.'

In the deep of the night, Dorcas had told Jubal what it entailed and his first reaction was to flee.

'We can leave,' he said simply 'you can't put your life, your very soul on the line for a bunch of people who don't even trust you enough to tend to their boils.'

'It is my destiny Jubal. I, apparently, have the makings of a truewitch, a full witch, total power.'

'And you want this?'

Dorcas did not know how to answer, but she knew that all her life she had been waiting for something to happen. Deep inside there was this other thing, a power that she had kept a tight grip on, only tapping into it in a very mild way.

'It is part of me' she said simply.

'Like hiding your scar? I saw it on May Day' he said in explanation to her puzzled look.

'It has always been inside me, trying to find a way out.'

'Like fur ball.' Zebulonus said.

'If you like. I have to use it, otherwise it will eventually consume me and kill me. The battle to keep it under control has become increasingly difficult over the last few years. I am somewhat glad that there may be a resolution to this.'

Jubal had read the quote from the leader of the Pagans and it was not exactly comforting reading. He knew now that Dorcas was going to go through with it and he had no choice but to stay with her and try to pull her out the other side. Now that he had found a woman he could trust he had no intention of letting her go.

*

Here in the chapel the Preacher Rowe tried, and failed miserably, to understand the goings on in this, his first parish. He would have to inform the authorities and his mind was racing ahead, planning his escape from this hellish town. They were all mad, of that he was certain, mad or under the fluence of the witch in their midst.

Dorcas stepped forward. The time for pussyfooting around had long since departed.

'See me not' she said.

The Preacher looked at the palm that was raised before him. As soon as he was fascinated, Dorcas uttered another incantation and he turned and left.

'Useful' Tregonning stated.

'He will not bother us; he will take up gardening and ignore what is going on around him. It will only last until my attention is directed elsewhere. There is much to be done now and we must make a start. We cannot have the whole of the southern church on our heels while we prepare.'

*

'One hundred and fifty-five,' Telfer reported the following week 'Marnie Tregunna is hanging on the brink but I think that Siddie can persuade her.'

'Not enough' Josiah said.

It was more than Dorcas had hoped but the Mayor was right, it was still not enough.

'My cousin in St Zenno would probably help, I'll go tomorrow' Jakey added.

The Pathworkers that Jubal had dubbed 'the cursing club' had worked hard, wheedling and coaxing the Pendarthans to join their cause. With a few exceptions, the response had been positive. Josiah had wondered why a spot of fascination would not draw in the rest of the numbers they needed.

'Free will' Dorcas had answered 'they have to be there by their own volition, I cannot fascinate the whole town Josiah, and I could not keep it up for long anyway.'

The day before Lammas, they came to a halt and Dorcas had only one choice left. She would have to try to contact the north and bring some more down here. There was just enough time for them to make the journey if she could get her message through.

Dorcas had judged the best time to deal with the Tulpa would be Samhain Sabbat, when the veil between the worlds was at its thinnest and she could tap into the natural power of both worlds and take the thing home to where it belonged. That was the plan.

Her coven had been the obvious choice to call and Maghda had stuck out above them all. Although Ginny had been her closest friend at Summerlands, it was Maghda with whom she felt the most affinity. She took the small silver pig from the dresser and rubbed it between her fingers. *Maghda.*

She had spent many hours reaching with her mind into the darkness, testing and probing. She knew Maghda was there, pictures of sties, straw and an overpowering smell of manure had come to her. Why would she not listen?

The child's song had come to her in a flash. Maghda had always been irritated by the mundane droning words of some of the everyday incantations that the students had to practice. Dorcas would drive her mad until she listened.

'Is it done?' Jubal asked on his return from the quay.

'As much as I can do. I just hope it is enough.'

*

By the time Mabon Sabbat arrived, Dorcas had all but given up hope of any help forthcoming from the north. She had spent the month trying to prepare the frightened townsfolk for the task ahead. Some had pulled out and others had come forward. The numbers had grown and diminished with the daily tides.

There was also a new problem to deal with. As word spread of the physical presence of the Tulpa in the sea, the fishermen became too afraid to take the boats out. Pendartha had become a dead port with no boats going out on the tide and none coming in. Nearly all the families in Pendartha relied on the sea for their sustenance in one way or another, but now there was nothing. If the fishermen could not get out to fish then Pendartha would slowly starve to death and the curse would have complete control.

Illness ripped through the population and there was a general air of despondency that no one seemed able to lift. On Dorcas's instructions, Josiah organised jolly gatherings to lift minds and spirits, but it was hardly worth the effort.

'These are dark times' Josiah said as they sat alone in the meeting hall. Violetta had gone to great lengths to provide a warm supper that was to coincide with a sing-song around the battered old piano.

'We cannot give up Chief, there is too much at stake. Pendartha will not survive the winter if we fail to raise the appropriate numbers for the coven' the witch said wearily.

Dorcas had tried to support all the events that they had arranged but her resources were diminished and she was losing hope. She was beyond exhaustion. She spent every day doing her rounds, trying to keep her coven healthy and happy, tending to their physical illnesses and their depressions. It was a task that took her away from home from morning until late at night and sometimes she never made it to her bed at all.

The Pensilvas all had the flu and she spent nearly two days administering steam inhalations and poultices to keep their lungs free of secondary infection. As she opened the door to leave the small cottage on the hill, she found a breathless Mordecai Leven panting on the step.

'Come, you have to come. The curse has taken flight over the sea.'

Dorcas groaned inwardly, she was in no fit state to deal with anything today.

As they reached the wharf Dorcas could see that the Pendarthans had done their usual and had come out in force to witness an impending disaster. Mordecai announced her passage through the crowd and she joined Jubal and the rest of the committee at the end of the quay. Many were clinging to each other and Jakey Moyle had even tethered himself to a post in case a freak wave should try to take him as it did Grenville Simmons.

Jubal pointed out to sea and Dorcas followed his directions. In the bright glare from the sinking sun there appeared to be what looked like a flock of black birds sitting in mid air just outside the sea entrance to Pendartha. They just hovered there, not retreating, but coming no nearer. It was as if they were waiting for something.

'Tis the curse, it is rising up from the sea, we are doomed' Violetta said dramatically, holding her hands in front of her face as if to ward off the impending evil.

Dorcas squinted out to sea and then laughed aloud.

'That is not the curse. That is my coven. They have come.'

Violetta fainted into her husband's arms and without thinking, Dorcas called for a broom. With a small incantation to the hastily-found, nearly-bare brush that Josiah kept in his office, Dorcas rose majestically into the air. She left the quay, and an astounded, silent crowd, behind her.

No one got much sleep that night. The Pendarthans lay awake in their beds trying to fathom what their eyes had seen and Dorcas lay on the floor of her bedroom, surrounded by things that were familiar and comforting to her. Jubal retreated to his own cottage leaving the Summerlands coven to unite once more.

'Did you see their faces?' Amberlynne laughed.

'I am surprised that we did not kill anyone, I thought some were just going to keel over and pop their clogs there and then' Nancy said.

Joan let out a snort of exasperation.

'How you have survived down here I'll never know.'

'And how do you understand a word that they are saying, it's like a foreign language?' Eliza said.

'I thought the dialect around Sallington was bad enough' Maghda added.

Their arrival certainly caused a stir. Floating gracefully in on their besoms, they landed on the quay like so many settling crows.

'Oops, bit out of practice with the landings, not much call for it in the mountains you know' were the first words that the townsfolk heard from her coven.

Violetta opened her fluttering eyes as the women dusted themselves off and smoothed down their black travelling cloaks. She promptly fainted again at the sight of Joan's tall pointed hat.

Dorcas looked around at them all. She had greeted each one individually and had been delighted that Ginnifer Belle was with them. Ignoring the amazed looks from the inhabitants of the town, the young women greeted each other noisily with hugs and kisses.

Josiah cleared the quay and they made their way straight to Dorcas's cottage. It was one thing to have one witch in their midst, but a gaggle of them was more than most could bear. This would take some getting used to.

The Summerlands coven did not stop talking for two days, glad to be back in each other's company and catching up on news of their travels and work.

'So how did you all get here, I mean, all together?'

'Well, after you had nearly driven me to plunge a knife into my heart, I went straight to Elshalamane at Masterbridge.' Maghda said 'They knew Dorcas, they knew all about you, and they have done for years.'

'We weren't supposed to know when we were all at Summerlands, that's the rules' Joan said.

'You are different now' Bridget said, she had been studying Dorcas for a while.

There were nods all round.

'In what way?' Dorcas asked.

'Free' Ginny said simply.

'That would be the spellweave that they placed around Dorcas to protect her and us' Joan said with authority. 'I read up on it as part of my studies. Truewitches have to find themselves with no help from anyone else.'

'That was why the High Druid put up such a fight against us coming here, otherwise we would have been here much sooner' Maghda said.

'Then how did you do it?'

'Ellen helped,' Manae said 'she was sent to Summerlands because of you, because of Mother Lylas who spotted you first. But it took Enid on the Lanshire Downs to confirm it, she is a truewitch herself.'

Dorcas took some time to soak in all this new information.

'That is why Ellen wore all those amulets and udjats, she was protecting herself from you! She had us all cleansed before we could take up our posts' Ginny laughed 'and you owe me a graduation ceremony by the way. I somehow missed mine.'

Ginny went on to explain as best she could.

'Ellen, had to get me away quickly, we were getting too close.'

'I still don't believe that a High Priestess needed protection from me?' Dorcas said.

'In case you leaked' Gwenna said as she smothered Dorcas's hands with a new mallow and rose hand-oil that she had just developed.

'And in case you pinched anybody's hands to make a cake!' Maghda giggled 'I didn't know what had come over me at Yule and it was you, wasn't it?'

Dorcas admitted to tapping into Maghda's skill and apologised.

'No apologies, I made seven cakes that day, the pigs were in heaven.'

Somewhere near dawn, just before they all finally went to sleep Dorcas asked a question.

'You know why I called you don't you?'

The coven sobered as she outlined the plan.

'We also know the risks Dorcas Fleming' Manae said.

'Then you know more than me' Dorcas smiled 'this is unknown.'

'Well, we can handle that I'm sure' Joan said quickly. There was no need for Dorcas to know that she held many souls in the palm of her hand. The Summerlands coven knew the risks, and each and every one of them had agreed to come without a moment's hesitation. Joan doubted they would have done the same for her.

'Anyway, that is a month away,' Eliza said 'we could have some fun before then.'

Dorcas was too tired to make any argument, she would explain her role in this town tomorrow, but she went to sleep with a slight dread in her heart. She knew exactly what her coven could be like when they all got together.

*

'Can you not keep them under control?' Josiah said with more than a hint of desperation in his voice.

Dorcas suppressed a rising giggle and solemnly told the committee that she would endeavour to set some ground rules for the witches.

'We can't have them running all over the place causing havoc. They are frightening people' Violetta said petulantly.

'I think they are bringing a much needed spark back to this town' Morwenna said decisively.

Dorcas was thankful to the old woman who had befriended most of the coven but she could see that they were a problem. Joan was the only one who was sensible enough not to upset anyone with displays of magick in the square, or to teach the children how to mesmerise frogs.

'I am taking them up the Hag Stone tomorrow, I think that should cool them off a bit.'

'It wasn't like that with you, you have really been no trouble at all' Violetta said.

'Thank you, that is why I was sent here, but they don't mean any harm.'

'That's as maybe but we can't have them running naked all over Pendartha.'

'Josiah, I hardly think that is true. They held an Esbat in my garden and yes it was sky clad but there was no one around except...'

Minnie Gembo had the decency to look a little ashamed.

'I will talk to them' she added.

Josiah did not know the half of it. The coven were having a riot and the local men were all in danger of losing their reputations. Nancy and Maegwyn were openly pursuing the Tremain brothers and Amber had taken a shine to Leven Portloe who helped Jubal out on the quay. She was stalking him with a determination that would outdo a panther.

'You have to stop' she said 'it is not like the north here.'

'We are only having a bit of fun' Maegwyn said sulkily 'it's like the old days in Brexham.'

'This is not the old days and this is not Brexham,' Dorcas said firmly 'they still hang witches down here you know. Besides which, I cannot teach you all the finer points of the ritual intended for Samhain when your minds are full of sex!'

Dorcas filled them in on her brush with southern law and the power of the church and they eased up for a while. She also found them jobs to do to keep them out of mischief. Gwenna and Anne helped with her rounds and Joan and Manae ran the chemist's shop in her kitchen. They had knocked out more poultices and infusions than she alone could have managed and Dorcas had to admit that both she, and the Pendarthans, were on the road to recovery. Maghda joined up with Jakey Moyle and was working with a sick horse and Amber was doing what Amber did best. Dorcas noticed very quickly that she had left her mark wherever she went and Violetta was positively glowing from the pampering she had received.

'Mad old bint' Amber had exclaimed when Dorcas had praised her ministrations to the Mayor's wife.

'Amber!'

'I don't know how you survive down here. They are so, well, antiquated, and all that gingham, yuk.'

Dorcas laughed.

'You get used to it.'

Dorcas had been trying to calm them down with a well-timed sighting of the Tulpa. She had eyes and ears on the sea in the form of Foggy Isaacs but he had seen nothing at all. It was almost as if the demon had known she was watching and kept its head down for a few days.

'Perhaps it has left' Maghda said,

It was true that there had been no more deaths but no soul had ventured on the sea for over a month now and Dorcas had the feeling that it was still lurking out there, somewhere. Deep in her mind's eye she could still see its black form boiling under the now calm waters of the harbour. This was not a time for complacency. If it had gone, she would know about it, she was sure of that. The time to call it forth was nearly upon her.

Jubal kept well away from the coven of witches holed up in Dorcas's house. Zebulonus, on the other hand, was spreading himself evenly amongst the newcomers and revelling in the attention that the northern women lavished on him. Dorcas herself could only take so much and she escaped every few nights and joined Jubal in his own cottage.

'Even I despair of their antics and I now realise why I so longed for peace and quiet at Summerlands.'

Jubal lay in bed looking at her.

'They are still talking about us you know.'

'Who?'

'Everyone. I think I had better make an honest woman out of you.'

Dorcas turned her face to the window and gazed out at the nearly full moon. It was two days until Samhain and her mind was filled with the duty ahead of her. She had sought solace with this man and now she was regretting it. It had been this way her whole life, never able to get close to anyone, for one reason or another. She forced her mouth to smile and her arm reached out to pat his hand.

'After the ritual' she said.

He seemed content with her answer and Dorcas sent him into a peaceful sleep. She watched as his face relaxed into dreams of the future knowing that this night she could not follow. The path in front of her was one way, there could be no turning back once she had set foot on it.

'And wherever I am after it is done Jubal Sancreed, I will know that at this moment in time I think I was loved, and it will have to be enough.'

This is magick at its purest.
Blessing, gift, misfortune, and iniquity all rolled into one.
Primordial power, older than the epoch, it uses the user and
can destroy kings and countries in the blink of an eye.
Truewitch beware, the blade is thin, and thy very soul is at
stake, drink not for long at the chalice of evil,
or be ruined and damned
— Book of Riuitha Dei Faiarh.

Chapter twenty-seven

Dorcas checked the circles once more. Maghda, Ginny, and Joan sat on nearby rocks and watched her every careful move. She finished the inner circle that encompassed the Hag Stone with a last sprinkling of salt, satisfied now that it was truly complete. Choosing to start the ritual in the daylight meant that there was less room for mistakes in the darkness. The circles were consecrated and one of the coven would keep watch until it was time. Dorcas placed her knife and salt pots on the grass and gazed out to sea. The wind was biting, blowing in from the sea but the skies were blue and clear. Dorcas could detect no malevolence before her but her soul recognised a signature. It was there, out there, waiting for her.

Joan shivered and pulled her cloak around her tightly. She, above the rest of the coven knew what Dorcas was going to have to face tonight. In her work at Masterbridge, she had gleaned much information from loose tongues and drunken conversations. Although still in the lowly position of apprentice, Joan had been privy to things that the rest of the coven could not imagine. In their world of Hedgewitchery, life was simple and straightforward, but in the bowels of the capital there were covens who wielded more power in a fingertip than a country witch would see in a lifetime. The great libraries held books that were under lock and key for their own safety and it was said that the High Druid had books in his offices that were as old as time itself. This knowledge had not helped Joan, she was now as nervous and jittery as the rest of the coven. She had expected Dorcas to be anxious as well but her coven sister now looked the epitome of calmness and serenity.

The previous two days had been hard and Dorcas had been snappy and irritable then. Josiah had come with the news that one of the Pendarthans was pulling out and it had sent her into a frenzy of panic.

'They cannot pull out now, they knew that they had to make a commitment and keep to it, so much depends on the numbers. Typical of this lot, heathen bastards.'

Ginny had taken her off for a couple of hours up into the wooded valley and she had returned with a calmer frame of mind.

'Minnie Gembo has been in your absence,' Maghda said 'her cousin is taking the place of the one who pulled out.'

'It will be all right. I'm sorry I lost my temper,' she said to the members of her coven who were gathered in the kitchen 'there is just so much to do.'

'Tell us Dorcas, we can't help unless you give us instructions. You cannot shoulder this alone and you do not have to. This is why we came, for one of our own' Eliza said gently.

'It is all in my head and I think if I impart any of it to you I will lose it.'

'Share,' Joan said 'we will hold it for you.'

'The trouble is I'm not sure that I am allowed to. This seems to be something I have to do on my own.'

Maghda pointed out that she had already called for help when she sent the rhyme to her. Dorcas relented and the women took some of the burden that was threatening to drag her under.

Maghda watched her casting the circles of power on the cliffs with a profound admiration. She had never seen a threefold circle that was so intricately laced with both sigils of power, and protection. Dorcas had used her athame to carve invisible runes on the four watchtowers of north, south, east and west and then add some ancient runic symbols that she had never seen before.

'How did you do that?' she asked, drawing alongside Dorcas's besom on the flight back to the cottage.

'It is in my head like a black outline on a white background. It was laid out on the grass, I just had to follow the drawing with the salt and water, and we will fill it in with the light later.'

'It will be all right' Maghda said after a while.

'I hope so. I have done as much as I can do, it will be up to you lot to hold me tonight.'

Two hours before sunset, Dorcas lay on her bed and wrote the last few lines in her Book of Shadows. She knew what she had written but it seemed unreal in a proper kind of way. The last pages contained her wishes for what was to be done with her things when this night was over. She had also written a long letter to Jubal that mostly contained advice for getting on with his life.

> *You know I have no choices but if I did, then I would spend the rest of my life with you. I know you have never told me that you loved me and here in the south it does not seem like a thing that people do so naturally in the north*
>
> *I love you Jubal Sancreed but I do not hold you to this love. Take it in your arms and then throw it out to the wind where I will be waiting. I know you do not hold with many of my beliefs and practices, but I know that you believe in me and I thank you for that.*
>
> *Merrypart Jubal, and may we meet in the otherworld where there will be no hindrance to our joining.*

With the final entry in her Book of Shadows complete, Dorcas pushed it under her pillow and dressed for the ritual. She had bathed and performed the cleansing ritual along with the rest of the coven. Done in silence and solemnity the coven were now as one as they had been for thirteen years at Summerlands.

The Pendarthans had left the town an hour before and as the witches flew over the darkening town it appeared deserted and ghost-like. Those who had declined to be one of the hundred and sixty-nine were now locked inside their houses praying that dawn would come quickly, if it came at all.

Dorcas felt the wind hit her face as they cut up over the cliff and past Foggy's cottage. He had placed a solitary candle in the window as if to wish them luck.

'*They will need that and more*' she thought.

The lights from the many torches glowed in the distance as the coven made their way over the barren cliff tops. Jubal had declined her offer of a lift on her broomstick preferring to keep his own two feet firmly planted on the earth.

'One day,' he had said 'when there is not so much at stake if I fall off.'

The coven landed to the side of the ring stone and they could see Manae talking to some of the townsfolk. The coven had kept vigil all day, swapping with each other every couple of hours, making sure that nothing was disturbed.

Josiah was a little in awe of the witches who were all dressed alike in their cloaks and hats with the points. Dorcas's new hat was finally getting its first outing and underneath she was wearing her purple velvet dress that had remained in a box from the day she bought it in Brexham. Floor length with long floating sleeves, she had added every silver amulet and udjat that she possessed. Around her wrists were thick silver bangles, engraved with the Eye of Horus and they clinked and jingled as she walked towards her waiting coven.

Jubal thought he had never seen her look so beautiful as she took off her cloak and hat and cast them aside. He saw that her long hair was unbound from its customary stringent bun and fell to her waist in a glossy sheet.

'You look like a High Priestess that I used to know' Maghda had teased before they left her cottage.

'I only steal from the best and besides I have to have every bit of providence with me tonight, I think I need it. Is it too much do you think?'

'It's your show, make the most of it' Maghda said.

'Good, then let us get on with it.'

The coven formed themselves into two circles. The outer one consisted of the ring of Pendarthans and the coven took the inner one. All had been careful to tread exactly where they were told as they took up their positions on the night when the veil between the worlds was opaque.

As they had been drilled, the whole coven performed the cleansing ritual, sharpening their minds and honing them to attune to Dorcas as she stepped into the middle. She stood facing out to sea and directly in front of the hole in the Hag Stone with the two circles around her.

'So, this is it, what I must do, what I must become, and what I must leave behind.'

With a deep breath, she addressed the waiting coven.

'Thirteen called this demon of the sea and thirteen times thirteen must witness its demise. Stay strong and do not waver even though you be tempted. Act as one together and bring the light to this sacred circle.'

The candles were lit and passed around; the circle of light was complete and whole, it was time. Silence enveloped the people gathered on the cliff top as Dorcas took up her athame and chanted the first part of the incantation.

Lords of the watchtowers,

Protect this circle as we call the name of the veiled ones.

We call on the Cailleach, wisdom is needed

We call on Aine, strength is needed.

Horus, bring us clarity

Sekhmet, give us courage.

In this time of Hecate, we call her name.

Bless us with your power of banishment.

So mote it be.

The circle remained tight as Dorcas spun three times deosil and drew a glyph in the air with her knife.

'Focus' she heard from the inner ring and recognised the authoritive voice as Joan's. Nothing had happened and some of the Pendarthans were starting to get cold and stiff.

'It's not coming, perhaps it is gone' a voice from the back said.

'Patience' Eliza hissed 'these things take time.'

Dorcas's senses were wide open as she strained to detect any change in the ether. Doubt started to creep in and she pushed it away as a tinge of blackness entered her mind. There was a gasp from Violetta as a coldness tangibly saturated the air.

'It cannot permeate the circle, it can only test you, be strong, and hold your God in your mind' Dorcas said.

When they were training, the Pendarthans had been surprised that Dorcas and her coven had positively encouraged them to focus on an image of their own God.

'They are all aspects John Boslowek, you southerners just choose to acknowledge the one.'

Dorcas hoped that they would be strong enough to hold that picture because something was starting to happen.

'Fill us with the power of your guiding light' Dorcas implored.

The air crackled for a minute and then all was still.

'Call it, it will come' came a voice that was not a voice, but swept through her mind like a silken scarf.

Dorcas looked at Jubal who stood directly in front of her. He was the only Pendarthan in the inner circle and his presence there was another loving essence to which she would try to journey back to when it was all over. She smiled, the voices of the Goddess were with her.

'Call it Dorcas Fleming. It will come to your bidding.'

Jubal had almost lost the power to focus. Dorcas was before him and she shimmered with the unbound power that she had kept locked up for so long. His mind flicked over the events that had shaped the man he was today. The witch had got under his skin and drawn him out of the tangle of emotions that he too had kept under lock and key. She had set him free, allowing him to feel again. Now it was too late to put those emotions into the words he longed to say to her.

'We bring it now' she called out.

The inner coven took over. The townsfolk had all been twitchy about calling the names of power and dread and were happy to let the trained witches do it on their own.

Djinn of the water
Tulpa of the sea
Servant of the negative
Thief of souls
Come forth and show thyself

All eyes were drawn to the boiling waters out to sea and in the grey light of night, the coven witnessed the rising Tulpa as it pulled itself from its watery nest. Unable to resist the call, it hung in the air, huge and dense, as a cloud of thick oily blackness.

'It comes, be strong' Dorcas demanded, feeling the horror that was already creeping through the ranks of her novice army.

Slowly, slowly it was hauled away from its comfort and was drawn to the Hag Stone from whence it had come.

Holey Stones were more than just a focus of power, in times gone by the wielders of the black arts had used them to draw influence through the hole where negative power was said to gather. Dorcas wished to draw the Tulpa through the hole to reduce its power and diminish its strength. Every ounce of her being was now fixed on luring the cunning demon to the place of its demise.

The power of the joined coven was strong, stronger than even Dorcas could have imagined and the thing came forward like a dog on its belly. Many of the Pendarthans shut their eyes as it came to a halt over their heads. It blotted out the moonlight, sucking some of the radiance from the circle of candles. It pulsed above them, obedient to the call of power, subservient to the wakening force that was housed in the truewitch below it.

Dorcas held her athame before her, mouthing another incantation as she sought to drag it down towards her. A bulge formed in the middle of the black cloud as the demon was drawn closer to the ground. As it got nearer Dorcas's ear picked up a new horror. Faint sounds of screaming, keening voices that pleaded, beseeching release. Their howls were nearly drowned in the wind that had come with the Tulpa but many in the circle heard them calling and joined their wails with ones of their own.

'Be strong, you must be strong, we have called it and it has come, it is under our fluence. It carries the souls of your loved ones.'

The coven groaned as the witch put their worst nightmares into words.

'And they must be freed,' Dorcas cried encouragingly 'we can send them back to your God, we have it now, work with me!'

A low snigger entered her mind and built into a malevolent threatening laugh.

'Caught I?' the voice of the Tulpa boomed 'Tis you that is trapped witch woman. You are mine. Now I will have thee.'

Dorcas stood in horror, the athame tumbling to the ground at her feet.

'Stop! We have been tricked. The demon answers for the deities. It comes on its own accord, not our calling.'

More laughter came from deep within the evil form.

'And you hoped to negate I? Small thing, thou knowest not mine power.'

Doubt, terror, and dread raced through Dorcas's mind. She had been so sure of the power of the coven but it would be much easier to give in now and let it do as it willed but the souls of the coven around her held her fast as she wavered.

Dorcas was knocked sideways and a seed of fascination planted itself, tugging at her soul and pulling her towards the dark side, tempting her with promises of power.

'We can use that power together, together we can be as one. No one shall harm us. Come to me, be with me,' it slavered 'I shall love you Dorcas Fleming, beyond all, and you shall be free'

'No!' she screamed but Dorcas was aware that her resolve was weakening.

'Freedom, you will be free of all this.'

The lure of the dark forces that could be at her disposal was persuasive and enticing.

'Be mine, be with me.'

Dorcas held on and called on the powers of the earth once again, and with each incantation, more voices joined with hers. They called on the Gods and Goddesses, imploring their help and protection but Dorcas was losing, her will was fading.

Only a step away, it could all be over. What do I care for these people? What have they done for me? I have no true friends here. My coven despises me as much as these inhabitants of this Goddess forsaken town.'

Dorcas took one more step towards the maw of the demon.

To the surrounding coven, many things happened at once. The Tulpa began to swirl above causing a stinking wind to whip up the hair and cloak of the mesmerised witch as it circled the coven. The demon spun faster, working itself into a maelstrom that dragged the air around it and drew it into its core. It was winning.

Dorcas found herself enveloped in light, and time, for a moment, stood still. The Tulpa was still above but Dorcas herself was cocooned in a moment of safety.

'Choices Dorcas, one must always look at the choices.'

'Lylas?'

The old woman nodded. Her form was wispy and opaque. Both women were bathed in the protective light that nothing could penetrate. She had been given a breathing space, the demon could not touch her, but it would not last for long.

'I called them Lylas, the deities, but they did not come. I cannot fight this on my own. It is winning, my resolve is fading, I know it.'

'They are here child, waiting.'

'Waiting!' Dorcas cried *'The time is now, do they not see this thing before us? Why do they not come to me, help me, I am nearly lost, I cannot hold out.'*

'They see Dorcas but they wait for your decision.'

'I have made my decision Lylas, tell them.'

Lylas smiled and Dorcas caught a glimpse of the old woman as she would have been in her younger days.

'I taught you the basics of good and evil, the yin, or the yang, the black or the white, which will be yours child?'

Without the influence of the Tulpa, Dorcas saw much more clearly, it was simple.

'It offers me a life' she said.

'I know.'

'I do not want to die.'

'I know.'

'But that is not my choice, is it?'

Lylas took her hand and drew her spirit around the two circles

'And you would give up everything for these people?'

'Yes' Dorcas said sadly *'I will and I must.'*

'For him?'

Dorcas looked at the immobile face of Jubal Sancreed.

'Especially for him.'

'Then you know who you must call and what you must do.'

Dorcas nodded and Lylas folded back into the light.

All her life Dorcas had struggled to keep herself under control; hiding the scar that denounced her as a truewitch and smothering the desires to wipe out those that crossed her. It had never been easy. The battle within her was constant, and since she had come to the south, the negative side of her had been harder to keep in check.

For a truewitch to use the dark power was allowing herself to cross over to the black, the balance would be broken and she would be lost forever. Dorcas had never realised the power within her was unusual. As a young girl she thought that all witches had the same battles; the same arguments with themselves. She also thought that everyone was capable of hiding a blemish or a scar.

Now it was time, time to put herself to the test and give herself over to the power that lay deep in her soul.

The surrounding coven came back into time and Dorcas opened her mouth and uttered the words that she had held inside.

'Cailleac Bhuer, hag, Hecate, wise one, Bridgid, high one, come to me, come to me now, I am open and ready and I welcome you to this battle.'

As the coven watched, the ancient Hag Stone came to life. A sulphurous light emanated from the granite and in the eerie radiance, Dorcas Fleming changed and deformed before their eyes.

Shoulders bent over and a hump appeared in her once straight back, legs bowed and her hands gnarled like oak branches as the powerful aspects of the Goddess herself enveloped her. A staff of primeval holly appeared in her right hand and on her shoulder appeared a dark, mangy crow, his hematite eyes casting about to fix on the few that still watched this dreadful transformation. The only thing that was recognisable as Dorcas Fleming was her hair, that and the vivid, bright red scar that had always run across her cheek. No longer under any sort of control, Dorcas was free, free and tremendous in her natural power. The crow screeched three times before Dorcas raised the staff of holly and ascended into the furious spinning turmoil above her head.

Silence cloaked the cliff top as the coven fought to keep each other from passing out or breaking the sacred circle. No sign or sound came from above to indicate the battle that was raging within. Even the wind had died back to release the familiar sounds of sea on rocks.

Dorcas became just one of four spirits who battled the elemental Tulpa. Strong in its evilness it flung away the spellweaves that were directed at it and knocked aside the blows from the staff of power. The one body cast about freeing the bound souls only to find that they crept back to their master as soon as he called.

'Too strong for you am I. I hath fed from the ether of life, it hath strengthened mine soul. No witch can hold me, no Goddess can touch me, come to me, come to me now, all of you join me.'

For a split second, Dorcas felt the four parts of her drawn to the open maw of wickedness, tempted with silken words from the beast. It was strong, very strong, trying in turn to split the four, divide their power, using every persuasion its dark mind could conjure. Dorcas was as a vessel that held the power of the deities that she had called. She was hurled this way and that as the battle grew. Shafts of light scored her skin and grazed her soul as the Tulpa gained control and tried to suck the life from the otherworld.

'He will not have it' screamed the deities.

'He shall not have it'

'He cannot have it, it is not his to have'

'It is mine.'

'Not so sister, it is mine.'

'I beg to differ, it is but mine and mine alone.'

Dorcas realised with growing horror that the spirits who were inside her were not only fighting the demon but also fighting themselves for power. Too strong in their own milieu, they could not bind to produce enough force to repel the noxious blasts from the black form. They squabbled like children, arguing and bickering for ultimate control, and all the time the Tulpa was growing and leeching their power. The blackness around her darkened, thickened, the demon was gaining strength from their weakness.

'Nearly mine.'

Dorcas saw her chance and came to the fore, seizing the power for herself, forcing them to her bidding. They struggled against this new power but she let go of the last vestiges of control that she had over her body and soul and wielded the staff in a blaze of furious light and energy. The power that had been born within her rose to the surface, pulling the deities together as her volcano erupted.

'Cailleac, Hecate, Bridgid. As One. Now!'

Dorcas let go of the last vestige of her control and set the monster within her free. The pure light burned the demon and it screamed. She struck again and it tried to escape back to the sea. Dorcas pulled it back, driving the light deep inside its foulness. It screeched and writhed horribly still trying to sway her mind to the very end. It pleaded, wheedled and implored now, but she would not, and could not, let go of the power that she had finally set free.

'**NO MORE. NO MORE, NO MORE ARE YOU!**' Dorcas screamed sending a final blow to the rapidly diminishing entity. The vile core exploded and the ensuing cataclysm of light and sound flung the deities back to the otherworld, ripping the life from her body in its wake. Dorcas Fleming fell to earth, an empty, broken shell. It was done.

As she lay on the windy cliff, her last thoughts reached out softly, to touch those she loved in this world. She had completed the task and Natural Law was balanced, the way that it should be. Her hand reached out over the damp grass and Dorcas Fleming slipped into the otherworld that was waiting for her as it always had been.

I am here.

I am now

Call me 'forever'

- Akashic records

Epilogue

Beltane morning dawned bright and clear. The sun sparkled off the sea giving promise to the fine weather ahead. The witch woke alone in the new bed in the new house. She now had an uninterrupted view of the calm blue and turquoise waters of the Lazardian Channel.

The day roused her with excitement in her heart and a rude song on her lips. It *was* May Day after all. Pendartha was going to celebrate and had put up a May pole in the square. They had not stopped celebrating since the Tulpa had been destroyed and had even embraced a few of the milder Pagan festivals as their own. The seas were now free and only inhabited by the normal kind of dangers that humans could deal with. The boats had gone back to work, the pilchard presses were working again, and Pendartha was slowly getting up off its knees.

Dorcas was not stupid; she knew it would not last. The church had already started to make enquiries into the goings on in its most southerly town but for now, they would all make the most of it. There would be time enough to revert to the heathen practices and time enough to go back to being a simple hedgewitch.

She remembered the day, two weeks after Samhain, when she had finally decided to come back to the land of the living. It had been a long struggle to find herself again and the temptation to stay in the otherworld was great. As her body lay in Pendartha with its soul in the afterlife, Dorcas revelled in the simplistic truths that were held beyond the world of the living. She was reacquainted with some of the souls who had touched her life. Mother Alice came and told the story of her birth and then Lylas returned once again. The old Mother spent many hours talking to her former protégé, persuading her that her life was only just beginning.

'You see child, we make choices, here, there, light, dark, life, or death. You have chosen now. Go back, there is still work to be

done and there seems to be one who would have you back.'
Dorcas finally returned.

'Glad to see you are awake, that lot just don't remember that I need the occasional fish for my poor hungry belly.'

'Hello Zebulonus, I am sorry for the inconvenience, I'm sure it can now be rectified but what happened? I am supposed to be with the spirits and unless I am very much mistaken, I am in my own bed in my own house. I have made my choice it appears.'

'Of course you have, there was no other way for you, and you don't think that the fisherman was going to let you go so easily do you? He breathed his life and his soul into your body and you came back to us, eventually.'

'Yes it seems I did, but where is everyone?'

'Your friends and half the people of the town have been taking it in turns to watch over you. The coven moved into town to give you more space but I don't know where Jubal is. He left.'

Ginny appeared at the door and gave a squeak, Maghda and Joan followed her in.

'There I said she would come back to us, doubting cat' she scolded as Zebulonus flicked his tail and made for the door.

'Not a breath in you, and in the dawn light you were, well, as pale as death itself' Joan said, as she filled in the rest of the story.

'Jubal stepped forward, pushed everyone aside, and breathed into you. He said you had done it for him and he was returning the favour' Maghda added.

'And he brought you back to life because of his love' Ginny smiled, a soppy look flooding her face.

The Tulpa was truly destroyed and the whole coven had watched for an hour as the trapped spirits left the dark and made their way to the waiting light. Their smoke-like forms drifted on the wind getting brighter before they eventually stepped over to the otherworld where they belonged. It was something that Pendartha would talk about for a very long time.

'So where is the love of my life now?'

'In St Zenno, making arrangements' Maghda smirked, but no one would fill in any more details.

It took Dorcas a long time to let herself remember what happened that night. The battle had been to the death but death had not wanted her, for now.

Jubal and Dorcas were married the following month when she was strong enough to jump the broom. They encompassed both of their religions by having a blessing in the chapel straight after their greenwood wedding. Dorcas would always swear that she had nothing to do with persuading the Preacher to accommodate them.

Here in her bed on the first day of May, Dorcas stroked her swelling stomach. The baby inside her was growing well and she would tell her husband today that his first child was to be a daughter.

The coven had arrived two days earlier for the Beltane celebrations and were causing their usual havoc around the town. No doubt, Josiah, at some point would beat a path to her door with moans about their outrageous behaviour. Ellen had come with them and she was looking forward to seeing them all later to catch up on their news from the north. Masterbridge was asking for more reports and some time in the future she would have to attend a meeting with Elshalamane himself; but that could all wait. Pendartha was her home now and it appeared that its inhabitants still needed, and wanted, their hedgewitch.

For now, she was content to lie in her bed, feeling smug and self-satisfied. With her cat by her side, the witch from the north kept one eye on the slow boiling kettle, and one eye on her husband out at sea, keeping him safe until he returned to her.

* * *

Witch facts

Akashic Records...*said to hold all the knowledge of the universe, reached during deep meditation on the astral plane*

Athame....*a witch's ritual knife*

Besom...*broomstick, used to aid a spellweave and used at handfasting (marriage) when a couple 'jump the broom'.*

Boline...*herb-cutting knife, used for spell preparation.*

Book of Shadows...*a witch's personal journal holding recipes, spells and rituals.*

Chalice...*a witch's sacred cup*

Censer or thurible...*a fireproof vessel for spell making*

Esbat...*observance of the full moon.*

Element   *Fire/south*
               Water/west
               Earth/north
               Air/east

Elemental witch...*a witch who has affinity with the elements.*

Fascination...*a spellweave of persuasion.*

Grimoire...*ancient spell book of both black and white magic*

Hag stone (Holey stone, witch stone) ...*a granite ring of power.*

Handfasting (jumping the broom)...*Pagan marriage*

Herbology...*knowledge and practice of medicinal herbs.*

Hedgewitch...*a witch who works with the gifts of the earth.*

Hexenbanner...*an individual who can ward off curses and spellweaves.*

Pentacle....*five side star, denoting the five elements enclosed within a circle of power.*

Pentagram....*five sided star representing protection.*

Scrying...*to look to the future, or past, using runes, mirror, crystal ball, tea leaves etc.*

Spellweave...*a working spell.*

Summerlands...*most renowned college of witchcraft in the north, also the common name for the otherworld.*

Truewitch...*the most powerful of all witches combining all talents.*

Tulpa...*negative elemental demon*

The wheel of the year/ The Eight Sabbats or festivals

Samhain (31ˢᵗ October) *-Goddess mourns for the God, veil between worlds is thin*

Yule   (21ˢᵗ December) *-Midwinter solstice, Goddess gives birth to the God, a time of re-birth*

Imbolg (2ⁿᵈ February) *-Goddess recovers from birth, the land awakens*

Oestara (21ˢᵗ March) *-Spring equinox, God and Goddess walk together, spring unfolds*

Beltane (1ˢᵗ May)*-May Day, God and Goddess unite, the land is fertile*

Litha (21ˢᵗ June) *-Summer solstice, God and Goddess celebrate, a time of healing*

Lammas (1ˢᵗ August) *-Goddess becomes pregnant, a time of hope for the future*

Mabon (21ˢᵗ September) *-Autumn equinox, God leaves and the Goddess rests, a time of thanksgiving*

The characters of Coven of One

At Summerlands:
High Priestess Ellen
Mother Elsie
Mother Susan
Mother Hedda
Mother Willamina
Mother Sarah
Mother Lylas – in the Otherworld

The Coven
Dorcas Fleming
Ginnifer Belle
Maghda Cotton
Joan Barton
Amberlynne Butts
Gwenna Johnson
Bridget Wainwright
Maegwyn Rogers
Eliza Ford
Breyone Wilding
Manae Carter
Nancy Potter
Anne Shields

At Masterbridge:
High Druid Elshalamane
Meredith Spooner – scryer
June Partridge – assistant scryer
Stanley Horton – carter

At Pendartha:
Chief /Mayor Josiah Penpol
Violetta Penpol - his wife
Morwenna Penpol – his mother
Reverend Trewidden
Jubal Sancreed – lobster fisherman
Denzell Richards – deceased
Tregonning – second mate
Foggy Isaacs – weatherman
Lizzy Mims
Minnie Gembo
Mordecai Leven - carpenter
Telfer Meriadoc – local store owner
Mags – his daughter
Jakey Moyle - blacksmith
Mary Moyle - Jakey's daughter
Anne Moyle - Jakey's daughter
Mrs Creed – baker's wife
Rosie Trevennen
Lily Trevennen
Morley Trewidden - the Reverend's brother
Sarah Trewidden - his wife
Avergila Pengelly - fishwife
John Boslowek – pilchard presser
Grenville Simmons - fisherman
Squire Flench – of Polempter
Royston Carleen – prison guard

More is coming . . . . . .

"....and then she was gone. Away in the swirling mists of autumn......"

'An if ye harm none, do as ye will'

33887868R00165

Printed in Great Britain
by Amazon